The plot has it all. I have no doubt that in a year's time I'm going to be saying that this is my favorite novel of 2012. Brilliant' Kate Atkinson

Flynn, an extraordinarily good writer, plays her readers with the finesse and delicacy of an expert angler. She wields her unreliable narrators to stunning effect, baffling, disturbing and delighting in turn, practically guaranteeing an immediate reread once her terrifying, wonderful conclusion is reached ... an early contender for thriller of the year, and an absolute must-read' Alison Flood, *Observer*

These voices are wonderfully authentic, to the point where the reader becomes a gawker at the full-spectrum of marital dysfunction. Excellent' John O'Connor, *Guardian*

Just about everyone I meet, and everyone on Twitter, is telling me it's brilliant, so I can't wait to see what the fuss is all about' S.J. Watson, *Sunday Express*

Read it and stay single' *Financial Times*

Flynn has created a gripping tale and a page-turner'
Literary Review

Immensely dark and deeply intelligent, *Gone Girl* is a book about how well one person can truly know another' *Metro*

Flynn is a brilliantly accomplished psychological crime writer and this latest book is so dark, so twisted and so utterly compelling that it actually messes with your mind'
Carla McKay, *Daily Mail*

You think you're reading a good, conventional thriller and then it grows into a fascinating portrait of one averagely mismatched relationship ... Nothing's as it seems – Flynn is a fabulous plotter, and a very sharp observer of modern life in the aftermath of the credit crunch' Kate Saunders, *The Times*

'Definitely a contender for thriller of the year ... Flynn is, without a doubt, at the front of the pack of American thriller writers' Doug Johnstone, *Independent on Sunday*

'Flynn's portrait of a woman trying to please an impossible husband is subtly drawn, but there are hints that all is not as it seems. One version of events hides another in a novel that cleverly manipulates the reader' Joan Smith, *Sunday Times*

'A chilling tale of a hip, New York couple's failing marriage, smart, suspenseful and brilliantly written, *Gone Girl* is a class act' *Independent*

'She skilfully manages to sustain tension and uncertainty to the end, as well as presenting a beautiful portrait of marriage disintegration' Marcel Berlins, *The Times*

'This is Flynn's third novel and she's more than found her voice, creating taut, thrilling, deeply intense narratives about characters very much on the edge'
Henry Sutton, *Daily Mirror*

'A near-masterpiece. Flynn is an extraordinary writer who, with every sentence, makes words do things that other writers merely dream of' Sophie Hannah, *Sunday Express*

'A brilliant switchback ride, you'll beg others to read it so you can discuss it with them'
John Williams, *Irish Mail on Sunday*

'Flynn keeps the accelerator firmly to the floor, ratcheting up the tension with wildly unexpected plot twists, contradictory stories and the tantalising feeling that nothing is as it seems. Deviously good' *Marie Claire*

'*Gone Girl* is superbly constructed, ingeniously paced and absolutely terrifying ... a five-star suspense mystery'
A.N. Wilson, *Reader's Digest*

'In this riveting noirish thriller and intense dissection of a marriage, nothing is as it seems' *Woman and Home*

'Gripping thriller: Nick's wife, Amy, is missing and he's a suspect. The story is told by Nick, then Amy, but who's telling the truth?' *Essentials*

'Funny, cunning thriller ... the tale takes some stomach-churning turns, right to its chilling conclusion' *Psychologies*

'A chilling, stylish read about another unknowable woman'
Elle

'In what is so much more than a straightforward crime novel (with a mid-story twist so shocking you'll drop the book), Flynn unpicks the minutiae of the couple's personalities and relationship' *Easy Living*

'A terrifically intelligent thriller with a gasp-inducing twist'
Good Housekeeping

'Ms Flynn's latest novel of psychological suspense will confound anyone trying to keep up with her quicksilver mind and diabolical rules of play' *International Herald Tribune*

Gillian Flynn's first novel, *Sharp Objects*, was the winner of the two CWA Dagger Awards and was shortlisted for the CWA Gold Dagger Award, and for an Edgar. Her second, *Dark Places*, was published to great critical acclaim. A former writer and critic for *Entertainment Weekly*, her novels have been published in twenty-eight countries. She lives in Chicago with her husband and son.

Also by Gillian Flynn

SHARP OBJECTS
DARK PLACES

GONE GIRL

GILLIAN FLYNN

PHOENIX

A PHOENIX PAPERBACK

First published in Great Britain in 2012
by Weidenfeld & Nicolson
This paperback edition published in 2012
by Phoenix,
an imprint of Orion Books Ltd,
Orion House, 5 Upper St Martin's Lane,
London WC2H 9EA

An Hachette UK company

15

A CIP catalogue record for this book
is available from the British Library.

ISBN 978-1-7802-2135-9

Typeset by Input Data Services Ltd, Bridgwater, Somerset

The Orion Publishing Group's policy is to use papers
that are natural, renewable and recyclable products and
made from wood grown in sustainable forests. The logging
and manufacturing processes are expected to conform to
the environmental regulations of the country of origin.

www.orionbooks.co.uk

To Brett: light of my life, senior and
Flynn: light of my life, junior

Love is the world's infinite mutability; lies, hatred, murder even, are all knit up in it; it is the inevitable blossoming of its opposites, a magnificent rose smelling faintly of blood.

Tony Kushner, THE ILLUSION

PART ONE

BOY LOSES GIRL

NICK DUNNE
THE DAY OF

When I think of my wife, I always think of her head. The shape of it, to begin with. The very first time I saw her, it was the back of the head I saw, and there was something lovely about it, the angles of it. Like a shiny, hard corn kernel or a riverbed fossil. She had what the Victorians would call *a finely shaped head*. You could imagine the skull quite easily.

I'd know her head anywhere.

And what's inside it. I think of that, too: her mind. Her brain, all those coils, and her thoughts shuttling through those coils like fast, frantic centipedes. Like a child, I picture opening her skull, unspooling her brain and sifting through it, trying to catch and pin down her thoughts. *What are you thinking, Amy?* The question I've asked most often during our marriage, if not out loud, if not to the person who could answer. I suppose these questions stormcloud over every marriage: *What are you thinking? How are you feeling? Who are you? What have we done to each other? What will we do?*

My eyes flipped open at exactly six a.m. This was no avian fluttering of the lashes, no gentle blink toward consciousness. The awakening was mechanical. A spooky ventriloquist-dummy click of the lids: The world is black and then, *showtime!* 6-0-0 the clock said – in my face, first thing I saw. 6-0-0. It felt different. I rarely woke at such a rounded time. I was a man of jagged risings: 8:43, 11:51, 9:26. My life was alarmless.

At that exact moment, 6-0-0, the sun climbed over the skyline of oaks, revealing its full summer angry-God self. Its reflection flared across the river toward our house, a long, blaring finger aimed at me through our frail bedroom curtains. Accusing: *You have been seen. You will be seen.*

I wallowed in bed, which was our New York bed in our new house, which we still called *the new house*, even though we'd been back here for two years. It's a rented house right along the Mississippi River, a house that screams Suburban Nouveau Riche, the kind of place I aspired to as a kid from my split-level, shag-carpet side of town. The kind of house that is immediately familiar: a generically grand, unchallenging, new, new, new house that my wife would – and did – detest.

'Should I remove my soul before I come inside?' Her first line upon arrival. It had been a compromise: Amy demanded we rent, not buy, in my little Missouri hometown, in her firm hope that we wouldn't be stuck here long. But the only houses for rent were clustered in this failed development: a miniature ghost town of bank-owned, recession-busted, price-reduced mansions, a neighborhood that closed before it ever opened. It was a compromise, but Amy didn't see it that way, not in the least. To Amy, it was a punishing whim on my part, a nasty, selfish twist of the knife. I would drag her, caveman-style, to a town she had aggressively avoided, and make her live in the kind of house she used to mock. I suppose it's not a compromise if only one of you considers it such, but that was what our compromises tended to look like. One of us was always angry. Amy, usually.

Do not blame me for this particular grievance, Amy. The Missouri Grievance. Blame the economy, blame bad luck, blame my parents, blame your parents, blame the Internet, blame people who use the Internet. I used to be a writer. I was a writer who wrote about TV and movies and books. Back when people read things on paper, back when anyone cared about what I thought. I'd arrived in New York in the late '90s, the last gasp of the glory days, although no one knew it then. New York was packed with writers, real writers, because there were magazines, real magazines, loads of them. This was back when the Internet was still some exotic pet kept in the corner of the publishing world – throw some kibble at it, watch it

4

dance on its little leash, oh quite cute, it definitely won't kill us in the night. Think about it: a time when newly graduated college kids could come to New York and *get paid to write*. We had no clue that we were embarking on careers that would vanish within a decade.

I had a job for eleven years and then I didn't, it was that fast. All around the country, magazines began shuttering, succumbing to a sudden infection brought on by the busted economy. Writers (my kind of writers: aspiring novelists, ruminative thinkers, people whose brains don't work quick enough to blog or link or tweet, basically old, stubborn blowhards) were through. We were like women's hat makers or buggy-whip manufacturers: Our time was done. Three weeks after I got cut loose, Amy lost her job, such as it was. (Now I can feel Amy looking over my shoulder, smirking at the time I've spent discussing my career, my misfortune, and dismissing her experience in one sentence. That, she would tell you, is typical. *Just like Nick*, she would say. It was a refrain of hers: *Just like Nick to* ... and whatever followed, whatever was *just like me*, was bad.) Two jobless grown-ups, we spent weeks wandering around our Brooklyn brownstone in socks and pajamas, ignoring the future, strewing unopened mail across tables and sofas, eating ice cream at ten a.m. and taking thick afternoon naps.

Then one day the phone rang. My twin sister was on the other end. Margo had moved back home after her own New York layoff a year before – the girl is one step ahead of me in everything, even shitty luck. Margo, calling from good ole North Carthage, Missouri, from the house where we grew up, and as I listened to her voice, I saw her at age ten, with a dark cap of hair and overall shorts, sitting on our grandparents' back dock, her body slouched over like an old pillow, her skinny legs dangling in the water, watching the river flow over fish-white feet, so intently, utterly self-possessed even as a child.

Go's voice was warm and crinkly even as she gave this cold news: Our indomitable mother was dying. Our dad was nearly gone – his (nasty) mind, his (miserable) heart, both murky as

5

he meandered toward the great gray beyond. But it looked like our mother would beat him there. About six months, maybe a year, she had. I could tell that Go had gone to meet with the doctor by herself, taken her studious notes in her slovenly handwriting, and she was teary as she tried to decipher what she'd written. Dates and doses.

'Well, fuck, I have no idea what this says, is it a nine? Does that even make sense?' she said, and I interrupted. Here was a task, a purpose, held out on my sister's palm like a plum. I almost cried with relief.

'I'll come back, Go. We'll move back home. You shouldn't have to do this all by yourself.'

She didn't believe me. I could hear her breathing on the other end.

'I'm serious, Go. Why not? There's nothing here.'

A long exhale. 'What about Amy?'

That is what I didn't take long enough to consider. I simply assumed I would bundle up my New York wife with her New York interests, her New York pride, and remove her from her New York parents – leave the frantic, thrilling futureland of Manhattan behind – and transplant her to a little town on the river in Missouri, and all would be fine.

I did not yet understand how foolish, how optimistic, how, yes, *just like Nick* I was for thinking this. The misery it would lead to.

'Amy will be fine. Amy ...' Here was where I should have said, 'Amy *loves* Mom.' But I couldn't tell Go that Amy loved our mother, because after all that time, Amy still barely knew our mother. Their few meetings had left them both baffled. Amy would dissect the conversations for days after – 'And what did she mean by ... ,' – as if my mother were some ancient peasant tribeswoman arriving from the tundra with an armful of raw yak meat and some buttons for bartering, trying to get something from Amy that wasn't on offer.

Amy didn't care to know my family, didn't want to know my birthplace, and yet for some reason, I thought moving home would be a good idea.

6

My morning breath warmed the pillow, and I changed the subject in my mind. Today was not a day for second-guessing or regret, it was a day for doing. Downstairs, I could hear the return of a long-lost sound: Amy making breakfast. Banging wooden cupboards (rump-thump!), rattling containers of tin and glass (ding-ring!), shuffling and sorting a collection of metal pots and iron pans (ruzz-shuzz!). A culinary orchestra tuning up, clattering vigorously toward the finale, a cake pan drumrolling along the floor, hitting the wall with a cymballic crash. Something impressive was being created, probably a crepe, because crepes are special, and today Amy would want to cook something special.

It was our five-year anniversary.

I walked barefoot to the edge of the steps and stood listening, working my toes into the plush wall-to-wall carpet Amy detested on principle, as I tried to decide whether I was ready to join my wife. Amy was in the kitchen, oblivious to my hesitation. She was humming something melancholy and familiar. I strained to make it out – a folk song? a lullabye? – and then realized it was the theme to *M.A.S.H.* Suicide is painless. I went downstairs.

I hovered in the doorway, watching my wife. Her yellow-butter hair was pulled up, the hank of ponytail swinging cheerful as a jumprope, and she was sucking distractedly on a burnt fingertip, humming around it. She hummed to herself because she was an unrivaled botcher of lyrics. When we were first dating, a Genesis song came on the radio: 'She seems to have an invisible touch, yeah.' And Amy crooned instead, 'She takes my hat and puts it on the *top* shelf.' When I asked her why she'd ever think her lyrics were remotely, possibly, vaguely right, she told me she always thought the woman in the song truly loved the man because she put his hat on the *top* shelf. I knew I liked her then, really liked her, this girl with an explanation for everything.

There's something disturbing about recalling a warm memory and feeling utterly cold.

7

Amy peered at the crepe sizzling in the pan and licked something off her wrist. She looked triumphant, wifely. If I took her in my arms, she would smell like berries and powdered sugar.

When she spied me lurking there in grubby boxers, my hair in full Heat Miser spike, she leaned against the kitchen counter and said, 'Well, hello, handsome.'

Bile and dread inched up my throat. I thought to myself: *Okay, go.*

I was very late getting to work. My sister and I had done a foolish thing when we both moved back home. We had done what we always talked about doing. We opened a bar. We borrowed money from Amy to do this, eighty thousand dollars, which was once nothing to Amy but by then was almost everything. I swore I would pay her back, with interest. I would not be a man who borrowed from his wife – I could feel my dad twisting his lips at the very idea. *Well, there are all kinds of men*, his most damning phrase, the second half left unsaid, *and you are the wrong kind.*

But truly, it was a practical decision, a smart business move. Amy and I both needed new careers; this would be mine. She would pick one someday, or not, but in the meantime, here was an income, made possible by the last of Amy's trust fund. Like the McMansion I rented, the bar featured symbolically in my childhood memories – a place where only grown-ups go, and do whatever grown-ups do. Maybe that's why I was so insistent on buying it after being stripped of my livelihood. It's a reminder that I am, after all, an adult, a grown man, a useful human being, even though I lost the career that made me all these things. I won't make that mistake again: The once plentiful herds of magazine writers would continue to be culled – by the Internet, by the recession, by the American public, who would rather watch TV or play video games or electronically inform friends that, like, *rain sucks!* But there's no app for a bourbon buzz on a warm day in a cool, dark bar. The world will always want a drink.

Our bar is a corner bar with a haphazard, patchwork aesthetic. Its best feature is a massive Victorian backbar, dragon heads and angel faces emerging from the oak – an extravagant work of wood in these shitty plastic days. The remainder of the bar is, in fact, shitty, a showcase of the shabbiest design offerings of every decade: an Eisenhower-era linoleum floor, the edges turned up like burnt toast; dubious wood-paneled walls straight from a '70s home-porn video; halogen floor lamps, an accidental tribute to my 1990s dorm room. The ultimate effect is strangely homey – it looks less like a bar than someone's benignly neglected fixer-upper. And jovial: We share a parking lot with the local bowling alley, and when our door swings wide, the clatter of strikes applauds the customer's entrance.

We named the bar The Bar. 'People will think we're ironic instead of creatively bankrupt,' my sister reasoned.

Yes, we thought we were being clever New Yorkers – that the name was a joke no one else would really get, not get like we did. Not *meta*-get. We pictured the locals scrunching their noses: Why'd you name it *The Bar*? But our first customer, a gray-haired woman in bifocals and a pink jogging suit, said, 'I like the name. Like in *Breakfast at Tiffany's* and Audrey Hepburn's cat was named Cat.'

We felt much less superior after that, which was a good thing.

I pulled into the parking lot. I waited until a strike erupted from the bowling alley – *thank you, thank you, friends* – then stepped out of the car. I admired the surroundings, still not bored with the broken-in view: the squatty blond-brick post office across the street (now closed on Saturdays), the unassuming beige office building just down the way (now closed, period). The town wasn't prosperous, not anymore, not by a long shot. Hell, it wasn't even original, being one of two Carthage, Missouris – ours is technically *North* Carthage, which makes it sound like a twin city, although it's hundreds of miles from the other and the lesser of the two: a quaint little 1950s town that bloated itself into a basic midsize suburb and dubbed it progress. Still, it was where my mom grew up and where she raised me and Go, so it had some history. Mine, at least.

As I walked toward the bar across the concrete-and-weed parking lot, I looked straight down the road and saw the river. That's what I've always loved about our town: We aren't built on some safe bluff overlooking the Mississippi – we are *on* the Mississippi. I could walk down the road and step right into the sucker, an easy three-foot drop, and be on my way to Tennessee. Every building downtown bears hand-drawn lines from where the river hit during the Flood of '61, '75, '84, '93, '07, '08, '11. And so on.

The river wasn't swollen now, but it was running urgently, in strong ropy currents. Moving apace with the river was a long single-file line of men, eyes aimed at their feet, shoulders tense, walking steadfastly nowhere. As I watched them, one suddenly looked up at me, his face in shadow, an oval blackness. I turned away.

I felt an immediate, intense need to get inside. By the time I'd gone twenty feet, my neck bubbled with sweat. The sun was still an angry eye in the sky. *You have been seen.*

My gut twisted, and I moved quicker. I needed a drink.

AMY ELLIOTT
JANUARY 8, 2005

– Diary entry –

Tra and la! I am smiling a big adopted-orphan smile as I write this. I am embarrassed at how happy I am, like some Technicolor comic of a teenage girl talking on the phone with my hair in a ponytail, the bubble above my head saying: *I met a* boy!

But I did. This is a technical, empirical truth. I met a boy, a great, gorgeous dude, a funny, cool-ass guy. Let me set the scene, because it deserves setting for posterity (no, please, I'm not that far gone, posterity! feh). But still. It's not New Year's, but still very much the new year. It's winter: early dark, freezing cold.

Carmen, a newish friend – semi-friend, barely friend, the kind of friend you can't cancel on – has talked me into going out to Brooklyn, to one of her writers' parties. Now, I like a writer party, I like writers, I am the child of writers, I am a writer. I still love scribbling that word – WRITER – any time a form, questionnaire, document asks for my occupation. Fine, I write personality quizzes, I don't write about the Great Issues of the Day, but I think it's fair to say I am a writer. I'm using this journal to get better: to hone my skills, to collect details and observations. To show don't tell and all that other writery crap. (*Adopted-orphan smile*, I mean, that's not bad, come on.) But really, I do think my quizzes alone qualify me on at least an honorary basis. Right?

At a party you find yourself surrounded by genuine talented writers, employed at high-profile, respected newspapers and magazines.

You merely write quizzes for women's rags. When someone asks what you do for a living, you:

a) Get embarrassed and say, 'I'm just a quiz writer, it's silly stuff!'
b) Go on the offense: 'I'm a writer now, but I'm considering something more challenging and worthwhile – why, what do you do?'
c) Take pride in your accomplishments: 'I write personality quizzes using the knowledge gleaned from my master's degree in psychology – oh, and fun fact: I am the inspiration for a beloved children's-book series, I'm sure you know it, *Amazing Amy?* Yeah, so suck it, snobdouche!

Answer: C, totally C

Anyway, the party is being thrown by one of Carmen's good friends who writes about movies for a movie magazine, and is very funny, according to Carmen. I worry for a second that she wants to set us up: I am not interested in being set up. I need to be ambushed, caught unawares, like some sort of feral love-jackal. I'm too self-conscious otherwise. I feel myself trying to be charming, and then I realize I'm obviously trying to be charming, and then I try to be even more charming to make up for the fake charm, and then I've basically turned into Liza Minnelli: I'm dancing in tights and sequins, begging you to love me. There's a bowler and jazz hands and lots of teeth.

But no, I realize, as Carmen gushes on about her friend: *She* likes him. Good.

We climb three flights of warped stairs and walk into a whoosh of body heat and writerness: many black-framed glasses and mops of hair; faux western shirts and heathery turtlenecks; black wool pea-coats flopped all across the couch, puddling to the floor; a German poster for The Getaway (*Ihre Chance war gleich Null!*) covering one paint-cracked wall. Franz Ferdinand on the stereo: 'Take Me Out.'

A clump of guys hovers near a card table where all the alcohol is set up, tipping more booze into their cups after every few sips, all too aware of how little is left to go around. I nudge in, aiming my plastic cup in the center like a busker, get a clatter of ice cubes and a splash of vodka from a sweet-faced guy wearing a Space Invaders T-shirt.

A lethal-looking bottle of green-apple liqueur, the host's ironic purchase, will soon be our fate unless someone makes a booze run, and that seems unlikely, as everyone clearly believes they made the run last time. It is a January party, definitely, everyone still glutted and sugar-pissed from the holidays, lazy and irritated simultaneously. A party where people drink too much and pick cleverly worded fights, blowing cigarette smoke out an open window even after the host asks them to go outside. We've already talked to one another at a thousand holiday parties, we have nothing left to say, we are collectively bored, but we don't want to go back into the January cold; our bones still ache from the subway steps.

I have lost Carmen to her host-beau – they are having an intense discussion in a corner of the kitchen, the two of them hunching their shoulders, their faces toward each other, the shape of a heart. Good. I think about eating to give myself something to do besides standing in the center of the room, smiling like the new kid in the lunchroom. But almost everything is gone. Some potato-chip shards sit in the bottom of a giant Tupperware bowl. A supermarket deli tray full of hoary carrots and gnarled celery and a semeny dip sits untouched on a coffee table, cigarettes littered throughout like bonus vegetable sticks. I am doing my thing, my impulse thing: What if I leap from the theater balcony right now? What if I tongue the homeless man across from me on the subway? What if I sit down on the floor of this party by myself and eat everything on that deli tray, including the cigarettes?

'Please don't eat anything in that area,' he says. It is *him* (bum bum BUMMM!), but I don't yet know it's *him* (bum-bum-bummm). I know it's a guy who will talk to me, he wears his cockiness like an ironic T-shirt, but it fits him better. He is the kind of guy who carries himself like he gets laid a lot, a guy who likes women, a guy who would actually fuck me properly. I would like to be fucked properly! My dating life seems to rotate around three types of men: preppy Ivy Leaguers who believe they're characters in a Fitzgerald novel; slick Wall Streeters with money signs in their eyes, their ears, their mouths; and sensitive smart-boys who are so self-aware that everything feels like a joke. The Fitzgerald fellows tend to be ineffectively porny in bed, a lot of noise and acrobatics to very little end. The finance guys turn rageful and flaccid. The smart-boys fuck like they're composing a piece of math rock: This hand strums around here, and then this finger offers a nice bass rhythm ... I sound quite slutty, don't I? Pause while I count how many ... eleven. Not bad. I've always thought twelve was a solid, reasonable number to end at.

'Seriously,' Number 12 continues. (Ha!) 'Back away from the tray. James has up to three other food items in his refrigerator. I could make you an olive with mustard. Just one olive, though.'

Just one olive, though. It is a line that is only a little funny, but it already has the feel of an inside joke, one that will get funnier with nostalgic repetition. I think: *A year from now, we will be walking along the Brooklyn Bridge at sunset and one of us will whisper, 'Just one olive, though,' and we'll start to laugh.* (Then I catch myself. Awful. If he knew I was doing *a year from now* already, he'd *run* and I'd be obliged to cheer him on.)

Mainly, I will admit, I smile because he's gorgeous. Distractingly gorgeous, the kind of looks that make your eyes pinwheel, that make you want to just address the elephant – 'You know you're gorgeous, right?' – and move on with the conversation. I bet dudes hate him: He looks like the rich-boy villain in an '80s teen movie – the one who bullies the sensitive misfit, the one who will end up with a pie in the puss, the whipped cream wilting his upturned collar as everyone in the cafeteria cheers.

He doesn't act that way, though. His name is Nick. I love

it. It makes him seem nice, and regular, which he is. When he tells me his name, I say, 'Now, that's a real name.' He brightens and reels off some line: 'Nick's the kind of guy you can drink a beer with, the kind of guy who doesn't mind if you puke in his car. Nick!'

He makes a series of awful puns. I catch three fourths of his movie references. Two thirds, maybe. (Note to self: Rent *The Sure Thing*.) He refills my drink without me having to ask, somehow ferreting out one last cup of the good stuff. He has claimed me, placed a flag in me: *I was here first, she's mine, mine*. It feels nice, after my recent series of nervous, respectful post-feminist men, to be a territory. He has a great smile, a cat's smile. He should cough out yellow Tweety Bird feathers, the way he smiles at me. He doesn't ask what I do for a living, which is fine, which is a change. (I'm a writer, did I mention?) He talks to me in his river-wavy Missouri accent; he was born and raised outside of Hannibal, the boyhood home of Mark Twain, the inspiration for *Tom Sawyer*. He tells me he worked on a steamboat when he was a teenager, dinner and jazz for the tourists. And when I laugh (bratty, bratty New York girl who has never ventured to those big unwieldy middle states, those States Where Many Other People Live), he informs me that *Missoura* is a magical place, the most beautiful in the world, no state more glorious. His eyes are mischievous, his lashes are long. I can see what he looked like as a boy.

We share a taxi home, the streetlights making dizzy shadows and the car speeding as if we're being chased. It is one a.m. when we hit one of New York's unexplained deadlocks twelve blocks from my apartment, so we slide out of the taxi into the cold, into the great What Next? and Nick starts walking me home, his hand on the small of my back, our faces stunned by the chill. As we turn the corner, the local bakery is getting its powdered sugar delivered, funneled into the cellar by the barrelful as if it were cement, and we can see nothing but the shadows of the deliverymen in the white, sweet cloud. The street is billowing, and Nick pulls me close and smiles that smile again, and he takes a single lock of my hair between two fingers and runs them all the way to the end, tugging twice, like he's ringing a bell. His eyelashes are trimmed with powder, and before he leans in, he brushes the sugar from my lips so he can taste me.

NICK DUNNE
THE DAY OF

I swung wide the door of my bar, slipped into the darkness, and took my first real deep breath of the day, took in the smell of cigarettes and beer, the spice of a dribbled bourbon, the tang of old popcorn. There was only one customer in the bar, sitting by herself at the far, far end: an older woman named Sue who had come in every Thursday with her husband until he died three months back. Now she came alone every Thursday, never much for conversation, just sitting with a beer and a crossword, preserving a ritual.

My sister was at work behind the bar, her hair pulled back in nerdy-girl barrettes, her arms pink as she dipped the beer glasses in and out of hot suds. Go is slender and strange-faced, which is not to say unattractive. Her features just take a moment to make sense: the broad jaw; the pinched, pretty nose; the dark globe eyes. If this were a period movie, a man would tilt back his fedora, whistle at the sight of her, and say, 'Now, there's a helluva *broad*!' The face of a '30s screwball-movie queen doesn't always translate in our pixie-princess times, but I know from our years together that men like my sister, a lot, which puts me in that strange brotherly realm of being both proud and wary.

'Do they still make pimento loaf?' she said by way of greeting, not looking up, just knowing it was me, and I felt the relief I usually felt when I saw her: Things might not be great, but things would be okay.

My twin, Go. I've said this phrase so many times, it has become a reassuring mantra instead of actual words: Mytwingo. We were born in the '70s, back when twins were rare, a bit

17

magical: cousins of the unicorn, siblings of the elves. We even have a dash of twin telepathy. Go is truly the one person in the entire world I am totally myself with. I don't feel the need to explain my actions to her. I don't clarify, I don't doubt, I don't worry. I don't tell her everything, not anymore, but I tell her more than anyone else, by far. I tell her as much as I can. We spent nine months back to back, covering each other. It became a lifelong habit. It never mattered to me that she was a girl, strange for a deeply self-conscious kid. What can I say? She was always just cool.

'Pimento loaf, that's like lunch meat, right? I think they do.'

'We should get some,' she said. She arched an eyebrow at me. 'I'm intrigued.'

Without asking, she poured me a draft of PBR into a mug of questionable cleanliness. When she caught me staring at the smudged rim, she brought the glass up to her mouth and licked the smudge away, leaving a smear of saliva. She set the mug squarely in front of me. 'Better, my prince?'

Go firmly believes that I got the best of everything from our parents, that I was the boy they planned on, the single child they could afford, and that she sneaked into this world by clamping onto my ankle, an unwanted stranger. (For my dad, a particularly unwanted stranger.) She believes she was left to fend for herself throughout childhood, a pitiful creature of random hand-me-downs and forgotten permission slips, tightened budgets and general regret. This vision could be somewhat true; I can barely stand to admit it.

'Yes, my squalid little serf,' I said, and fluttered my hands in royal dispensation.

I huddled over my beer. I needed to sit and drink a beer or three. My nerves were still singing from the morning.

'What's up with you?' she asked. 'You look all twitchy.' She flicked some suds at me, more water than soap. The air-conditioning kicked on, ruffling the tops of our heads. We spent more time in The Bar than we needed to. It had become the childhood clubhouse we never had. We'd busted open the storage boxes in our mother's basement one drunken night last year, back when she was alive but right near the end, when we were in need of comfort, and we revisited the toys and games with much oohing and ahhing between sips of canned beer. Christmas in August. After Mom died, Go moved into our old house, and we slowly relocated our toys, piecemeal, to The Bar: a Strawberry Shortcake doll, now scentless, pops up on a stool one day (my gift to Go). A tiny Hot Wheels El Camino, one wheel missing, appears on a shelf in the corner (Go's to me).

We were thinking of introducing a board game night, even though most of our customers were too old to be nostalgic for our Hungry Hungry Hippos, our Game of Life with its tiny plastic cars to be filled with tiny plastic pinhead spouses and tiny plastic pinhead babies. I couldn't remember how you won. (Deep Hasbro thought for the day.)

Go refilled my beer, refilled her beer. Her left eyelid drooped slightly. It was exactly noon, 12–00, and I wondered how long she'd been drinking. She's had a bumpy decade. My speculative sister, she of the rocket-science brain and the rodeo spirit, dropped out of college and moved to Manhattan in the late '90s. She was one of the original dot-com phenoms – made crazy money for two years, then took the Internet bubble bath in 2000. Go remained unflappable. She was closer to twenty than thirty; she was fine. For act two, she got her degree and joined the gray-suited world of investment banking. She was midlevel, nothing flashy, nothing blameful, but she lost her job – fast – with the 2008 financial meltdown. I didn't even know she'd left New York until she phoned me from Mom's house: *I give up.* I begged her, cajoled her to return, hearing nothing but peeved silence on the other end. After I hung up, I made an anxious pilgrimage to her apartment in the Bowery and saw Gary, her beloved ficus tree, yellow-dead on the fire escape, and knew she'd never come back.

The Bar seemed to cheer her up. She handled the books, she poured the beers. She stole from the tip jar semi-regularly, but then she did more work than me. We never talked about our old lives. We were Dunnes, and we were done, and strangely content about it.

'So, what?' Go said, her usual way of beginning a conversation.

'*Eh.*'

'Eh, what? Eh, bad? You look bad.'

I shrugged a yes; she scanned my face.

'Amy?' she asked. It was an easy question. I shrugged again – a confirmation this time, a *whatcha gonna do?* shrug.

Go gave me her amused face, both elbows on the bar, hands cradling chin, hunkering down for an incisive dissection of my marriage. Go, an expert panel of one. 'What about her?'

'Bad day. It's just a bad day.'

'Don't let her worry you.' Go lit a cigarette. She smoked exactly one a day. 'Women are crazy.' Go didn't consider herself part of the general category of *women*, a word she used derisively.

I blew Go's smoke back to its owner. 'It's our anniversary today. Five years.'

'Wow.' My sister cocked her head back. She'd been a bridesmaid, all in violet – 'the gorgeous, raven-haired, amethyst-draped *dame*,' Amy's mother had dubbed her – but anniversaries weren't something she'd remember. 'Jeez. Fuck. Dude. That came fast.' She blew more smoke toward me, a lazy game of cancer catch. 'She going to do one of her, uh, what do you call it, not scavenger hunt—'

'Treasure hunt,' I said.

My wife loved games, mostly mind games, but also actual games of amusement, and for our anniversary she always set up an elaborate treasure hunt, with each clue leading to the hiding place of the next clue until I reached the end, and my present. It was what her dad always did for her mom on their anniversary, and don't think I don't see the gender roles here, that I don't get the hint. But I did not grow up in Amy's household, I grew up in mine, and the last present I remember my dad giving my mom was an iron, set on the kitchen counter, no wrapping paper.

'Should we make a wager on how pissed she's going to get at you this year?' Go asked, smiling over the rim of her beer.

The problem with Amy's treasure hunts: I never figured out the clues. Our first anniversary, back in New York, I went two for seven. That was my best year. The opening parley:

This place is a bit of a hole in the wall,
But we had a great kiss there one Tuesday last fall.

Ever been in a spelling bee as a kid? That snowy second after the announcement of the word as you sift your brain to see if you can spell it? It was like that, the blank panic.

'An Irish bar in a not-so-Irish place,' Amy nudged.

I bit the side of my lip, started a shrug, scanning our living room as if the answer might appear. She gave me another very long minute.

'We were lost in the rain,' she said in a voice that was pleading on the way to peeved.

I finished the shrug.

'*McMann's*, Nick. Remember, when we got lost in the rain in Chinatown trying to find that dim sum place, and it was supposed to be near the statue of Confucius but it turns out there are two statues of Confucius, and we ended up at that random Irish bar all soaking wet, and we slammed a few whiskeys, and you grabbed me and kissed me, and it was—'

'Right! You should have done a clue with Confucius, I would have gotten that.'

'The statue wasn't the point. The place was the point. The moment. I just thought it was special.' She said these last words in a childish lilt that I once found fetching.

'It *was* special.' I pulled her to me and kissed her. 'That smooch right there was my special anniversary reenactment. Let's go do it again at McMann's.'

At McMann's, the bartender, a big, bearded bear-kid, saw us come in and grinned, poured us both whiskeys, and pushed over the next clue.

When I'm down and feeling blue
There's only one place that will do.

That one turned out to be the Alice in Wonderland statue at Central Park, which Amy had told me – she'd *told* me, she *knew* she'd told me *many* times – lightened her moods as a child. I do not remember any of those conversations. I'm being honest here, I just don't. I have a dash of ADD, and I've always found my wife a bit dazzling, in the purest sense of the word: to lose clear vision, especially from looking at bright light. It was enough to be near her and hear her talk, it didn't always matter what she was saying. It should have, but it didn't.

By the time we got to the end of the day, to exchanging our actual presents – the traditional paper presents for the first year of marriage – Amy was not speaking to me.

'I love you, Amy. You know I love you,' I said, tailing her in and out of the family packs of dazed tourists parked in the middle of the sidewalk, oblivious and openmouthed. Amy was slipping through the Central Park crowds, maneuvering between laser-eyed joggers and scissor-legged skaters, kneeling parents and toddlers careering like drunks, always just ahead of me, tight-lipped, hurrying nowhere. Me trying to catch up, grab her arm. She stopped finally, gave me a face unmoved as I explained myself, one mental finger tamping down my exasperation: 'Amy, I don't get why I need to prove my love to you by remembering the exact same *things* you do, the exact same *way* you do. It doesn't mean I don't love our life together.'

A nearby clown blew up a balloon animal, a man bought a rose, a child licked an ice cream cone, and a genuine tradition was born, one I'd never forget: Amy always going overboard, me never, ever worthy of the effort. Happy anniversary, asshole.

'I'm guessing – five years – she's going to get *really* pissed,' Go continued. 'So I hope you got her a really good present.'

'On the to-do list.'

'What's the, like, symbol, for five years? Paper?'

'Paper is first year,' I said. At the end of Year One's

22

unexpectedly wrenching treasure hunt, Amy presented me with a set of posh stationery, my initials embossed at the top, the paper so creamy I expected my fingers to come away moist. In return, I'd presented my wife with a bright red dime-store paper kite, picturing the park, picnics, warm summer gusts. Neither of us liked our presents; we'd each have preferred the other's. It was a reverse O. Henry.

'Silver?' guessed Go. 'Bronze? Scrimshaw? Help me out.'

'Wood,' I said. 'There's no romantic present for wood.'

At the other end of the bar, Sue neatly folded her newspaper and left it on the bartop with her empty mug and a five-dollar bill. We all exchanged silent smiles as she walked out.

'I got it,' Go said. 'Go home, fuck her brains out, then smack her with your penis and scream, "There's some wood for you, bitch!"'

We laughed. Then we both flushed pink in our cheeks in the same spot. It was the kind of raunchy, unsisterly joke that Go enjoyed tossing at me like a grenade. It was also the reason why, in high school, there were always rumors that we secretly screwed. Twincest. We were too tight: our inside jokes, our edge-of-the-party whispers. I'm pretty sure I don't need to say this, but you are not Go, you might misconstrue, so I will: My sister and I have never screwed or even thought of screwing. We just really like each other.

Go was now pantomiming dick-slapping my wife.

No, Amy and Go were never going to be friends. They were each too territorial. Go was used to being the alpha girl in my life, Amy was used to being the alpha girl in everyone's life. For two people who lived in the same city – the same city twice: first New York, now here – they barely knew each other. They flitted in and out of my life like well-timed stage actors, one going out the door as the other came in, and on the rare occasions when they both inhabited the same room, they seemed somewhat bemused at the situation.

Before Amy and I got serious, got engaged, got married, I would get glimpses of Go's thoughts in a sentence here or there. *It's funny, I can't quite get a bead on her, like who she really is.* And: *You just seem kind of not yourself with her.* And: *There's a difference between really loving someone and loving the idea of her.* And finally: *The important thing is she makes you really happy.*

Back when Amy made me really happy.

Amy offered her own notions of Go: *She's very ... Missouri, isn't she?* And: *You just have to be in the right mood for her.* And: *She's a little needy about you, but then I guess she doesn't have anyone else.*

I'd hoped when we all wound up back in Missouri, the two would let it drop – agree to disagree, free to be you and me. Neither did. Go was funnier than Amy, though, so it was a mismatched battle. Amy was clever, withering, sarcastic. Amy could get me riled up, could make an excellent, barbed point, but Go always made me laugh. It is dangerous to laugh at your spouse.

'Go, I thought we agreed you'd never mention my genitalia again,' I said. 'That within the bounds of our sibling relationship, I have no genitalia.'

The phone rang. Go took one more sip of her beer and answered, gave an eyeroll and a smile. 'He sure *is* here, one moment, please!' To me, she mouthed: 'Carl.'

Carl Pelley lived across the street from me and Amy. Retired three years. Divorced two years. Moved into our development right after. He'd been a traveling salesman – children's party supplies – and I sensed that after four decades of motel living, he wasn't quite at home being home. He showed up at the bar nearly every day with a pungent Hardee's bag, complaining about his budget until he was offered a first drink on the house. (This was another thing I learned about Carl from his days in The Bar – that he was a functioning but serious alcoholic.) He had the good grace to accept whatever we were 'trying to get rid of,' and he meant it: For one full month Carl drank nothing but dusty Zimas, circa 1992, that we'd discovered in the basement. When a hangover kept Carl home, he'd find a reason to call: *Your mailbox looks awfully full today, Nicky, maybe a package came.* Or: *It's supposed to rain, you might want to close your windows*. The reasons were bogus. Carl just needed to hear the clink of glasses, the glug of a drink being poured.

I picked up the phone, shaking a tumbler of ice near the receiver so Carl could imagine his gin.

'Hey, Nicky,' Carl's watery voice came over. 'Sorry to bother you. I just thought you should know … your door is wide open, and that cat of yours is outside. It isn't supposed to be, right?'

I gave a non-commital grunt.

'I'd go over and check, but I'm a little under the weather,' Carl said heavily.

'Don't worry,' I said. 'It's time for me to go home anyway.'

It was a fifteen-minute drive, straight north along River Road. Driving into our development occasionally makes me shiver, the sheer number of gaping dark houses – homes that have never known inhabitants, or homes that have known owners and seen them ejected, the house standing triumphantly voided, humanless.

When Amy and I moved in, our only neighbors descended on us: one middle-aged single mom of three, bearing a casserole; a young father of triplets with a six-pack of beer (his wife left at home with the triplets); an older Christian couple who lived a few houses down; and of course, Carl from across the street. We sat out on our back deck and watched the river, and they all talked ruefully about ARMs, and zero percent interest, and zero money down, and then they all remarked how Amy and I were the only ones with river access, the only ones without children. 'Just the two of you? In this whole big house?' the single mom asked, doling out a scrambled-egg something.

'Just the two of us,' I confirmed with a smile, and nodded in appreciation as I took a mouthful of wobbly egg.

'Seems lonely.'

On that she was right.

Four months later, the *whole big house* lady lost her mortgage battle and disappeared in the night with her three kids. Her house has remained empty. The living room window still has

25

a child's picture of a butterfly taped to it, the bright Magic Marker sun-faded to brown. One evening not long ago, I drove past and saw a man, bearded, bedraggled, staring out from behind the picture, floating in the dark like some sad aquarium fish. He saw me see him and flickered back into the depths of the house. The next day I left a brown paper bag full of sandwiches on the front step; it sat in the sun untouched for a week, decaying wetly, until I picked it back up and threw it out.

Quiet. The complex was always disturbingly quiet. As I neared our home, conscious of the noise of the car engine, I could see the cat was definitely on the steps. Still on the steps, twenty minutes after Carl's call. This was strange. Amy loved the cat, the cat was declawed, the cat was never let outside, never ever, because the cat, Bleecker, was sweet but extremely stupid, and despite the LoJack tracking device pelleted somewhere in his fat furry rolls, Amy knew she'd never see the cat again if he ever got out. The cat would waddle straight into the Mississippi River – deedle-de-dum – and float all the way to the Gulf of Mexico into the maw of a hungry bull shark.

But it turned out the cat wasn't even smart enough to get past the steps. Bleecker was perched on the edge of the porch, a pudgy but proud sentinel – Private Tryhard. As I pulled in to the drive, Carl came out and stood on his own front steps, and I could feel the cat and the old man both watching me as I got out of the car and walked toward the house, the red peonies along the border looking fat and juicy, asking to be devoured.

I was about to go into blocking position to get the cat when I saw that the front door was open. Carl had said as much, but seeing it was different. This wasn't taking-out-the-trash-back-in-a-minute open. This was wide-gaping-ominous open.

Carl hovered across the way, waiting for my response, and like some awful piece of performance art, I felt myself enacting Concerned Husband. I stood on the middle step and frowned,

26

then took the stairs quickly, two at a time, calling out my wife's name.

Silence.

'Amy, you home?'

I ran straight upstairs. No Amy. The ironing board was set up, the iron still on, a dress waiting to be pressed.

'Amy!'

As I ran back downstairs, I could see Carl still framed in the open doorway, hands on hips, watching. I swerved into the living room, and pulled up short. The carpet glinted with shards of glass, the coffee table shattered. End tables were on their sides, books slid across the floor like a card trick. Even the heavy antique ottoman was belly-up, its four tiny feet in the air like something dead. In the middle of the mess was a pair of good sharp scissors.

'Amy!'

I began running, bellowing her name. Through the kitchen, where a kettle was burning, down to the basement, where the guest room stood empty, and then out the back door. I pounded across our yard onto the slender boat deck leading out over the river. I peeked over the side to see if she was in our rowboat, where I had found her one day, tethered to the dock, rocking in the water, her face to the sun, eyes closed, and as I'd peered down into the dazzling reflections of the river, at her beautiful, still face, she'd suddenly opened her blue eyes and said nothing to me, and I'd said nothing back and gone into the house alone.

'Amy!'

She wasn't on the water, she wasn't in the house. Amy was not there.

Amy was gone.

AMY ELLIOTT
SEPTEMBER 18, 2005

– Diary entry –

Well, well, well. Guess who's back? Nick Dunne, Brooklyn party boy, sugar-cloud kisser, disappearing act. Eight months, two weeks, couple of days, no word, and then he resurfaces, like it was all part of the plan. Turns out, he'd lost my phone number. His cell was out of juice, so he'd written it on a stickie. Then he'd tucked the stickie into his jeans pocket and put the jeans in the washer, and it turned the stickie into a piece of cyclone-shaped pulp. He tried to unravel it but could only see a 3 and an 8. (He said.)

And then work clobbered him and suddenly it was March and too embarrassingly late to try to find me. (He said.)

Of course I *was* angry. I had *been* angry. But now I'm not. Let me set the scene. (She said.) Today. Gusty September winds. I'm walking along Seventh Avenue, making a lunchtime contemplation of the sidewalk bodega bins – endless plastic containers of cantaloupe and honeydew and melon perched on ice like the day's catch – and I could feel a man barnacling himself to my side as I sailed along, and I corner-eyed the intruder and realized who it was. It was *him*. The boy in 'I met a boy!'

I didn't break my stride, just turned to him and said:

a) 'Do I know you?' (manipulative, challenging)
b) 'Oh, wow, I'm so happy to see you!' (eager, doormatlike)
c) 'Go fuck yourself.' (aggressive, bitter)

28

d) 'Well, you certainly take your time about it, don't you, Nick?' (light, playful, laid-back)

Answer: D

And now we're together. Together, together. It was that easy.

It's interesting, the timing. Propitious, if you will. (And I will.) Just last night was my parents' book party. *Amazing Amy and the Big Day*. Yup, Rand and Marybeth couldn't resist. They've given their daughter's namesake what they can't give their daughter: a husband! Yes, for book twenty, Amazing Amy is getting married! Wheeeeeee. No one cares. No one wanted Amazing Amy to grow up, least of all me. Leave her in kneesocks and hair ribbons and let *me* grow up, unencumbered by my literary alter ego, my paper-bound better half, the me I was supposed to be.

But *Amy* is the Elliott bread and butter, and she's served us well, so I suppose I can't begrudge her a perfect match. She's marrying good old Able Andy, of course. They'll be just like my parents: happy-happy.

Still, it was unsettling, the incredibly small order the publisher put in. A new *Amazing Amy* used to get a first print of a hundred thousand copies back in the '80s. Now ten thousand. The book-launch party was, accordingly, unfabulous. Off-tone. How do you throw a party for a fictional character who started life as a precocious moppet of six and is now a thirty-year-old bride-to-be who still speaks like a child? ('*Sheesh,*' *thought Amy, 'my dear fiancé sure is a grouch-monster when he doesn't get his way . . .*' That is an actual quote. The whole book made me want to punch Amy right in her stupid, spotless vagina.) The book is a nostalgia item, intended to be purchased by women who grew up with *Amazing Amy*, but I'm not sure who will actually want to read it. I read it, of course. I gave the book my blessing – multiple times. Rand and Marybeth feared that I might take Amy's marriage as some jab at my perpetually single state. ('I, for one, don't think women should marry before thirty-five,' said my mom, who married my dad at twenty-three.)

My parents have always worried that I'd take *Amy* too personally – they always tell me not to read too much into her. And yet I can't fail to notice that whenever I screw something up, Amy does it right: When I finally quit violin at age twelve, Amy was revealed as a prodigy in the next book. ('Sheesh, violin can be hard work, but hard work is the only way to get better!') When I blew off the junior tennis championship at age sixteen to do a beach weekend with friends, Amy recommitted to the game. ('Sheesh, I know it's fun to spend time with friends, but I'd be letting myself and everyone else down if I didn't show up for the tournament.') This used to drive me mad, but after I went off to Harvard (and *Amy* correctly chose my parents' alma mater), I decided it was all too ridiculous to think about. That my parents, two *child psychologists*, chose this particular public form of passive-aggressiveness toward *their child* was not just fucked up but also stupid and weird and kind of hilarious. So be it.

The book party was as schizophrenic as the book – at Bluenight, off Union Square, one of those shadowy salons with wingback chairs and art deco mirrors that are supposed to make you feel like a Bright Young Thing. Gin martinis wobbling on trays lofted by waiters with rictus smiles. Greedy journalists with knowing smirks and hollow legs, getting the free buzz before they go somewhere better.

My parents circulate the room hand in hand – their love story is always part of the *Amazing Amy* story: husband and wife in mutual creative labor for a quarter century. Soul mates. They really call themselves that, which makes sense, because I guess they are. I can vouch for it, having studied them, little lonely only child, for many years. They have no harsh edges with each other, no spiny conflicts, they ride through life like conjoined jellyfish – expanding and contracting instinctively, filling each other's spaces liquidly. Making it look easy, the soul-mate thing. People say children from broken homes have it hard, but the children of charmed marriages have their own particular challenges.

Naturally, I have to sit on some velvety banquette in the corner of the room, out of the noise, so I can give a few interviews to a sad handful of kid interns who've gotten stuck with the 'grab a quote' assignment from their editors.

How does it feel to see Amy finally married to Andy? Because you're not married, right?

Question asked by:

a) a sheepish, bug-eyed kid balancing a notebook on top of his messenger bag
b) an overdressed, sleek-haired young thing with fuck-me stilettos
c) an eager, tattooed rockabilly girl who seemed way more interested in *Amy* than one would guess a tattooed rockabilly girl would be
d) all of the above

Answer: D

Me: *'Oh, I'm thrilled for Amy and Andy, I wish them the best. Ha, ha.'*

My answers to all the other questions, in no particular order:

'Some parts of Amy are inspired by me, and some are just fiction.'

'I'm happily single right now, no Able Andy in my life!'

'No, I don't think Amy oversimplifies the male-female dynamic.'

'No, I wouldn't say Amy is dated; I think the series is a classic.'

'Yes, I am single. No Able Andy in my life right now.'

'Why is Amy amazing and Andy's just able? Well, don't you know a lot of powerful, fabulous women who settle for regular guys, Average Joes and Able Andys? No, just kidding, don't write that.'

'Yes, I am single.'

'Yes, my parents are definitely soul mates.'

31

'Yes, I would like that for myself one day.'

'Yep, single, motherfucker.'

Same questions over and over, and me trying to pretend they're thought-provoking. And them trying to pretend they're thought-provoking. Thank God for the open bar.

Then no one else wants to talk to me – that fast – and the PR girl pretends it's a good thing: *Now you can get back to your party!* I wriggle back into the (small) crowd, where my parents are in full hosting mode, their faces flushed – Rand with his toothy prehistoric-monster-fish smile, Marybeth with her chickeny, cheerful head bobs, their hands intertwined, making each other laugh, enjoying each other, *thrilled* with each other – and I think, *I am so fucking lonely.*

I go home and cry for a while. I am almost thirty-two. That's not old, especially not in New York, but fact is, it's been *years* since I even really liked someone. So how likely is it I'll meet someone I love, much less someone I love enough to marry? I'm tired of not knowing who I'll be with, or if I'll be with anyone.

I have many friends who are married – not many who are happily married, but many married friends. The few happy ones are like my parents: They're baffled by my singleness. A smart, pretty, nice girl like me, a girl with so many *interests* and *enthusiasms*, a cool job, a loving family. And let's say it: money. They knit their eyebrows and pretend to think of men they can set me up with, but we all know there's no one left, no one *good* left, and I know that they secretly think there's something wrong with me, something hidden away that makes me unsatisfiable, unsatisfying.

The ones who are not soul-mated – the ones who have *settled* – are even more dismissive of my singleness: It's not that hard to find someone to marry, they say. No relationship is perfect, they say – they, who make do with dutiful sex and gassy bedtime rituals, who settle for TV as conversation, who believe that husbandly capitulation – yes, honey, okay, honey – is the same as concord. *He's doing what you tell him to do because he doesn't care enough to argue*, I think. *Your petty*

demands simply make him feel superior, or resentful, and someday
he will fuck his pretty, young coworker who asks nothing of him,
and you will actually be shocked. Give me a man with a little
fight in him, a man who calls me on my bullshit. (But who
also kind of likes my bullshit.) And yet: Don't land me in one
of those relationships where we're always pecking at each other,
disguising insults as jokes, rolling our eyes and 'playfully'
scrapping in front of our friends, hoping to lure them to our
side of an argument they could not care less about. Those
awful *if only* relationships: *This marriage would be great if only*
... and you sense the *if only* list is a lot longer than either of
them realizes.

So I know I am right not to settle, but it doesn't make me
feel better as my friends pair off and I stay home on Friday
night with a bottle of wine and make myself an extravagant
meal and tell myself, *This is perfect*, as if I'm the one dating
me. As I go to endless rounds of parties and bar nights,
perfumed and sprayed and hopeful, rotating myself around the
room like some dubious dessert. I go on dates with men who
are nice and good-looking and smart – perfect-on-paper men
who make me feel like I'm in a foreign land, trying to explain
myself, trying to make myself known. Because isn't that the
point of every relationship: to be known by someone else, to
be understood? He *gets* me. She *gets* me. Isn't that the simple
magic phrase?

So you suffer through the night with the perfect-on-paper
man – the stutter of jokes misunderstood, the witty remarks
lobbed and missed. Or maybe he understands that you've made
a witty remark but, unsure of what to do with it, he holds it
in his hand like some bit of conversational phlegm he will wipe
away later. You spend another hour trying to find each other,
to recognize each other, and you drink a little too much and
try a little too hard. And you go home to a cold bed and think,
That was fine. And your life is a long line of fine.

And then you run into Nick Dunne on Seventh Avenue as
you're buying diced cantaloupe, and pow, you are known, you
are recognized, the both of you. You both find the exact same

things worth remembering. *(Just one olive, though)*. You have the same rhythm. Click. You just know each other. All of a sudden you see *reading in bed* and *waffles on Sunday* and *laughing at nothing* and *his mouth on yours*. And it's so far beyond fine that you know you can never go back to fine. That fast. You think: *Oh, here is the rest of my life. It's finally arrived.*

NICK DUNNE
THE DAY OF

I waited for the police first in the kitchen, but the acrid smell of the burnt teakettle was curling up in the back of my throat, underscoring my need to retch, so I drifted out on the front porch, sat on the top stair, and willed myself to be calm. I kept trying Amy's cell, and it kept going to voice mail, that quick-clip cadence swearing she'd phone right back. Amy always phoned right back. It had been three hours, and I'd left five messages, and Amy had not phoned back.

I didn't expect her to. I'd tell the police: Amy would never have left the house with the teakettle on. Or the door open. Or anything waiting to be ironed. The woman got shit done, and she was not one to abandon a project (say, her fixer-upper husband, for instance), even if she decided she didn't like it. She'd made a grim figure on the Fiji beach during our two-week honeymoon, battling her way through a million mystical pages of *The Wind-Up Bird Chronicle*, casting pissy glances at me as I devoured thriller after thriller. Since our move back to Missouri, the loss of her job, her life had revolved (devolved?) around the completion of endless tiny, incon-sequential projects. The dress would have been ironed.

And there was the living room, *signs pointing to a struggle*. I already knew Amy wasn't phoning back. I wanted the next part to start.

It was the best time of day, the July sky cloudless, the slowly setting sun a spotlight on the east, turning everything golden and lush, a Flemish painting. The police rolled up. It felt casual, me sitting on the steps, an evening bird singing in the tree, these two cops getting out of their car at a leisurely pace, as if they were dropping by a neighborhood picnic. Kid cops, mid-twenties, confident and uninspired, accustomed to soothing worried parents of curfew-busting teens. A Hispanic girl, her hair in a long dark braid, and a black guy with a marine's stance. Carthage had become a bit (a very tiny bit) less Caucasian while I was away, but it was still so severely segregated that the only people of color I saw in my daily routine tended to be occupational roamers: delivery men, medics, postal workers. Cops. ('This place is so white, it's disturbing,' said Amy, who, back in the melting pot of Manhattan, counted a single African-American among her friends. I accused her of craving ethnic window dressing, minorities as backdrops. It did not go well.)

'Mr Dunne? I'm Officer Velásquez,' said the woman, 'and this is Officer Riordan. We understand you're concerned about your wife?'

Riordan looked down the road, sucking on a piece of candy. I could see his eyes follow a darting bird out over the river. Then he snapped his gaze back toward me, his curled lips telling me he saw what everyone else did. I have a face you want to punch: I'm a working-class Irish kid trapped in the body of a total trust-fund douchebag. I smile a lot to make up for my face, but this only sometimes works. In college, I even wore glasses for a bit, fake spectacles with clear lenses that I thought would lend me an affable, unthreatening vibe. 'You do realize that makes you even more of a dick?' Go reasoned. I threw them out and smiled harder.

I waved in the cops: 'Come inside the house and see.'

The two climbed the steps, accompanied by the squeaking and shuffling noises of their belts and guns. I stood in the entry to the living room and pointed at the destruction.

'*Oh,*' said Officer Riordan, and gave a brisk crack of his knuckles. He suddenly looked less bored.

Riordan and Velásquez leaned forward in their seats at the dining room table as they asked me all the initial questions: who, where, how long. Their ears were literally pricked. A call had been made out of my hearing, and Riordan informed me that detectives were being dispatched. I had the grave pride of being taken seriously.

Riordan was asking me for the second time if I'd seen any strangers in the neighborhood lately, was reminding me for the third time about Carthage's roving bands of homeless men, when the phone rang. I launched myself across the room and grabbed it.

A surly woman's voice: 'Mr Dunne, this is Comfort Hill Assisted Living.' It was where Go and I boarded our Alzheimer's-riddled father.

'I can't talk right now, I'll call you back,' I snapped, and hung up. I despised the women who staffed Comfort Hill: unsmiling, uncomforting. Underpaid, gruelingly underpaid, which was probably why they never smiled or comforted. I knew my anger toward them was misdirected – it absolutely infuriated me that my father lingered on while my mom was in the ground.

It was Go's turn to send the check. I was pretty sure it was Go's turn for July. And I'm sure she was positive it was mine. We'd done this before. Go said we must be mutually subliminally forgetting to mail those checks, that what we really wanted to forget was our dad.

I was telling Riordan about the strange man I'd seen in our neighbor's vacated house when the doorbell rang. The doorbell rang. It sounded so normal, like I was expecting a pizza.

The two detectives entered with end-of-shift weariness. The man was rangy and thin, with a face that tapered severely into a dribble of a chin. The woman was surprisingly ugly – brazenly, beyond the scope of everyday ugly: tiny round eyes set tight as buttons, a long twist of a nose, skin spackled with tiny bumps, long lank hair the color of a dust bunny. I have an affinity for ugly women. I was raised by a trio of women who were hard on the eyes – my grandmother, my mom, her sister – and they were all smart and kind and funny and sturdy, good, good women. Amy was the first pretty girl I ever dated, really dated.

The ugly woman spoke first, an echo of Miss Officer Velásquez. 'Mr Dunne? I'm Detective Rhonda Boney. This is my partner, Detective Jim Gilpin. We understand there are some concerns about your wife.'

My stomach growled loud enough for us all to hear it, but we pretended we didn't.

'We take a look around, sir?' Gilpin said. He had fleshy bags under his eyes and scraggly white whiskers in his mustache. His shirt wasn't wrinkled, but he wore it like it was; he looked like he should stink of cigarettes and sour coffee, even though he didn't. He smelled like Dial soap.

I led them a few short steps to the living room, pointed once again at the wreckage, where the two younger cops were kneeling carefully, as if waiting to be discovered doing something useful. Boney steered me toward a chair in the dining room, away from but in view of the *signs of struggle*.

Rhonda Boney walked me through the same basics I'd told Velásquez and Riordan, her attentive sparrow eyes on me. Gilpin squatted down on a knee, assessing the living room.

'Have you phoned friends or family, people your wife might be with?' Rhonda Boney asked.

'I . . . No. Not yet. I guess I was waiting for you all.'

'Ah.' She smiled. 'Let me guess: baby of the family.'

'What?'

'You're the baby.'

'I have a twin sister.' I sensed some internal judgment being made. 'Why?' Amy's favorite vase was lying on the floor, intact, bumped up against the wall. It was a wedding present, a Japanese masterwork that Amy put away each week when our housecleaner came because she was sure it would get smashed.

'Just a guess of mine, why you'd wait for us: You're used to someone else always taking the lead,' Boney said. 'That's what my little brother is like. It's a birth-order thing.' She scribbled something on a notepad.

'Okay.' I gave an angry shrug. 'Do you need my sun sign too, or can we get started?'

Boney smiled at me kindly, waiting.

'I waited to do something because, I mean, she's obviously not with a friend,' I said, pointing at the disarray in the living room.

'You've lived here, what, Mr Dunne, two years?' she asked.

'Two years September.'

'Moved from where?'

'New York.'

'City?'

'Yes.'

She pointed upstairs, asking permission without asking, and I nodded and followed her, Gilpin following me.

'I was a writer there,' I blurted out before I could stop myself. Even now, two years back here, and I couldn't bear for someone to think this was my only life.

Boney: 'Sounds impressive.'

Gilpin: 'Of what?'

I timed my answer to my stair climbing: I wrote for a magazine (step), I wrote about pop culture (step) for a men's magazine (step). At the top of the stairs, I turned to see Gilpin looking back at the living room. He snapped to.

'Pop culture?' he called up as he began climbing. 'What exactly does that entail?'

'Popular culture,' I said. We reached the top of the stairs, Boney waiting for us. 'Movies, TV, music, but, uh, you know, not high arts, nothing hifalutin.' I winced: *hifalutin*? How patronizing. You two bumpkins probably need me to translate my English, Comma, Educated East Coast into English, Comma, Midwest Folksy. *Me do sum scribbling of stuffs I get in my noggin after watchin' them movin' pitchers!*

'She loves movies,' Gilpin said, gesturing toward Boney. Boney nodded: *I do.*

'Now I own The Bar, downtown,' I added. I taught a class at the junior college too, but to add that suddenly felt too needy. I wasn't on a date.

Boney was peering into the bathroom, halting me and Gilpin in the hallway. 'The Bar?' she said. 'I know the place. Been meaning to drop by. Love the name. Very meta.'

39

'Sounds like a smart move,' Gilpin said. Boney made for the bedroom, and we followed. 'A life surrounded by beer ain't too bad.'

'Sometimes the answer *is* at the bottom of a bottle,' I said, then winced again at the inappropriateness.

We entered the bedroom.

Gilpin laughed. 'Don't I know that feeling.'

'See how the iron is still on?' I began.

Boney nodded, opened the door of our roomy closet, and walked inside, flipping on the light, fluttering her latexed hands over shirts and dresses as she moved toward the back. She made a sudden noise, bent down, turned around – holding a perfectly square box covered in elaborate silver wrapping.

My stomach seized.

'Someone's birthday?' she asked.

'It's our anniversary.'

Boney and Gilpin both twitched like spiders and pretended they didn't.

By the time we returned to the living room, the kid officers were gone. Gilpin got down on his knees, eyeing the overturned ottoman.

'Uh, I'm a little freaked out, obviously,' I started.

'I don't blame you at all, Nick,' Gilpin said earnestly. He had pale blue eyes that jittered in place, an unnerving tic.

'Can we do something? To find my wife. I mean, because she's clearly not here.'

Boney pointed at the wedding portrait on the wall: me in my tux, a block of teeth frozen on my face, my arms curved formally around Amy's waist; Amy, her blond hair tightly coiled and sprayed, her veil blowing in the beach breeze of Cape Cod, her eyes open too wide because she always blinked at the last minute and she was trying so hard not to blink. The day after Independence Day, the sulfur from the fireworks mingling with the ocean salt – summer.

The Cape had been good to us. I remember discovering several months in that Amy, my girlfriend, was also quite

40

wealthy, a treasured only child of creative-genius parents. An icon of sorts, thanks to a namesake book series that I thought I could remember as a kid. *Amazing Amy*. Amy explained this to me in calm, measured tones, as if I were a patient waking from a coma. As if she'd had to do it too many times before and it had gone badly – the admission of wealth that's greeted with too much enthusiasm, the disclosure of a secret identity that she herself didn't create.

Amy told me who and what she was, and then we went out to the Elliotts' historically registered home on Nantucket Sound, went sailing together, and I thought: *I am a boy from Missouri, flying across the ocean with people who've seen much more than I have. If I began seeing things now, living big, I could still not catch up with them.* It didn't make me feel jealous. It made me feel content. I never aspired to wealth or fame. I was not raised by big-dreamer parents who pictured their child as a future president. I was raised by pragmatic parents who pictured their child as a future office worker of some sort, making a living of some sort. To me, it was heady enough to be in the Elliotts' proximity, to skim across the Atlantic and return to a plushly restored home built in 1822 by a whaling captain, and there to prepare and eat meals of organic, healthful foods whose names I didn't know how to pronounce. Quinoa. I remember thinking quinoa was a kind of fish.

So we married on the beach on a deep blue summer day, ate and drank under a white tent that billowed like a sail, and a few hours in, I sneaked Amy off into the dark, toward the waves, because I was feeling so unreal, I believed I had become merely a shimmer. The chilly mist on my skin pulled me back, Amy pulled me back, toward the golden glow of the tent, where the Gods were feasting, everything ambrosia. Our whole courtship was just like that.

Boney leaned in to examine Amy. 'Your wife is very pretty.'

'She is, she's beautiful,' I said, and felt my stomach lilt.

'What anniversary today?' she asked.

'Five.'

I was jittering from one foot to another, wanting to *do*

41

something. I didn't want them to discuss how lovely my wife was, I wanted them to go out and search for my fucking wife. I didn't say this out loud, though; I often don't say things out loud, even when I should. I contain and I compartmentalize to a disturbing degree: In my belly-basement are hundreds of bottles of rage, despair, fear, but you'd never guess from looking at me.

'Five, big one. Let me guess, reservations at Houston's?' Gilpin asked. It was the only upscale restaurant in town. *You all really need to try Houston's*, my mom had said when we moved back, thinking it was Carthage's unique little secret, hoping it might please my wife.

'Of course, Houston's.'

It was my fifth lie to the police. I was just starting.

AMY ELLIOTT DUNNE
JULY 5, 2008

I am fat with love! Husky with ardor! Morbidly obese with devotion! A happy, busy bumblebee of marital enthusiasm. I positively hum around him, fussing and fixing. I have become a strange thing. I have become a wife. I find myself steering the ship of conversations – bulkily, unnaturally – just so I can say his name aloud. I have become a wife, I have become a bore, I have been asked to forfeit my Independent Young Feminist card. I don't care. I balance his checkbook, I trim his hair. I've gotten so retro, at one point I will probably use the word *pocketbook*, shuffling out the door in my swingy tweed coat, my lips painted red, on the way to the *beauty parlor*. Nothing bothers me. Everything seems like it will turn out fine, every bother transformed into an amusing story to be told over dinner. *So I killed a hobo today, honey ... hahahaha! Ah, we have fun!*

Nick is like a good stiff drink: He gives everything the correct perspective. Not a different perspective, the correct perspective. With Nick, I realize it actually, truly doesn't matter if the electricity bill is a few days late, if my latest quiz turns out a little lame. (My most recent, I'm not joking: 'What kind of tree would you be?' Me, I'm an apple tree! This means nothing!) It doesn't matter if the new *Amazing Amy* book has been well and duly scorched, the reviews vicious, the sales a stunning plummet after a limp start. It doesn't matter what color I paint our room, or how late traffic makes me, or whether our recycling really, truly does get recycled. (Just level with me, New York, does it?) It doesn't matter, because I have found my match. It's Nick, laid-back and calm, smart and fun and uncomplicated. Untortured, happy. Nice. Big penis.

All the stuff I don't like about myself has been pushed to the back of my brain. Maybe that is what I like best about him, the way he makes me. Not makes me feel, just makes me. I am fun. I am playful. I am game. I feel naturally happy and entirely satisfied. I am a wife! It's weird to say those words. (Seriously, about the recycling, New York – come on, just a wink.)

We do silly things, like last weekend we drove to Delaware because neither of us have ever had sex in Delaware. Let me set the scene, because now it really is for posterity. We cross the state line – *Welcome to Delaware!*, the sign says, and also: *Small Wonder*, and also: *The First State*, and also: *Home of Tax-Free Shopping*.

Delaware, a state of many rich identities.

I point Nick down the first dirt road I see, and we rumble five minutes until we hit pine trees on all sides. We don't speak. He pushes his seat back. I pull up my skirt. I am not wearing undies, I can see his mouth turn down and his face go slack, the drugged, determined look he gets when he's turned on. I climb atop him, my back to him, facing the windshield. I'm pressed against the steering wheel, and as we move together, the horn emits tiny bleats that mimic me, and my hand makes a smearing noise as I press it against the windshield. Nick and I can come anywhere; neither of us gets stage fright, it's something we're both rather proud of. Then we drive right back home. I eat beef jerky and ride with bare feet on the dashboard.

We love our house. The house that *Amazing Amy* built. A Brooklyn brownstone my parents bought for us, right on the Promenade, with the big wide-screen view of Manhattan. It's extravagant, it makes me feel guilty, but it's perfect. I battle the spoiled-rich-girl vibe where I can. Lots of DIY. We painted the walls ourselves over two weekends: spring green and pale yellow and velvety blue. In theory. None of the colors turned out like we thought they would, but we pretend to like them anyway. We fill our home with knickknacks from flea markets;

we buy records for Nick's record player. Last night we sat on the old Persian rug, drinking wine and listening to the vinyl scratches as the sky went dark and Manhattan switched on, and Nick said, 'This is how I always pictured it. This is exactly how I pictured it.'

On weekends, we talk to each other under four layers of bedding, our faces warm under a sunlit yellow comforter. Even the floorboards are cheerful: There are two old creaky slats that call out to us as we walk in the door. I love it, I love that it is ours, that we have a great story behind the ancient floor lamp, or the misshapen clay mug that sits near our coffeepot, never holding anything but a single paper clip. I spend my days thinking of sweet things to do for him – go buy a peppermint soap that will sit in his palm like a warm stone, or maybe a slim slice of trout that I could cook and serve to him, an ode to his riverboat days. I know, I am ridiculous. I love it, though – I never knew I was capable of being ridiculous over a man. It's a relief. I even swoon over his socks, which he manages to shed in adorably tangled poses, as if a puppy carried them in from another room.

It is our one-year anniversary and I am fat with love, even though people kept telling and telling us the first year was going to be so hard, as if we were naive children marching off to war. It wasn't hard. We are meant to be married. It is our one-year anniversary, and Nick is leaving work at lunchtime; my treasure hunt awaits him. The clues are all about us, about the past year together:

Whenever my sweet hubby gets a cold
It is this dish that will soon be sold.

Answer: the torn yum soup from Thai Town on President Street. The manager will be there this afternoon with a taster bowl and the next clue.

Also McMann's in Chinatown and the Alice statue at Central Park. A grand tour of New York. We'll end at the Fulton Street fish market, where we'll buy a pair of beautiful lobsters, and I will hold the container in my lap as Nick jitters nervously in the cab beside me. We'll rush home, and I will drop them in a new pot on our old stove with all the finesse of a girl who has lived many Cape summers while Nick giggles and pretends to hide in fear outside the kitchen door.

I had suggested we get burgers. Nick wanted us to go out – fivestar, fancy – somewhere with a clockwork of courses and name-dropping waiters. So the lobsters are a perfect in-between, the lobsters are what everyone tells us (and tells us and tells us) that marriage is about: compromise!

We'll eat lobster with butter and have sex on the floor while a woman on one of our old jazz records sings to us in her far-side-of-the-tunnel voice. We'll get slowly lazy-drunk on good Scotch, Nick's favorite. I'll give him his present – the mono-grammed stationery he's been wanting from Crane & Co. with the clean sans-serif font set in hunter green, on the thick creamy stock that will hold lush ink and his writer's words. Stationery for a writer, and a writer's wife who's maybe angling for a love letter or two.

Then maybe we'll have sex again. And a late-night burger. And more Scotch. Voilà: happiest couple on the block! And they say marriage is such hard work.

NICK DUNNE
THE NIGHT OF

Boney and Gilpin moved our interview to the police station, which looks like a failing community bank. They left me alone in a little room for forty minutes, me willing myself not to move. To pretend to be calm is to be calm, in a way. I slouched over the table, put my chin on my arm. Waited.

'Do you want to call Amy's parents?' Boney had asked.

'I don't want to panic them,' I said. 'If we don't hear from her in an hour, I'll call.'

We'd done three rounds of that conversation.

Finally, the cops came in and sat at the table across from me. I fought the urge to laugh at how much it felt like a TV show. This was the same room I'd seen surfing through late-night cable for the past ten years, and the two cops – weary, intense – acted like the stars. Totally fake. Epcot Police Station. Boney was even holding a paper coffee cup and a manila folder that looked like a prop. Cop prop. I felt giddy, felt for a moment we were all pretend people: *Let's play the Missing Wife game!*

'You okay there, Nick?' Boney asked.

'I'm okay, why?'

'You're smiling.'

The giddiness slid to the tiled floor. 'I'm sorry, it's all just—'

'I know,' Boney said, giving me a look that was like a hand pat. 'It's too strange, I know.' She cleared her throat. 'First of all, we want to make sure you're comfortable here. You need anything, just let us know. The more information you can give us right now, the better, but you can leave at any time, that's not a problem, either.'

'Whatever you need.'

'Okay, great, thank you,' she said. 'Um, okay. I want to get the annoying stuff out of the way first. The crap stuff. If your wife was indeed abducted – and we don't know that, but if it comes to that – we want to catch the guy, and when we catch the guy, we want to nail him, hard. No way out. No wiggle room.'

'Right.'

'So we have to rule you out real quick, real easy. So the guy can't come back and say we didn't rule you out, you know what I mean?'

I nodded mechanically. I didn't really know what she meant, but I wanted to seem as cooperative as possible. 'Whatever you need.'

'We don't want to freak you out,' Gilpin added. 'We just want to cover all the bases.'

'Fine by me.' *It's always the husband*, I thought. *Everyone knows it's always the husband, so why can't they just say it: We suspect you because you are the husband, and it's always the husband. Just watch* Dateline.

'Okay, great, Nick,' Boney said. 'First let's get a swab of the inside of your cheek so we can rule out all of the DNA in the house that isn't yours. Would that be okay?'

'Sure.'

'I'd also like to take a quick sweep of your hands for gun shot residue. Again, just in case—'

'Wait, wait, wait. Have you found something that makes you think my wife was—'

'Nonono, Nick,' Gilpin interrupted. He pulled a chair up to the table and sat on it backward. I wondered if cops actually did that. Or did some clever actor do that, and then cops began doing it because they'd seen the actors playing cops do that and it looked cool?

'It's just smart protocol,' Gilpin continued. 'We try to cover every base: Check your hands, get a swab, and if we could check out your car too . . .'

'Of course. Like I said, whatever you need.'

48

'Thank you, Nick. I really appreciate it. Sometimes guys, they make things hard for us just because they can.'

I was exactly the opposite. My father had infused my childhood with unspoken blame; he was the kind of man who skulked around looking for things to be angry at. This had turned Go defensive and extremely unlikely to take unwarranted shit. It had turned me into a knee-jerk suckup to authority. Mom, Dad, teachers: *Whatever makes your job easier, sir or madam.* I craved a constant stream of approval. 'You'd literally lie, cheat, and steal – hell, kill – to convince people you are a good guy,' Go once said. We were in line for knishes at Yonah Schimmel's, not far from Go's old New York apartment – that's how well I remember the moment – and I lost my appetite because it was so completely true and I'd never realized it, and even as she was saying it, I thought: *I will never forget this, this is one of those moments that will be lodged in my brain forever.*

We made small talk, the cops and I, about the July Fourth fireworks and the weather, while my hands were tested for gunshot residue and the slick inside of my cheek was cotton-tipped. Pretending it was normal, a trip to the dentist.

When it was done, Boney put another cup of coffee in front of me, squeezed my shoulder. 'I'm sorry about that. Worst part of the job. You think you're up to a few questions now? It'd really help us.'

'Yes, definitely, fire away.'

She placed a slim digital tape recorder on the table in front of me. 'You mind? This way you won't have to answer the same questions over and over and over ...' She wanted to tape me so I'd be nailed to one story. *I should call a lawyer*, I thought, *but only guilty people need lawyers*, so I nodded: *No problem.*

'So: Amy,' Boney said. 'You two been living here how long?'

'Just about two years.'

'And she's originally from New York. City.'

'Yes.'

'She work, got a job?' Gilpin said.

'No. She used to write personality quizzes.'

The detectives swapped a look: *Quizzes?*

'For teen magazines, women's magazines,' I said. 'You know: "Are you the jealous type? Take our quiz and find out! Do guys find you too intimidating? Take our quiz and find out!"'

'Very cool, I love those,' Boney said. 'I didn't know that was an actual job. Writing those. Like, a career.'

'Well, it's not. Anymore. The Internet is packed with quizzes for free. Amy's were smarter – she had a master's in psychology – *has* a master's in psychology.' I guffawed uncomfortably at my gaffe. 'But smart can't beat free.'

'Then what?'

I shrugged. 'Then we moved back here. She's just kind of staying at home right now.'

'Oh! You guys got kids, then?' Boney chirped, as if she had discovered good news.

'No.'

'Oh. So then what does she do most days?'

That was my question too. Amy was once a woman who did a little of everything, all the time. When we moved in together, she'd made an intense study of French cooking, displaying hyper-quick knife skills and an inspired boeuf bourguignon. For her thirty-fourth birthday, we flew to Barcelona, and she stunned me by rolling off trills of conversational Spanish, learned in months of secret lessons. My wife had a brilliant, popping brain, a greedy curiosity. But her obsessions tended to be fueled by competition: She needed to dazzle men and jealous-ify women: *Of course Amy can cook French cuisine and speak fluent Spanish and garden and knit and run marathons and day-trade stocks and fly a plane and look like a runway model doing it.* She needed to be Amazing Amy, all the time. Here in Missouri, the women shop at Target, they make diligent, comforting meals, they laugh about how little high school Spanish they remember. Competition doesn't interest them. Amy's relentless achieving is greeted with open-palmed acceptance and maybe a bit of pity. It was about the worst outcome possible for my competitive wife: A town of contented also-rans.

'She has a lot of hobbies,' I said.

'Anything worrying you?' Boney asked, looking worried. 'You're not concerned about drugs or drinking? I'm not speaking ill of your wife. A lot of housewives, more than you'd guess, they pass the day that way. The days, they get long when you're by yourself. And if the drinking turns to drugs – and I'm not talking heroin but even prescription painkillers – well, there are some pretty awful characters selling around here right now.'

'The drug trade has gotten bad,' Gilpin said. 'We've had a bunch of police layoffs – one fifth of the force, and we were tight to begin with. I mean, it's *bad*, we're overrun.'

'Had a housewife, nice lady, get a tooth knocked out last month over some Oxycontin,' Boney prompted.

'No, Amy might have a glass of wine or something, but not drugs.'

Boney eyed me; this was clearly not the answer she wanted. 'She have some good friends here? We'd like to call some of them, just make sure. No offense. Sometimes a spouse is the last to know when drugs are involved. People get ashamed, especially women.'

Friends. In New York, Amy made and shed friends weekly; they were like her projects. She'd get intensely excited about them: Paula who gave her singing lessons and had a wicked good voice (Amy went to boarding school in Massachusetts; I loved the very occasional times she got all New England on me: *wicked good*); Jessie from the fashion-design course. But then I'd ask about Jessie or Paula a month later, and Amy would look at me like I was making up words.

Then there were the men who were always rattling behind Amy, eager to do the husbandly things that her husband failed to do. Fix a chair leg, hunt down her favorite imported Asian tea. Men who she swore were her friends, just good friends. Amy kept them at exactly an arm's distance – far enough away that I couldn't get too annoyed, close enough that she could crook a finger and they'd do her bidding.

51

In Missouri ... good God, I really didn't know. It only occurred to me just then. *You truly are an asshole*, I thought. Two years we'd been here, and after the initial flurry of meet-and-greets, those manic first months, Amy had no one she regularly saw. She had my mom, who was now dead, and me – and our main form of conversation was attack and rebuttal. When we'd been back home for a year, I'd asked her faux gallantly: 'And how are you liking North Carthage, Mrs Dunne?' '*New* Carthage, you mean?' she'd replied. I refused to ask her the reference, but I knew it was an insult.

'She has a few good friends, but they're mostly back east.'

'Her folks?'

'They live in New York. City.'

'And you still haven't called any of these people?' Boney asked, a bemused smile on her face.

'I've been doing everything *else* you've been asking me to do. I haven't had a chance.' I'd signed away permission to trace credit cards and ATMs and track Amy's cell phone, I'd handed over Go's cell number and the name of Sue, the widow at The Bar, who could presumably attest to the time I arrived.

'Baby of the family.' She shook her head. 'You really do remind me of my little brother.' A beat. 'That's a compliment, I swear.'

'She dotes on him,' Gilpin said, scribbling in a notebook. 'Okay, so you left the house at about seven-thirty a.m., and you showed up at The Bar at about noon, and in between, you were at the beach.'

There's a beachhead about ten miles north of our house, a not overly pleasant collection of sand and silt and beer-bottle shards. Trash barrels overflowing with Styrofoam cups and dirty diapers. But there is a picnic table upwind that gets nice sun, and if you stare directly at the river, you can ignore the other crap.

'I sometimes bring my coffee and the paper and just sit. Gotta make the most of summer.'

No, I hadn't talked to anyone at the beach. No, no one saw me.

'It's a quiet place midweek,' Gilpin allowed.

If the police talked to anyone who knew me, they'd quickly learn that I rarely went to the beach and that I never sometimes brought my coffee to just enjoy the morning. I have Irish-white skin and an impatience for navel-gazing: A beach boy I am not. I told the police that because it had been Amy's idea, for me to go sit in the spot where I could be alone and watch the river I loved and ponder our life together. She'd said this to me this morning, after we'd eaten her crepes. She leaned forward on the table and said, 'I know we are having a tough time. I still love you so much, Nick, and I know I have a lot of things to work on. I want to be a good wife to you, and I want you to be my husband and be happy. But you need to decide what you want.'

She'd clearly been practicing the speech; she smiled proudly as she said it. And even as my wife was offering me this kindness, I was thinking, *Of course she has to stage-manage this. She wants the image of me and the wild running river, my hair ruffling in the breeze as I look out onto the horizon and ponder our life together. I can't just go to Dunkin' Donuts.*

You need to decide what you want. Unfortunately for Amy, I had decided already.

Boney looked up brightly from her notes: 'Can you tell me what your wife's blood type is?' she asked.

'Uh, no, I don't know.'

'You don't know your wife's blood type?'

'Maybe O?' I guessed.

Boney frowned, then made a drawn-out yoga-like sound. 'Okay, Nick, here are the things *we* are doing to help.' She listed them: Amy's cell was being monitored, her photo circulated, her credit cards tracked. Known sex offenders in the area were being interviewed. Our sparse neighborhood was being canvassed. Our home phone was tapped, in case any ransom calls came in.

I wasn't sure what to say now. I raked my memory for the lines: What does the husband say at this point in the movie? Depends on whether he's guilty or innocent.

'I can't say that reassures me. Are you – is this an abduction, or a missing persons case, or what exactly is going on?' I knew the statistics, knew them from the same TV show I was starring in: If the first forty-eight hours didn't turn up something in a case, it was likely to go unsolved. The first forty-eight hours were crucial. 'I mean, my wife is gone. My wife: *is gone!*' I realized it was the first time I'd said it the way it should have been said: panicked and angry. My dad was a man of infinite varieties of bitterness, rage, distaste. In my lifelong struggle to avoid becoming him, I'd developed an inability to demonstrate much negative emotion at all. It was another thing that made me seem like a dick – my stomach could be all oiled eels, and you would get nothing from my face and less from my words. It was a constant problem: too much control or no control at all.

'Nick, we are taking this *extremely* seriously,' Boney said. 'The lab guys are over at your place as we speak, and that will give us more information to go on. Right now, the more you can tell us about your wife, the better. What is she like?'

The usual husband phrases came into my mind: *She's sweet, she's great, she's nice, she's supportive.*

'What is she like *how?*' I asked.

'Give me an idea of her personality,' Boney prompted. 'Like, what did you get her for your anniversary? Jewelry?'

'I hadn't gotten anything quite yet,' I said. 'I was going to do it this afternoon.' I waited for her to laugh and say 'baby of the family' again, but she didn't.

'Okay. Well, then, tell me about her. Is she outgoing? Is she – I don't know how to say this – is she New Yorky? Like what might come off to some as rude? Might rub people the wrong way?'

'I don't know. She's not a never-met-a-stranger kind of person, but she's not – not abrasive enough to make someone ... hurt her.'

This was my eleventh lie. The Amy of today was abrasive enough to want to hurt, sometimes. I speak specifically of the Amy of today, who was only remotely like the woman I fell in

54

love with. It had been an awful fairy-tale reverse transformation. Over just a few years, the old Amy, the girl of the big laugh and the easy ways, literally shed herself, a pile of skin and soul on the floor, and out stepped this new, brittle, bitter Amy. My wife was no longer my wife but a razor-wire knot daring me to unloop her, and I was not up to the job with my thick, numb, nervous fingers. Country fingers. Flyover fingers untrained in the intricate, dangerous work of *solving Amy*. When I'd hold up the bloody stumps, she'd sigh and turn to her secret mental notebook on which she tallied all my deficiencies, forever noting disappointments, frailties, shortcomings. My old Amy, damn, she was fun. She was funny. She made me laugh. I'd forgotten that. And *she* laughed. From the bottom of her throat, from right behind that small finger-shaped hollow, which is the best place to laugh from. She released her grievances like handfuls of birdseed: They are there, and they are gone.

She was not the thing she became, the thing I feared most: an angry woman. I was not good with angry women. They brought something out in me that was unsavory.

'She bossy?' Gilpin asked. 'Take-charge?'

I thought of Amy's calendar, the one that went three years into the future, and if you looked a year ahead, you would actually find appointments: dermatologist, dentist, vet. 'She's a planner – she doesn't, you know, wing anything. She likes to make lists and check things off. Get things done. That's why this doesn't make sense—'

'That can drive you crazy,' Boney said sympathetically. 'If you're not that type. You seem very B-personality.'

'I'm a little more laid-back, I guess,' I said. Then I added the part I was supposed to add: 'We round each other out.'

I looked at the clock on the wall, and Boney touched my hand.

'Hey, why don't you go ahead and give a call to Amy's parents? I'm sure they'd appreciate it.'

It was past midnight. Amy's parents went to sleep at nine p.m.; they were strangely boastful about this early bedtime.

They'd be deep asleep by now, so this would be an urgent middle-of-the-night call. Cells went off at 8:45 always, so Rand Elliott would have to walk from his bed all the way to the end of the hall to pick up the old heavy phone; he'd be fumbling with his glasses, fussy with the table lamp. He'd be telling himself all the reasons not to worry about a late-night phone call, all the harmless reasons the phone might be ringing.

I dialed twice and hung up before I let the call ring through. When I did, it was Marybeth, not Rand, who answered, her deep voice buzzing my ears. I'd only gotten to 'Marybeth, this is Nick' when I lost it.

'What is it, Nick?'

I took a breath.

'Is it Amy? Tell me.'

'I uh – I'm sorry I should have called—'

'Tell me, goddamn it!'

'We c-can't find Amy,' I stuttered.

'You can't *find* Amy?'

'I don't know—'

'Amy is missing?'

'We don't know that for sure, we're still—'

'Since when?'

'We're not sure. I left this morning, a little after seven—'

'And you waited till now to call us?'

'I'm sorry, I didn't want to—'

'Jesus Christ. We played tennis tonight. *Tennis*, and we could have been … My God. Are the police involved? You've notified them?'

'I'm at the station right now.'

'Put on whoever's in charge, Nick. Please.'

Like a kid, I went to fetch Gilpin. *My mommy-in-law wants to talk to you.*

Phoning the Elliotts made it official. The emergency – *Amy is gone* – was spreading to the outside.

I was heading back to the interview room when I heard my father's voice. Sometimes, in particularly shameful moments,

I heard his voice in my head. But this was my father's voice, here. His words emerged in wet bubbles like something from a rancid bog. *Bitch bitch bitch.* My father, out of his mind, had taken to flinging the word at any woman who even vaguely annoyed him: *bitch bitch bitch.* I peered inside a conference room, and there he sat on a bench against the wall. He had been a handsome man once, intense and cleft-chinned. *Jarringly dreamy* was how my aunt had described him. Now he sat muttering at the floor, his blond hair matted, trousers muddy and arms scratched, as if he'd fought his way through a thornbush. A line of spittle glimmered down his chin like a snail's trail, and he was flexing and unflexing arm muscles that had not yet gone to seed. A tense female officer sat next to him, her lips in an angry pucker, trying to ignore him: *Bitch bitch bitch I told you bitch.*

'What's going on?' I asked her. 'This is my father.'

'You got our call?'

'What call?'

'To come get your father.' She overenunciated, as if I were a dim ten-year-old.

'I – My wife is missing. I've been *here* most of the night.'

She stared at me, not connecting in the least. I could see her debating whether to sacrifice her leverage and apologize, inquire. Then my father started up again, *bitch bitch bitch*, and she chose to keep the leverage.

'Sir, Comfort Hill has been trying to contact you all day. Your father wandered out a fire exit early this morning. He's got a few scratches and scrapes, as you can see, but no damage. We picked him up a few hours ago, walking down River Road, disoriented. We've been trying to reach you.'

'I've been right here,' I said. 'Right goddamn next door, how did no one put this together?'

Bitch bitch bitch, said my dad.

'Sir, please don't take that tone with me.'

Bitch bitch bitch.

*

Boney ordered an officer – male – to drive my dad back to the home so I could finish up with them. We stood on the stairs outside the police station, watched him get settled into the car, still muttering. The entire time he never registered my presence. When they drove off, he didn't even look back.

'You guys not close?' she asked.

'We are the definition of not close.'

The police finished with their questions and hustled me into a squad car at about two a.m. with advice to get a good night's sleep and return at eleven a.m. for a 12-noon press conference.

I didn't ask if I could go home. I had them take me to Go's, because I knew she'd stay up and have a drink with me, fix me a sandwich. It was, pathetically, all I wanted right then: a woman to fix me a sandwich and not ask me any questions.

'You don't want to go look for her?' Go offered as I ate. 'We can drive around.'

'That seems pointless,' I said dully. 'Where do I look?'

'Nick, this is really fucking serious.'

'I know, Go.'

'Act like it, okay, *Lance*? Don't fucking *myuhmyuhmyuh*.' It was a thick-tongued noise, the noise she always made to convey my indecisiveness, accompanied by a dazed rolling of the eyes and the dusting off of my legal first name. No one who has my face needs to be called Lance. She handed me a tumbler of Scotch. 'And drink this, but only this. You don't want to be hungover tomorrow. Where the fuck could she be? God, I feel sick to my stomach.' She poured herself a glass, gulped, then tried to sip, pacing around the kitchen. 'Aren't you worried, Nick? That some guy, like, saw her on the street and just, just decided to take her? Hit her on the head and—'

I started. 'Why did you say *hit her on the head*, what the fuck is that?'

'I'm sorry, I didn't mean to paint a picture, I just ... I don't know, I just keep thinking. About some crazy person.' She splashed some more Scotch into her tumbler.

'Speaking of crazy people,' I said, 'Dad got out again today, they found him wandering down River Road. He's back at Comfort now.'

She shrugged: *okay*. It was the third time in six months that our dad had slipped out. Go was lighting a cigarette, her thoughts still on Amy. 'I mean, isn't there someone we can go talk to?' she asked. 'Something we can do?'

'Jesus, Go! You really need me to feel more fucking impotent than I do right now?' I snapped. 'I have no idea what I'm supposed to be doing. There's no "When Your Wife Goes Missing 101." The police told me I could leave. I left. I'm just doing what they tell me.'

'Of course you are,' murmured Go, who had a long-stymied mission to turn me into a rebel. It wouldn't take. I was the kid in high school who made curfew; I was the writer who hit my deadlines, even the fake ones. I respect rules, because if you follow rules, things go smoothly, usually.

'Fuck, Go, I'm back at the station in a few hours, okay? Can you please just be nice to me for a second? I'm scared shitless.'

We had a five-second staring contest, then Go filled up my glass one more time, an apology. She sat down next to me, put a hand on my shoulder.

'Poor Amy,' she said.

AMY ELLIOTT DUNNE
APRIL 21, 2009

– Diary entry –

Poor me. Let me set the scene: Campbell and Insley and I are all down in Soho, having dinner at Tableau. Lots of goat-cheese tarts, lamb meatballs and rocket greens, I'm not sure what all the fuss is about. But we are working backward: dinner first, then drinks in one of the little nooks Campbell has reserved, a mini-closet where you can lounge expensively in a place that's not too different from, say, your living room. But fine, it's fun to do the silly, trendy things sometimes. We are all overdressed in our little flashy frocks, our slasher heels, and we all eat small plates of food bites that are as decorative and insubstantial as we are.

We've discussed having our husbands drop by to join us for the drinks portion. So there we are, post-dinner, tucked into our nook, mojitos and martinis and my bourbon delivered to us by a waitress who could be auditioning for the small role of Fresh-faced Girl Just Off the Bus.

We are running out of things to say; it is a Tuesday, and no one is feeling like it is anything but. The drinks are being carefully drunk: Insley and Campbell both have vague appointments the next morning, and I have work, so we aren't gearing up for a big night, we are winding down, and we are getting dull-witted, bored. We would leave if we weren't waiting for the possible appearance of the men. Campbell keeps peeking at her BlackBerry, Insley studies her flexed calves from different angles. John arrives first – huge apologies to Campbell, big smiles and kisses for us all, a man just thrilled to be here, just delighted to arrive at the tail-end of a cocktail hour across town so he can guzzle a drink and head home with his wife. George shows up about twenty minutes later – sheepish, tense, a terse excuse about work, Insley snapping at him, 'You're *forty* minutes late,' him nipping back, 'Yeah, sorry about making us money.' The two barely talking to each other as they make conversation with everyone else.

Nick never shows; no call. We wait another forty-five minutes, Campbell solicitous ('Probably got hit with some last-minute deadline,' she says, and smiles toward good old John, who never lets last-minute deadlines interfere with his wife's plans); Insley's anger thawing toward her husband as she realizes he is only the second-biggest jackass of the group ('You sure he hasn't even texted, sweetie?').

Me, I just smile: 'Who knows where he is – I'll catch him at home.' And then it is the men of the group who look stricken: *You mean that was an option? Take a pass on the night with no nasty consequences? No guilt or anger or sulking?*

Well, maybe not for you guys.

Nick and I, we sometimes laugh, laugh out loud, at the horrible things women make their husbands do to prove their love. The pointless tasks, the myriad sacrifices, the endless small surrenders. We call these men the *dancing monkeys*.

Nick will come home, sweaty and salty and beer-loose from a day at the ballpark, and I'll curl up in his lap, ask him about the game, ask him if his friend Jack had a good time, and he'll say, 'Oh, he came down with a case of the dancing monkeys – poor Jennifer was having a "real stressful week" and *really* needed him at home.'

Or his buddy at work, who can't go out for drinks because his girlfriend really needs him to stop by some bistro where she is having dinner with a friend from out of town. So they can finally meet. And so she can show how obedient her monkey is: *He comes when I call, and look how well groomed!*

Wear this, don't wear that. Do this chore now and do this chore when you get a chance and by that I mean now. And definitely, definitely, give up the things you love for me, so I will have proof that you love me best. It's the female pissing contest – as we swan around our book clubs and our cocktail hours, there are few things women love more than being able to detail the sacrifices our men make for us. A call-and-response, the response being: 'Ohhh, that's so *sweet.*'

I am happy not to be in that club. I don't partake, I don't get off on emotional coercion, on forcing Nick to play some happy-hubby role – the shrugging, cheerful, dutiful *taking out the trash, honey!* role. Every wife's dream man, the counterpoint to every man's fantasy of the sweet, hot, laid-back woman who loves sex and a stiff drink.

I like to think I am confident and secure and mature enough to know Nick loves me without him constantly proving it. I don't need pathetic dancing-monkey scenarios to repeat to my friends, I am content with letting him be himself.

I don't know why women find that so hard.

When I get home from dinner, my cab pulls up just as Nick is getting out of his own taxi, and he stands in the street with his arms out to me and a huge grin on his face – 'Baby!' – and I run and I jump up into his arms and he presses a stubbly cheek against mine.

'What did you do tonight?' I ask.

'Some guys were playing poker after work, so I hung around for a bit. Hope that was okay.'

'Of course,' I say. 'More fun than my night.'

'Who all showed up?'

'Oh, Campbell and Insley and their dancing monkeys. Boring. You dodged a bullet. A really lame bullet.'

He squeezes me into him – those strong arms – and hauls me up the stairs. 'God, I love you,' he says.

Then comes sex and a stiff drink and a night of sleep in a sweet, exhausted rats' tangle in our big, soft bed. Poor me.

NICK DUNNE
ONE DAY GONE

I didn't listen to Go about the booze. I finished half the bottle sitting on her sofa by myself, my eighteenth burst of adrenaline kicking in just when I thought I'd finally go to sleep: My eyes were shutting, I was shifting my pillow, my eyes were closed, and then I saw my wife, blood clotting her blond hair, weeping and blind in pain, scraping herself along our kitchen floor. Calling my name. *Nick, Nick, Nick!*

I took repeated tugs on the bottle, psyching myself up for sleep, a losing routine. Sleep is like a cat: It only comes to you if you ignore it. I drank more and continued my mantra. *Stop thinking*, swig, *empty your head*, swig, *now, seriously, empty your head, do it now*, swig. *You need to be sharp tomorrow, you need to sleep*! Swig. I got nothing more than a fussy nap toward dawn, woke up an hour later with a hangover. Not a disabling hangover, but decent. I was tender and dull. Fuggy. Maybe still a little drunk. I stutter-walked to Go's Subaru, the movement feeling alien, like my legs were on backward. I had temporary ownership of the car; the police had graciously accepted my gently used Jetta for inspection along with my laptop – all just a formality, I was assured. I drove home to get myself some decent clothes.

Three police cruisers sat on my block, our very few neighbors milling around. No Carl, but there was Jan Teverer – the Christian lady – and Mike, the father of the three-year-old IVF triplets – Taylor, Topher, and Talullah. ('I hate them all, just by name,' said Amy, a grave judge of anything trendy. When I mentioned that the name Amy was once trendy, my

63

wife said, 'Nick, you *know* the story of my name.' I had no idea what she was talking about.)

Jan nodded from a distance without meeting my eyes, but Mike strode over to me as I got out of my car. 'I'm so sorry, man, anything I can do, you let me know. Anything. I did the mowing this morning, so at least you don't needta worry about that.'

Mike and I took turns mowing all the abandoned foreclosed properties in the complex – heavy rains in the spring had turned yards into jungles, which encouraged an influx of raccoons. We had raccoons everywhere, gnawing through our garbage late at night, sneaking into our basements, lounging on our porches like lazy house pets. The mowing didn't seem to make them go away, but we could at least see them coming now.

'Thanks, man, thank you,' I said.

'Man, my wife, she's been hysterical since she heard,' he said. 'Absolutely hysterical.'

'I'm so sorry to hear that,' I said. 'I gotta—' I pointed at my door.

'Just sitting around, crying over pictures of Amy.'

I had no doubt that a thousand Internet photos had popped up overnight, just to feed the pathetic needs of women like Mike's wife. I had no sympathy for drama queens.

'Hey, I gotta ask—' Mike started.

I patted his arm and pointed again at the door, as if I had pressing business. I turned away before he could ask any questions and knocked on the door of my own house.

Officer Velásquez escorted me upstairs, into my own bedroom, into my own closet – past the silvery perfect-square gift box – and let me rifle through my things. It made me tense, selecting clothes in front of this young woman with the long brown braid, this woman who had to be judging me, forming an opinion. I ended up grabbing blindly: The final look was business-casual, slacks and short sleeves, like I was going to a convention. It would make an interesting essay, I thought, picking out appropriate clothes when a loved one

64

goes missing. The greedy, angle-hungry writer in me, impossible to turn off.

I jammed it all into a bag and turned back around, looking at the gift box on the floor. 'Could I look inside?' I asked her.

She hesitated, then played it safe. 'No, I'm sorry, sir. Better not right now.'

The edge of the gift wrapping had been carefully slit. 'Has somebody looked inside?'

She nodded.

I stepped around Velásquez toward the box. 'If it's already been looked at then—'

She stepped in front of me. 'Sir, I can't let you do that.'

'This is ridiculous. It's *for* me from *my* wife—'

I stepped back around her, bent down, and had one hand on the corner of the box when she slapped an arm across my chest from behind. I felt a momentary spurt of fury, that this *woman* presumed to tell me what to do in *my own home*. No matter how hard I try to be my mother's son, my dad's voice comes into my head unbidden, depositing awful thoughts, nasty words.

'Sir, this is a crime scene, you—'

Stupid bitch.

Suddenly her partner, Riordan, was in the room and on me too, and I was shaking them off – *fine, fine, fuck* – and they were forcing me down the stairs. A woman was on all fours near the front door, squirreling along the floorboards, searching, I assume for blood spatter. She looked up at me impassively, then back down.

I forced myself to decompress as I drove back to Go's to dress. This was only one in a long series of annoying and asinine things the police would do in the course of this investigation (I like rules that make sense, not rules without logic), so I needed to calm down: *Do not antagonize the cops,* I told myself. Repeat if necessary: *Do not antagonize the cops.*

I ran into Boney as I entered the police station, and she said, 'Your in-laws are here, Nick' in an encouraging tone, like she was offering me a warm muffin.

Marybeth and Rand Elliott were standing with their arms around each other. Middle of the police station, they looked like they were posing for prom photos. That's how I always saw them, hands patting, chins nuzzling, cheeks rubbing. Whenever I visited the Elliott home, I became an obsessive throat-clearer – *I'm about to enter* – because the Elliotts could be around any corner, cherishing each other. They kissed each other full on the mouth whenever they were parting, and Rand would cup his wife's rear as he passed her. It was foreign to me. My parents divorced when I was twelve, and I think maybe, when I was very young, I witnessed a chaste cheek kiss between the two when it was impossible to avoid. Christmas, birthdays. Dry lips. On their best married days, their communications were entirely transactional: *We're out of milk again. (I'll get some today.) I need this ironed properly. (I'll do that today.) How hard is it to buy milk? (Silence.) You forgot to call the plumber. (Sigh.) Goddammit, put on your coat, right now, and go out and get some goddamn milk. Now.* These messages and orders brought to you by my father, a mid-level phone-company manager who treated my mother at best like an incompetent employee. At worst? He never beat her, but his pure, inarticulate fury would fill the house for days, weeks, at a time, making the air humid, hard to breathe, my father stalking around with his lower jaw jutting out, giving him the look of a wounded, vengeful boxer, grinding his teeth so loud you could hear it across the room. Throwing things near her but not exactly at her. I'm sure he told himself: *I never hit her.* I'm sure because of this technicality he never saw himself as an abuser. But he turned our family life into an endless road trip with bad directions and a rage-clenched driver, a vacation that never got a chance to be fun. *Don't make me turn this car around.* Please, really, turn it around.

I don't think my father's issue was with my mother in particular. He just didn't like women. He thought they were stupid, inconsequential, irritating. *That dumb bitch.* It was his favorite phrase for any woman who annoyed him: a fellow motorist, a waitress, our grade school teachers, none of whom

66

he ever actually met, parent-teacher conferences stinking of the female realm as they did. I still remember when Geraldine Ferraro was named the 1984 vice presidential candidate, us all watching it on the news before dinner. My mother, my tiny, sweet mom, put her hand on the back of Go's head and said, *Well, I think it's wonderful.* And my dad flipped the TV off and said, *It's a joke. You know it's a goddamn joke. Like watching a monkey ride a bike.*

It took another five years before my mother finally decided she was done. I came home from school one day and my father was gone. He was there in the morning and gone by the afternoon. My mom sat us down at the dining table and announced, 'Your father and I have decided it would be best for everyone if we live apart,' and Go burst into tears and said, 'Good, I hate you both!' and then, instead of running to her room like the script called for, she went to my mom and hugged her.

So my father went away and my thin, pained mother got fat and happy – fairly fat and extremely happy – as if she were supposed to be that way all along: a deflated balloon taking in air. Within a year, she'd morphed into the busy, warm, cheerful lady she'd be till she died, and her sister said things like 'Thank God the old Maureen is back,' as if the woman who raised us was an imposter.

As for my father, for years I spoke to him on the phone about once a month, the conversations polite and newsy, a recital of *things that happened.* The only question my father ever asked about Amy was 'How is Amy?,' which was not meant to elicit any answer beyond 'She's fine.' He remained stubbornly distant even as he faded into dementia in his sixties. *If you're always early, you're never late.* My dad's mantra, and that included the onset of Alzheimer's – a slow decline into a sudden, steep drop that forced us to move our independent, misogynistic father to a giant home that stank of chicken broth and piss, where he'd be surrounded by women helping him at all times. Ha.

My dad had limitations. That's what my good-hearted mom

always told us. He had limitations, but he meant no harm. It was kind of her to say, but he did do harm. I doubt my sister will ever marry: If she's sad or upset or angry, she needs to be alone – she fears a man dismissing her womanly tears. I'm just as bad. The good stuff in me I got from my mom. I can joke, I can laugh, I can tease, I can celebrate and support and praise – I can operate in sunlight, basically – but I can't deal with angry or tearful women. I feel my father's rage rise up in me in the ugliest way. Amy could tell you about that. She would definitely tell you, if she were here.

I watched Rand and Marybeth for a moment before they saw me. I wondered how furious they'd be with me. I had committed an unforgivable act, not phoning them for so long. Because of my cowardice, my in-laws would always have that night of tennis lodged in their imagination: the warm evening, the lazy yellow balls bumping along the court, the squeak of tennis shoes, the average Thursday night they'd spent while their daughter was disappeared.

'Nick,' Rand Elliott said, spotting me. He took three big strides toward me, and as I braced myself for a punch, he hugged me desperately hard.

'How are you holding up?' he whispered into my neck, and began rocking. Finally, he gave a high-pitched gulp, a swallowed sob, and gripped me by the arms. 'We're going to find Amy, Nick. It can't go any other way. Believe that, okay?' Rand Elliott held me in his blue stare for a few more seconds, then broke up again – three girlish gasps burst from him like hiccups – and Marybeth moved into the huddle, buried her face in her husband's armpit.

When we parted, she looked up at me with giant stunned eyes. 'It's just a – just a goddamn *night*mare,' she said. 'How are you, Nick?'

When Marybeth asked *How are you*, it wasn't a courtesy, it was an existential question. She studied my face, and I was sure she was studying me, and would continue to note my every thought and action. The Elliotts believed that every trait should be considered, judged, categorized. It all means something, it can all be used. Mom, Dad, Baby, they were three advanced people with three advanced degrees in psychology – they thought more before nine a.m. than most people thought all month. I remember once declining cherry pie at dinner, and Rand cocked his head and said, 'Ahh! Iconoclast. Disdains the easy, symbolic patriotism.' And when I tried to laugh it off and said, well, I didn't like cherry cobbler either, Marybeth touched Rand's arm: 'Because of the divorce. All those comfort foods, the desserts a family eats together, those are just bad memories for Nick.'

It was silly but incredibly sweet, these people spending so much energy trying to figure me out. The answer: I don't like cherries.

By eleven-thirty, the station was a rolling boil of noise. Phones were ringing, people were yelling across the room. A woman whose name I never caught, whom I registered only as a chattering bobblehead of hair, suddenly made her presence known at my side. I had no idea how long she'd been there: '... and the main point of this, Nick, is just to get people looking for Amy and knowing she has a family who loves her and wants her back. This will be very controlled. Nick, you will need to – Nick?'

'Yep.'

'People will want to hear a quick statement from her husband.'

From across the room, Go was darting toward me. She'd dropped me at the station, then run by The Bar to take care of bar things for thirty minutes, and now she was back, acting like she'd abandoned me for a week, zigzagging between desks, ignoring the young officer who'd clearly been assigned to usher her in, neatly, in a hushed, dignified manner.

'Okay so far?' Go said, squeezing me with one arm, the dude hug. The Dunne kids don't perform hugs well. Go's thumb landed on my right nipple. 'I wish Mom was here,' she whispered, which was what I'd been thinking. 'No news?' she asked when she pulled away.

'Nothing, fucking nothing—'

'You look like you feel awful.'

'I feel like fucking shit.' I was about to say what an idiot I was, not listening to her about the booze.

'I would have finished the bottle, too.' She patted my back.

'It's almost time,' the PR woman said, again appearing magically. 'It's not a bad turnout for a July fourth weekend.' She started herding us all toward a dismal conference room – aluminum blinds and folding chairs and a clutch of bored reporters – and up onto the platform. I felt like a third-tier speaker at a mediocre convention, me in my business-casual blues, addressing a captive audience of jet-lagged people daydreaming about what they'd eat for lunch. But I could see the journalists perk up when they caught sight of me – let's say it: a young, decent-looking guy – and then the PR woman placed a cardboard poster on a nearby easel, and it was a blown-up photo of Amy at her most stunning, that face that made you keep double-checking: *She can't be that good-looking, can she?* She could, she was, and I stared at the photo of my wife as the cameras snapped photos of me staring at the photo. I thought of that day in New York when I found her again: the blond hair, the back of her head, was all I could see, but I knew it was her, and I saw it as a sign. How many millions of heads had I seen in my life, but I knew this was Amy's pretty skull floating down Seventh Avenue in front of me. I knew it was her, and that we would be together.

Cameras flashed. I turned away and saw spots. It was surreal. That's what people always say to describe moments that are merely unusual. I thought: *You have no fucking idea what surreal is.* My hangover was really warming up now, my left eye throbbing like a heart.

The cameras were clicking, and the two families stood together, all of us with mouths in thin slits, Go the only one looking even close to a real person. The rest of us looked like placeholder humans, bodies that had been dollied in and propped up. Amy, over on her easel, looked more present. We'd all seen these news conferences before – when other women went missing. We were being forced to perform the scene that TV viewers expected: the worried but hopeful family. Caffeine-dazed eyes and ragdoll arms.

My name was being said; the room gave a collective gulp of expectation. *Showtime*.

When I saw the broadcast later, I didn't recognize my voice. I barely recognized my face. The booze floating, sludgelike, just beneath the surface of my skin made me look like a fleshy wastrel, just sensuous enough to be disreputable. I had worried about my voice wavering, so I overcorrected and the words came out clipped, like I was reading a stock report. 'We just want Amy to get home safe ...' Utterly unconvincing, disconnected. I might as well have been reading numbers at random.

Rand Elliott stepped up and tried to save me: 'Our daughter, Amy, is a sweetheart of a girl, full of life. She's our only child, and she's smart and beautiful and kind. She really is Amazing Amy. And we want her back. Nick wants her back.' He put a hand on my shoulder, wiped his eyes, and I involuntarily turned steel. My father again: *Men* don't cry.

Rand kept talking: 'We all want her back where she belongs, with her family. We've set up a command center over at the Days Inn ...'

The news reports would show Nick Dunne, husband of the missing woman, standing metallically next to his father-in-law, arms crossed, eyes glazed, looking almost bored as Amy's parents wept. And then worse. My longtime response, the need to remind people I wasn't a dick, I was a nice guy despite the affectless stare, the haughty, douchebag face.

So there it came, out of nowhere, as Rand begged for his daughter's return: a killer smile.

AMY ELLIOTT DUNNE
JULY 5, 2010

– Diary entry –

I won't blame Nick. I don't blame Nick. I refuse – refuse! –
to turn into some pert-mouthed, strident angry-girl. I made
two promises to myself when I married Nick. One: no dancing-
monkey demands. Two: I would never, ever say, *Sure, that's
fine by me (if you want to stay out later, if you want to do a
boys' weekend, if you want to do something you want to do)* and
then punish him for doing what I said was *fine by me.* I worry
I am coming perilously close to violating both of those promises.

But still. It is our third wedding anniversary and I am alone
in our apartment, my face all mask-tight from tears because,
well, because: Just this afternoon, I get a voice mail from Nick,
and I already know it's going to be bad, I know the second the
voice mail begins because I can tell he's calling from his cell
and I can hear men's voices in the background and a big,
roomy gap, like he's trying to decide what to say, and then
I hear his taxi-blurred voice, a voice that is already wet and
lazy with booze, and I know I am going to be angry – that
quick inhale, the lips going tight, the shoulders up, the *I so
don't want to be mad but I'm going to be* feeling. Do men not
know that feeling? You don't want to be mad, but you're
obligated to be, almost. Because a rule, a good rule, a nice rule
is being broken. Or maybe *rule* is the wrong word. Protocol?
Nicety? But the rule/protocol/nicety – our anniversary – is
being broken for a good reason, I understand, I do. The rumors
were true: Sixteen writers have been laid off at Nick's magazine.
A third of the staff. Nick has been spared, for now, but of

course he feels obliged to take the others out to get drunk. They are men, piled in a cab, heading down Second Avenue, pretending to be brave. A few have gone home to their wives, but a surprising number have stayed out. Nick will spend the night of our anniversary buying these men drinks, going to strip clubs and cheesy bars, flirting with twenty-two-year-olds (*My friend here just got laid off, he could use a hug*). These jobless men will proclaim Nick a great guy as he buys their drinks on a credit card linked to my bank account. Nick will have a grand old time on our anniversary, which he didn't even mention in the message. Instead, he said, *I know we had plans but . . .*

I am being a girl. I just thought it'd be a tradition: All across town, I have strewn little love messages, reminders of our past year together, my treasure hunt. I can picture the third clue, fluttering from a piece of scotch tape in the crook of the V of the Robert Indiana love sculpture up near Central Park. Tomorrow, some bored twelve-year-old tourist stumbling along behind his parents is going to pick it off, read it, shrug, and let it float away like a gum wrapper.

My treasure-hunt finale was perfect, but isn't now. It's an absolutely gorgeous vintage briefcase. Leather. Third anniversary is leather. A work-related gift may be a bad idea, given that work isn't exactly happy right now. In our kitchen, I have two live lobsters, like always. Or like what was supposed to be like always. I need to phone my mom and see if they can keep for a day, scrambling dazedly around their crate, or if I need to stumble in, and with my wine-lame eyes, battle them and boil them in my pot for no good reason. I'm killing two lobsters I won't even eat.

Dad phoned to wish us happy anniversary, and I picked up the phone and I was going to play it cool, but then I started crying when I started talking – I was doing the awful chick talk-cry: *mwaha-waah-gwwahh-and-waaa-wa* – so I had to tell him what happened, and he told me I should open a bottle of wine and wallow in it for a bit. Dad is always a proponent of a good indulgent sulk. Still, Nick will be angry that I told

Rand, and of course Rand will do his fatherly thing, pat Nick on the shoulder and say, 'Heard you had some emergency drinking to do on your anniversary, Nicky.' And chuckle. So Nick will know, and he will be angry with me because he wants my parents to believe he's perfect – he beams when I tell them stories about what a flawless son-in-law he is.

Except for tonight. I know, I know, I'm being a girl.

It's five a.m. The sun is coming up, almost as bright as the streetlights outside that have just blinked off. I always like that switch, when I'm awake for it. Sometimes, when I can't sleep, I'll pull myself out of bed and walk through the streets at dawn, and when the lights click off, all together, I always feel like I've seen something special. *Oh, there go the streetlights!* I want to announce. In New York it's not three or four a.m. that's the quiet time – there are too many bar stragglers, calling out to each other as they collapse into taxis, yelping into their cell phones as they frantically smoke that one last cigarette before bed. Five a.m., that's the best time, when the clicking of your heels on the sidewalk sounds illicit. All the people have been put away in their boxes, and you have the whole place to yourself.

Here's what happened: Nick got home just after four, a bulb of beer and cigarettes and fried-egg odor attached to him, a placenta of stink. I was still awake, waiting for him, my brain ca-thunking after a marathon of *Law and Order*. He sat down on our ottoman and glanced at the present on the table and said nothing. I stared at him back. He clearly wasn't going to even graze against an apology – *hey, sorry things got screwy today*. That's all I wanted, just a quick acknowledgment.

'Happy day after anniversary,' I start.

He sighs, a deep aggrieved moan. 'Amy, I've had the crappiest day ever. Please don't lay a guilt trip on me on top of it.'

Nick grew up with a father who never, ever apologized, so when Nick feels he has screwed up, he goes on offense. I know this, and I can usually wait it out, usually.

74

'I was just saying happy anniversary.'

'Happy anniversary, my asshole husband who neglected me on my big day.'

We sit silent for a minute, my stomach knotting. I don't want to be the bad guy here. I don't deserve that. Nick stands up.

'Well, how was it?' I ask dully.

'How was it? It was fucking awful. Sixteen of my friends now have no jobs. It was miserable. I'll probably be gone too, another few months.'

Friends. He doesn't even like half the guys he was out with, but I say nothing.

'I know it feels dire right now, Nick. But—'

'It's not dire for you, Amy. Not for you, it never will be dire. But for the rest of us? It's very different.'

The same old. Nick resents that I've never had to worry about money and I never will. He thinks that makes me softer than everyone else, and I wouldn't disagree with him. But I do work. I clock in and clock back out. Some of my girlfriends have literally never had a job; they discuss people with jobs in the pitying tones you talk about a fat girl with 'such a nice face.' They will lean forward and say, 'But of course, Ellen has to work,' like something out of a Noël Coward play. They don't count me, because I can always quit my job if I want to. I could build my days around charity committees and home decoration and gardening and volunteering, and I don't think there's anything wrong with building a life around those things. Most beautiful, good things are done by women people scorn. But I work.

'Nick, I'm on your side here. We'll be okay no matter what. My money is your money.'

'Not according to the prenup.'

He is drunk. He only mentions the prenup when he's drunk. Then all the resentment comes back. I've told him hundreds, literally *hundreds of times*, I've said the words: The prenup is pure business. It's not for me, it's not even for my parents, it's for my parents' lawyers. It says nothing about us, not you and me.

He walks over toward the kitchen, tosses his wallet and wilted dollars on the coffee table, crumples a piece of notepaper and tosses it in the trash with a series of credit-card receipts.

'That's a shitty thing to say, Nick.'

'It's a shitty way to feel, Amy.'

He walks to our bar – in the careful, swamp-wading gait of a drunk – and actually pours himself another drink.

'You're going to make yourself sick,' I say.

He raises his glass in an up-yours cheers to me. 'You just don't get it, Amy. You just can't. I've worked since I was fourteen years old. I didn't get to go to fucking tennis camp and creative-writing camp and SAT prep and all that shit that apparently everyone else in New York City did, because I was wiping down tables at the mall and I was mowing lawns and I was driving to Hannibal and fucking dressing like Huck Finn for the tourists and I was cleaning the funnel-cake skillets at midnight.'

I feel an urge to laugh, actually to guffaw. A big belly laugh that would sweep up Nick, and soon we'd both be laughing and this would be over. This litany of crummy jobs. Being married to Nick always reminds me: People have to do awful things for money. Ever since I've been married to Nick, I always wave to people dressed as food.

'I've had to work so much harder than anyone else at the magazine to even *get* to the magazine. Twenty years, basically, I've been working to get where I am, and now it's all going to be gone, and there's not a fucking thing I know how to do instead, unless I want to go back home, be a river rat again.'

'You're probably too old to play Huck Finn,' I say.

'Fuck you, Amy.'

And then he goes to the bedroom. He's never said that to me before, but it came out of his mouth so smoothly that I assume – and this never crossed my mind – I assume he's thought it. Many times. I never thought I'd be the kind of woman who'd be told to fuck herself by her husband. And we've sworn never to go to bed angry. Compromise, communicate, and never go to bed angry – the three pieces of advice gifted and regifted to all newlyweds. But lately it seems I am the only one who compromises; our communications don't solve anything; and Nick is very good at going to bed angry. He can turn off his emotions like a spout. He is already snoring.

And then I can't help myself, even though it's none of my business, even though Nick would be furious if he knew: I cross over to the trash can and pull out the receipts, so I can picture where he's been all night. Two bars, two strip clubs. And I can see him in each one, talking about me with his friends, because he must have already talked about me for all that petty, smeared meanness to come out so easily. I picture them at one of the pricier strip clubs, the posh ones that make men believe they are still designed to rule, that women are meant to serve them, the deliberately bad acoustics and thwumping music so no one has to talk, a stretch-titted woman straddling my husband (who swears it's all in fun), her hair trailing down her back, her lips wet with gloss, but I'm not supposed to be threatened, no it's just boyish hijinks, I am supposed to laugh about it, I am supposed to be a *good sport*.

Then I unroll the crumpled piece of notebook paper and see a girl's handwriting – Hannah – and a phone number. I wish it were like the movies, the name something silly, CanDee or Bambie, something you could roll your eyes at. Misti with two hearts over the I's. But it's Hannah, which is a real woman, presumably like me. Nick has never cheated on me, he has sworn it, but I also know he has ample opportunity. I could ask him about Hannah, and he'd say, *I have no idea why she gave me her number, but I didn't want to be rude, so I took it.* Which may be true. Or not. He could cheat on me and he would never tell me, and he would think less and less of me for not figuring it out. He would see me across the breakfast table, innocently slurping cereal, and know that I am a fool, and how can anyone respect a fool?

Now I am crying again, with Hannah in my hand.

It's a very female thing, isn't it, to take one boys' night and snowball it into a marital infidelity that will destroy our marriage?

I don't know what I am supposed to do. I'm feeling like a shrill fishwife, or a foolish doormat – I don't know which. I don't want to be angry, I can't even figure out if I should be angry. I consider checking in to a hotel, let him wonder about *me* for a change.

I stay where I am for a few minutes, and then I take a breath and wade into our booze-humid bedroom, and when I get in bed, he turns to me and wraps his arms around me and buries his face in my neck, and at the same time we both say, 'I'm sorry.'

NICK DUNNE
ONE DAY GONE

Flashbulbs exploded, and I dropped the smile, but not soon enough. I felt a wave of heat roll up my neck, and beads of sweat broke out on my nose. *Stupid, Nick, stupid*. And then, just as I was pulling myself together, the press conference was over, and it was too late to make any other impression.

I walked out with the Elliotts, my head ducked low as more flash-bulbs popped. I was almost to the exit when Gilpin trotted across the room toward me, flagging me down: 'Canna grab a minute, Nick?'

He updated me as we headed toward a back office: 'We checked out that house in your neighborhood that was broken into, looks like people camped out there, so we've got lab there. And we found another house on the edge of your complex, had some squatters.'

'I mean, that's what worries me,' I said. 'Guys are camped out everywhere. This whole town is overrun with pissed-off, unemployed people.'

Carthage was, until a year ago, a company town and that company was the sprawling Riverway Mall, a tiny city unto itself that once employed four thousand locals – one fifth the population. It was built in 1985, a destination mall meant to attract shoppers from all over the Middle West. I still remember the opening day: me and Go, Mom and Dad, watching the festivities from the very back of the crowd in the vast tarred parking lot, because our father always wanted to be able to leave quickly, from anywhere. Even at baseball games, we parked by the exit and left at the eighth inning, me and Go a predictable set of mustard-smeared whines, petulant and sun-fevered: *We never get to see the end*. But this time our faraway vantage was desirable, because we got to take in the full scope of the Event: the impatient crowd, leaning collectively from one foot to another; the mayor atop a red-white-and-blue dais; the booming words – *pride, growth, prosperity, success* – rolling over us, soldiers on the battlefield of consumerism, armed with vinyl-covered checkbooks and quilted handbags. And the doors opening. And the rush into the air-conditioning, the Muzak, the smiling salespeople who were our neighbors. My father actually let us go inside that day, actually waited in line and bought us something that day: sweaty paper cups brimming with Orange Julius.

For a quarter century, the Riverway Mall was a given. Then the recession hit, washed away the Riverway store by store until the whole mall finally went bust. It is now two million square feet of echo. No company came to claim it, no businessman promised a resurrection, no one knew what to do with it or what would become of all the people who'd worked there, including my mother, who lost her job at Shoe-Be-Doo-Be – two decades of kneeling and kneading, of sorting boxes and collecting moist foot hosiery, gone without ceremony.

The downfall of the mall basically bankrupted Carthage. People lost their jobs, they lost their houses. No one could see anything good coming anytime soon. *We never get to see the end*. Except it looked like this time Go and I would. We all would.

The bankruptcy matched my psyche perfectly. For several years, I had been bored. Not a whining, restless child's boredom (although I was not above that) but a dense, blanketing malaise. It seemed to me that there was nothing new to be discovered ever again. Our society was utterly, ruinously derivative (although the word *derivative* as a criticism is itself derivative). We were the first human beings who would never see anything for the first time. We stare at the wonders of the world, dull-eyed, underwhelmed. Mona Lisa, the Pyramids, the Empire State Building. Jungle animals on attack, ancient icebergs collapsing, volcanoes erupting. I can't recall a single amazing thing I have seen firsthand that I didn't immediately reference to a movie or TV show. A fucking commercial. You know the awful singsong of the blasé: *Seeeen it.* I've literally seen it all, and the worst thing, the thing that makes me want to blow my brains out, is: The secondhand experience is always better. The image is crisper, the view is keener, the camera angle and the soundtrack manipulate my emotions in a way reality can't anymore. I don't know that we are actually human at this point, those of us who are like most of us, who grew up with TV and movies and now the Internet. If we are betrayed, we know the words to say; when a loved one dies, we know the words to say. If we want to play the stud or the smart-ass or the fool, we know the words to say. We are all working from the same dog-eared script.

It's a very difficult era in which to be a person, just a real, actual person, instead of a collection of personality traits selected from an endless automat of characters.

And if all of us are play-acting, there can be no such thing as a soul mate, because we don't have genuine souls.

It had gotten to the point where it seemed like nothing matters, because I'm not a real person and neither is anyone else.

I would have done anything to feel real again.

Gilpin opened the door to the same room where they'd questioned me the night before. In the center of the table sat Amy's silvery gift box.

I stood staring at the box sitting in the middle of the table, so ominous in this new setting. A sense of dread descended on me. Why hadn't I found it before? I should have found it.

'Go ahead,' Gilpin said. 'We wanted you to take a look at this.'

I opened it as gingerly as if a head might be inside. I found only a creamy blue envelope marked FIRST CLUE.

Gilpin smirked. 'Imagine our confusion: A missing persons case, and here we find an envelope marked FIRST CLUE.'

'It's for a treasure hunt that my wife—'

'Right. For your anniversary. Your father-in-law mentioned it.'

I opened the envelope, pulled out a thick sky-blue piece of paper – Amy's signature stationery – folded once. Bile crept up my throat. These treasure hunts had always amounted to a single question: Who is Amy? (What is my wife thinking? What was important to her this past year? What moments made her happiest? Amy, Amy, Amy, let's think about Amy.)

I read the first clue with clenched teeth. Given our marital mood the past year, it was going to make me look awful. I didn't need anything else that made me look awful.

I picture myself as your student,
With a teacher so handsome and wise
My mind opens up (not to mention my thighs!)
If I were your pupil, there'd be no need for flowers
Maybe just a naughty appointment during your office hours
So hurry up, get going, please do
And this time I'll teach you a thing or two.

It was an itinerary for an alternate life. If things had gone according to my wife's vision, yesterday she would have hovered near me as I read this poem, watching me expectantly, the hope emanating from her like a fever: *Please get this. Please get me.*

And she would finally say, *So?* And I would say:

'Oh, I actually know this! She must mean my office. At the junior college. I'm an adjunct professor there. Huh. I mean, it must be, right?' I squinted and reread. 'She took it easy on me this year.'

'You want me to drive you over?' Gilpin asked.

'Nah, I've got Go's car.'

'I'll follow you then.'

'You think it's important?'

'Well, it shows her movements the day or two before she went missing. So it's not unimportant.' He looked at the stationery. 'It's sweet, you know? Like something out of a movie: a treasure hunt. My wife and I, we give each other a card and maybe get a bite to eat. Sounds like you guys were doing it right. Preserve the romance.'

Then Gilpin looked at his shoes, got bashful, and jingled his keys to leave.

The college had rather grandly presented me with a coffin of an office, big enough for a desk, two chairs, some shelves. Gilpin and I wended our way through the summer-school students, a combination of impossibly young kids (bored yet busy, their fingers clicking out texts or dialing up music) and earnest older people I had to assume were mall layoffs, trying to retrain for a new career.

'What do you teach?' Gilpin asked.

'Journalism, magazine journalism.' A girl texting and walking forgot the nuances of the latter and almost ran into me. She stepped to the side without glancing up. It made me feel cranky, *off my lawn!* old.

'I thought you didn't do journalism anymore.'

'He who can't do ....' I smiled.

I unlocked my office, stepped into the close-smelling, dust-moted air. I'd taken the summer off; it had been weeks since I'd been here. On my desk sat another envelope, marked SECOND CLUE.

'Your key always on your key chain?' Gilpin asked.

'Yup.'

'So Amy could have borrowed that to get in?'

I tore down the side of the envelope.

'And we have a spare at home.' Amy made doubles of everything – I tended to misplace keys, credit cards, cell phones, but I didn't want to tell Gilpin this, get another baby-of-the-family jab. 'Why?'

'Oh, just wanted to make sure she wouldn't have had to go through, I don't know, a janitor or someone.'

'No Freddy Krueger types here, that I've noticed.'

'Never saw those movies,' Gilpin replied.

Inside the envelope were two folded slips of paper. One was marked with a heart; the other was labeled CLUE.

Two notes. Different. My stomach clenched. God knew what Amy was going to say. I opened the note with the heart. I wished I hadn't let Gilpin come, and then I caught the first words.

My Darling Husband,

I figured this was the perfect place – these hallowed halls of learning! – to tell you I think you are a brilliant man. I don't tell you enough, but I am amazed by your mind: the weird statistics and anecdotes, the strange facts, the disturbing ability to quote from any movie, the quick wit, the beautiful way you have of wording things. After years together, I think a couple can forget how wonderful they find each other. I remember when we first met, how dazzled I was by you, and so I want to take a moment to tell you I still am and it's one of my favorite things about you: You are BRILLIANT.

My mouth watered. Gilpin was reading over my shoulder, and he actually sighed. 'Sweet lady,' he said. Then he cleared his throat. 'Um, hah, these yours?'

He used the eraser end of a pencil to pick up a pair of women's underwear (technically, they were panties – stringy, lacy, red – but I know women get creeped out by that word – just Google *hate the word* panties). They'd been hanging off a knob on the AC unit.

'Oh, jeez. That's embarrassing.'

Gilpin waited for an explanation.

'Uh, one time Amy and I, well, you read her note. We kinda, you know, you sometimes gotta spice things up a little.'

Gilpin grinned. 'Oh I get it, randy professor and naughty student. I get it. You two really were doing it right.' I reached for the underwear, but Gilpin was already producing an evidence bag from his pocket and sliding them in. 'Just a precaution,' he said inexplicably.

'Oh, please don't,' I said. 'Amy would die—' I caught myself.

'Don't worry, Nick, it's all protocol, my friend. You wouldn't believe the hoops we gotta jump through. *Just in case, just in case*. Ridiculous. What's the clue say?'

I let him read over my shoulder again, his jarringly fresh smell distracting me.

'So what's that one mean?' he asked.

'I have no idea,' I lied.

I finally rid myself of Gilpin, then drove aimlessly down the highway so I could make a call on my disposable. No pickup. I didn't leave a message. I sped for a while longer, as if I could get anywhere, and then drove the 45 minutes back toward town to meet the Elliotts at the Days Inn. I walked into a lobby packed with members of the Midwest Payroll Vendors Association – wheelie bags parked everywhere, their owners slurping complimentary drinks in small plastic cups and networking, forced guttural laughs and pockets fished for business cards. I rode up the elevator with four men, all balding and khaki'd and golf-shirted, lanyards bouncing off round married bellies.

Marybeth opened the door while talking on her cell phone; she pointed toward the TV and whispered to me, 'We have a cold-cut tray if you want, sweetheart,' then went into the bathroom and closed the door, her murmurs continuing.

She emerged a few minutes later, just in time for the local five o'clock news from St. Louis, which led with Amy's disappearance. 'Perfect photo,' Marybeth murmured at the screen, where Amy peered back at us. 'People will see it and really know what Amy looks like.'

I'd thought the portrait – a head shot from Amy's brief fling with acting – beautiful but unsettling. Amy's pictures gave a sense of her actually watching you, like an old-time haunted-house portrait, the eyes moving from left to right.

'We should get them some candid photos too,' I said. 'Some everyday ones.'

The Elliotts nodded in tandem but said nothing, watching. When the spot was done, Rand broke the silence: 'I feel sick.'

'I know,' Marybeth said.

'How are you holding up, Nick?' Rand asked, hunched over, hands on both knees, as if he were preparing to get up from the sofa but couldn't quite do it.

'I'm a goddamn mess, to tell the truth. I feel so useless.'

'You know, I gotta ask, what about your employees, Nick?' Rand finally stood. He went to the minibar, poured himself a ginger ale, then turned to me and Marybeth. 'Anyone? Something? Anything?' I shook my head; Marybeth asked for a club soda.

'Want some gin with it too, babe?' Rand asked, his deep voice going high on the final word.

'Sure. Yes. I do.' Marybeth closed her eyes, bent in half, and brought her face between her knees; then she took a deep breath and sat back up in her exact previous position, as if it were all a yoga exercise.

'I gave them lists of everyone,' I said. 'But it's a pretty tame business, Rand. I just don't think that's the place to look.'

Rand put a hand across his mouth and rubbed upward, the flesh of his cheeks bunching up around his eyes. 'Of course, we're doing the same with our business, Nick.'

Rand and Marybeth always referred to the *Amazing Amy* series as a business, which on the surface never failed to strike me as silly: They are children's books, about a perfect little girl who's pictured on every book cover, a cartoonish version of my own Amy. But of course they are (were) a business, big business. They were elementary-school staples for the better part of two decades, largely because of the quizzes at the end of every chapter.

In third grade, for instance, Amazing Amy caught her friend Brian overfeeding the class turtle. She tried to reason with him, but when Brian persisted in the extra helpings, Amy had no choice but to narc on him to her teacher: 'Mrs Tibbles, I don't want to be a tattletale, but I'm not sure what to do.

I've tried talking to Brian myself, but now ... I guess I might need help from a grown-up ...' The fallout:

1) *Brian told Amy she was an untrustworthy friend and stopped talking to her.*
2) *Her timid pal Suzy said Amy shouldn't have told; she should have secretly fished out the food without Brian knowing.*
3) *Amy's archrival, Joanna, said Amy was jealous and just wanted to feed the turtle herself.*
4) *Amy refused to back down – she felt she did the proper thing.*

Who is right?!

Well, that's easy, because Amy is always right, in every story. (Don't think I haven't brought this up in my arguments with my real Amy, because I have, more than once.)

The quizzes – written by *two psychologists, who are also parents like you!* – were supposed to tease out a child's personality traits: Is your wee one a sulker who can't stand to be corrected, like Brian? A spineless enabler, like Suzy? A pot-stirrer, like Joanna? Or perfect, *like Amy*? The books became extremely trendy among the rising yuppie class: They were the Pet Rock of parenting. The Rubik's Cube of child rearing. The Elliotts got rich. At one point it was estimated that every school library in America had an *Amazing Amy* book.

'Do you have worries that this might link back to the *Amazing Amy* business?' I asked.

'We do have a few people we thought might be worth checking out,' Rand began.

I coughed out a laugh. 'Do you think Judith Viorst kidnapped Amy for Alexander so he wouldn't have any more Terrible, Horrible, No Good, Very Bad Days?'

Rand and Marybeth turned matching surprised-disappointed faces toward me. It was a gross, tasteless thing to say – my brain had been burping up such inappropriate thoughts at inopportune moments. Mental gas I couldn't control. Like, I'd started internally singing the lyrics to 'Bony Moronie' whenever I saw my cop friend. *She's as skinny as a stick of macaroni*, my brain would bebop as Detective Rhonda Boney was telling me about dragging the river for my missing wife. *Defense mechanism*, I told myself, *just a weird defense mechanism*. I'd like it to stop.

I rearranged my leg delicately, spoke delicately, as if my words were an unwieldy stack of fine china. 'I'm sorry, I don't know why I said that.'

'We're all tired,' Rand offered.

'We'll have the cops round up Viorst,' Marybeth tried. 'And that bitch Beverly Cleary too.' It was less a joke than a pardon.

'I guess I should tell you,' I said. 'The cops, it's normal in this kind of case—'

'To look at the husband first, I know,' Rand interrupted. 'I told them they're wasting their time. The questions they asked us—'

'They were offensive,' Marybeth finished.

'So they have spoken with you? About me?' I moved over to the minibar, casually poured a gin. I swallowed three belts in a row and felt immediately worse. My stomach was working its way up my esophagus. 'What kind of stuff did they ask?'

'Have you ever hurt Amy, has Amy ever mentioned you threatening her?' Marybeth ticked off. 'Are you a womanizer, has Amy ever mentioned you cheating on her? Because that sounds like Amy, right? I told them we didn't raise a doormat.'

Rand put a hand on my shoulder. 'Nick, what we should have said, first of all, is: We know you would never, ever hurt Amy. I even told the police, told them the story about you saving the mouse at the beach house, saving it from the glue trap.' He looked over at Marybeth as if she didn't know the story, and Marybeth obliged with her rapt attention. 'Spent an hour trying to corner the damn thing, and then literally drove the little rat bastard out of town. Does that sound like a guy who would hurt his wife?'

I felt a burst of intense guilt, self-loathing. I thought for a second I might cry, finally.

'We love you, Nick,' Rand said, giving me a final squeeze.

'We do, Nick,' Marybeth echoed. 'You're our son. We are

so incredibly sorry that on top of Amy being gone, you have to deal with this – cloud of suspicion.'

I didn't like the phrase *cloud of suspicion*. I much preferred *routine investigation* or *a mere formality*.

'They did wonder about your restaurant reservations that night,' Marybeth said, an overly casual glance.

'My reservations?'

'They said you told them you had reservations at Houston's, but they checked it out, and there were no reservations. They seemed really interested in that.'

I had no reservation, and I had no gift. Because if I planned on killing Amy that day, I wouldn't have needed reservations for that night or a gift I'd never need to give her. The hallmarks of an extremely pragmatic killer.

I am pragmatic to a fault – my friends could certainly tell the police that.

'Uh, no. No, I never made reservations. They must have misunderstood me. I'll let them know.'

I collapsed on the couch across from Marybeth. I didn't want Rand to touch me again.

'Oh, okay. Good,' Marybeth said. 'Did she, uh, did you get a treasure hunt this year?' Her eyes turned red again. 'Before . . .'

'Yeah, they gave me the first clue today. Gilpin and I found the second one in my office at the college. I'm still trying to figure it out.'

'Can we take a look?' my mother-in-law asked.

'I don't have it with me,' I lied.

'Will you . . . will you try to solve it, Nick?' Marybeth asked.

'I will, Marybeth. I'll solve it.'

'I just hate the idea of things she touched, left out there, all alone—'

My phone rang, the disposable, and I flicked a glance at the display, then shut it off. I needed to get rid of the thing, but I couldn't yet.

'You should pick up every call, Nick,' Marybeth said.

'I recognized this one – just my college alum fund looking for money.'

89

Rand sat beside me on the couch. The ancient, much abused cushions sank severely under our weight, so we ended up pushed toward each other, arms touching, which was fine with Rand. He was one of those guys who'd pronounce *I'm a hugger* as he came at you, neglecting to ask if the feeling was mutual.

Marybeth returned to business: 'We do think it's possible an *Amy* obsessive took her.' She turned to me, as if pleading a case. 'We've had 'em over the years.'

Amy had been fond of recollecting stories of men obsessed with her. She described the stalkers in hushed tones over glasses of wine at various periods during our marriage – men who were still out there, always thinking about her and wanting her. I suspected these stories were inflated: The men always came off as dangerous to a very precise degree – enough for me to worry about but not enough to require us to involve the police. In short, a play world where I could be Amy's chest-puffed hero, defending her honor. Amy was too independent, too modern, to be able to admit the truth: She wanted to play damsel.

'Lately?'

'Not lately, no,' Marybeth said, chewing her lip. 'But there was a very disturbed girl back in high school.'

'Disturbed how?'

'She was obsessed with Amy. Well, with *Amazing Amy*. Her name was Hilary Handy – she modeled herself after Amy's best friend in the books, Suzy. At first it was cute, I guess. And then it was like that wasn't good enough anymore – she wanted to be Amazing Amy, not Suzy the sidekick. So she began imitating *our* Amy. She dressed like Amy, she colored her hair blond, she'd linger outside our house in New York. One time I was walking down the street and she came running up to me, this strange girl, and she looped her arm through mine and said, "I'm going to be your daughter now. I'm going to kill Amy and be your new Amy. Because it doesn't really matter to you, does it? As long as you have *an Amy*." Like our daughter was a piece of fiction she could rewrite.'

'We finally got a restraining order because she threw Amy

down a flight of stairs at school,' Rand said. 'Very disturbed girl. That kind of mentality doesn't go away.'

'And then Desi,' Marybeth said.

'And Desi,' Rand said.

Even I knew about Desi. Amy had attended a Massachusetts boarding school called Wickshire Academy – I had seen the photos, Amy in lacrosse skirts and headbands, always with autumn colors in the background, as if the school were based not in a town but in a month. October. Desi Collings attended the boys' boarding school that was paired with Wickshire. In Amy's stories, he was a pale, Romantic figure, and their courtship had been of the boarding-school variety: chilly football games and overheated dances, lilac corsages and rides in a vintage Jaguar. Everything a little bit midcentury.

Amy dated Desi, quite seriously, for a year. But she began to find him alarming: He talked as if they were engaged, he knew the number and gender of their children. They were going to have four kids, all boys. Which sounded suspiciously like Desi's own family, and when he brought his mother down to meet her, Amy grew queasy at the striking resemblance between herself and Mrs Collings. The older woman had kissed her cheek coldly and murmured calmly in her ear, 'Good luck.' Amy couldn't tell if it was a warning or a threat.

After Amy cut it off with Desi, he still lingered around the Wickshire campus, a ghostly figure in dark blazers, leaning against wintry, leafless oak trees. Amy returned from a dance one February night to find him lying on her bed, naked, on top of the covers, groggy from a very marginal pill overdose. Desi left school shortly after.

But he still phoned her, even now, and several times a year sent her thick, padded envelopes that Amy tossed unopened after showing them to me. They were postmarked St. Louis. Forty minutes away. 'It's just a horrible, miserable coincidence,' she'd told me. Desi had the St. Louis family connections on his mother's side. This much she knew but didn't care to know more. I'd picked through the trash to retrieve one, read the letter, sticky with alfredo sauce, and it had been utterly banal:

talk of tennis and travel and other things preppy. Spaniels. I tried to picture this slender dandy, a fellow in bow ties and tortoiseshell glasses, busting into our house and grabbing Amy with soft, manicured fingers. Tossing her in the trunk of his vintage roadster and taking her ... antiquing in Vermont. Desi. Could anyone believe it was Desi?

'Desi lives not far away, actually,' I said. 'St. Louis.'

'Now, *see*?' Rand said. 'Why are the cops not all over this?'

'Someone needs to be,' I said. 'I'll go. After the search here tomorrow.'

'The police definitely seem to think it's ... close to home,' Marybeth said. She kept her eyes on me one beat too long, then shivered, as if shaking off a thought.

AMY ELLIOTT DUNNE
AUGUST 23, 2010

– Diary entry –

Summer. Birdies. Sunshine. I spent today shuffling around Prospect Park, my skin tender, my bones brittle. Misery-battling. It is an improvement, since I spent the previous three days in our house in the same crusty pajama set, marking time until five, when I could have a drink. Trying to make myself remember the suffering in Darfur. Put things into perspective. Which, I guess, is just further exploiting the people of Darfur.

So much has unraveled the past week. I think that's what it is, that it's all happened at once, so I have the emotional bends. Nick lost his job a month ago. The recession is supposed to be winding down, but no one seems to know that. So Nick lost his job. Second round of layoffs, just like he predicted – just a few weeks after the first round. *Oops, we didn't fire nearly enough people.* Idiots.

At first I think Nick might be okay. He makes a massive list of things he's always meant to do. Some of it's tiny stuff: He changes watch batteries and resets clocks, he replaces a pipe beneath our sink and repaints all the rooms we painted before and didn't like. Basically, he does a lot of things over. It's nice to take some actual do-overs, when you get so few in life. And then he starts on bigger stuff: He reads *War and Peace*. He flirts with taking Arabic lessons. He spends a lot of time trying to guess what skills will be marketable over the next few decades. It breaks my heart, but I pretend it doesn't for his sake.

I keep asking him: 'Are you sure you're okay?'

93

At first I try it seriously, over coffee, eye contact, my hand on his. Then I try it breezily, lightly, in passing. Then I try it tenderly, in bed, stroking his hair.

He has the same answer always: 'I'm fine. I don't really want to talk about it.'

I wrote a quiz that was perfect for the times: 'How Are You Handling Your Layoff?'

a) I sit in my pajamas and eat a lot of ice cream – sulking is therapeutic!
b) I write nasty things about my old boss online, everywhere – venting feels great!
c) Until a new job comes along, I try to find useful things to do with my newfound time, like learning a marketable language or finally reading *War and Peace*.

It was a compliment to Nick – C was the correct answer – but he just gave a sour smile when I showed it to him.

A few weeks in, the bustling stopped, the usefulness stopped, as if he woke up one morning under a decrepit, dusty sign that read, *Why Fucking Bother?* He went dull-eyed. Now he watches TV, surfs porn, watches porn on TV. He eats a lot of delivery food, the Styrofoam shells propped up near the overflowing trash can. He doesn't talk to me, he behaves as if the act of talking physically pains him and I am a vicious woman to ask it of him.

He barely shrugs when I tell him I was laid off. Last week.

'That's awful, I'm sorry,' he says. 'At least you have your money to fall back on.'

'*We* have the money. I liked my job, though.'

He starts singing 'You Can't Always Get What You Want,' off-key, high-pitched, with a little stumbling dance, and I realize he is drunk. It is late afternoon, a beautiful blue-blue day, and our house is dank, thick with the sweet smell of rotting Chinese food, the curtains all drawn over, and I begin walking room to room to air it out, pulling back the drapes, scaring the dust motes, and when I reach the darkened den, I stumble over a bag on the floor, and then another and another, like the cartoon cat who walks into a room full of mousetraps. When I switch on the lights, I see dozens of shopping bags, and they are from places laid-off people don't go. They are the high-end men's stores, the places that hand-tailor suits, where salespeople carry ties individually, draped over an arm, to male shoppers nestled in leather armchairs. I mean, the shit is *bespoke*.

'What is all this, Nick?'

'For job interviews. If anyone ever starts hiring again.'

'You needed so much?'

'We *do* have the money.' He smiles at me grimly, his arms crossed.

'Do you at least want to hang them up?' Several of the plastic coverings have been chewed apart by Bleecker. A tiny mound of cat vomit lies near one three-thousand-dollar suit; a tailored white shirt is covered in orange fur where the cat has napped.

'Not really, nope,' he says. He grins at me.

I have never been a nag. I have always been rather proud of my un-nagginess. So it pisses me off, that Nick is forcing me to nag. I am willing to live with a certain amount of sloppiness, of laziness, of the lackadaisical life. I realize that I am more type A than Nick, and I try to be careful not to inflict my neat-freaky, to-do-list nature on him. Nick is not the kind of guy who is going to think to vacuum or clean out the fridge. He truly doesn't *see* that kind of stuff. Fine. Really. But I do like a certain standard of living – I think it's fair to say the garbage shouldn't literally overflow, and the plates shouldn't sit in the sink for a week with smears of bean burrito dried on them. That's just being a good grown-up roommate. And Nick's not doing anything anymore, so I have to nag, and it pisses me off: *You are turning me into what I never have been and never wanted to be, a nag, because you are not living up to your end of a very basic compact. Don't do that, it's not okay to do.*

I know, I know, I *know* that losing a job is incredibly stressful, and particularly for a man, they say it can be like a

95

death in the family, and especially for a man like Nick, who has always worked, so I take a giant breath, roll my anger up into a red rubber ball, and mentally kick it out into space. 'Well, do you mind if I hang these up? Just so they stay nice for you?'

'Knock yourself out.'

His-and-her layoffs, isn't that sweet? I know we are luckier than most: I go online and check my trust fund whenever I get nervous. I never called it a trust fund before Nick did; it's actually not that grand. I mean, it's nice, it's great – $785,404 that I have in savings thanks to my parents. But it's not the kind of money that allows you to stop working forever, especially not in New York. My parents' whole point was to make me feel secure enough so I didn't need to make choices based on money – in schooling, in career – but not so well off that I could be tempted to check out. Nick makes fun, but I think it's a great gesture for parents to make. (And appropriate, considering they plagiarized my childhood for the books.)

But I'm still feeling sick about the layoff, *our layoffs*, when my dad calls and asks if he and Mom can stop by. They need to talk with us. This afternoon, now, actually, if it's okay. Of course it's okay, I say, and in my head, I think, *Cancer cancer cancer.*

My parents appear at the door, looking like they've put up an effort. My father is thoroughly pressed and tucked and shined, impeccable except for the grooves beneath his eyes. My mother is in one of her bright purple dresses that she always wore to speeches and ceremonies, back when she got those invitations. She says the color demands confidence of the wearer.

They look great, but they seem ashamed. I usher them to the sofa, and we all sit silently for a second.

'Kids, your mother and I, we seem to have—' my father finally starts, then stops to cough. He places his hands on his knees; his big knuckles pale. 'Well, we seem to have gotten ourselves into a hell of a financial mess.'

I don't know what my reaction is supposed to be: shocked,

consoling, disappointed? My parents have never confessed any troubles to me. I don't think they've had many troubles.

'The fact of the matter is, we've been irresponsible,' Marybeth continues. 'We've been living the past decade like we were making the same kind of money we did for the previous two decades, and we weren't. We haven't made half that, but we were in denial. We were ... *optimistic* may be a kind way to put it. We just kept thinking the next *Amy* book would do the trick. But that hasn't happened. And we kept making bad decisions. We invested foolishly. We spent foolishly. And now.'

'We're basically broke,' Rand says. 'Our house, as well as *this* house, it's all underwater.'

I'd thought – assumed – they'd bought this house for us outright. I had no idea they were making payments on it. I feel a sting of embarrassment that I am as sheltered as Nick says.

'Like I said, we made some serious judgment errors,' Marybeth says. 'We should write a book: *Amazing Amy and the Adjustable Rate Mortgage*. We would flunk every quiz. We'd be the cautionary tale. Amy's friend, Wendy Want It Now.'

'Harry Head in the Sand,' Rand adds.

'So what happens next?' I ask.

'That is entirely up to you,' my dad says. My mom fishes out a homemade pamphlet from her purse and sets it on the table in front of us – bars and graphs and pie charts created on their home computer. It kills me to picture my parents squinting over the user's manual, trying to make their proposition look pretty for me.

Marybeth starts the pitch: 'We wanted to ask if we could borrow some money from your trust while we figure out what to do with the rest of our lives.'

My parents sit in front of us like two eager college kids hoping for their first internship. My father's knee jiggles until my mother places a gentle fingertip on it.

'Well, the trust fund is your money, so of course you can borrow from it,' I say. I just want this to be over; the hopeful look on my parents' faces, I can't stand it. 'How much do you think you need, to pay everything off and feel comfortable for a while?'

My father looks at his shoes. My mother takes a deep breath. 'Six hundred and fifty thousand,' she says.

'Oh.' It is all I can say. It is almost everything we have.

'Amy, maybe you and I should discuss—' Nick begins.

'No, no, we can do this,' I say. 'I'll just go grab my checkbook.'

'Actually,' Marybeth says, 'if you could wire it to our account tomorrow, that would be best. Otherwise there's a ten-day waiting period.'

That's when I know they are in serious trouble.

NICK DUNNE
TWO DAYS GONE

I woke up on the pullout couch in the Elliotts' suite, exhausted. They'd insisted I stay over – my home had not yet been reopened to me – insisted with the same urgency they once applied to snapping up the check at dinner: hospitality as ferocious force of nature. *You must let us do this for you.* So I did. I spent the night listening to their snores through the bedroom door, one steady and deep – a hearty lumberjack of a snore – the other gaspy and arrhythmic, as if the sleeper were dreaming of drowning.

I could always turn myself off like a light. *I'm going to sleep*, I'd say, my hands in prayer position against my cheek, *Zzzzzz*, the deep sleep of a NyQuiled child – while my insomniac wife fussed in bed next to me. Last night, though, I felt like Amy, my brain still going, my body on edge. I was, most of the time, a man who was literally comfortable in his own skin. Amy and I would sit on the couch to watch TV, and I'd turn to melted wax, my wife twitching and shifting constantly next to me. I asked her once if she might have restless leg syndrome – an ad for the disease was running, the actors' faces all furrowed in distress as they shook their calves and rubbed their thighs – and Amy said, *I have restless everything syndrome*.

I watched the ceiling of the hotel room turn gray then pink then yellow and finally pulled myself up to see the sun blaring right at me, across the river, again, a solar third degree. Then the names popped in my head – bing! Hilary Handy. Such an adorable name to be accused of such disturbing acts. Desi Collings, a former obsessive who lived an hour away. I had claimed them both as mine. It is a do-it-yourself era: health care, real estate, police investigation. Go online and fucking figure it out for yourself because everyone's overworked and understaffed. I was a *journalist*. I spent over ten years interviewing people for a living and getting them to reveal themselves. I was up to the task, and Marybeth and Rand believed so too. I was thankful they let me know I was still in their trust, the husband under a wispy cloud of suspicion. Or do I fool myself to use the word *wispy*?

The Days Inn had donated an underused ballroom to serve as the Find Amy Dunne headquarters. It was unseemly – a place of brown stains and canned smells – but just after dawn, Marybeth set about pygmalioning it, vacuuming and saniwiping, arranging bulletin boards and phone banks, hanging a large headshot of Amy on one wall. The poster – with Amy's cool, confident gaze, those eyes that followed you – looked like something from a presidential campaign. In fact, by the time Marybeth was done, the whole room buzzed with efficiency – the urgent hopefulness of a seriously underdog politician with a lot of true believers refusing to give up.

Just after ten a.m., Boney arrived, talking into her cell phone. She patted me on the shoulder and began fiddling with a printer. The volunteers arrived in bunches: Go and a half dozen of our late mother's friends. Five forty-something women, all in capri pants, like they were rehearsing a dance show: two of them – slender and blond and tanned – vying for the lead, the others cheerfully resigned to second string. A group of loudmouthed white-haired old ladies, each trying to talk over the next, a few of them texting, the kind of elderly people who have a baffling amount of energy, so much youthful vigor you had to wonder if they were trying to rub it in. Only one man showed up, a good-looking guy about my age, well dressed, alone, failing to realize that his presence could use some explaining. I watched Loner Guy as he sniffed around the pastries, sneaking glances at the poster of Amy.

Boney finished setting up the printer, grabbed a brannylooking muffin, and came to stand by me.

'Do you guys keep an eye on everyone who reports to volunteer?' I asked. 'I mean, in case it's someone—'

'Someone who seems to have a suspicious amount of interest? Absolutely.' She broke off the edges of the muffin and popped them in her mouth. She dropped her voice. 'But to tell the truth, serial killers watch the same TV shows we do. They know that *we* know they like to—'

'Insert themselves into the investigation.'

'That's it, yup.' She nodded. 'So they're more careful about that kind of thing now. But yeah, we sift through all the kinda-weirdos to make sure they're just, you know, kinda-weirdos.'

I raised an eyebrow.

'Like, Gilpin and I were lead detectives on the Kayla Holman case few years back. Kayla Holman?'

I shook my head: no bell.

'Anyway, you'll find some ghouls get attracted to stuff like this. And watch out for those two—' Boney pointed toward the two pretty forty-something women. 'Because they look like the type. To get a little too interested in consoling the worried husband.'

'Oh, come on—'

'You'd be surprised. Handsome guy like you. It happens.'

Just then one of the women, the blonder and tanner, looked over at us, made eye contact, and smiled the gentlest, shyest smile at me, then ducked her head like a cat waiting to be petted.

'She'll work hard, though; she'll be Little Miss Involved,' Boney said. 'So that's good.'

'How'd the Kayla Holman case turn out?' I asked.

She shook her head: *no.*

Four more women filed in, passing a bottle of sunblock among themselves, slathering it on bare arms and shoulders and noses. The room smelled like coconuts.

'By the way, Nick,' Boney said. 'Remember when I asked if Amy had friends in town – what about Noelle Hawthorne? You didn't mention her.' She left us two messages.

I gave her a blank stare.

'Noelle in your complex? Mother of triplets?'

'No, they aren't friends.'

'Oh, funny. She definitely seems to think they are.'

'That happens to Amy a lot,' I said. 'She talks to people once, and they latch on. It's creepy.'

'That's what her parents said.'

I debated asking Boney directly about Hilary Handy and Desi Collings. Then I decided not to; I'd look better if I were the one leading the charge. I wanted Rand and Marybeth to see me in action-hero mode. I couldn't shake the look Marybeth had given me: *The police definitely seem to think it's ... close to home.*

'People think they know her because they read the books growing up,' I said.

'I can see that,' Boney said, nodding. 'People want to believe they know other people. Parents want to believe they know their kids. Wives want to believe they know their husbands.'

Another hour and the volunteer center began feeling like a family picnic. A few of my old girlfriends dropped by to say hello, introduce their kids. One of my mom's best friends, Vicky, came by with three of her granddaughters, bashful tweens all in pink.

Grandkids. My mom had talked about grandkids a lot, as if it were doubtlessly going to happen – whenever she bought a new piece of furniture, she'd explain she favored that particular style because 'it'll work for when there's grandkids.' She wanted to live to see some grandkids. All her friends had some to spare. Amy and I once had my mom and Go over for dinner to mark The Bar's biggest week ever. I'd announced that we had reason to celebrate, and Mom had leapt from her seat, burst into tears, and hugged Amy, who also began weeping, murmuring from beneath my mom's smothering nuzzle, 'He's talking about The Bar, he's just talking about The Bar.' And then my mom tried hard to pretend she was just as excited about that. '*Plenty* of time for babies,' she'd said in her most consoling voice, a voice that just made Amy start to cry again.

Which was strange, since Amy had decided she didn't want kids, and she'd reiterated this fact several times, but the tears gave me a perverse wedge of hope that maybe she was changing her mind. Because there wasn't really plenty of time. Amy was thirty-seven when we moved to Carthage. She'd be thirty-nine in October.

And then I thought: We'll have to throw some fake birthday party or something if this is still going on. *We'll have to mark it somehow, some ceremony, for the volunteers, the media — something to revive attention. I'll have to pretend to be hopeful.*

'The prodijal son returns,' said a nasally voice, and I turned to see a skinny man in a stretched-out T-shirt next to me, scratching a handlebar mustache. My old friend Stucks Buckley, who had taken to calling me a prodigal son despite not knowing how to pronounce the word, or what its meaning was. I assume he meant it as a fancy synonym for jackass. Stucks Buckley, it sounded like a baseball player's name, and that was what Stucks was supposed to be, except he never had the talent, just the hard wish. He was the best in town, growing up, but that wasn't good enough. He got the shock of his life in college when he was cut from the team, and it all went to shit after. Now he was an odd-job stoner with twitchy moods. He had dropped by The Bar a few times to try to pick up work, but he shook his head at every crappy day-job chore I offered, chewing on the inside of his cheek, annoyed: *Come on, man, what else you got, you got to have something else.*

'Stucks,' I said by way of greeting, waiting to see if he was in a friendly mood.

'Hear the police are botching this royally,' he said, tucking his hands into his armpits.

'It's a little early to say that.'

'Come on, man, these little pansy-ass searches? I seen more effort put into finding the mayor's dog.' Stuck's face was sunburned; I could feel the heat coming off him as he leaned in closer, giving me a blast of Listerine and chaw. 'Why ain't they rounded up some people? Plenty of people in town to choose from, they ain't brought a single one in? Not a *single* one? What about the Blue Book Boys? That's what I asked the lady detective: What about the Blue Book Boys? She wouldn't even answer me.'

'What are the Blue Book Boys? A gang?'

'All those guys got laid off from the Blue Book plant last winter. No severance, nothing. You see some of the homeless guys wandering around town in packs, looking real, real pissed? Probably Blue Book Boys.'

'I'm still not following you: Blue Book plant?'

'You know: River Valley Printworks. On edge of town? They made those blue books you used for essays and shit in college.'

'Oh. I didn't know.'

'Now colleges use computers, whatnot, so – phwet! – bye-bye, Blue Book Boys.'

'God, this whole town is shutting down,' I muttered.

'The Blue Book Boys, they drink, drug, harass people. I mean, they did that before, but they always had to stop, go back to work on Monday. Now they just run wild.'

Stucks grinned his row of chipped teeth at me. He had paint flecks in his hair; his summer job since high school, housepainting. *I specialize in trim work*, he'd say, and wait for you to get the joke. If you didn't laugh, he'd explain it.

'So, the cops been out to the mall?' Stucks asked. I started a confused shrug.

'Shit, man, didn't you used to be a reporter?' Stucks always seemed angry at my former occupation, like it was a lie that had stood too long. 'The Blue Book Boys, they all made themselves a nice little town over in the mall. Squatting. Drug deals. The police run them out every once in a while, but they're always back next day. Anyway, that's what I told the lady detective: *Search the fucking mall*. Because some of them, they gang-raped a girl there a month ago. I mean, you get a bunch of angry men together, and things aren't too good for a woman that comes across them.'

On my drive to the afternoon search area, I phoned Boney, started in as soon as she said hello.

'Why isn't the mall being searched?'

'The mall will be searched, Nick. We have cops heading over there right now.'

'Oh. Okay. Because a buddy of mine—'

'Stucks, I know, I know him.'

'He was talking about all the—'

'The Blue Book Boys, I know. Trust us, Nick, we got this. We want to find Amy as much as you do.'

'Okay, uh, thanks.'

My righteousness deflated, I gulped down my giant Styrofoam cup of coffee and drove to my assigned area. Three spots were being searched this afternoon: the Gully boat launch (now known as the Place Nick Spent the Morning of, Unseen by Anyone); the Miller Creek woods (which hardly deserved the name; you could see fast-food restaurants through the treeline); and Wolky Park, a nature spot with hiking and horse trails. I was assigned to Wolky Park.

When I arrived, a local officer was addressing a crowd of about twelve people, all thick legs in tight shorts, sunglasses, and hats, zinc oxide on noses. It looked like opening day of camp.

Two different TV crews were out to capture images for local stations. It was the July 4th weekend; Amy would be squeezed in between state fair stories and barbecue cookoffs. One cub reporter kept mosquitoing around me, peppering me with pointless questions, my body going immediately stiff, inhuman, with the attention, my 'concerned' face looking fake. A waft of horse manure hung in the air.

The reporters soon left to follow the volunteers into the trails. (What kind of journalist finds a suspicious husband ripe for the picking and *leaves*? A bad low-pay journalist left behind after all the decent ones have been laid off.) A young uniform cop told me to stand – right here – at the entry to the various trails, near a bulletin board that held a mess of ancient flyers, as well as a missing person notice for Amy, my wife staring out of that photo. She'd been everywhere today, following me.

'What should I be doing?' I asked the officer. 'I feel like a jackass here. I need to do something.' Somewhere in the woods, a horse whinnied mournfully.

'We really need you right here, Nick. Just be friendly, be encouraging,' he said, and pointed to the bright orange thermos next to me. 'Offer water. Just point anyone who comes in my way.' He turned and walked toward the stables. It occurred to me that they were intentionally barring me from any possible crime scene. I wasn't sure what that meant.

As I stood aimlessly, pretending to busy myself with the cooler, a latecomer SUV rolled in, shiny red as nail polish. Out poured the fortysomethings from headquarters. The prettiest woman, the one Boney picked as a groupie, was holding her hair up in a ponytail so one of her friends could bug-spray the back of her neck. The woman waved at the fumes elaborately. She glanced at me out of the corner of her eye. Then she stepped away from her friends, let her hair fall down around her shoulders, and began picking her way over to me, that stricken, sympathetic smile on her face, the *I'm so sorry* smile. Giant brown pony eyes, her pink shirt ending just above crisp white shorts. High-heeled sandals, curled hair, gold hoops. *This*, I thought, *is how you* not *dress for a search*.

Please don't talk to me, lady.

'Hi, Nick, I'm Shawna Kelly. *I'm so sorry.*' She had an unnecessarily loud voice, a bit of a bray, like some enchanted, hot donkey. She held out her hand, and I felt a flick of alarm as Shawna's friends started ambling down the trail, casting girl-clique glances back toward us, the couple.

I offered what I had: my thanks, my water, my lip-swallowing awkwardness. Shawna didn't make any move to leave, even though I was staring ahead, toward the trail where her friends had disappeared.

'I hope you have friends, relatives, who are looking out for you during this, Nick,' she said, swatting a horsefly. 'Men forget to take care of themselves. Comfort food is what you need.'

'We've been eating mostly cold cuts – you know, fast, easy.' I could still taste the salami in the back of my throat, the fumes floating up from my belly. I became aware that I hadn't brushed my teeth since the morning.

'Oh, you poor man. Well, cold cuts, that won't do it.' She shook her head, the gold hoops flickering sunlight. 'You need to keep up your strength. Now, you are lucky, because *I* make a mean chicken Frito pie. You know what? I am going to put that together and drop it by the volunteer center tomorrow. You can just microwave it whenever you want a nice warm dinner.'

'Oh, that sounds like too much trouble, really. We're fine. We really are.'

'You'll be more fine after you eat a good meal,' she said, patting my arm.

Silence. She tried another angle.

'I really hope it doesn't end up having anything to do ... with our homeless problem,' she said. 'I swear, I have filed complaint after complaint. One broke into my garden last month. My motion sensor went off, so I peeked outside and there he was, kneeling in the dirt, just guzzling tomatoes. Gnawing at them like apples, his face and shirt were covered in juice and seeds. I tried to scare him off, but he loaded up at least twenty before he ran off. They were on the edge anyway, those Blue Book guys. No other skills.'

I felt a sudden affinity for the troop of Blue Book men, pictured myself walking into their bitter encampment, waving a white flag: *I am your brother, I used to work in print too. The computers stole my job too.*

'Don't tell me you're too young to remember Blue Books, Nick,' Shawna was saying. She poked me in the ribs, making me jump more than I should have.

'I'm so old, I'd forgotten about Blue Books until you reminded me.'

She laughed: 'What are you, thirty-one, thirty-two?'

'Try thirty-four.'

'A baby.'

The trio of energetic elderly ladies arrived just then, tromping toward us, one working her cell phone, all wearing sturdy canvas garden skirts, Keds, and sleeveless golf tops revealing wobbly arms. They nodded at me respectfully, then flicked a glance of disapproval when they saw Shawna. We looked like a couple hosting a backyard barbecue. We looked inappropriate.

Please go away, Shawna, I thought.

'So anyway, the homeless guys, they can be really aggressive, like, threatening, toward women,' Shawna said. 'I mentioned it to Detective Boney, but I get the feeling she doesn't like me very much.'

'Why do you say that?' I already knew what she was going to say, the mantra of all attractive women.

'Women don't like me all that much.' She shrugged. 'Just one of those things. Did – does Amy have a lot of friends in town?'

A number of women – friends of my mom's, friends of Go's – had invited Amy to book clubs and Amway parties and girls' nights at Chili's. Amy had predictably declined all but a few, which she attended and hated: 'We ordered a million little fried things and drank cocktails made from *ice cream.*'

Shawna was watching me, wanting to know about Amy, wanting to be grouped together with my wife, who would hate her.

'I think she may have the same problem you do,' I said in a clipped voice.

She smiled.

Leave, Shawna.

'It's hard to come to a new town,' she said. 'Hard to make friends, the older you get. Is she your age?'

'Thirty-eight.'

That seemed to please her too.

Go the fuck away.

'Smart man, likes them older women.'

She pulled a cell phone out of her giant chartreuse handbag, laughing. 'Come here,' she said, and pulled an arm around me. 'Give me a big chicken-Frito casserole smile.'

I wanted to smack her, right then, the obliviousness, the *girliness*, of her: trying to get an ego stroke from the husband of a missing woman. I swallowed my rage, tried to hit reverse, tried to overcompensate and *be nice*, so I smiled robotically as she pressed her face against my cheek and took a photo with her phone, the fake camera-click sound waking me.

She turned the phone around, and I saw our two sunburned faces pressed together, smiling as if we were on a date at the baseball game. Looking at my smarmy grin, my hooded eyes, I thought, *I would hate this guy.*

AMY ELLIOTT DUNNE
SEPTEMBER 15, 2010

– Diary entry –

I am writing from somewhere in Pennsylvania. Southwest corner. A motel off the highway. Our room overlooks the parking lot, and if I peek out from behind the stiff beige curtains, I can see people milling about under the fluorescent lights. It's the kind of place where people mill about. I have the emotional bends again. Too much has happened, and so fast, and now I am in southwest Pennsylvania, and my husband is enjoying a defiant sleep amid the little packets of chips and candies he bought from the vending machine down the hall. Dinner. He is angry at me for not being a good sport. I thought I was putting up a convincing front – hurray, a new adventure! – but I guess not.

Now that I look back, it was like we were waiting for something to happen. Like Nick and I were sitting under a giant soundproof, windproof jar, and then the jar fell over and – there was something to do.

Two weeks ago, we are in our usual unemployed state: partly dressed, thick with boredom, getting ready to eat a silent breakfast that we'll stretch over the reading of the newspaper in its entirety. We even read the auto supplement now.

Nick's cell phone rings at ten a.m., and I can tell by his voice that it is Go. He sounds springy, boyish, the way he always does when he talks to her. The way he used to sound with me.

He heads into the bedroom and shuts the door, leaving me holding two freshly made eggs Benedicts quivering on the plates. I place his on the table and sit opposite, wondering if I should wait to eat. If it were me, I think, I would come back out and tell him to eat, or else I'd raise a finger: *Just one minute*. I'd be aware of the other person, my spouse, left in the kitchen with plates of eggs. I feel bad that I was thinking that. Because soon I can hear worried murmurs and upset exclamations and gentle reassurances from behind the door, and I begin wondering if Go is having some back-home boy troubles. Go has a lot of breakups. Even the ones that she instigates require much handholding and goo-gawing from Nick.

So I have my usual *Poor Go* face on when Nick emerges, the eggs hardened on the plate. I see him and know this isn't just a Go problem.

'My mom,' he starts, and sits down. 'Shit. My mom has cancer. Stage four, and it's spread to the liver and bones. Which is bad, which is . . .'

He puts his face in his hands, and I go over and put my arms around him. When he looks up, he is dry-eyed. Calm. I've never seen my husband cry.

'It's too much for Go, on top of my dad's Alzheimer's.'

'Alzheimer's? *Alzheimer's?* Since when?'

'Well, a while. At first they thought it was some sort of early dementia. But it's more, it's worse.'

I think, immediately, that there is something wrong with us, perhaps unfixable, if my husband wouldn't think to tell me this. Sometimes I feel it's his personal game, that he's in some sort of undeclared contest for impenetrability. 'Why didn't you say anything to me?'

'My dad isn't someone I like to talk about that much.'

'But still—'

'Amy. Please.' He has that look, like I am being unreasonable, like he is so sure I am being unreasonable that I wonder if I am.

'But now. Go says with my mom, she'll need chemo but . . . she'll be really, really sick. She'll need help.'

'Should we start looking for in-home care for her? A nurse?'

'She doesn't have that kind of insurance.'

He stares at me, arms crossed, and I know what he is daring: daring me to offer to pay, and we can't pay, because I've given my money to my parents.

'Okay, then, babe,' I say. 'What do you want to do?'

We stand across from each other, a showdown, as if we are in a fight and I haven't been informed. I reach out to touch him, and he just looks at my hand.

'We have to move back.' He glares at me, opening his eyes wide. He flicks his fingers out as if he is trying to rid himself of something sticky. 'We'll take a year and we'll go do the right thing. We have no jobs, we have no money, there's nothing holding us here. Even you have to admit that.'

'Even *I* have to?' As if I am already being resistant. I feel a burst of anger that I swallow.

'This is what we're going to do. We are going to do the right thing. We are going to help *my* parents for once.'

Of course that's what we have to do, and of course if he had presented the problem to me like I wasn't his enemy, that's what I would have said. But he came out of the door already treating me like a problem that needed to be dealt with. I was the bitter voice that needed to be squelched.

My husband is the most loyal man on the planet until he's not. I've seen his eyes literally turn a shade darker when he's felt betrayed by a friend, even a dear longtime friend, and then the friend is never mentioned again. He looked at me then like I was an object to be jettisoned if necessary. It actually chilled me, that look.

So it is decided that quickly, with that little of a debate: We are leaving New York. We are going to Missouri. To a house in Missouri by the river where we will live. It is surreal, and I'm not one to misuse the word *surreal*.

I know it will be okay. It's just so far from what I pictured. When I pictured my life. That's not to say bad, just ... If you gave me a million guesses where life would take me, I wouldn't have guessed. I find that alarming.

The packing of the U-Haul is a mini-tragedy: Nick, determined and guilty, his mouth a tight line, getting it done, unwilling to look at me. The U-Haul sits for hours, blocking traffic on our little street, blinking its hazard lights – danger, danger, danger – as Nick goes up and down the stairs, a one-man assembly line, carrying boxes of books, boxes of kitchen supplies, chairs, side tables. We are bringing our vintage sofa – our broad old chesterfield that Dad calls our pet, we dote on it so much. It is to be the last thing we pack, a sweaty, awkward two-person job. Getting the massive thing down our stairs (*Hold on, I need to rest. Lift to the right. Hold on, you're going too fast. Watch out, my fingers my fingers!*) will be its own much-needed team-building exercise. After the sofa, we'll pick up lunch from the corner deli, bagel sandwiches to eat on the road. Cold soda.

Nick lets me keep the sofa, but our other big items are staying in New York. One of Nick's friends will inherit the bed; the guy will come by later to our empty home – nothing but dust and cable cords left – and take the bed, and then he'll live his New York life in our New York bed, eating two a.m. Chinese food and having lazy-condomed sex with tipsy, brass-mouthed girls who work in PR. (Our home itself will be taken over by a noisy couple, hubby-wife lawyers who are shamelessly, brazenly gleeful at this buyers'-market deal. I hate them.)

I carry one load for every four that Nick grunts down. I move slowly, shuffling, like my bones hurt, a feverish delicacy descending on me. Everything does hurt. Nick buzzes past me, going up or down, and throws his frown at me, snaps, 'You okay?' and keeps moving before I answer, leaving me gaping, a cartoon with a black mouth-hole. I am not okay. I will be okay, but right now I am not okay. I want my husband to put his arms around me, to console me, to baby me a little bit. Just for a second.

Inside the back of the truck, he fusses with the boxes. Nick prides himself on his packing skills: He is (was) the loader of the dishwasher, the packer of the holiday bags. But by hour three, it is clear that we've sold or gifted too many of our belongings. The U-Haul's massive cavern is only half full. It gives me my single satisfaction of the day, that hot, mean satisfaction right in the belly, like a nib of mercury. *Good*, I think. *Good.*

'We can take the bed if you really want to,' Nick says, looking past me down the street. 'We have enough room.'

'No, you promised it to Wally, Wally should have it,' I say primly.

I was wrong. Just say: *I was wrong, I'm sorry, let's take the bed. You should have your old, comforting bed in this new place.* Smile at me and be nice to me. Today, be nice to me.

Nick blows out a sigh. 'Okay, if that's what you want. Amy? Is it?' He stands, slightly breathless, leaning on a stack of boxes, the top one with Magic Marker scrawl: *Amy Clothes Winter.* 'This is the last I'll hear about the bed, Amy? Because I'm offering right now. I'm happy to pack the bed for you.'

'How gracious of you,' I say, just a whiff of breath, the way I say most retorts: a puff of perfume from a rank atomizer. I am a coward. I don't like confrontation. I pick up a box and start toward the truck.

'What did you say?'

I shake my head at him. I don't want him to see me cry, because it will make him more angry.

Ten minutes later, the stairs are pounding – bang! bang! bang! Nick is dragging our sofa down by himself.

I can't even look behind me as we leave New York, because the truck has no back window. In the side mirror, I track the skyline (the *receding skyline* – isn't that what they write in Victorian novels where the doomed heroine is forced to leave her ancestral home?), but none of the good buildings – not the Chrysler or the Empire State or the Flatiron, they never appear in that little shining rectangle.

My parents dropped by the night before, presented us with the family cuckoo clock that I'd loved as a child, and the three of us cried and hugged as Nick shuffled his hands in his pockets and promised to take care of me.

He promised to take care of me, and yet I feel afraid. I feel like something is going wrong, very wrong, and that it will get even worse. I don't feel like Nick's wife. I don't feel like a person at all: I am something to be loaded and unloaded, like a sofa or a cuckoo clock. I am something to be tossed into a junkyard, thrown into the river, if necessary. I don't feel real anymore. I feel like I could disappear.

NICK DUNNE
THREE DAYS GONE

The police weren't going to find Amy unless someone wanted her found. That much was clear. Everything green and brown had been searched: miles of the muddy Mississippi River, all the trails and hiking paths, our sad collection of patchy woods. If she were alive, someone would need to return her. If she were dead, nature would have to give her up. It was a palpable truth, like a sour taste on the tongue tip. I arrived at the volunteer center and realized everyone else knew this too: There was a listlessness, a defeat, that hung over the place. I wandered aimlessly over to the pastries station and tried to convince myself to eat something. Danish. I'd come to believe there was no food more depressing than Danish, a pastry that seemed stale upon arrival.

'I still say it's the river,' one volunteer was saying to his buddy, both of them picking through the pastries with dirty fingers. 'Right behind the guy's house, what easier way?'

'She would have turned up in an eddy by now, a lock, something.'

'Not if she's been cut. Chop off the legs, the arms ... the body can shoot all the way to the Gulf. Tunica, at least.'

I turned away before they noticed me.

A former teacher of mine, Mr Coleman, sat at a card table, hunched over the tip-line phone, scribbling down information. When I caught his eye, he made the cuckoo signal: finger circling his ear, then pointing at the phone. He had greeted me yesterday by saying, 'My granddaughter was killed by a drunk driver, so ...' We'd murmured and patted each other awkwardly.

My cell rang, the disposable – I couldn't figure out where to keep it, so I kept it on me. I'd made a call, and the call was being returned, but I couldn't take it. I turned the phone off, scanned the room to make sure the Elliotts hadn't seen me do it. Marybeth was clicking away on her BlackBerry, then holding it at arm's length so she could read the text. When she saw me, she shot over in her tight quick steps, holding the BlackBerry in front of her like a talisman.

'How many hours from here is Memphis?' she asked.

'Little under five hours, driving. What's in Memphis?'

'Hilary Handy lives in Memphis. Amy's *stalker* from high school. How much of a coincidence is that?'

I didn't know what to say: none?

'Yeah, Gilpin blew me off too. *We can't authorize the expense for something that happened twenty-some years ago.* Asshole. Guy always treats me like I'm on the verge of hysteria; he'll talk to Rand when I'm right there, totally ignore me, like I need my husband to explain things to little dumb me. *Ass*hole.'

'The city's broke,' I said. 'I'm sure they really don't have the budget, Marybeth.'

'Well, we do. I'm serious, Nick, this girl was off her rocker. And I know she tried to contact Amy over the years. Amy told me.'

'She never told me that.'

'What's it cost to drive there? Fifty bucks? Fine. Will you go? You said you'd go. Please? I won't be able to stop thinking until I know someone's talked to her.'

I knew this to be true, at least, because her daughter suffered from the same tenacious worry streak: Amy could spend an entire evening out fretting that she left the stove on, even though we didn't cook that day. Or was the door locked? Was I sure? She was a worst-case scenarist on a grand scale. Because it was never just that the door was unlocked, it was that the door was unlocked, and men were inside, and they were waiting to rape and kill her.

I felt a layer of sweat shimmer to the surface of my skin, because, finally, my wife's fears had come to fruition. Imagine the awful satisfaction, to know that all those years of worry had paid off.

'Of course I'll go. And I'll stop by St. Louis, see the other one, Desi, on the way. Consider it done.' I turned around, started my dramatic exit, got twenty feet, and suddenly, there was Stucks again, his entire face still slack with sleep.

'Heard the cops searched the mall yesterday,' he said, scratching his jaw. In his other hand he held a glazed donut, unbitten. A bagel-shaped bulge sat in the front pocket of his cargo pants. I almost made a joke: *Is that a baked good in your pocket or are you . . .*

'Yeah. Nothing.'

'Yester*day*. They went yester*day*, the jackasses.' He ducked, looked around, as if he worried they'd overheard him. He leaned closer to me. 'You go at night, that's when they're there. Daytime, they're down by the river, or out flying a flag.'

'Flying a flag?'

'You know, sitting by the exits on the highway with those signs: *Laid Off, Please Help, Need Beer Money*, whatever,' he said, scanning the room. 'Flying a flag, man.'

'Okay.'

'At night they're at the mall,' he said.

'Then let's go tonight,' I said. 'You and me and whoever.'

'Joe and Mikey Hillsam,' Stucks said. 'They'd be up for it.' The Hillsams were three, four years older than me, town badasses. The kind of guys who were born without the fear gene, impervious to pain. Jock kids who sped through the summers on short, muscled legs, playing baseball, drinking beer, taking strange dares: skateboarding into drainage ditches, climbing water towers naked. The kind of guys who would peel up, wild-eyed, on a boring Saturday night and you knew something would happen, maybe nothing good, but something. Of course the Hillsams would be up for it.

'Good,' I said. 'Tonight we go.'

My phone rang in my pocket. The thing didn't turn off right. It rang again.

'You gonna get that?' Stucks asked.

'Nah.'

'You should answer every call, man. You really should.'

There was nothing to do for the rest of the day. No searches planned, no more flyers needed, the phones fully manned. Marybeth started sending volunteers home; they were just standing around, eating, bored. I suspected Stucks of leaving with half the breakfast table in his pockets.

'Anyone hear from the detectives?' Rand asked.

'Nothing,' Marybeth and I both answered.

'That may be good, right?' Rand asked, hopeful eyes, and Marybeth and I both indulged him. Yes, sure.

'When are you leaving for Memphis?' she asked me.

'Tomorrow. Tonight my friends and I are doing another search of the mall. We don't think it was done right yesterday.'

'Excellent,' Marybeth said. 'That's the kind of action we need. We suspect it wasn't done right the first time, we do it ourselves. Because I just – I'm just not that impressed with what's been done so far.'

Rand put a hand on his wife's shoulder, a signal this refrain had been expressed and received many times.

'I'd like to come with you, Nick,' he said. 'Tonight. I'd like to come.' Rand was wearing a powder-blue golf shirt and olive slacks, his hair a gleaming dark helmet. I pictured him trying to hail-fellow the Hillsam brothers, doing his slightly desperate one-of-the-guys routine – *hey, I love a good beer too, and how about that sports team of yours?* – and felt a flush of impending awkwardness.

'Of course, Rand. Of course.'

I had a good ten unscheduled hours to work with. My car was being released back to me – having been processed and vacuumed and printed, I assume – so I hitched a ride to the police station with an elderly volunteer, one of those bustling grandmotherly types who seemed slightly nervous to be alone with me.

'I'm just driving Mr Dunne to the police station, but I will be back in less than half an hour,' she said to one of her friends. 'No more than half an hour.'

Gilpin had not taken Amy's second note into evidence; he'd been too thrilled with the underwear to bother. I got in my car, flung the door open, and sat as the heat drooled out, reread my wife's second clue:

> *Picture me: I'm crazy about you*
> *My future is anything but hazy with you*
> *You took me here so I could hear you chat*
> *About your boyhood adventures: crummy jeans and visor hat*
> *Screw everyone else, for us they're all ditched*
> *And let's sneak a kiss ... pretend we just got hitched.*

It was Hannibal, Missouri, boyhood home of Mark Twain, where I'd worked summers growing up, where I'd wandered the town dressed as Huck Finn, in an old straw hat and faux-ragged pants, smiling scampishly while urging people to visit the Ice Cream Shoppe. It was one of those stories you dine out on, at least in New York, because no one else could match it. No one could ever say: *Oh yeah, me too.*

The 'visor hat' comment was a little inside joke: When I'd first told Amy I played Huck, we were out to dinner, into our second bottle of wine, and she'd been adorably tipsy. Big grin and the flushed cheeks she got when she drank. Leaning across the table as if I had a magnet on me. She kept asking me if I still had the visor, would I wear the visor for her, and when I asked her why in the name of all that was holy would she think that Huck Finn wore a visor, she swallowed once and said, 'Oh, I meant a straw hat!' As if those were two entirely interchangeable words. After that, any time we watched tennis, we always complimented the players' sporty straw hats.

Hannibal was a strange choice for Amy, however, as I don't remember us having a particularly good or bad time there, just a time. I remember us ambling around almost a full year ago, pointing at things and reading placards and saying, 'That's interesting,' while the other one agreed, 'That is.' I'd been there since then without Amy (my nostalgic streak uncrushable) and had a glorious day, a wide-grin, right-with-the-world day. But with Amy, it had been still, rote. A bit embarrassing. I remember at one point starting a goofy story about a childhood field trip here, and I saw her eyes go blank, and I got secretly furious, spent ten minutes just winding myself up – because at this point of our marriage, I was so used to being angry with her, it felt almost enjoyable, like gnawing on a cuticle: You know you should stop, that it doesn't really feel as good as you think, but you can't quit grinding away. On the surface, of course, she saw nothing. We just kept walking, and reading placards, and pointing.

It was a fairly awful reminder, the dearth of good memories we had since our move, that my wife was forced to pick Hannibal for her treasure hunt.

I reached Hannibal in twenty minutes, drove past the glorious Gilded Age courthouse that now held only a chicken-wing place in its basement, and headed past a series of shuttered businesses – ruined community banks and defunct movie houses – toward the river. I parked in a lot right on the Mississippi, smack in front of the *Mark Twain* riverboat. Parking was free. (I never failed to thrill to the novelty, the generosity of free parking.) Banners of the white-maned man hung listlessly from lamp poles, posters curled up in the heat. It was a blow-dryer-hot day, but even so, Hannibal seemed disturbingly quiet. As I walked along the few blocks of souvenir stores – quilts and antiques and taffy – I saw more for-sale signs. Becky Thatcher's house was closed for renovations, to be paid with money that had yet to be raised. For ten bucks, you could graffiti your name on Tom Sawyer's whitewashed fence, but there were few takers.

I sat in the doorstep of a vacant storefront. It occurred to me that I had brought Amy to the end of everything. We were literally experiencing the end of a way of life, a phrase I'd applied only to New Guinea tribesmen and Appalachian glassblowers. The recession had ended the mall.

Computers had ended the Blue Book plant. Carthage had gone bust; its sister city Hannibal was losing ground to brighter, louder, cartoonier tourist spots. My beloved Mississippi River was being eaten in reverse by Asian carp flip-flopping their way up toward Lake Michigan. *Amazing Amy* was done. It was the end of my career, the end of hers, the end of my father, the end of my mom. The end of our marriage. The end of Amy.

The ghost wheeze of the steamboat horn blew out from the river. I had sweated through the back of my shirt. I made myself stand up. I made myself buy my tour ticket. I walked the route Amy and I had taken, my wife still beside me in my mind. It was hot that day too. *You are BRILLIANT.* In my imagination, she strolled next to me, and this time she smiled. My stomach went oily.

I mind-walked my wife around the main tourist drag. A gray-haired couple paused to peer into the Huckleberry Finn House but didn't bother to walk in. At the end of the block, a man dressed as Twain – white hair, white suit – got out of a Ford Focus, stretched, looked down the lonely street, and ducked into a pizza joint. And then there we were, at the clapboard building that had been the courtroom of Samuel Clemens's dad. The sign out front read: *J. M. Clemens, Justice of the Peace.*

Let's sneak a kiss … pretend we just got hitched.

You're making these so nice and easy, Amy. As if you actually want me to find them, to feel good about myself. Keep this up and I'll break my record.

No one was inside. I got down on my knees on the dusty floorboards and peered under the first bench. If Amy left a clue in a public place, she always taped it to the underside of things, in between the wadded gum and the dust, and she was always vindicated, because no one likes to look at the underside of things. There was nothing under the first bench, but there was a flap of paper hanging down from the bench behind. I climbed over and tugged down the Amy-blue envelope, a piece of tape winging off it.

Hi Darling Husband,

You found it! Brilliant man. It may help that I decided to not make this year's treasure hunt an excruciating forced march through my arcane personal memories.

I took a cue from your beloved Mark Twain: 'What ought to be done to the man who invented the celebrating of anniversaries? Mere killing would be too light.'

I finally get it, what you've said year after year, that this treasure hunt should be a time to celebrate us, not a test about whether you remember everything I think or say throughout the year. You'd think that would be something a grown woman would realize on her own, but ... I guess that's what husbands are for. To point out what we can't see for ourselves, even if it takes five years.

So I wanted to take a moment now, in the childhood stomping grounds of Mark Twain, and thank you for your WIT. You are truly the cleverest, funniest person I know. I have a wonderful sense memory: of all the times over the years you've leaned in to my ear – I can feel your breath tickling my lobe, right now, as I'm writing this – and whispered something just to me, just to make me laugh. What a generous thing that is, I realize, for a husband to try to make his wife laugh. And you always picked the best moments. Do you remember when Insley and her dancing-monkey husband made us come over to admire their baby, and we did the obligatory visit to their strangely perfect, overflowered, overmuffined house for brunch and baby-meeting and they were so self-righteous and patronizing of our childless state, and meanwhile there was their hideous boy, covered in streaks of slobber and stewed carrots and maybe some feces – naked except for a frilly bib and a pair of knitted booties – and as I sipped my orange juice, you leaned over and whispered, 'That's what I'll be wearing later.' And I literally did a spit take. It was one of those moments where you saved me, you made me laugh at just the right time. Just one olive, though. So let me say it again: You are WITTY. Now kiss me!

I felt my soul deflate. Amy was using the treasure hunt to steer us back to each other. And it was too late. While she had been writing these clues, she'd had no idea of my state of mind. *Why, Amy, couldn't you have done this sooner?*

Our timing had never been good.

I opened the next clue, read it, tucked it in my pocket, then headed back home. I knew where to go, but I wasn't ready yet. I couldn't handle another compliment, another kind word from my wife, another olive branch. My feelings for her were veering too quickly from bitter to sweet.

I went back to Go's, spent a few hours alone, drinking coffee and flipping around the TV, anxious and pissy, killing time till my eleven p.m. carpool to the mall. My twin got home just after seven, looking wilted from her solo bar shift. Her glance at the TV told me I should turn it off. 'What'd you do today?' she asked, lighting a cigarette and flopping down at our mother's old card table.

'Manned the volunteer center ... then we go search the mall at eleven,' I said. I didn't want to tell her about Amy's clue. I felt guilty enough.

Go doled out some solitaire cards, the steady slap of them on the table a rebuke. I began pacing. She ignored me.

'I was just watching TV to distract myself.'

'I know, I do.'

She flipped over a Jack.

'There's got to be something I can *do*,' I said, stalking around her living room.

'Well, you're searching the mall in a few hours,' Go said, and gave no more encouragement. She flipped over three cards.

'You sound like you think it's a waste of time.'

'Oh. No. Hey, everything is worth checking out. They got Son of Sam on a parking ticket, right?'

Go was the third person who'd mentioned this to me; it must be the mantra for cases going cold. I sat down across from her.

'I haven't been upset enough about Amy,' I said. 'I know that.'

'Maybe not.' She finally looked up at me. 'You're being weird.'

'I think that instead of panicking, I've just focused on being pissed at her. Because we were in such a bad place lately. It's like it feels wrong for me to worry too much because I don't have the right. I guess.'

'You've been weird, I can't lie,' Go said. 'But it's a weird situation.' She stubbed out her cigarette. 'I don't care how you are with me. Just be careful with everyone else, okay? People judge. Fast.'

She went back to her solitaire, but I wanted her attention. I kept talking.

'I should probably check in on Dad at some point,' I said. 'I don't know if I'll tell him about Amy.'

'No,' she said. 'Don't. He was even weirder about Amy than you are.'

'I always felt like she must remind him of an old girlfriend or something – the one who got away. After he—' I made the downward swoop of a hand that signified his Alzheimer's – 'he was kind of rude and awful, but . . .'

'Yeah, but he kind of wanted to impress her at the same time,' she said. 'Your basic jerky twelve-year-old boy trapped in a sixty-eight-year-old asshole's body.'

'Don't women think that all men are jerky twelve-year-olds at heart?'

'Hey, if the heart fits.'

Eleven-oh-eight p.m., Rand was waiting for us just inside the automatic sliding doors to the hotel, his face squinting into the dark to make us out. The Hillsams were driving their pick-up; Stucks and I both rode in the bed. Rand came trotting up to us in khaki golf shorts and a crisp Middlebury T-shirt. He hopped in the back, planted himself on the wheel cover with surprising ease, and handled the introductions like he was the host of his own mobile talk show.

'I'm really sorry about Amy, Rand,' Stucks said loudly, as we hurtled out of the parking lot with unnecessary speed and hit the highway. 'She's such a sweet person. One time she saw me out painting a house, sweating my ba – my butt off, and she drove on to 7-Eleven, got me a giant pop, and brought it back to me, right up on the ladder.'

This was a lie. Amy cared so little for Stucks or his refreshment that she wouldn't have bothered to piss in a cup for him.

'That sounds like her,' Rand said, and I was flush with unwelcome, ungentlemanly annoyance. Maybe it was the journalist in me, but facts were facts, and people didn't get to turn Amy into everyone's beloved best friend just because it was emotionally expedient.

'Middlebury, huh?' Stucks continued, pointing at Rand's T-shirt. 'Got a hell of a rugby team.'

'That's *right* we do,' Rand said, the big smile again, and he and Stucks began an improbable discussion of liberal-arts rugby over the noise of the car, the air, the night, all the way to the mall.

Joe Hillsam parked his truck outside the giant cornerstone Mervyns. We all hopped out, stretched our legs, shook ourselves awake. The night was muggy and moon-slivered. I noticed Stucks was wearing – maybe ironically, possibly not – a T-shirt that read *Save Gas, Fart in a Jar*.

'So, this place, what we're doing, it's freakin' dangerous, I don't want to lie,' Mikey Hillsam began. He had beefed up over the years, as had his brother; they weren't just barrel-chested but barrel-everythinged. Standing side by side, they were about five hundred pounds of dude.

'We came here once, me and Mikey, just for – I don't know, to see it, I guess, see what it had become, and we almost got our asses handed to us,' said Joe. 'So tonight we take no chances.' He reached into the cab for a long canvas bag and unzipped it to reveal half a dozen baseball bats. He began handing them out solemnly. When he got to Rand, he hesitated. 'Uh, you want one?'

'Hell yes, I do,' Rand said, and they all nodded and smiled approval, the energy in the circle a friendly backslap, a *good for you old man*.

'Come on,' Mike said, and led us along the exterior. 'There's a door with a lock smashed off down here near the Spencer's.'

Just then we passed the dark windows of Shoe-Be-Doo-Be, where my mom had worked for more than half my life. I still remember the thrill of her going to apply for a job at that most wondrous of places – the mall! – leaving one Saturday morning for the job fair in her bright peach pantsuit, a forty-year-old woman looking for work for the first time, and her coming home with a flushed grin: We couldn't imagine how busy the mall was, so many different kinds of stores! And who knew which one she might work in? She applied to nine! Clothing stores and stereo stores and even a designer popcorn store. When she announced a week later that she was officially a shoe saleslady, her kids were underwhelmed.

'You'll have to touch all sorts of stinky feet,' Go complained.

'I'll get to meet all sorts of interesting people,' our mom corrected.

I peered into the gloomy window. The place was entirely vacant except for a shoe sizer lined pointlessly against the wall.

'My mom used to work here,' I told Rand, forcing him to linger with me.

'What kind of place was it?'

'It was a nice place, they were good to her.'

'I mean what did they do here?'

'Oh, shoes. They did shoes.'

'That's right! Shoes. I like that. Something people actually need. And at the end of the day, you know what you've done: You've sold five people shoes. Not like writing, huh?'

'Dunne, come on!' Stucks was leaning against the open door ahead; the others had gone inside.

I'd expected the mall smell as we entered: that temperature-controlled hollowness. Instead, I smelled old grass and dirt, the scent of the outdoors inside, where it had no place being. The building was heavy-hot, almost fuzzy, like the inside of a mattress. Three of us had giant camping flashlights, the glow illuminating jarring images: It was suburbia, post-comet, post-zombie, post-humanity. A set of muddy shopping-cart tracks looped crazily along the white flooring. A raccoon chewed on a dog treat in the entry to a women's bathroom, his eyes flashing like dimes.

The whole mall was quiet; Mikey's voice echoed, our footsteps echoed, Stucks' drunken giggle echoed. We would not be a surprise attack, if attack was what we had in mind.

When we reached the central promenade of the mall, the whole area ballooned: four stories high, escalators and elevators crisscrossing in the black. We all gathered near a dried-up fountain and waited for someone to take the lead.

'So, guys,' Rand said doubtfully, 'what's the plan here? You all know this place, and I don't. We need to figure out how to systematically—'

We heard a loud metal rattle right behind us, a security gate going up.

'Hey, there's one!' Stucks yelled. He trained his flashlight on a man in a billowing rain slicker, shooting out from the entry of Claire's, running full speed away from us.

'Stop him!' Joe yelled, and began running after him, thick tennis shoes slapping against the ceramic tile floors, Mikey right behind him, flashlight trained on the stranger, the two brothers calling gruffly – *hold up there, hey, guy, we just have a question.* The man didn't even give a backward glance. *I said hold on, motherfucker!* The runner remained silent amid the yelling, but he picked up speed and shot down the mall corridor, in and out of the flashlight's glow, his slicker flapping behind him like a cape. Then the guy turned acrobatic: leaping over a trash can, shimmying off the edge of a fountain, and finally slipping under a metal security gate to the Gap and disappearing.

'Fucker!' The Hillsams had turned heart-attack red in the face, the neck, the fingers. They took turns grunting at the gate, straining to lift it.

I reached down with them, but there was no budging it

over half a foot. I lay down on the floor and tried threading myself under the gate: toes, calves, then stuck at my waist.

'Nope, no go.' I grunted. 'Fuck!' I pulled up and shone my flash-light into the store. The showroom was empty except for a pile of clothing racks someone had dragged to the center, as if to start a bonfire. 'All the stores connect in the back to passageways for trash, plumbing,' I said. 'He's probably at the other end of the mall by now.'

'Come out, you fuckers!' Joe yelled, his head tilted back, eyes scrunched. His voice echoed through the building. We began walking ragtag, trailing our bats alongside us, except for the Hillsams, who used theirs to bang against security gates and doors, like they were on military patrol in a particularly nasty war zone.

'Better you come to us than we come to you!' Mikey called. 'Oh, *hell*o!' In the entryway to a pet shop, a man and woman huddled on a few army blankets, their hair wet with sweat. Mikey loomed over them, breathing heavily, wiping his brow. It was the scene in the war movie when the frustrated soldiers come across innocent villagers and bad things happen.

'The fuck you want?' the man on the floor asked. He was emaciated, his face so thin and drawn it looked like it was melting. His hair was tangled to his shoulders, his eyes mournful and upturned: a despoiled Jesus. The woman was in better shape, with clean, plump arms and legs, her lank hair oily but brushed.

'You a Blue Book Boy?' Stucks asked.

'Ain't no boy, anyhow,' the man muttered, folding his arms.

'Have some fucking respect,' the woman snapped. Then she looked like she might cry. She turned away from us, pretending to look at something in the distance. 'I'm sick of *no one* having *no respect*.'

'We asked you a question, buddy,' Mikey said, moving closer to the guy, kicking the sole of his foot.

'I ain't Blue Book,' the man said. 'Just down on my luck.'

'Bullshit.'

'Lots of different people here, not just Blue Books. But if that's who you're looking for ...'

'Go on, go on, then, and find them,' the woman said, her mouth turning down. 'Go bother them.'

'They deal down in the Hole,' the man said. When we looked blank, he pointed. 'The Mervyns, far end, past where the carousel used to be.'

'And fuck you very much,' the woman muttered.

A crop-circle stain marked where the carousel once was. Amy and I had taken a ride just before the mall shut down. Two grown-ups, side by side on levitating bunny rabbits, because my wife wanted to see the mall where I spent so much of my childhood. Wanted to hear my stories. It wasn't all bad with us.

The barrier gate to the Mervyns had been busted through, so the store was open as wide and welcoming as the morning of a Presidents' Day sale. Inside, the place was cleared out except for the islands that once held cash registers and now held about a dozen people in various states of drug highs, under signs that read *Jewelry* and *Beauty* and *Bedding*. They were illuminated by gas camping lamps that flickered like tiki torches. A few guys barely opened an eye as we passed, others were out cold. In a far corner, two kids not long out of their teens were manically reciting the Gettysburg Address. *Now we are engaged in a great civil war ...* One man sprawled out on the rug in immaculate jean shorts and white tennis shoes, like he was on the way to his kid's T-ball game. Rand stared at him as if he might know the guy.

Carthage had a bigger drug epidemic than I ever knew: The cops had been here just yesterday, and already the druggies had resettled, like determined flies. As we made our way through the piles of humans, an obese woman shushed up to us on an electric scooter. Her face was pimply and wet with sweat, her teeth catlike.

'You buying or leaving, because this ain't a show-and-tell,' she said.

Stucks shone a flashlight on her face.

'Get that fucking thing off me.' He did.

'I'm looking for my wife,' I began. 'Amy Dunne. She's been missing since Thursday.'

'She'll show up. She'll wake up, drag herself home.'

'We're not worried about drugs,' I said, 'we're more concerned about some of the men here. We've heard rumors.'

'It's okay, Melanie,' a voice called. At the edge of the juniors section, a rangy man leaned against a naked mannequin torso, watching us, a sideways grin on his face.

Melanie shrugged, bored, annoyed, and motored away.

The man kept his eyes on us but called toward the back of the juniors section, where four sets of feet poked out from the dressing rooms, men camped out in their individual cubicles.

'Hey, Lonnie! Hey, all! The assholes are back. Five of 'em,' the man said. He kicked an empty beer can toward us. Behind him, three sets of feet began moving, men pulling themselves up. One set remained still, their owner asleep or passed out.

'Yeah, fuckos, we're back,' Mikey Hillsam said. He held his bat like a pool cue and punched the mannequin torso between the breasts. She tottered toward the ground, the Blue Book guy removing his arm gracefully as she fell, as if it were all part of a rehearsed act. 'We want some information on a missing girl.'

The three men from the dressing rooms joined their friends. They all wore Greek-party T-shirts: *Pi Phi Tie-Dye* and *Fiji Island*. Local Goodwills got inundated with these come summer – university graduates shedding their old souvenirs.

The men were all wiry-strong, muscular arms rivered with popping blue veins. Behind them, a guy with a long, drooping mustache and hair in a ponytail – Lonnie – came out of the largest corner dressing room, dragging a long length of pipe, wearing a Gamma Phi T-shirt. We were looking at mall security.

'What's up?' Lonnie called.

We cannot dedicate, we cannot consecrate, we cannot hallow this ground ... the kids were reciting in a pitch that was close to screaming.

'We're looking for Amy Dunne, you probably seen her on the news, missing since Thursday,' Joe Hillsam said. 'Nice, pretty, sweet lady, stolen from her own home.'

'I heard about it. So?' said Lonnie.

'She's my wife,' I said.

'We know what you guys've been getting into out here,' Joe continued, addressing only Lonnie, who was tossing his ponytail behind him, squaring his jaw. Faded green tattoos covered his fingers. 'We know about the gang rape.'

I glanced at Rand to see if he was all right; he was staring at the naked mannequin on the floor.

'Gang rape,' Lonnie said, jerking his head back. 'The fuck you talking about a gang rape.'

'You guys,' Joe said. 'You Blue Book Boys—'

'Blue Book Boys, like we're some kind of crew.' Lonnie sniffed. 'We're not animals, asshole. We don't steal women. People want to feel okay for not helping us. *See, they don't deserve it, they're a bunch of rapists*. Well, bull*shit*. I'd get the fuck out of this town if the plant would give me my back pay. But I got nothing. None of us got nothing. So here we are.'

'We'll give you money, good money, if you can tell us anything about Amy's disappearance,' I said. 'You guys know a lot of people, maybe you heard something.'

I pulled out her photo. The Hillsams and Stucks looked surprised, and I realized – of course – this was only a macho diversion for them. I pushed the photo in Lonnie's face, expecting him to barely glance. Instead, he leaned in closer.

'Oh, shit,' he said. '*Her?*'

'You recognize her?'

He actually looked stricken. 'She wanted to buy a gun.'

AMY ELLIOTT DUNNE
OCTOBER 16, 2010

– Diary entry –

Happy anniversary to me! One full month as a Missouri resident, and I am on my way to becoming a good midwesterner. Yep, I have gone cold turkey off all things East Coast and I have earned my thirty-day chip (here it would be a potato chip). I am taking notes, I am honoring traditions. I am the Margaret Mead of the goddamn Mississip.

Let's see, what's new? Nick and I are currently embroiled in what I have taken to calling (to myself) the Cuckoo Clock Conundrum. My parents' cherished heirloom looks ridiculous in the new house. But then all our New York stuff does. Our dignified elephant of a chesterfield with its matching baby ottoman sits in the living room looking stunned, as if it got sleep-darted in its natural environment and woke up in this strange new captivity, surrounded by faux-posh carpet and synthetic wood and unveined walls. I do miss our old place – all the bumps and ridges and hairline fractures left by the decades. (Pause for attitude adjustment.) But new is nice, too! Just different. The clock would disagree. The cuckoo is also having a tough time adjusting to its new space: The little bird lurches out drunkenly at ten minutes after the hour; seventeen minutes before; forty-one past. It emits a dying wail – coo-crrrrww – that every time brings Bleecker trotting in from some hideaway, eyes wild, all business, his tail a bottle-brush as he tilts his head toward the feathers and mewls.

'Wow, your parents must really hate me,' Nick says whenever we're both in earshot of the noise, though he's smart enough not to recommend ridding ourselves of the thing just yet. I actually want to trash it too. I am the one (the jobless) at home all day, just waiting for its squawk, a tense moviegoer steeling myself for the next outburst from the crazy patron behind me – both relieved (there it is!) and angry (there it is!) each time it comes.

Much to-do was made over the clock at the housewarming (*oh, look at that, an antique clock!*), which Mama Maureen Dunne insisted on. Actually, not insisted on; Mama Mo does not insist. She simply makes things a reality by assuming they are such: From the first morning after the move, when she appeared on our doorstep with a welcome-home egg scramble and a family pack of toilet paper (which didn't speak well for the egg scramble), she'd spoken of the housewarming as if it were a fact. *So when do you want to do your housewarming? Have you thought about who I should invite to the housewarming? Do you want a housewarming or something fun, like a stock-the-bar party? But a traditional housewarming is always nice.*

And then suddenly there was a date, and the date was today, and Dunne family and friends were shaking off the October drizzle from umbrellas and carefully, conscientiously wiping their feet on the floor mat Maureen had brought for us this morning. The rug says: *All Are Friends Who Enter Here*. It is from Costco. I have learned about bulk shopping in my four weeks as a Mississippi River resident. Republicans go to Sam's Club, Democrats go to Costco. But everyone buys bulk because – unlike Manhattanites – they all have space to store twenty-four jars of sweet pickles. And – unlike Manhattanites – they all have uses for twenty-four jars of sweet pickles. (No gathering is complete without a lazy Susan full of pickles and Spanish olives right from the jar. And a salt lick.)

I set the scene: It is one of those big-smelling days, when people bring the outdoors in with them, the scent of rain on their sleeves, in their hair. The older women – Maureen's friends – present varying food items in plastic, dishwasher-safe containers they will later ask to be returned. And ask and ask. I know, now, that I am supposed to wash out the containers and drop each of them back by their proper homes – a Ziploc carpool – but when I first came here, I was unaware of the protocol. I dutifully recycled all the plastic containers, and so I had to go buy all new ones. Maureen's best friend, Vicky, immediately noticed her container was brand-new, store-bought, an imposter, and when I explained my confusion, she widened her eyes in amazement: *So* that's *how they do it in New York.*

But the housewarming: The older women are Maureen's friends from long-ago PTA meetings, from book clubs, from the Shoe-Be-Doo-Be at the mall, where she spent forty hours a week slipping sensible block heels onto women of a certain age. (She can size a foot on sight – women's 8, narrow! – it's her go-to party trick.) All Mo's friends love Nick, and they all have stories about sweet things Nick has done for them over the years.

The younger women, the women representing the pool of possible Amy-friends, all sport the same bleached-blond wedge haircut, the same slip-on mules. They are the daughters of Maureen's friends, and they all love Nick, and they all have stories about sweet things Nick has done for them over the years. Most of them are out of work from the mall closings, or their husbands are out of work from the mall closings, so they all offer me recipes for 'cheap and easy eats' that usually involve a casserole made from canned soup, butter, and a snack chip.

The men are nice and quiet and hunker in circles, talking about sports and smiling benevolently toward me.

Everyone is nice. They are literally *as nice as they can be.* Maureen, the tristate's hardiest cancer patient, introduces me to all her friends the same way you'd show off a slightly dangerous new pet: 'This is Nick's wife, Amy, who was *born and raised* in New York City.' And her friends, plump and welcoming, immediately suffer some strange Tourettesian episode: They repeat the words – *New York City*! – with clasped hands and say something that defies response: *That must have been neat.* Or, in reedy voices, they sing '*New York,*

135

New York,' rocking side to side with tiny jazz hands. Maureen's friend from the shoe store, Barb, drawls '*Nue* York *Ceety*! Get a rope,' and when I squint at her in confusion, she says, 'Oh, it's from that old salsa commercial!' and when I still fail to connect, she blushes, puts a hand on my arm, and says, 'I wouldn't really hang you.'

Ultimately, everyone trails off into giggles and confesses they've never been to New York. Or that they've been – once – and didn't care for it much. Then I say something like: *You'd like it* or *It's definitely not for everyone* or *Mmm*, because I've run out of things to say.

'Be friendly, Amy,' Nick spits into my ear when we're refilling drinks in the kitchen (midwesterners love two liters of soda, always two liters, and you pour them into big red plastic Solo cups, always).

'I *am*,' I whine. It really hurts my feelings, because if you asked anyone in that room whether I'd been friendly, I know they'd say yes.

Sometimes I feel like Nick has decided on a version of me that doesn't exist. Since we've moved here, I've done girls' nights out and charity walks, I've cooked casseroles for his dad and helped sell tickets for raffles. I tapped the last of my money to give to Nick and Go so they could buy the bar they've always wanted, and I even put the check inside a card shaped like a mug of beer – *Cheers to You!* – and Nick just gave a flat begrudging thanks. I don't know what to do. I'm trying.

We deliver the soda pops, me smiling and laughing even harder, a vision of grace and good cheer, asking everyone if I can get them anything else, complimenting women on ambrosia salads and crab dips and pickle slices wrapped in cream cheese wrapped in salami.

Nick's dad arrives with Go. They stand silently on the doorstep, Midwest Gothic, Bill Dunne wiry and still handsome, a tiny Band-Aid on his forehead, Go grim-faced, her hair in barrettes, her eyes averted from her father.

'Nick,' Bill Dunne says, shaking his hand, and he steps

inside, frowning at me. Go follows, grabs Nick, and pulls him back behind the door, whispering, 'I have no idea where he is right now, headwise. Like if he's having a bad day or if he's just being a jackass. No idea.'

'Okay, okay. Don't worry, I'll keep an eye on him.'

Go shrugs pissily.

'I'm serious, Go. Grab a beer and take a break. You are relieved of Dad duty for the next hour.'

I think: *If that had been me, he'd complain that I was being too sensitive.*

The older women keep swirling around me, telling me how Maureen has always said what a wonderful couple Nick and I are and she is right, we are clearly made for each other.

I prefer these well-meant clichés to the talk we heard before we got married. *Marriage is compromise and hard work, and then more hard work and communication and compromise. And then work.* Abandon all hope, ye who enter.

The engagement party back in New York was the worst for this, all the guests hot with wine and resentment, as if every set of spouses had gotten into an argument on the way to the club. Or they remembered some argument. Like Binks. Binks Moriarty, my mom's best friend's eighty-eight-year-old mother, stopped me at the bar – bellowed, 'Amy! I must talk to you!' in an emergency-room voice. She twisted her precious rings on overknuckled fingers – twist, turn, creak – and fondled my arm (that old-person grope – cold fingers coveting your nice, soft, warm, new skin), and then Binks told me how her late husband of sixty-three years had trouble 'keeping it in his pants.' Binks said this with one of those *I'm almost dead, I can say this kind of stuff* grins and cataract-clouded eyes. 'He just couldn't keep it in his pants,' the old lady said urgently, her hand chilling my arm in a death grip. 'But he loved me more than any of them. *I* know it, and *you* know it.' The moral to the story being: Mr Binks was a cheating dickweasel, but, you know, marriage is compromise.

I retreated quickly and began circulating through the crowd, smiling at a series of wrinkled faces, that baggy, exhausted, disappointed look that people get in middle age, and all the faces were like that. Most of them were also drunk, dancing steps from their youth – swaying to country-club funk – and that seemed even worse. I was making my way to the French windows for some air, and a hand squeezed my arm. Nick's mom, Mama Maureen, with her big black laser eyes, her eager pug-dog face. Thrusting a wad of goat cheese and crackers into her mouth, Maureen managed to say: 'It's not easy, pairing yourself off with someone forever. It's an admirable thing, and I'm glad you're both doing it, but, boy-oh-girl-oh, there will be days you wish you'd never done it. And those will be the good times, when it's only *days* of regret and not *months*.' I must have looked shocked – I was definitely shocked – because she said quickly: 'But then you have good times, too. I know you will. *You two*. A *lot* of good times. So just ... forgive me, sweetheart, what I said before. I'm just being a silly old divorced lady. Oh, mother of pearl, I think I had too much *wine*.' And she fluttered a goodbye at me and scampered away through all the other disappointed couples.

'You're not supposed to be here,' Bill Dunne was suddenly saying, and he was saying it to me. 'Why are you here? You're not allowed here.'

'I'm Amy,' I say, touching his arm as if that might wake him. Bill has always liked me; even if he could think of nothing to say to me, I could tell he liked me, the way he watched me like I was a rare bird. Now he is scowling, thrusting his chest toward me, a caricature of a young sailor ready to brawl. A few feet away, Go sets down her food and gets ready to move toward us, quietly, like she is trying to catch a fly.

'Why are you in our house?' Bill Dunne says, his mouth grimacing. 'You've got some nerve, lady.'

'Nick?' Go calls behind her, not loudly but urgently.

'Got it,' Nick says, appearing. 'Hey, Dad, this is my wife, Amy. Remember Amy? We moved back home so we could see you more. This is our new house.'

Nick glares at me: I was the one who insisted we invite his dad.

'All I'm saying, Nick,' Bill Dunne says, pointing now, jabbing an index finger toward my face, the party going hushed, several men moving slowly, cautiously, in from the other room, their hands twitching, ready to move, 'is *she* doesn't belong here. Little bitch thinks she can do whatever she wants.'

Mama Mo swoops in then, her arm around her ex-husband, always, always rising to the occasion. 'Of course she belongs here, Bill. It's her house. She's your son's wife. Remember?'

'I want her out of here, do you understand me, Maureen?' He shrugs her off and starts moving toward me again. 'Dumb bitch. Dumb bitch.'

It's unclear if he means me or Maureen, but then he looks at me and tightens his lips. 'She doesn't *belong* here.'

'I'll go,' I say, and turn away, walk straight out the door, into the rain. *From the mouths of Alzheimer's patients*, I think, trying to make light. I walk a loop around the neighborhood, waiting for Nick to appear, to guide me back to our house. The rain spackles me gently, dampening me. I really believe Nick will come after me. I turn toward the house and see only a closed door.

Rand and I sat in the vacant Find Amy Dunne headquarters at five in the morning, drinking coffee while we waited for the cops to check out Lonnie. Amy stared at us from her poster perch on the wall. Her photo looked distressed.

'I just don't understand why she wouldn't say something to you if she was afraid,' Rand said. 'Why wouldn't she tell you?'

Amy had come to the mall to buy a gun on Valentine's Day, of all days, that's what our friend Lonnie had said. She was a little abashed, a little nervous: *Maybe I'm being silly, but ... I just really think I need a gun.* Mostly, though, she was scared. Someone was unnerving her, she told Lonnie. She gave no more details, but when he asked her what kind of gun she wanted, she said: *One that stops someone fast.* He told her to come back in a few days, and she did. He hadn't been able to get her one ('It's not really my bag, man'), but now he wished he had. He remembered her well; over the months, he'd wondered how she was now and then, this sweet blonde with the fearful face, trying to get a gun on Valentine's Day.

'Who would she be afraid of?' Rand asked.

'Tell me about Desi again, Rand,' I said. 'Did you ever meet him?'

'He came to the house a few times.' Rand frowned, remembering. 'He was a nice-looking kid, very solicitous of Amy – treated her like a princess. But I just never liked him. Even when things were good with them – young love, Amy's first love – even then I disliked him. He was very rude to me, inexplicably so. Very possessive of Amy, arms around her at all times. I found it strange, very strange, that he wouldn't try to be nice to us. Most young men want to get in good with the parents.'

'I wanted to.'

'And you did!' He smiled. 'You were just the right amount of nervous, it was very sweet. Desi wasn't anything but nasty.'

'Desi's less than an hour out of town.'

'True. And Hilary Handy?' Rand said, rubbing his eyes. 'I don't want to be sexist here – she was scarier than Desi. Because that Lonnie guy at the mall, he didn't say Amy was afraid of a man.'

'No, he just said she was afraid,' I said. 'There *is* that Noelle Hawthorne girl – the one who lives near us. She told the police she was best friends with Amy when I know she wasn't. They weren't even *friends*. Her husband says she's been in hysterics. That she was looking at pictures of Amy, crying. At the time I thought they were Internet photos, but ... what if they were actual photos she had of Amy? What if she was stalking Amy?'

'She tried to talk with me when I was a little busy yesterday,' Rand said. 'She quoted some *Amazing Amy* stuff at me. *Amazing Amy and the Best Friend War*, actually. "Best friends are the people who know us best."'

'Sounds like Hilary,' I said. 'All grown up.'

We met Boney and Gilpin just after seven a.m. at an IHOP out along the highway for a showdown: It was ridiculous that we were doing their job for them. It was insane that we were the ones discovering leads. It was time to call in the FBI if the local cops couldn't handle it.

A plump, amber-eyed waitress took our orders, poured us coffee, and, clearly recognizing me, lingered within eavesdropping distance until Gilpin scatted her away. She was like a determined housefly, though. Between drink refills and dispensing of utensils and the magically quick arrival of our food, our entire harangue came in limp bursts. *This is unacceptable ... no more coffee, thanks ... it's unbelievable that ... uh, sure, rye is fine ...*

Before we were done, Boney interrupted. 'I understand, guys, it's natural to want to feel involved. But what you did was dangerous. You have got to let us handle this kind of thing.'

'That's just it, though, you aren't handling it,' I said. 'You'd never have gotten this information, about the gun, if we didn't go out there last night. What did Lonnie say when you talked to him?'

'Same thing you said he said,' Gilpin said. 'Amy wanted to buy a gun, she was scared.'

'You don't seem that impressed by this information,' I snapped. 'Do you think he was lying?'

'We don't think he was lying,' Boney said. 'There's no reason for the guy to invite police attention to himself. He seemed very struck by your wife. Very ... I don't know, rattled that this had happened to her. He remembered specific details. Nick, he said she was wearing a green scarf that day. You know, not a winter scarf but a fashion-statement scarf.' She made fluttery moves with her fingers to show she thought fashion to be childish, unworthy of her attention. 'Emerald green. Ring a bell?'

I nodded. 'She has one she wears with blue jeans a lot.'

'And a pin on her jacket – a gold cursive A?'

'Yes.'

Boney shrugged: *Well, that settles it.*

'You don't think he might have been so struck by her that he ... kidnapped her?' I asked.

'He has an alibi. Rock-solid,' Boney said, giving me a pointed look. 'To tell the truth, we've begun to look for ... a different kind of motive.'

'Something more ... personal,' Gilpin added. He looked dubiously at his pancakes, topped with strawberries and puffs of whipped cream. He began scraping them to the side of his plate.

'More personal,' I said. 'So does that mean you're finally going to talk to Desi Collings, or Hilary Handy? Or do I need to?' I had, in fact, promised Marybeth I'd go today.

'Sure, we will,' Boney said. She had the placating tone of a girl promising her pesky mom to eat better. 'We doubt it's a lead – but we'll talk to them.'

'Well, great, thanks for doing your job, kind of,' I said. 'And what about Noelle Hawthorne? If you want someone close to home, she's right in our complex, and she seems a little obsessed with Amy.'

'I know, she's called us, and she's on our list.' Gilpin nodded. 'Today.'

'Good. What else are you doing?'

'Nick, we'd actually like you to make some time for us, let us pick your brain a bit more,' Boney said. 'Spouses often know more than they realize. We'd like you to think a bit more about the argument – that barnburner your neighbor Mrs, uh, Teverer overheard you and Amy having the night before she went missing.'

Rand's head jerked toward me.

Jan Teverer, the Christian casserole lady who wouldn't meet my eye anymore.

'I mean, could it have been because – I know this is hard to hear, Mr Elliott – because Amy was under the influence of something?' Boney asked. Innocent eyes. 'I mean, maybe she *has* had contact with less savory elements in town. There are plenty of other drug dealers. Maybe she got in over her head, and that's why she wanted a gun. There's got to be a reason she wants a gun for protection and doesn't tell her husband. And Nick, we'd like you to think harder about where you were between that time – the time of the argument, about eleven p.m., the last anyone heard Amy's voice—'

'Besides me.'

'Besides you – and noon, when you arrived at your bar. If you were out and about in this town, driving to the beach, hanging around the dock area, someone must have seen you. Even if it was someone just, you know, walking his dog. If you can help us, I think that would be really ...'

'Helpful,' Gilpin finished. He speared a strawberry.

They both watched me attentively, congenially. 'It'd be

super-helpful, Nick,' Gilpin repeated more pleasantly. First time I'd heard about the argument – that they knew about it – and they chose to tell me in front of Rand – and they chose to pretend it wasn't a gotcha.

'Sure thing,' I said.

'You mind telling us what it was about?' Boney asked. 'The argument?'

'What did Mrs Teverer tell you it was about?'

'I hate to take her word when I got you right here.' She poured some cream into her coffee.

'It was such a nothing argument,' I began. 'That's why I never mentioned it. Just both of us scrapping at each other, the way couples do sometimes.'

Rand looked at me as if he had no clue what I was talking about: *Scrapping? What is this* scrapping *of which you speak?*

'It was just – about dinner,' I lied. 'About what we'd do for dinner for our anniversary. You know, Amy is a traditionalist about these things—'

'The lobster!' Rand interrupted. He turned to the cops. 'Amy cooks lobster every year for Nick.'

'Right. But there's nowhere to get lobster in this town, not alive, from the tank, so she was frustrated. I had the Houston's reservation—'

'I thought you said you *didn't* have a Houston's reservation.' Rand frowned.

'Well, yes, sorry, I'm getting confused. I just had the idea of the Houston's reservation. But I really should have just arranged to have some lobster flown in.'

The cops, each of them, raised an accidental eyebrow. *How very fancy.*

'It's not that expensive to do. Anyway, we were at this rotten loggerheads, and it was one of those arguments that got bigger than it should have.' I took a bite of my pancakes. I could feel the heat rushing from under my collar. 'We were laughing about it within the hour.'

'Hunh' was all Boney said.

'And where are you on the treasure hunt?' Gilpin asked.

I stood up, put down some money, ready to go. I wasn't the one who was supposed to be playing defense here. 'Nowhere, not right yet – it's hard to think clearly with so much going on.'

'Okay,' Gilpin said. 'It's less likely the treasure hunt is an angle, now that we know she was already feeling threatened months ago. But keep me in the loop anyway, okay?'

We all shuffled out into the heat. As Rand and I got into our car, Boney called out, 'Hey, is Amy still a two, Nick?'

I frowned at her.

'A size two?' she repeated.

'Yes, she is, I think,' I said. 'Yes. She is.'

Boney made a face that said, *Hmmmm*, and got in her car.

'What do you think that was about?' Rand asked.

'Those two, who knows?'

We remained silent for most of the way to the hotel, Rand staring out the window at the rows of fast-food restaurants blinking by, me thinking about my lie – my lies. We had to circle to find a space at the Days Inn; the payroll convention was apparently a hot ticket.

'You know, it's funny, how provincial I am, lifetime New Yorker,' Rand said, fingers on the door handle. 'When Amy talked about moving back here, back along the *Ole* Mississippi River, with you, I pictured … green, farmland, apple trees, and those great old red barns. I have to tell you, it's really quite ugly here.' He laughed. 'I can't think of a single thing of beauty in this whole town. Except for my daughter.'

He got out and strode quickly toward the hotel, and I didn't try to catch up. I entered the headquarters a few minutes behind him, took a seat at a secluded table toward the back of the room. I needed to complete the treasure hunt before the clues disappeared, figure out where Amy had been taking me. After a few hours' stint here, I'd deal with the third clue. In the meantime, I dialed.

'Yeah,' came an impatient voice. A baby was crying in the background. I could hear the woman blow the hair off her face.

'Hi, is this – is this Hilary Handy?'

She hung up. I phoned back.

'Hell*o*?'

'Hi there. I think we got cut off before.'

'Would you put this number on your *do not call* list—'

'Hilary, I'm not selling anything, I'm calling about Amy Dunne – Amy Elliott.'

Silence. The baby squawked again, a mewl that wavered dangerously between laughter and tantrum.

'What about her?'

'I don't know if you've seen this on TV, but she's gone missing. She went missing on July fifth under potentially violent circumstances.'

'Oh. I'm sorry.'

'I'm Nick Dunne, her husband. I've just been calling old friends of hers.'

'Oh yeah?'

'I wondered if you'd had any contact with her. Recently.'

She breathed into the phone, three deep breaths. 'Is this because of that, that bullshit back in high school?' Farther in the background, a child's wheedling voice yelled out, 'Moo-oom, I nee-eed you.'

'In a minute, Jack,' she called into the void behind her. Then returned to me with a bright red voice: 'Is it? Is that why you're calling me? Because that was twenty goddamn years ago. More.'

'I know. I know. Look, I have to ask. I'd be an asshole not to ask.'

'Jesus fucking Christ. I'm a mother of *three kids* now. I haven't talked to Amy since high school. I learned my lesson. If I saw her on the street, I'd run the other way.' The baby howled. 'I gotta go.'

'Just real quick, Hilary—'

She hung up, and immediately, my disposable vibrated. I ignored it. I had to find a place to stow the damn thing.

I could feel the presence of someone, a woman, near me, but I didn't look up, hoping she would go away.

146

'It's not even noon, and you already look like you've had a full day, poor baby.'

Shawna Kelly. She had her hair pulled up in a high bubble-gum-girl ponytail. She aimed glossed lips at me in a sympathetic pout. 'You ready for some of my Frito pie?' She was bearing a casserole dish, holding it just below her breasts, the saran wrap dappled with sweat. She said the words like she was the star of some '80s hair-rock video: You want summa my *pie*?

'Big breakfast. Thanks, though. That's really kind of you.'

Instead of going away, she sat down. Under a turquoise tennis skirt, her legs were lotioned so well they reflected. She kicked me with the toe of an unblemished Tretorn. 'You sleeping, sweetie?'

'I'm holding up.'

'You've got to sleep, Nick. You're no good to anyone if you're exhausted.'

'I might leave in a little bit, see if I can grab a few hours.'

'I think you should. I really do.'

I felt a sudden keen gratitude to her. It was my mama's-boy attitude, rising up. Dangerous. *Crush it, Nick.*

I waited for her to go. She needed to go – people were beginning to watch us.

'If you want, I can drive you home right now,' she said. 'A nap might be just the thing for you.'

She reached out to touch my knee, and I felt a burst of rage that she didn't realize she needed to go. *Leave the casserole, you clingy groupie whore, and go.* Daddy's-boy attitude, rising up. Just as bad.

'Why don't you check in with Marybeth?' I said brusquely, and pointed to my mother-in-law by the Xerox, making endless copies of Amy's photo.

'Okay.' She lingered, so I began ignoring her outright. 'I'll leave you to it, then. Hope you like the pie.'

The dismissal had stung her, I could tell, because she made no eye contact as she left, just turned and sauntered off. I felt bad, debated apologizing, making nice. *Do not go after that woman*, I ordered myself.

147

'Any news?' It was Noelle Hawthorne, entering the same space Shawna had just vacated. She was younger than Shawna but seemed older – a plump body with dour, wide-spaced mounds for breasts. A frown on her face.

'Not so far.'

'You sure seem to be handling it all okay.'

I twitched my head at her, unsure what to say.

'Do you even know who I am?' she asked.

'Of course. You're Noelle Hawthorne.'

'I'm Amy's *best* friend here.'

I had to remind the police: There were only two options with Noelle. She was either a lying publicity whore – she liked the cachet of being pals with a missing woman – or she was crazy. A stalker determined to befriend Amy, and when Amy shirked her …

'Do you have any information about Amy, Noelle?' I asked.

'Of course I do, *Nick*. She was my *best friend*.'

We stared each other down for a few seconds.

'Are you going to share it?' I asked.

'The police know where to find me. If they ever get around to it.'

'That's super-helpful, Noelle. I'll make sure they talk to you.'

Her cheeks blazed red, two expressionist splatters of color.

She went away. I thought the unkind thought, one of those that burbled up beyond my control. I thought: *Women are fucking crazy.* No qualifier: Not *some* women, not *many* women. Women are crazy.

Once night fell fully, I drove to my dad's vacant house, Amy's clue on the seat beside me.

Maybe you feel guilty for bringing me here
I must admit it felt a bit queer
But it's not like we had the choice of many a place
We made the decision: We made this our space.
Let's take our love to this little brown house
Gimme some goodwill, you hot lovin' spouse!

This one was more cryptic than the others, but I was sure I had it right. Amy was conceding Carthage, finally forgiving me for moving back here. *Maybe you feel guilty for bringing me here ... [but] We made this our space.* The little brown house was my father's house, which was actually blue, but Amy was making another inside joke. I'd always liked our inside jokes the best – they made me feel more connected to Amy than any amount of confessional truth-telling or passionate love-making or talk-till-sunrising. The little brown house story was about my father, and Amy is the only person I'd ever told it to: that after the divorce, I saw him so seldom that I decided to think of him as a character in a storybook. He was not my actual father – who would have loved me and spent time with me – but a benevolent and vaguely important figure named Mr Brown, who was very busy doing very important things for the United States and who (very) occasionally used me as a cover to move more easily about town. Amy got tears in her eyes when I told her this, which I hadn't meant, I'd meant it as a *kids are funny* story. She told me she was my family now, that she loved me enough to make up for ten crappy fathers, and that *we* were now the Dunnes, the two of us. And then she whispered in my ear, 'I do have an assignment you might be good for ...'

As for bringing back the goodwill, that was another con-ciliation. After my father was completely lost to the Alz-heimer's, we decided to sell his place, so Amy and I went through his house, putting together boxes for Goodwill. Amy, of course, was a whirling dervish of doing – pack, store, toss – while I sifted through my father's things glacially. For me, everything was a clue. A mug with deeper coffee stains than the others must be his favorite. Was it a gift? Who gave it to him? Or did he buy it himself? I pictured my father finding the very act of shopping emasculating. Still, an inspection of his closet revealed five pairs of shoes, shiny new, still in their boxes. Had he bought these himself, picturing a different, more social Bill Dunne than the one slowly unspooling alone? Did he go to Shoe-Be-Doo-Be, get my mother to help him, just another in a long line of her casual kindnesses? Of course, I didn't share any of these musings with Amy, so I'm sure I came off as the goldbricker I so often am.

'Here. A box. For Goodwill,' she said, catching me on the floor, leaning against a wall, staring at a shoe. 'You put the shoes in the box. Okay?' I was embarrassed, I snarled at her, she snapped at me, and … the usual.

I should add, in Amy's defense, that she'd asked me twice if I wanted to talk, if I was sure I wanted to do this. I sometimes leave out details like that. It's more convenient for me. In truth, I wanted her to read my mind so I didn't have to stoop to the womanly art of articulation. I was sometimes as guilty of playing the figure-me-out game as Amy was. I've left that bit of information out, too.

I'm a big fan of the lie of omission.

I pulled up in front of my dad's house just after ten p.m. It was a tidy little place, a good starter home (or ender home). Two bedrooms, two baths, dining room, dated but decent kitchen. A for-sale sign rusted in the front yard. One year and not a bite.

I entered the stuffy house, the heat rolling over me. The budget alarm system we installed after the third break-in began beeping, like a bomb countdown. I input the code, the one that drove Amy insane because it went against every rule about codes. It was my birthday: 81577.

Code rejected. I tried again. *Code rejected.* A bead of sweat rolled down my back. Amy had always threatened to change the code. She said it was pointless to have one that was so guessable, but I knew the real reason. She resented that it was my birthday and not our anniversary: Once again I'd chosen *me* over *us*. My semi-sweet nostalgia for Amy disappeared. I stabbed my finger at the numbers again, growing more panicked as the alarm beeped and beeped and beeped its countdown – until it went into full intruder blare.

Woooonk-woooonk-woooonk!

My cell phone was supposed to ring so I could give the all-clear: *Just me, the idiot.* But it didn't. I waited a full minute, the alarm reminding me of a torpedoed-submarine movie. The canned heat of a closed house in July shimmered over me. My shirt back was already soaked. *Goddammit, Amy.* I scanned the alarm for the company's number and found nothing. I pulled over a chair and began yanking at the alarm; I had it off the wall, hanging by the cords, when my phone finally rang. A bitchy voice on the other end demanded Amy's first pet's name.

Woooonk-woooonk-woooonk!

It was exactly the wrong tone – smug, petulant, utterly unconcerned – and exactly the wrong question, because I didn't know the answer, which infuriated me. No matter how many clues I solved, I'd be faced with some Amy trivia to unman me.

'Look, this is Nick Dunne, this is my dad's house, this account was set up by me,' I snapped. 'So it doesn't really fucking matter what my wife's first pet's name was.'

Woooonk-woooonk-woooonk!

'Please don't take that tone with me, sir.'

'Look, I just came in to grab one thing from my dad's house, and now I'm leaving, okay?'

'I have to notify the police immediately.'

'Can you just turn off the goddamn alarm so I can think?'

Woooonk-woooonk-woooonk!

'The alarm's off.'

'The alarm is not off.'

'Sir, I warned you once, do not take that tone with me.'

You fucking bitch.

'You know what? Fuck it, fuck it, *fuck it.*'

I hung up just as I remembered Amy's cat's name, the very first one: Stuart.

I called back, got a different operator, a reasonable operator, who turned off the alarm and, God bless her, called off the police. I really wasn't in the mood to explain myself.

I sat on the thin, cheap carpet and made myself breathe, my heart clattering. After a minute, after my shoulders untensed and my jaw unclenched and my hands unfisted and my heart returned to normal, I stood up and momentarily debated just leaving, as if that would teach Amy a lesson. But as I stood up, I saw a blue envelope left on the kitchen counter like a Dear John note.

I took a deep breath, blew it out – new attitude – and opened the envelope, pulled out the letter marked with a heart.

Hi Darling,
  So we both have things we want to work on. For me, it'd be my perfectionism, my occasional (wishful thinking?) self-righteousness. For you? I know you worry that you're sometimes too distant, too removed, unable to be tender or nurturing. Well, I want to tell you – here in your father's house – that isn't true. You are not your father. You need to know that you are a good man, you are a sweet man, you are kind. I've punished you for not being able to read my mind sometimes, for not being able to act in exactly the way I wanted you to act right at exactly that moment. I punished you for being a real, breathing *man*. I ordered you around instead of trusting you to find your way. I didn't give you the benefit of the doubt: that no matter how much you and I blunder, you always love me and want me to be happy. And that should be enough for any girl, right? I worry I've said things about you that aren't actually true, and that you've come to believe them. So I am here to say now: You are WARM. You are my sun.

If Amy were with me, as she'd planned on being, she would have nuzzled into me the way she used to do, her face in the crook of my neck, and she would have kissed me and smiled and said, *You are, you know. My sun.* My throat tight, I took a final look around my father's house and left, closing the door on the heat. In my car, I fumbled open the envelope marked FOURTH CLUE. We had to be near the end.

Picture me: I'm a girl who is very bad
I need to be punished, and by punished, *I mean* had

It's where you store goodies for anniversary five
Pardon me if this is getting contrived!
A good time was had here right at sunny midday
Then out for a cocktail, all so terribly gay.
So run there right now, full of sweet sighs,
And open the door for your big surprise.

My stomach seized. I didn't know what this one meant. I reread it. I couldn't even guess. Amy had stopped taking it easy on me. I wasn't going to finish the treasure hunt after all.

I felt a surge of angst. What a fucking day. Boney was out to get me, Noelle was insane, Shawna was pissed, Hilary was resentful, the woman at the security company was a bitch, and my wife had stumped me finally. It was time to end this goddamn day. There was only one woman I could stand to be around right now.

Go took one look at me – rattled, tight-lipped, and heat-exhausted from my dad's – and parked me on the couch, announced she'd make some late dinner. Five minutes later, she was stepping carefully toward me, balancing my meal on an ancient TV tray. An old Dunne standby: grilled cheese and BBQ chips, a plastic cup of . . .

'It's not Kool-Aid,' Go said. 'It's beer. Kool-Aid seemed a little too regressive.'

'This is very nurturing and strange of you, Go.'

'You're cooking tomorrow.'

'Hope you like canned soup.'

She sat down on the couch next to me, stole a chip from my plate, and asked, too casually: 'Any thoughts on why the cops would ask *me* if Amy was still a size two?'

'Jesus, they won't fucking let that go,' I said.

'Doesn't it freak you out? Like, they found her clothes or something?'

'They'd have asked me to identify them. Right?'

She thought about that a second, her face pinched. 'That makes sense,' she said. Her face remained pinched until she caught me looking, then she smiled. 'I taped the ball game, wanna watch? You okay?'

'I'm okay.' I felt awful, my stomach greasy, my psyche crackling. Maybe it was the clue I couldn't figure out, but I suddenly felt like I'd overlooked something. I'd made some huge mistake, and my error would be disastrous. Maybe it was my conscience, scratching back to the surface from its secret oubliette.

Go pulled up the game and, for the next ten minutes, remarked on the game only, and only between sips of her beer. Go didn't like grilled cheese; she was scooping peanut butter out of the jar onto saltines. When a commercial break came on, she paused and said, 'If I had a dick, I would fuck this peanut butter,' deliberately spraying cracker bits toward me.

'I think if you had a dick, all sorts of bad things would happen.'

She fast-forwarded through a nothing inning. Cards trailing by five. When it was time for the next commercial break, Go paused, said, 'So I called to change my cell-phone plan today, and the hold song was Lionel Richie – do you ever listen to Lionel Richie? I like "Penny Lover," but the song wasn't "Penny Lover," but anyway, then a woman came on the line, and she said the customer-service reps are all based in Baton Rouge, which was strange because she didn't have an accent, but she said she grew up in New Orleans, and it's a little-known fact that – what do you call someone from New Orleans, a New Orleansean? – anyway, that they don't have much of an accent. So she said for my package, package A ...'

Go and I had a game inspired by our mom, who had a habit of telling such outrageously mundane, endless stories that Go was positive she had to be secretly fucking with us. For about ten years now, whenever Go and I hit a conversation lull, one of us would break in with a story about appliance repair or coupon fulfillment. Go had more stamina than I did, though. Her stories could drone on, seamlessly, forever – they went on so long that they became genuinely annoying and then swung back around to hilarious.

Go was moving on to a story about her refrigerator light and showed no signs of faltering. Filled with a sudden, heavy gratefulness, I leaned across the couch and kissed her on the cheek.

'What's that for?'

'Just, thanks.' I felt my eyes get full with tears. I looked away for a second to blink them off, and Go said, 'So I needed a triple-A battery, which, as it turns out, is different from a *transistor* battery, so I had to find the receipt to return the transistor battery ...'

We finished watching the game. Cards lost. When it was over, Go switched the TV to mute. 'You want to talk, or you want more distraction? Whatever you need.'

'You go on to bed, Go. I'm just going to flip around. Probably sleep. I need to sleep.'

'You want an Ambien?' My twin was a staunch believer in the easiest way. No relaxation tapes or whale noises for her; pop a pill, get unconscious.

'Nah.'

'They're in the medicine cabinet if you change your mind. If there was ever a time for assisted sleep ...' She hovered over me for just a few seconds, then, Go-like, trotted down the hall, clearly not sleepy, and closed her door, knowing the kindest thing was to leave me alone.

A lot of people lacked that gift: knowing when to fuck off. People love talking, and I have never been a huge talker. I carry on an inner monologue, but the words often don't reach my lips. *She looks nice today*, I'd think, but somehow it wouldn't occur to me to say it out loud. My mom talked, my sister talked. I'd been raised to listen. So, sitting on the couch by myself, not talking, felt decadent. I leafed through one of Go's magazines, flipped through TV channels, finally alighting on an old black-and-white show, men in fedoras scribbling notes while a pretty housewife explained that her husband was away in Fresno, which made the two cops look at each other significantly and nod. I thought of Gilpin and Boney and my stomach lurched.

In my pocket, my disposable cell phone made a mini-jackpot sound that meant I had a text:

im outside open the door

– Diary entry –

Just got to keep on keeping on, that's what Mama Mo says, and when she says it – her sureness, each word emphasized, as if it really were a viable life strategy – the cliché stops being a set of words and turns into something real. Valuable. *Keep on keeping on, exactly!* I think.

I do love that about the Midwest: People don't make a big deal about everything. Not even death. Mama Mo will just keep on keeping on until the cancer shuts her down, and then she will die.

So I'm *keeping my head down* and *making the best of a bad situation*, and I mean that in the deep, literal Mama Mo usage. I keep my head down and do my work: I drive Mo to doctor's appointments and chemo appointments. I change the sickly water in the flower vase in Nick's father's room, and I drop off cookies for the staff so they take good care of him.

I'm making the best of a really bad situation, and the situation is mostly bad because my husband, who brought me here, who uprooted me to be closer to his ailing parents, seems to have lost all interest in both me and said ailing parents.

Nick has written off his father entirely: He won't even say the man's name. I know every time we get a phone call from Comfort Hill, Nick is hoping it's the announcement that his dad is dead. As for Mo, Nick sat with his mom during a single chemo session and pronounced it unbearable. He said he hated hospitals, he hated sick people, he hated the slowly ticking time, the IV bag dripping molasses-slow. He just couldn't do it. And when I tried to talk him back into it, when I tried to stiffen his spine with some *gotta do what you gotta do*, he told me to do it. So I did, I have. Mama Mo, of course, takes on the burden of his blame. We sat one day, partly watching a romantic comedy on my computer but mostly chatting, while the IV dripped … so … slowly, and as the spunky heroine tripped over a sofa, Mo turned to me and said, 'Don't be too hard on Nick. About not wanting to do this kind of thing. I just always doted on him, I babied him – how could you *not*? That *face*. And so he has trouble doing hard things. But I truly don't mind, Amy. Truly.'

'You should mind,' I said.

'Nick doesn't have to prove his love for me,' she said, patting my hand. 'I know he loves me.'

I admire Mo's unconditional love, I do. So I don't tell her what I have found on Nick's computer, the book proposal for a memoir about a Manhattan magazine writer who returns to his Missouri roots to care for both his ailing parents. Nick has all sorts of bizarre things on his computer, and sometimes I can't resist a little light snooping – it gives me a clue as to what my husband is thinking. His search history gave me the latest: noir films and the website of his old magazine and a study on the Mississippi River, whether it's possible to free-float from here to the Gulf. I know what he pictures: floating down the Mississippi, like Huck Finn, and writing an article about it. Nick is always looking for angles.

I was nosing through all this when I found the book proposal.

Double Lives: A Memoir of Ends and Beginnings will especially resonate with Gen X males, the original man-boys, who are just beginning to experience the stress and pressures involved with caring for aging parents. In *Double Lives*, I will detail:

- My growing understanding of a troubled, once-distant father
- My painful, forced transformation from a carefree young man into the head of a family as I deal with the imminent death of a much loved mother

- The resentment my Manhattanite wife feels at this detour in her previously charmed life. My wife, it should be mentioned, is Amy Elliott Dunne, the inspiration for the best-selling *Amazing Amy* series.

The proposal was never completed, I assume because Nick realized he wasn't going to ever understand his once-distant father; and because Nick was shirking all 'head of the family' duties; and because I wasn't expressing any anger about my new life. A little frustration, yes, but no book-worthy rage. For so many years, my husband has lauded the emotional solidity of midwesterners: stoic, humble, without affectation! But these aren't the kinds of people who provide good memoir material. Imagine the jacket copy: *People behaved mostly well and then they died.*

Still, it stings a bit, 'the resentment my Manhattanite wife feels.' Maybe I do feel . . . stubborn. I think of how consistently lovely Maureen is, and I worry that Nick and I were not meant to be matched. That he would be happier with a woman who thrills at husband care and homemaking, and I'm not disparaging these skills: I wish I had them. I wish I cared more that Nick always has his favorite toothpaste, that I know his collar size off the top of my head, that I am an unconditionally loving woman whose greatest happiness is making my man happy.

I was that way, for a while, with Nick. But it was unsustainable. I'm not selfless enough. Only child, as Nick points out regularly.

But I try. I keep on keeping on, and Nick runs around town like a kid again. He's happy to be back in his rightful prom-king place – he dropped about ten pounds, he got a new haircut, he bought new jeans, he looks freakin' great. But I only know that from the glimpses of him coming home or going back out, always in a pretend hurry. *You wouldn't like it*, his standard response any time I ask to come with him, wherever it is he goes. Just like he jettisoned his parents when they were of no use to him, he's dropping me because I don't fit in his

159

new life. He'd have to work to make me comfortable here, and he doesn't want to do that. He wants to enjoy himself.

Stop it, stop it. I must *look on the bright side*. Literally. I must take my husband out of my dark shadowy thoughts and shine some cheerful golden light on him. I must do better at adoring him like I used to. Nick responds to adoration. I just wish it felt more equal. My brain is so busy with Nick thoughts, it's a swarm inside my head: *Nicknicknicknicknick!* And when I picture his mind, I hear my name as a shy crystal ping that occurs once, maybe twice, a day and quickly subsides. I just wish he thought about me as much as I do him.

Is that wrong? I don't even know anymore.

NICK DUNNE
FOUR DAYS GONE

She was standing there in the orange glow of the streetlight, in a flimsy sundress, her hair wavy from the humidity. Andie. She rushed through the doorway, her arms splayed to hug me, and I hissed, 'Wait, wait!' and shut it just before she wrapped herself around me. She pressed her cheek against my chest, and I put my hand on her bare back and closed my eyes. I felt a queasy mixture of relief and horror: when you finally stop an itch and realize it's because you've ripped a hole in your skin.

I have a mistress. Now is the part where I have to tell you I have a mistress and you stop liking me. If you liked me to begin with. I have a pretty, young, very young mistress, and her name is Andie.

I know. It's bad.

'Baby, why the *fuck* haven't you called me?' she said, her face still pressed against me.

'I know, sweetheart, I know. You just can't imagine. It's been a nightmare. How did you find me?'

She held onto me. 'Your house was dark, so I figured try Go's.'

Andie knew my habits, knew my habitats. We've been together a while. I have a pretty, very young mistress, and we've been together a while.

'I was worried about you, Nick. *Frantic*. I'm sitting at Madi's house, and the TV is, like, just on, and all of a sudden on the TV, I see this, like, *guy* who looks like you talking about his missing wife. And then I realize: It *is* you. Can you imagine how freaked out I was? And you didn't even try to reach me?'

'I called you.'

'*Don't say anything, sit tight, don't say anything till we talk.* That's an order, that's not you trying to *reach* me.'

'I haven't been alone much; people have been around me all the time. Amy's parents, Go, the police.' I breathed into her hair.

'Amy's just gone?' she asked.

'She's just gone.' I pulled myself from her and sat down on the couch, and she sat beside me, her leg pressed against mine, her arm brushing against mine. 'Someone took her.'

'Nick? Are you okay?'

Her chocolatey hair fell in waves over her chin, collarbone, breasts, and I watched one single strand shake in the stream of her breathing.

'No, not really.' I gave her the shhh sign and pointed toward the hallway. 'My sister.'

We sat side by side, silent, the TV flickering the old cop show, the men in fedoras making an arrest. I felt her hand wriggle into mine. She leaned in to me as if we were settling in for a movie night, some lazy, carefree couple, and then she pulled my face toward her and kissed me.

'Andie, no,' I whispered.

'Yes, I need you.' She kissed me again and climbed onto my lap, where she straddled me, her cotton dress slipping up around her knees, one of her flip-flops falling to the floor. 'Nick, I've been so worried about you. I need to feel your hands on me, that's all I've been thinking about. I'm scared.'

Andie was a physical girl, and that's not code for *It's all about the sex*. She was a hugger, a toucher, she was prone to running her fingers through my hair or down my back in a friendly scratch. She got reassurance and comfort from touching. And yes, fine, she also liked sex.

With one quick tug, she yanked down the top of her sundress and moved my hands onto her breasts. My canine-loyal lust surfaced.

I want to fuck you, I almost said aloud. *You are WARM*,

my wife said in my ear. I lurched away. I was so tired, the room was swimming.

'Nick?' Her bottom lip was wet with my spit. 'What? Are *we* not okay? Is it because of Amy?'

Andie had always felt young – she was twenty-three, of course she felt young – but right then I realized how grotesquely young she was, how irresponsibly, disastrously young she was. Ruinously young. Hearing my wife's name on her lips always jarred me. She said it a lot. She liked to discuss Amy, as if Amy were the heroine on a nighttime soap opera. Andie never made Amy the enemy; she made her a character. She asked questions, all the time, about our life together, about Amy: *What did you guys do, together in New York, like what did you do on the weekends?* Andie's mouth went O once when I told her about going to the opera. *You went to the* opera? *What did she wear? Full-length? And a wrap or a fur? And her jewelry and her hair?* Also: What were Amy's friends like? What did we talk about? What was Amy like, like, *really* like? Was she like the girl in the books, perfect? It was Andie's favorite bedtime story: Amy.

'My sister is in the other room, sweetheart. You shouldn't even be here. God, I want you here, but you really shouldn't have come, babe. Until we know what we're dealing with.'

YOU ARE BRILLIANT YOU ARE WITTY YOU ARE WARM. Now kiss me!

Andie remained atop me, her breasts out, nipples going hard from the air-conditioning.

'Baby, what we're dealing with right now is I need to make sure we're okay. That's all I need.' She pressed against me, warm and lush. 'That's all I need. Please, Nick, I'm freaked out. I know you: I know you don't want to talk right now, and that's fine. But I need you ... to be with me.'

And I wanted to kiss her then, the way I had that very first time: our teeth bumping, her face tilted to mine, her hair tickling my arms, a wet and tonguey kiss, me thinking of nothing but the kiss, because it would be dangerous to think of anything but how good it felt. The only thing that kept me from dragging her into the bedroom now was not how wrong it was – it had been many shades of wrong all along – but that now it was actually dangerous.

And because there was Amy. Finally, there was Amy, that voice that had made its home in my ear for half a decade, my wife's voice, but now it wasn't chiding, it was sweet again. I hated that three little notes from my wife could make me feel this way, soggy and sentimental.

I had absolutely no right to be sentimental.

Andie was burrowing into me, and I was wondering if the police had Go's house under surveillance, if I should be listening for a knock at the door. I have a very young, very pretty mistress.

My mother had always told her kids: If you're about to do something, and you want to know if it's a bad idea, imagine seeing it printed in the paper for all the world to see.

Nick Dunne, a onetime magazine writer still pride-wounded from a 2010 layoff, agreed to teach a journalism class for North Carthage Junior College. The older married man promptly exploited his position by launching a torrid fuckfest of an affair with one of his impressionable young students.

I was the embodiment of every writer's worst fear: a cliché.

Now let me string still more clichés together for your amusement: It happened gradually. I never meant to hurt anyone. I got in deeper than I thought I would. But it was more than a fling. It was more than an ego boost. I really love Andie. I do.

The class I was teaching – 'How to Launch a Magazine Career' – contained fourteen students of varying degrees of skill. All girls. I'd say women, but I think *girls* is factually correct. They all wanted to work in magazines. They weren't smudgy newsprint girls, they were glossies. They'd seen the movie: They pictured themselves dashing around Manhattan, latte in one hand, cell phone in the other, adorably breaking a designer heel while hailing a cab, and falling into the arms of a charming, disarming soul mate with winningly floppy hair. They had no clue about how foolish, how ignorant, their choice of a major was. I'd been planning on telling them as much, using my layoff as a cautionary tale. Although I had no interest in being the tragic figure. I pictured delivering the story nonchalantly, jokingly – no big deal. More time to work on my novel.

Then I spent the first class answering so many awestruck questions, and I turned into such a preening gasbag, such a needy fuck, that I couldn't bear to tell the real story: the call into the managing editor's office on the second round of layoffs, the hiking of that doomed path down the long rows of cubicles, all eyes shifting toward me, dead man walking, me still hoping I was going to be told something different – that the magazine needed me *now more than ever* – yes! it would be a buck-up speech, an all-hands-on-deck speech! But no, my boss just said: *I guess you know, unfortunately, why I called you in here*, rubbing his eyes under his glasses, to show how weary and dejected he was.

I wanted to feel like a shiny-cool winner, so I didn't tell my students about my demise. I told them we had a family illness that required my attention here, which was true, yes, I told myself, entirely true, and very heroic. And pretty, freckled Andie sat a few feet in front of me, wide-set blue eyes under chocolatey waves of hair, cushiony lips parted just a bit, ridiculously large, real breasts, and long thin legs and arms – an alien fuck-doll of a girl, it must be said, as different from my elegant, patrician wife as could be – and Andie was radiating body heat and lavender, clicking notes on her laptop, asking questions in a husky voice like 'How do you get a source to trust you, to open up to you?' And I thought to myself, right then: *Where the fuck did this girl come from? Is this a joke?*

You ask yourself, *Why?* I'd been faithful to Amy always. I was the guy who left the bar early if a woman was getting too flirty, if her touch was feeling too nice. I was not a cheater. I don't (didn't?) like cheaters: dishonest, disrespectful, petty, spoiled. I had never succumbed. But that was back when I was happy. I hate to think the answer is that easy, but I had been happy all my life, and now I was not, and Andie was there, lingering after class, asking me questions about myself that Amy never had, not lately. Making me feel like a worthwhile man, not the idiot who lost his job, the dope who forgot to put the toilet seat down, the blunderer who just could never quite get it right, whatever it was.

Andie brought me an apple one day. A Red Delicious (title of the memoir of our affair, if I were to write one). She asked me to give her story an early look. It was a profile of a stripper at a St. Louis club, and it read like a *Penthouse* Forum piece, and Andie began eating my apple while I read it, leaning over my shoulder, the juice sitting ludicrously on her lip, and then I thought, *Holy shit, this girl is trying to seduce me*, foolishly shocked, an aging Benjamin Braddock.

It worked. I began thinking of Andie as an escape, an opportunity. An option. I'd come home to find Amy in a tight ball on the sofa, Amy staring at the wall, silent, never saying the first word to me, always waiting, a perpetual game of icebreaking, a constant mental challenge – what will make Amy happy today? I would think: *Andie wouldn't do that*. As if I knew Andie. *Andie would laugh at that joke, Andie would like that story*. Andie was a nice, pretty, bosomy Irish girl from my hometown, unassuming and jolly. Andie sat in the front row of my class, and she looked soft, and she looked interested.

When I thought about Andie, my stomach didn't hurt the way it did with my wife – the constant dread of returning to my own home, where I wasn't welcome.

I began imagining how it might happen. I began craving her touch – yes, it was like that, just like a lyric from a bad '80s single – I craved her touch, I craved touch in general, because my wife avoided mine: At home she slipped past me like a fish, sliding just out of grazing distance in the kitchen or the stairwell. We watched TV silently on our two sofa cushions, as separate as if they were life rafts. In bed, she turned away from me, pushed blankets and sheets between us. I once woke up in the night and, knowing she was asleep, pulled aside her halter strap a bit, and pressed my cheek and a palm against her bare shoulder. I couldn't get back to sleep that night, I was so disgusted with myself. I got out of bed and masturbated in the shower, picturing Amy, the lusty way she used to look at me, those heavy-lidded moonrise eyes taking me in, making me feel seen. When I was done, I sat down in the bathtub and stared at the drain through the spray. My penis lay pathetically along my left thigh, like some small animal washed ashore. I sat at the bottom of the bathtub, humiliated, trying not to cry.

So it happened. In a strange, sudden snowstorm in early April. Not April of this year, April of *last* year. I was working the bar alone because Go was having a Mom Night; we took turns not working, staying home with our mother and watching bad TV. Our mom was going fast, she wouldn't last the year, not even close.

I was actually feeling okay right at that moment – my mom and Go were snuggled up at home watching an Annette Funicello beach movie, and The Bar had had a busy, lively night, one of those nights where everyone seemed to have come off a good day. Pretty girls were nice to homely guys. People were buying rounds for strangers just because. It was festive. And then it was the end of the night, time to close, everybody out. I was about to lock the door when Andie flung it wide and stepped in, almost on top of me, and I could smell the light-beer sweetness on her breath, the scent of woodsmoke in her hair. I paused for that jarring moment when you try to process someone you've seen in only one setting, put them in a new context. Andie in The Bar. Okay. She laughed a pirate-wench laugh and pushed me back inside.

'I just had the most fantastically awful date, and you have to have a drink with me.' Snowflakes gathered in the dark waves of her hair, her sweet scattering of freckles glowed, her cheeks were bright pink, as if someone had double-slapped her. She has this great voice, this fuzzy-duckling voice, that starts out ridiculously cute and ends up completely sexy. 'Please, Nick, I've got to get that bad-date taste out of my mouth.'

I remember us laughing, and thinking what a relief it was to be with a woman and hear her laugh. She was wearing jeans and a cashmere V-neck; she is one of those girls who look better in jeans than a dress. Her face, her body, is casual in the best way. I assumed my position behind the bar, and she slid onto a bar stool, her eyes assessing all the liquor bottles behind me.

'Whaddya want, lady?'

'Surprise me,' she said.

'Boo,' I said, the word leaving my lips kiss-puckered.

'Now surprise me with a drink.' She leaned forward so her cleavage was leveraged against the bar, her breasts pushed upward. She wore a pendant on a thin gold chain; the pendant slid between her breasts down under her sweater. *Don't be that guy*, I thought. *The guy who pants over where the pendant ends.*

'What flavor you feel like?' I asked.

'Whatever you give me, I'll like.'

It was that line that caught me, the simplicity of it. The idea that I could do something and it would make a woman happy, and it would be easy. *Whatever you give me, I'll like.* I felt an overwhelming wave of relief. And then I knew I didn't love Amy anymore.

I don't love my wife anymore, I thought, turning to grab two tumblers. *Not even a little bit. I am wiped clean of love, I am spotless.* I made my favorite drink: Christmas Morning, hot coffee and cold peppermint schnapps. I had one with her, and when she shivered and laughed – that big whoop of a laugh – I poured us another round. We drank together an hour past closing time, and I mentioned the word *wife* three times, because I was looking at Andie and picturing taking her clothes off. A warning for her, the least I could do: *I have a wife. Do with that what you will.*

She sat in front of me, her chin in her hands, smiling up at me.

'Walk me home?' she said. She'd mentioned before how close she lived to downtown, how she needed to stop by The Bar some night and say hello, and did she mention how close she lived to The Bar? My mind had been primed: Many times I'd mentally strolled the few blocks toward the bland brick apartments where she lived. So when I suddenly was out the door, walking her home, it didn't seem unusual at all – there wasn't that warning bell that told me: *This is unusual, this is not what we do.*

I walked her home, against the wind, snow flying everywhere, helping her rewrap her red knitted scarf once, twice, and on the third time, I was tucking her in properly and our faces were close, and her cheeks were a merry holiday-sledding pink, and it was the kind of thing that could never have happened in another hundred nights, but that night it was possible. The conversation, the booze, the storm, the scarf.

We grabbed each other at the same time, me pushing her up against a tree for better leverage, the spindly branches dumping a pile of snow on us, a stunning, comical moment that only made me more insistent on touching her, touching everything at once, one hand up inside her sweater, the other between her legs. And her letting me.

She pulled back from me, her teeth chattering. 'Come up with me.'

I paused.

'Come up with me,' she said again. 'I want to be with you.'

The sex wasn't that great, not the first time. We were two bodies used to different rhythms, never quite getting the hang of each other, and it had been so long since I'd been inside a woman, I came first, quickly, and kept moving, thirty crucial seconds as I began wilting inside her, just long enough to get her taken care of before I went entirely slack.

So it was nice but disappointing, anticlimactic, the way girls must feel when they give up their virginity: *That was what all the fuss was about?* But I liked how she wrapped herself around me, and I liked that she was as soft as I'd imagined. New skin. *Young*, I thought disgracefully, picturing Amy and her constant lotioning, sitting in bed and slapping away at herself angrily.

I went into Andie's bathroom, took a piss, looked at myself

in the mirror, and made myself say it: *You are a cheater. You have failed one of the most basic male tests. You are not a good man.* And when that didn't bother me, I thought: *You're really not a good man.*

The horrifying thing was, if the sex had been outrageously mind-blowing, that might have been my sole indiscretion. But it was only decent, and now I was a cheater, and I couldn't ruin my record of fidelity on something merely average. So I knew there would be a next. I didn't promise myself never again. And then the next was very, very good, and the next after that was great. Soon Andie became a physical counterpoint to all things Amy. She laughed with me and made me laugh, she didn't immediately contradict me or second-guess me. She never scowled at me. She was easy. It was all so fucking easy. And I thought: *Love makes you want to be a better man – right, right. But maybe love, real love, also gives you permission to just be the man you are.*

I was going to tell Amy. I knew it had to happen. I continued not to tell Amy, for months and months. And then more months. Most of it was cowardice. I couldn't bear to have the conversation, to have to *explain* myself. I couldn't imagine having to discuss the divorce with Rand and Marybeth, as they certainly would insert themselves into the fray. But part of it, in truth, was my strong streak of pragmatism – it was almost grotesque, how practical (self-serving?) I could be. I hadn't asked Amy for a divorce, in part, because Amy's money had financed The Bar. She basically owned it, she would certainly take it back. And I couldn't bear to look at my twin trying to be brave as she lost another couple years of her life. So I let myself drift on in the miserable situation, assuming that at some point Amy would take charge, Amy would demand a divorce, and then I would get to be the good guy.

This desire – to escape the situation without blame – was despicable. The more despicable I became, the more I craved Andie, who knew that I wasn't as bad as I seemed, if my story were published in the paper for strangers to read. *Amy will divorce you*, I kept thinking. *She can't let it linger on much longer.* But as spring faded away and summer came, then fall, then winter, and I became a cheating man of all seasons – a cheat with a pleasantly impatient mistress – it became clear that something would have to be done.

'I mean, I love you, Nick,' Andie said, here, surreally, on my sister's sofa. 'No matter what happens. I don't really know what else to say, I feel pretty ...' She threw her hands up. 'Stupid.'

'Don't feel stupid,' I said. 'I don't know what to say either. There's nothing to say.'

'You can say that you love me no matter what happens.'

I thought: *I can't say that out loud anymore.* I'd said it once or twice, a spitty mumble against her neck, homesick for something. But the words were out there, and so was a lot more. I thought then of the trail we'd left, our busy, semi-hidden love affair that I hadn't worried enough about. If her building had a security camera, I was on it. I'd bought a disposable phone just for her calls, but those voice mails and texts went to her very permanent cell. I'd written her a dirty valentine that I could already see splashed across the news, me rhyming *besot* with *twat.* And more: Andie was twenty-three. I assumed my words, voice, even photos of me were captured on various electronica. I'd flipped through the photos on her phone one night, jealous, possessive, curious, and seen plenty of shots of an ex or two smiling proudly in her bed, and I assumed at one point I'd join the club – I kind of *wanted* to join the club – and for some reason that hadn't worried me, even though it could be downloaded and sent to a million people in the space of a vengeful second.

'This is an extremely weird situation, Andie. I just need you to be patient.'

She pulled back from me. 'You can't say you love me, no matter what happens?'

'I love you, Andie. I do.' I held her eyes. Saying *I love you* was dangerous right now, but so was not saying it.

'Fuck me, then,' she whispered. She began tugging at my belt.

'We have to be real careful right now. I ... It's a bad, bad place for me if the police find out about us. It looks beyond bad.'

'That's what you're worried about?'

'I'm a man with a missing wife and a secret ... girlfriend. Yeah, it looks bad. It looks criminal.'

'That makes it sound sleazy.' Her breasts were still out.

'People don't know us, Andie. They *will* think it's sleazy.'

'God, it's like some bad noir movie.'

I smiled. I'd introduced Andie to noir – to Bogart and *The Big Sleep*, *Double Indemnity*, all the classics. It was one of the things I liked best about us, that I could show her things.

'Why don't we just tell the police?' she said. 'Wouldn't that be better—'

'No. Andie, don't even think about it. No.'

'They're going to find out—'

'Why? Why would they? Have you told anyone about us, sweetheart?'

She gave me a twitchy look. I felt bad: This was not how she thought the night would go. She had been excited to see me, she had been imagining a lusty reunion, physical reassurance, and I was busy covering my ass.

'Sweetheart, I'm sorry, I just need to know,' I said.

'Not by name.'

'What do you mean, not by name?'

'I mean,' she said, pulling up her dress finally, 'my friends, my mom, they know I'm seeing someone, but not by name.'

'And not by any kind of description, right?' I said it more urgently than I wanted to, feeling like I was holding up a collapsing ceiling. 'Two people know about this, Andie. You and me. If you help me, if you love me, it will just be us knowing, and then the police will never find out.'

She traced a finger along my jawline. 'And what if – if they never find Amy?'

'You and I, Andie, we'll be together no matter what happens. But *only* if we're careful. If we're not careful, it's possible – It looks bad enough that I could go to prison.'

'Maybe she ran off with someone,' she said, leaning her cheek against my shoulder. 'Maybe—'

I could feel her girl-brain buzzing, turning Amy's disappearance into a frothy, scandalous romance, ignoring any reality that didn't suit the narrative.

'She didn't run off. It's much more serious than that.' I put a finger under her chin so she looked at me. 'Andie? I need you to take this very seriously, okay?'

'Of course I'm taking it seriously. But I need to be able to talk to you more often. To see you. I'm freaking out, Nick.'

'We just need to sit tight for now.' I gripped both her shoulders so she had to look at me. 'My wife is missing, Andie.'

'But you don't even—'

I knew what she was about to say – *you don't even love her* – but she was smart enough to stop.

She put her arms around me. 'Look, I don't want to fight. I know you care about Amy, and I know you must be really worried. I am too. I know you are under ... I can't imagine the pressure. So I'm fine keeping an even lower profile than I did before, if that's possible. But remember, this affects me, too. I need to hear from you. Once a day. Just call when you can, even if it's only for a few seconds, so I can hear your voice. Once a day, Nick. Every single day. I'll go crazy otherwise. I'll go crazy.'

She smiled at me, whispered, 'Now kiss me.'

I kissed her very softly.

'I love you,' she said, and I kissed her neck and mumbled my reply. We sat in silence, the TV flickering.

I let my eyes close. *Now kiss me*, who had said that?

I lurched awake just after five a.m. Go was up, I could hear her down the hall, running water in the bathroom. I shook Andie – *It's five a.m., it's five a.m.* – and with promises of love and phone calls, I hustled her toward the door like a shameful one-nighter.

'Remember, call every day,' Andie whispered.

I heard the bathroom door open.

'Every day,' I said, and ducked behind the door as I opened it and Andie left.

When I turned back around, Go was standing in the living room. Her mouth had dropped open, stunned, but the rest of her body was in full fury: hands on hips, eyebrows V'ed.

'Nick. You fucking idiot.'

AMY ELLIOTT DUNNE
JULY 21, 2011

I am such an idiot. Sometimes I look at myself and I think: *No wonder Nick finds me ridiculous, frivolous, spoiled, compared to his mom.* Maureen is dying. She hides her disease behind big smiles and roomy embroidered sweatshirts, answering every question about her health with: 'Oh, I'm just fine, but how are *you* doing, sweetie?' She is dying, but she is not going to admit it, not yet. So yesterday she phones me in the morning, asks me if I want to go on a field trip with her and her friends – she is having a good day, she wants to get out of the house as much as she can – and I agree immediately, even though I knew they'd be doing nothing that particularly interested me: pinochle, bridge, some church activity that usually requires sorting things.

'We'll be there in fifteen minutes,' she says. 'Wear short sleeves.'

Cleaning. It had to be cleaning. Something requiring elbow grease. I throw on a short-sleeve shirt, and in exactly fifteen minutes, I am opening the door to Maureen, bald under a knitted cap, giggling with her two friends. They are all wearing matching appliquéd T-shirts, all bells and ribbons, with the words *The PlasMamas* airbrushed across their chests.

I think they've started a do-wop group. But then we all climb into Rose's old Chrysler – *old*-old, one of those where the front seat goes all the way across, a grandmotherly car that smells of lady cigarettes – and off we merrily go to the *plasma donation center.*

'We're Mondays and Thursdays,' Rose explains, looking at me in the rearview.

'Oh,' I say. How else does one reply? *Oh, those are awesome plasma days!*

'You're allowed to give twice a week,' says Maureen, the bells on her sweatshirt jingling. 'The first time you get twenty dollars, the second time you get thirty. That's why everyone's in such a good mood today.'

'You'll love it,' Vicky says. 'Everyone just sits and chats, like a beauty salon.'

Maureen squeezes my arm and says quietly, 'I can't give anymore, but I thought you could be my proxy. It might be a nice way for you to get some pin money – it's good for a girl to have a little cash of her own.'

I swallow a quick gust of anger: *I used to have more than a little cash of my own, but I gave it to your son.*

A scrawny man in an undersize jean jacket hangs around the parking lot like a stray dog. Inside, though, the place is clean. Well lit, piney-smelling, with Christian posters on the wall, all doves and mist. But I know I can't do it. Needles. Blood. I can't do either. I don't really have any other phobias, but those two are solid – I am the girl who swoons at a paper cut. Something about the opening of skin: peeling, slicing, piercing. During chemo with Maureen, I never looked when they put in the needle.

'Hi, Cayleese!' Maureen calls out as we enter, and a heavy black woman in a vaguely medical uniform calls back, 'Hi there, Maureen! How you feeling?'

'Oh, I'm fine, just fine – but how are *you*?'

'How long have you been doing this?' I ask.

'A while,' Maureen says. 'Cayleese is everyone's favorite, she gets the needle in real smooth. Which was always good for me, because I have rollers.' She proffers her forearm with its ropey blue veins. When I first met Mo, she was fat, but no more. It's odd, she actually looks better fat. 'See, try to put your finger on one.'

I look around, hoping Cayleese is going to usher us in.

'Go on, try.'

I touch a fingertip to the vein and feel it roll out from under. A rush of heat overtakes me.

'So, is this our new recruit?' Cayleese asks, suddenly beside me. 'Maureen brags on you all the time. So, we'll need you to fill out some paperwork—'

'I'm sorry, I can't. I can't do needles, I can't do blood. I have a serious phobia. I *literally* can't do it.'

I realize I haven't eaten today, and a wave of wooziness hits me. My neck feels weak.

'Everything here is very hygienic, you're in very good hands,' Cayleese says.

'No, it's not that, truly. I've never given blood. My doctor gets angry at me because I can't even handle a yearly blood test for, like, cholesterol.'

Instead, we wait. It takes two hours, Vicky and Rose strapped to churning machines. Like they are being harvested. They've even been branded on their fingers, so they can't give more than twice in a week anywhere – the marks show up under a purple light.

'That's the James Bond part,' Vicky says, and they all giggle. Maureen hums the Bond theme song (I think), and Rose makes a gun with her fingers.

'Can't you old biddies keep it down for once?' calls a white-haired woman four chairs down. She leans up over the reclined bodies of three oily men – green-blue tattoos on their arms, stubble on their chins, the kind of men I pictured donating plasma – and gives a finger wave with her loose arm.

'Mary! I thought you were coming tomorrow!'

'I was, but my unemployment doesn't come for a week, and I was down to a box of cereal and a can of creamed corn!'

They all laugh like near-starvation is amusing – this town is sometimes too much, so desperate and so in denial. I begin to feel ill, the sound of blood churning, the long plastic ribbons of blood coursing from bodies to machines, the people being, what, being *farmed*. Blood everywhere I look, out in the open, where blood isn't supposed to be. Deep and dark, almost purple.

I get up to go to the bathroom, throw cold water on my face. I take two steps and my ears close up, my vision pinholes, I feel my own heartbeat, my own blood, and as I fall, I say, 'Oh. Sorry.'

I barely remember the ride home. Maureen tucks me into bed, a glass of apple juice, a bowl of soup, at the bedside. We try to call Nick. Go says he's not at The Bar, and he doesn't pick up his cell.

The man disappears.

'He was like that as a boy too – he's a wanderer,' Maureen says. 'Worst thing you could ever do is ground him to his room.' She positions a cool washcloth on my forehead; her breath has the tangy smell of aspirin. 'Your job is to rest, okay? I'll keep calling till I get that boy home.'

When Nick gets home, I'm asleep. I wake up to hear him taking a shower, and I check the time: 11:04 p.m. He must have gone by The Bar after all – he likes to shower after a shift, get the beer and salty popcorn smell off his skin. (He says.)

He slips into bed, and when I turn to him with open eyes, he looks dismayed I'm awake.

'We've been trying to reach you for hours,' I say.

'My phone was out of juice. You fainted?'

'I thought you said your phone was out of juice.'

He pauses, and I know he is about to lie. The worst feeling: when you just have to wait and prepare yourself for the lie. Nick is old-fashioned, he needs his freedom, he doesn't like to explain himself. He'll know he has plans with the guys for a week, and he'll still wait until an hour before the poker game to tell me nonchalantly, 'Hey, so I thought I'd join the guys for poker tonight, if that's okay with you,' and leave me to be the bad guy if I've made other plans. You don't ever want to be the wife who keeps her husband from playing poker – you don't want to be the shrew with the hair curlers and the rolling pin. So you swallow your disappointment and say okay. I don't think he does this to be mean, it's just how he was raised. His dad did his own thing, always, and his mom put up with it. Until she divorced him.

He begins his lie. I don't even listen.

NICK DUNNE
FIVE DAYS GONE

I leaned against the door, staring at my sister. I could still smell Andie, and I wanted that moment to myself for one second, because now that she was gone, I could enjoy the idea of her. She always tasted like butterscotch and smelled like lavender. Lavender shampoo, lavender lotion. *Lavender's for luck*, she explained to me once. I'd need luck.

'How old is she?' Go was demanding, hands on hips.

'That's where you want to start?'

'How *old* is she, Nick?'

'Twenty-three.'

'Twenty-three. Brilliant.'

'Go, don't—'

'Nick. Do you not realize how *fucked* you are?' Go said. 'Fucked and *dumb*.' She made *dumb* – a kid's word – hit me as hard as if I were a ten-year-old again.

'It's not an ideal situation,' I allowed, my voice quiet.

'Ideal situation! You are . . . you're a *cheater*, Nick. I mean, what happened to you? You were always one of the good guys. Or have I just been an idiot all along?'

'No.' I stared at the floor, at the same spot I stared at as a kid when my mom sat me down on the sofa and told me I was better than whatever I'd just done.

'Now? You're a *man who cheats on his wife*, you can't ever undo that,' Go said. 'God, even *Dad* didn't cheat. You're so – I mean, your wife is missing, Amy's who knows where, and you're here making time with a little—'

'Go, I enjoy this revisionist history in which you're Amy's

180

champion. I mean, you never liked Amy, not even early on, and since all this happened, it's like—'

'It's like I have sympathy for your missing wife, yeah, Nick. I have concern. Yeah, I do. Remember how before, when I said you were being weird? You're— It's insane, the way you're acting.'

She paced the room, chewing a thumbnail. 'The police find out about this, and I just don't even know,' she said. 'I'm fucking *scared*, Nick. This is the first time I'm really scared for you. I can't believe they haven't found out yet. They must have pulled your phone records.'

'I used a disposable.'

She paused at that. 'That's even worse. That's ... like premeditation.'

'Premeditated cheating, Go. Yes, I am guilty of that.'

She succumbed for a second, collapsed on the sofa, the new reality settling on her. In truth, I was relieved that Go knew.

'How long?' she asked.

'A little over a year.' I made myself pull my eyes from the floor and look at her directly.

'Over a *year*? And you never told me.'

'I was afraid you'd tell me to stop. That you'd think badly of me and then I'd have to stop. And I didn't want to. Things with Amy—'

'Over a year,' Go said. 'And I never even guessed. Eight thousand drunk conversations, and you never trusted me enough to tell me. I didn't know you could do that, keep something from me that totally.'

'That's the only thing.'

Go shrugged: *How can I believe you now?* 'You love her?' She gave it a jokey spin to show how unlikely it was.

'Yeah. I really think I do. I did. I do.'

'You do realize, that if you actually dated her, saw her on a regular basis, *lived* with her, that she would find some fault with you, right? That she would find some things about you that drove her crazy. That she'd make demands of you that you wouldn't like. That she'd get angry at you?'

'I'm not ten, Go, I know how relationships work.'

She shrugged again: *Do you?* 'We need a lawyer,' she said. 'A good lawyer with some PR skills, because the networks, some cable shows, they're sniffing around. We need to make sure the media doesn't turn you into the evil philandering husband, because if that happens, I just think it's all over.'

'Go, you're sounding a little drastic.' I actually agreed with her, but I couldn't bear to hear the words aloud, from Go. I had to discredit them.

'Nick, this is a little drastic. I'm going to make some calls.'

'Whatever you want, if it makes you feel better.'

Go jabbed me in the sternum with two hard fingers. 'Don't you fucking pull that with me, *Lance*. "Oh, girls get so overexcited." That's bullshit. You are in a really bad place, my friend. Get your head out of your ass and start helping me fix this.'

Beneath my shirt, I could feel the spot embering on my skin as Go turned away from me and, thank God, went back to her room. I sat on her couch, numb. Then I lay down as I promised myself I'd get up.

I dreamed of Amy: She was crawling across our kitchen floor, hands and knees, trying to make it to the back door, but she was blind from the blood, and she was moving so slowly, too slowly. Her pretty head was strangely misshapen, dented in on the right side. Blood was dripping from one long hank of hair, and she was moaning my name.

I woke and knew it was time to go home. I needed to see the place – the scene of the crime – I needed to face it.

No one was out in the heat. Our neighborhood was as vacant and lonely as the day Amy disappeared. I stepped inside my front door and made myself breathe. Weird that a house so new could feel haunted, and not in the romantic Victorian-novel way, just really gruesomely, shittily ruined. A house with a history, and it was only three years old. The lab technicians had been all over the place; surfaces were smeared and sticky and smudged. I sat down on the sofa, and it smelled like someone, like an actual person, with a stranger's scent, a spicy aftershave. I opened the windows despite the heat, get in some air. Bleecker trotted down the stairs, and I picked him up and petted him while he purred. Someone, some cop, had overfilled his bowl for me. A nice gesture, after dismantling my home. I set him down carefully on the bottom step, then climbed up to the bedroom, unbuttoning my shirt. I lay down across the bed and put my face in the pillow, the same navy blue pillowcase I'd stared into the morning of our anniversary, the Morning Of.

My phone rang. Go. I picked up.

'*Ellen Abbott* is doing a special noon-day show. It's about Amy. You. I, uh, it doesn't look good. You want me to come over?'

'No, I can watch it alone, thanks.'

We both hovered on the line. Waiting for the other to apologize.

'Okay, let's talk after,' Go said.

Ellen Abbott Live was a cable show specializing in missing, murdered women, starring the permanently furious Ellen Abbott, a former prosecutor and victims' rights advocate. The show opened with Ellen, blow-dried and lip-glossed, glaring at the camera. 'A shocking story to report today: a beautiful, young woman who was the inspiration for the *Amazing Amy* book series. *Missing*. House torn *apart*. Hubby is Lance Nicholas Dunne, an *unemployed writer* who now owns a *bar* he *bought* with his wife's *money*. Want to know how worried he is? These are photos taken since his wife, Amy Elliott Dunne, went missing July fifth – their *five-year anniversary*.'

Cut to the photo of me at the press conference, the jackass grin. Another of me waving and smiling like a pageant queen as I got out of my car (I was waving *back* to Marybeth; I was smiling because I smile when I wave).

Then up came the cell-phone photo of me and Shawna Kelly, Frito-pie baker. The two of us cheek to cheek, beaming pearly whites. Then the real Shawna appeared on-screen, tanned and sculpted and somber as Ellen introduced her to America. Pinpricks of sweat erupted all over me.

ELLEN: So, Lance Nicholas Dunne – can you describe his demeanor for us, Shawna? You meet him as everyone is out searching for his missing wife, and Lance Nicholas Dunne is ... what?

SHAWNA: He was very calm, very friendly.

ELLEN: *Excuse* me, *excuse* me. He was *friendly* and *calm*? His wife is *missing*, Shawna. What kind of man is *friendly* and *calm*?

The grotesque photo appeared on-screen again. We somehow looked even more cheerful.

SHAWNA: He was actually a little flirty ...

You should have been nicer to her, Nick. You should have eaten the fucking pie.

ELLEN: *Flirty?* While his wife is God knows *where* and Lance Dunne is ... well, I'm sorry, Shawna, but this photo is just ... I don't know a better word than *disgusting*. This is not how an *innocent man* looks ...

The rest of the segment was basically Ellen Abbott, professional hatemonger, obsessing over my lack of alibi: '*Why* doesn't *Lance Nicholas Dunne* have an alibi until *noon*? Where was he that *morning*?' she drawled in her Texas sheriff's accent. Her panel of guests agreed that it didn't look good.

I phoned Go and she said, 'Well, you made it almost a week without them turning on you,' and we cursed for a while. *Fucking Shawna crazy bitch whore.*

'Do something really, really useful today, active,' Go advised. 'People will be watching now.'

'I couldn't sit still if I wanted to.'

*

I drove to St. Louis in a near rage, replaying the TV segment in my head, answering all of Ellen's questions, shutting her up. *Today, Ellen Abbott, you fucking cunt, I tracked down one of Amy's stalkers. Desi Collings. I tracked him down to get the truth.* Me, the hero husband. If I had soaring theme music, I would have played it. Me, the nice working-class guy, taking on the spoiled rich kid. The media would have to bite at that: Obsessive stalkers are more intriguing than run-of-the-mill wife killers. The Elliotts, at least, would appreciate it. I dialed Marybeth, but just got voice mail. Onward.

As I rolled into his neighborhood, I had to change my Desi vision from rich to extremely, sickly wealthy. The guy lived in a mansion in Ladue that probably cost at least $5 million. White-washed brick, black lacquer shutters, gaslight, and ivy. I'd dressed for the meeting, a decent suit and tie, but I realized as I rang his doorbell that a four-hundred-dollar suit in this neighborhood was more poignant than if I'd shown up in jeans. I could hear a clattering of dress shoes coming from the back of the house to the front, and the door opened with a desuctioning sound, like a refrigerator. Cold air rolled out toward me.

Desi looked the way I had always wanted to look: like a very handsome, very decent fellow. Something in the eyes, or the jaw. He had deep-set almond eyes, teddy-bear eyes, and dimples in both cheeks. If you saw the two of us together you'd assume he was the good guy.

'Oh,' Desi said, studying my face. 'You're Nick. Nick Dunne. Good God, I'm so sorry about Amy. Come in, come in.'

He ushered me into a severe living room, manliness as envisioned by a decorator. Lots of dark, uncomfortable leather. He pointed me toward an armchair with a particularly rigid back; I tried to make myself comfortable, as urged, but found the only posture the chair allowed was that of a chastised student: *Pay attention and sit up.*

Desi didn't ask me why I was in his living room. Or explain how he'd immediately recognized me. Although they were becoming more common, the double takes and cupped whispers.

'May I get you a drink?' Desi asked, pressing two hands together: business first.

'I'm fine.'

He sat down opposite me. He was dressed in impeccable shades of navy and cream; even his shoelaces looked pressed. He carried it all off, though. He wasn't the dismissible fop I'd been hoping for. Desi seemed the definition of a gentleman: a guy who could quote a great poet, order a rare Scotch, and buy a woman the right piece of vintage jewelry. He seemed, in fact, a man who knew inherently what women wanted – across from him, I felt my suit wilt, my manner go clumsy. I had a swelling urge to discuss football and fart. These were the kinds of guys who always got to me.

'Amy. Any leads?' Desi asked.

He looked like someone familiar, an actor, maybe.

'No good ones.'

'She was taken ... from the home. Is that correct?'

'From our home, yes.'

Then I knew who he was: He was the guy who'd shown up alone the first day of searches, the guy who kept sneaking looks at Amy's photo.

'You were at the volunteer center, weren't you? The first day.'

'I was,' Desi said, reasonable. 'I was about to say that. I wish I'd been able to meet you that day, express my condolences.'

'Long way to come.'

'I could say the same to you.' He smiled. 'Look, I'm really fond of Amy. Hearing what had happened, well, I had to do something. I just— It's terrible to say this, Nick, but when I saw it on the news, I just thought, *Of course.*'

'Of course?'

'Of course someone would ... want her,' he said. He had a deep voice, a fireside voice. 'You know, she always had that way. Of making people want her. Always. You know that old cliché: Men want her, and women want to be her. With Amy, that was true.'

Desi folded large hands across his trousers. Not pants, trousers. I couldn't decide if he was fucking with me. I told myself to tread lightly. It's the rule of all potentially prickly interviews: Don't go on the offense until you have to, first see if they'll hang themselves all on their own.

'You had a very intense relationship with Amy, right?' I asked.

'It wasn't only her looks,' Desi said. He leaned on a knee, his eyes distant. 'I've thought about this a lot, of course. First love. I've definitely thought about it. The navel-gazer in me. Too much philosophy.' He cracked a self-effacing grin. The dimples popped. 'See, when Amy likes you, when she's interested in you, her attention is so warm and reassuring and entirely enveloping. Like a warm bath.'

I raised my eyebrows.

'Bear with me,' he said. 'You feel good about yourself. Completely good, for maybe the first time. And then she sees your flaws, she realizes you're just another regular person she has to deal with – you are in actuality Able Andy, and in real life, Able Andy would never make it with Amazing Amy. So her interest fades, and you stop feeling good, you can feel that old coldness again, like you're naked on the bathroom floor, and all you want is to get back in the bath.'

I knew that feeling – I'd been on the bathroom floor for about three years – and I felt a rush of disgust for sharing this emotion with this other man.

'I'm sure you know what I mean,' Desi said, and smiled winkily at me.

What an odd man, I thought. *Who compares another man's wife to a bath he wants to sink into? Another man's missing wife?*

Behind Desi was a long, polished end table bearing several silver-framed photos. In the center was an oversize one of Desi and Amy back in high school, in tennis whites – the two so preposterously stylish, so monied-lush they could have been a frame from a Hitchcock movie. I pictured Desi, teenage Desi, slipping into Amy's dorm room, dropping his clothes to the floor, settling onto the cold sheets, swallowing plastic-coated pills. Waiting to be found. It was a form of punishment, of rage, but not the kind that occurred in my house. I could see why the police weren't that interested. Desi trailed my glance.

'Oh, well, you can't blame me for that.' He smiled. 'I mean, would *you* throw away a photo that perfect?'

'Of a girl I hadn't known for twenty years?' I said before I could stop. I realized my tone sounded more aggressive than was wise.

'I know Amy,' Desi snapped. He took a breath. 'I knew her. I knew her very well. There aren't any leads? I have to ask ... Her father, is he ... there?'

'Of course he is.'

'I don't suppose ... He was definitely in New York when it happened?'

'He was in New York. Why?'

Desi shrugged: *Just curious, no reason.* We sat in silence for a half minute, playing a game of eye-contact chicken. Neither of us blinked.

'I actually came here, Desi, to see what you could tell me.'

I tried again to picture Desi making off with Amy. Did he have a lake house somewhere nearby? All these types did. Would it be believable, this refined, sophisticated man keeping Amy in some preppy basement rec room, Amy pacing the carpet, sleeping on a dusty sofa in some bright, clubby '60s color, lemon yellow or coral. I wished Boney and Gilpin were here, had witnessed the proprietary tone of Desi's voice: *I know Amy.*

'Me?' Desi laughed. *He laughed richly.* The perfect phrase to describe the sound. 'I can't tell you anything. Like you said, I don't know her.'

'But you just said you did.'

'I certainly don't know her like you know her.'

'You stalked her in high school.'

'I *stalked* her? Nick. She was my girlfriend.'

'Until she wasn't,' I said. 'And you wouldn't go away.'

'Oh, I probably did pine for her. But nothing out of the ordinary.'

'You call trying to kill yourself in her dorm room ordinary?'

He jerked his head, squinted his eyes. He opened his mouth to speak, then stared down at his hands. 'I'm not sure what you're talking about, Nick,' he finally said.

'I'm talking about you stalking my wife. In high school. Now.'

'That's *really* what this is about?' He laughed again. 'Good God, I thought you were raising money for a reward fund or something. Which I'm happy to cover, by the way. Like I said, I've never stopped wanting the best for Amy. Do I love her? No. I don't know her anymore, not really. We exchange the occasional letter. But it is interesting, you coming here. You confusing the issue. Because I have to tell you, Nick, on TV, hell, *here*, now, you don't seem to be a grieving, worried husband. You seem ... smug. The police, by the way, already talked with me, thanks, I guess to you. Or Amy's parents. Strange you didn't know – you'd think they'd tell the husband everything if he were in the clear.'

My stomach clenched. 'I'm here because I wanted to see for myself your face when you talked about Amy,' I said. 'I gotta tell you, it worries me. You get a little ... moony.'

'One of us has to,' Desi said, again reasonably.

'Sweetheart?' A voice came from the back of the house, and another set of expensive shoes clattered toward the living room. 'What was the name of that *book*—'

The woman was a blurry vision of Amy, Amy in a steam-fogged mirror – exact coloring, extremely similar features, but a quarter century older, the flesh, the features, all let out a bit like a fine fabric. She was still gorgeous, a woman who chose to age gracefully. She was shaped like some sort of origami creation: elbows in extreme points, a clothes-hanger collarbone. She wore a china-blue sheath dress and had the same pull Amy did: When she was in a room, you kept turning your head back her way. She gave me a rather predatory smile.

'Hello, I'm Jacqueline Collings.'

'Mother, this is Amy's husband, Nick,' Desi said.

'Amy.' The woman smiled again. She had a bottom-of-a-well voice, deep and strangely resonant. 'We've been quite interested in that story around here. Yes, very interested.' She turned coldly to her son. 'We can never stop thinking about the superb Amy Elliott, can we?'

'Amy Dunne now,' I said.

'Of course,' Jacqueline agreed. 'I'm so sorry, Nick, for what you're going through.' She stared at me a moment. 'I'm sorry, I must ... I didn't picture Amy with such an ... *American* boy.' She seemed to be speaking neither to me nor to Desi. 'Good God, he even has a cleft chin.'

'I came over to see if your son had any information,' I said. 'I know he's written my wife a lot of letters over the years.'

'Oh, the *letters*!' Jacqueline smiled angrily. 'Such an interesting way to spend one's time, don't you think?'

'Amy shared them with you?' Desi asked. 'I'm surprised.'

'No,' I said, turning to him. 'She threw them away unopened, always.'

'All of them? Always? You know that?' Desi said, still smiling.

'Once I went through the trash to read one.' I turned back to Jacqueline. 'Just to see what exactly was going on.'

'Good for you,' Jacqueline said, purring at me. 'I'd expect nothing less of my husband.'

'Amy and I always wrote each other letters,' Desi said. He had his mother's cadence, the delivery that indicated everything he said was something you'd want to hear. 'It was our thing. I find e-mail so ... cheap. And no one saves them. No one saves an e-mail, because it's so inherently impersonal. I worry about posterity in general. All the great love letters – from Simone de Beauvoir to Sartre, from Samuel Clemens to his wife, Olivia – I don't know, I always think about what will be lost—'

'Have you kept all my letters?' Jacqueline asked. She was standing at the fireplace, looking down on us, one long sinewy arm trailing along the mantelpiece.

'Of course.'

She turned to me with an elegant shrug. 'Just curious.'

I shivered, was about to reach out toward the fireplace for warmth, but remembered that it was July. 'It seems to me a rather strange devotion to keep up all these years,' I said. 'I mean, she didn't write you back.'

That lit up Desi's eyes. 'Oh' was all he said, the sound of someone who spied a surprise firework.

'It strikes me as odd, Nick, that you'd come here and ask Desi about his relationship – or lack thereof – with your wife,' Jacqueline Collings said. 'Are you and Amy not close? I can guarantee you: Desi has had no genuine contact with Amy in decades. Decades.'

'I'm just checking in, Jacqueline. Sometimes you have to see something for yourself.'

Jacqueline started walking toward the door; she turned and gave me a single twist of her head to assure me that it was time to go.

'How very *intrepid* of you, Nick. Very do-it-yourself. Do you build your own *decks* too?' She laughed at the word and opened the door for me. I stared at the hollow of her neck and wondered why she wasn't wearing a noose of pearls. Women like these always have thick strands of pearls to click and clack. I could smell her, though, a female scent, vaginal and strangely lewd.

'It was interesting to meet you, Nick,' she said. 'Let's all hope Amy gets home safely. Until then, the next time you want to get in touch with Desi?'

She pressed a thick, creamy card into my hands. 'Call our lawyer, please.'

AMY ELLIOTT DUNNE
AUGUST 17, 2011

– Diary entry –

I know this sounds the stuff of moony teenage girls, but I've been tracking Nick's moods. Toward me. Just to make sure I'm not crazy. I've got a calendar, and I put hearts on any day Nick seems to love me again, and black squares when he doesn't. The past year was all black squares, pretty much.

But now? Nine days of hearts. In a row. Maybe all he needed to know was how much I loved him and how unhappy I'd become. Maybe he had a *change of heart*. I've never loved a phrase more.

Quiz: After over a year of coldness, your husband suddenly seems to love you again. You:

a) Go on and on about how much he's hurt you so he can apologize some more.
b) Give him the cold shoulder for a while longer – so he learns his lesson!
c) Don't press him about his new attitude – know that he will confide in you when the time comes, and in the meantime, shower him with affection so he feels secure and loved, because that's how this marriage thing works.
d) Demand to know what went wrong; make him talk and talk about it in order to calm your own neuroses.

Answer: C

It's August, so sumptuous that I couldn't bear any more

black squares, but no, it's been nothing but hearts, Nick acting like my husband, sweet and loving and goofy. He orders me chocolates from my favorite shop in New York for a treat, and he writes me a silly poem to go with them. A limerick, actually:

> *There once was a girl from Manhattan*
> *Who slept only on sheets made of satin*
> *Her husband slipped and he slided*
> *And their bodies collided*
> *So they did something dirty in Latin.*

It would be funnier if our sex life were as carefree as the rhyme would suggest. But last week we did ... *fuck? Do it?* Something more romantic that *have sex* but less cheesy than *make love.* He came home from work and kissed me full on the lips, and he touched me as if I were really there. I almost cried, I'd been so lonely. To be kissed on the lips by your husband is the most decadent thing.

What else? He takes me swimming in the same pond he's gone to since he was a child. I can picture little Nick flapping around manically, face and shoulders sunburned red because (just like now) he refuses to wear sunscreen, forcing Mama Mo to chase after him with lotion that she swipes on whenever she can reach him.

He's been taking me on a full tour of his boyhood haunts, like I asked him to for ages. He walks me to the edge of the river, and he kisses me as the wind whips my hair ('My two favorite things to look at in the world,' he whispers in my ear). He kisses me in a funny little playground fort that he once considered his own clubhouse ('I always wanted to bring a girl here, a perfect girl, and look at me now,' he whispers in my ear). Two days before the mall closes for good, we ride carousel bunnies side by side, our laughter echoing through the empty miles.

He takes me for a sundae at his favorite ice cream parlor, and we have the place to ourselves in the morning, the air all sticky with sweets. He kisses me and says this place is where he stuttered and suffered through so many dates, and he wishes he could have told his high school self that he would be back here with the girl of his dreams someday. We eat ice cream until we have to roll home and get under the covers. His hand on my belly, an accidental nap.

The neurotic in me, of course, is asking: Where's the catch? Nick's turnaround is so sudden and so grandiose, it feels like ... it feels like he must want something. Or he's already done something and he is being preemptively sweet for when I find out. I worry. I caught him last week shuffling through my thick file box marked *THE DUNNES!* (written in my best cursive in happier days), a box filled with all the strange paperwork that makes up a marriage, a combined life. I worry that he is going to ask me for a second mortgage on The Bar, or to borrow against our life insurance, or to sell off some not-to-be-touched-for-thirty-years stock. He said he just wanted to make sure everything was in order, but he said it in a fluster. My heart would break, it really would, if, midbite of bubblegum ice cream, he turned to me and said: *You know, the interesting thing about a second mortgage is ...*

I had to write that, I had to let that out. And just seeing it, I know it sounds crazy. Neurotic and insecure and suspicious.

I will not let my worst self ruin my marriage. My husband loves me. He loves me and he has come back to me and that is why he is treating me so nice. That is the only reason.

Just like that: *Here is my life. It's finally returned.*

NICK DUNNE
FIVE DAYS GONE

I sat in the billowing heat of my car outside Desi's house, the windows rolled down, and checked my phone. A message from Gilpin: 'Hi, Nick. We need to touch base today, update you on a few things, go over a few questions. Meet us at four at your house, okay? Uh ... thanks.'

It was the first time I'd been ordered. Not *Could we, we'd love to, if you don't mind.* But *We need to. Meet us ...*

I glanced at my watch. Three o'clock. Best not be late.

The summer air show – a parade of jets and prop planes spinning loops up and down the Mississippi, buzzing the tourist steamboats, rattling teeth – was three days off, and the practice runs were in high gear by the time Gilpin and Rhonda arrived. We were all back in my living room for the first time since The Day Of.

My home was right on a flight path; the noise was somewhere between jackhammer and avalanche. My cop buddies and I tried to jam a conversation in the spaces between the blasts. Rhonda looked more birdlike than usual – favoring one leg, then another, her head moving all around the room as her gaze alighted on different objects, angles – a magpie looking to line her nest. Gilpin hovered next to her, chewing his lip, tapping a foot. Even the room felt restive: The afternoon sun lit up an atomic flurry of dust motes. A jet shot over the house, that awful sky-rip noise.

'Okay, couple of things here,' Rhonda said when the silence returned. She and Gilpin sat down as if they both had suddenly decided to stay awhile. 'Some stuff to get clear on, some stuff to tell you. All very routine. And as always, if you want a lawyer—'

But I knew from my TV shows, my movies, that only guilty guys lawyered up. Real, grieving, worried, innocent husbands did not.

'I don't, thanks,' I said. 'I actually have some information to share with you. About Amy's former stalker, the guy she dated back in high school.'

'Desi – uh, Collins,' began Gilpin.

'Collings. I know you all talked to him, I know you for some reason aren't that interested in him, so I went to visit him myself today. To make sure he seemed ... okay. And I don't think he is okay. I think he's someone you all should look into. Really look into. I mean, he moves to St. Louis—'

'He was living in St. Louis three years before you all moved back,' Gilpin said.

'Fine, but he's in St. Louis. Easy drive. Amy bought a gun because she was afraid—'

'Desi's okay, Nick. Nice guy,' Rhonda said. 'Don't you think? He reminds me of you, actually. Real golden boy, baby of the family.'

'I'm a twin. Not the baby. I'm actually three minutes older.'

Rhonda was clearly trying to nip at me, see if she could get a rise, but even knowing this didn't prevent the angry blood flush to my stomach every time she accused me of being a baby.

'Anyway,' Gilpin interrupted. 'Both he and his mother deny that he ever stalked Amy, or that he even had much contact with her these past years except the occasional note.'

'My wife would tell you differently. He wrote Amy for years – *years* – and then he shows up *here* for the search, Rhonda. Did you know that? He was here that first day. You talked about keeping an eye out for men inserting themselves into the investigation—'

'Desi Collings is not a suspect,' she interrupted, one hand up.

'But—'

'Desi Collins is not a suspect,' she repeated.

The news stung. I wanted to accuse her of being swayed by *Ellen Abbott*, but *Ellen Abbott* was probably best left unmentioned.

'Okay, well what about all these, these *guys* who've clogged up our tip line?' I walked over and grabbed the sheet of names and numbers that I'd carelessly tossed on the dining room table. I began reading names. 'Inserting themselves into the investigation: David Samson, Murphy Clark – those are old boyfriends – Tommy O'Hara, Tommy O'Hara, Tommy O'Hara, that's three calls, Tito Puente – that's just a dumb joke.'

'Have you phoned any of them back?' Boney asked.

'No. Isn't that your job? I don't know which are worthwhile and which are crazies. I don't have time to call some jackass pretending to be Tito Puente.'

'I wouldn't put too much emphasis on the tip line, Nick,' Rhonda said. 'It's kind of a woodwork situation. I mean, we've fielded a lot of phone calls from your old *girlfriends*. Just want to say hi. See how you are. People are strange.'

'Maybe we should get started on our questions,' Gilpin nudged.

'Right. Well, I guess we should begin with where you were the morning your wife went missing,' Boney said, suddenly apologetic, deferential. She was playing good cop, and we both knew she was playing good cop. Unless she was actually on my side. It seemed possible that sometimes a cop was just on your side. Right?

'When I was *at the beach*.'

'And you still can't recall anyone seeing you there?' Boney asked. 'It'd help us so much if we could just cross this little thing off our list.' She allowed a sympathetic silence. Rhonda could not only keep quiet, she could infuse the room with a mood of her choosing, like an octopus and its ink.

'Believe me, I'd like that as much as you. But no. I don't remember anyone.'

Boney smiled a worried smile. 'It's strange, we've mentioned –

just in passing – your being at the beach to a few people, and they all said . . . They were all surprised, let's put it that way. Said that didn't sound like you. You aren't a beach guy.'

I shrugged. 'I mean, do I go to the beach and lay out all day? No. But to sip my coffee in the morning? Sure.'

'Hey, this might help,' Boney said brightly. 'Where'd you buy your coffee that morning?' She turned to Gilpin as if to seek approval.

'Could tighten the time frame at least, right?'

'I made it here,' I said.

'Oh.' She frowned. 'That's weird, because you don't have any coffee here. Nowhere in the house. I remember thinking it was odd. A caffeine addict notices these things.'

Right, just something you happened to notice, I thought. *I knew a cop named Boney Moronie . . . Her traps are so obvious, they're clearly phony . . .*

'I had a leftover cup in the fridge I heated up.' I shrugged again: *No big deal.*

'Huh. Must have been there a long time – I noticed there's no coffee container in the trash.'

'Few days. Still tastes good.'

We both smiled at each other: *I know and you know. Game on.* I actually thought those idiotic words: *Game on.* Yet I was pleased in a way: The next part was starting.

Boney turned to Gilpin, hands on knees, and gave a little nod. Gilpin chewed his lip some more, then finally pointed: toward the ottoman, the end table, the living room now righted. 'See, here's our problem, Nick,' he started. 'We've seen dozens of home invasions—'

'Dozens upon dozens upon dozens,' Boney interrupted.

'Many home invasions. This – all this area right there, in the living room – remember it? The upturned ottoman, the overturned table, the vase on the floor' – he slapped down a photo of the scene in front of me – 'this whole area, it was supposed to look like a struggle, right?'

My head expanded and snapped back into place. *Stay calm.* 'Supposed to?'

'It looked wrong,' Gilpin continued. 'From the second we saw it. To be honest, the whole thing looked staged. First of all, there's the fact that it was all centered in this one spot. Why wasn't anything messed up *anywhere* but this room? It's odd.' He proffered another photo, a close-up. 'And look here, at this pile of books. They should be in front of the end table – the end table is where they were stacked, right?'

I nodded.

'So when the end table was knocked over, they should have spilled mostly in front of it, following the trajectory of the falling table. Instead, they're back behind it, as if someone swept them off *before* knocking over the table.'

I stared dumbly at the photo.

'And watch this. This is very curious to me,' Gilpin continued. He pointed at three slender antique frames on the mantelpiece. He stomped heavily, and they all flopped facedown immediately. 'But somehow they stayed upright through everything else.'

He showed a photo of the frames upright. I had been hoping – even after they caught my Houston's dinner slipup – that they were dumb cops, cops from the movies, local rubes aiming to please, trusting the local guy: *Whatever you say, buddy.* I didn't get dumb cops.

'I don't know what you want me to say,' I mumbled. 'It's totally – I just don't know what to think about this. I just want to find my wife.'

'So do we, Nick, so do we,' Rhonda said. 'But here's another thing. The ottoman – remember how it was flipped upside down?' She patted the squatty ottoman, pointed at its four peg legs, each only an inch high. 'See, this thing is bottom-heavy because of those tiny legs. The cushion practically sits on the floor. Try to push it over.' I hesitated. 'Go on, try it,' Boney urged.

I gave it a push, but it slid across the carpet instead of turning over. I nodded. I agreed. It was bottom-heavy.

'Seriously, get down there if you need to, and knock that thing upside down,' Boney ordered.

I knelt down, pushed from lower and lower angles, finally put a hand underneath the ottoman, and flipped it. Even then it lifted up, one side hovering, and fell back into place; I finally had to pick it up and turn it over manually.

'Weird, huh?' Boney said, not sounding all that puzzled.

'Nick, you do any housecleaning the day your wife went missing?' Gilpin asked.

'No.'

'Okay, because the tech did a Luminol sweep, and I'm sorry to tell you, the kitchen floor lit up. A good amount of blood was spilled there.'

'Amy's type – *B positive*,' Boney interrupted. 'And I'm not talking a little cut, I'm talking *blood*.'

'Oh my God.' A clot of heat appeared in the middle of my chest. 'But—'

'Yes, so your wife made it out of this room,' Gilpin said. 'Somehow, in theory, she made it into the kitchen – without disturbing any of those gewgaws on that table just outside the kitchen – and then she collapsed in the kitchen, where she lost a lot of blood.'

'And then someone carefully mopped it up,' Rhonda said, watching me.

'Wait. Wait. Why would someone try to hide blood but then mess up the living room—'

'We'll figure that out, don't worry, Nick,' Rhonda said quietly.

'I don't get it, I just don't—'

'Let's sit down,' Boney said. She pointed me toward a dining room chair. 'You eat anything yet? Want a sandwich, something?'

I shook my head. Boney was taking turns playing different female characters: powerful woman, doting caregiver, to see what got the best results.

'How's your marriage, Nick?' Rhonda asked. 'I mean, five years, that's not far from the seven-year itch.'

'The marriage was fine,' I repeated. 'It's fine. Not perfect, but good, good.'

She wrinkled her nose: *You lie.*

'You think she might have run off?' I asked, too hopefully. 'Made this look like a crime scene and took off? Runaway-wife thing?'

Boney began ticking off reasons no: 'She hasn't used her cell, she hasn't used her credit cards, ATM cards. She made no major cash withdrawals in the weeks before.'

'And there's the blood,' Gilpin added. 'I mean, again, I don't want to sound harsh, but the amount of blood spilled? That would take some serious ... I mean, I couldn't have done it to myself. I'm talking some deep wounds there. Your wife got nerves of steel?'

'Yes. She does.' She also had a deep phobia of blood, but I'd wait and let the brilliant detectives figure that out.

'It seems extremely unlikely,' Gilpin said. 'If she were to wound herself that seriously, why would she mop it up?'

'So really, let's be honest, Nick,' Boney said, leaning over on her knees so she could make eye contact with me as I stared at the floor. 'How was your marriage currently? We're on your side, but we need the truth. The only thing that makes you look bad is you holding out on us.'

'We've had bumps.' I saw Amy in the bedroom that last night, her face mottled with the red hivey splotches she got when she was angry. She was spitting out the words – mean, wild words – and I was listening to her, trying to accept the words because they were true, they were technically true, everything she said.

'Describe the bumps for us,' Boney said.

'Nothing specific, just disagreements. I mean, Amy is a blow-stack. She bottles up a bunch of little stuff and – whoom! – but then it's over. We never went to bed angry.'

'Not Wednesday night?' Boney asked.

'Never,' I lied.

'Is it money, what you mostly argue about?'

'I can't even think what we'd argue about. Just stuff.'

'What stuff was it the night she went missing?' Gilpin said

it with a sideways grin, like he'd uttered the most unbelievable *gotcha*.

'Like I told you, there was the lobster.'

'What else? I'm sure you didn't scream about the lobster for a whole hour.'

At that point Bleecker waddled partway down the stairs and peered through the railings.

'Other household stuff, too. Married-couple stuff. The cat box,' I said. 'Who would clean the cat box.'

'You were in a screaming argument about a cat box,' Boney said.

'You know, the principle of the thing. I work a lot of hours, and Amy doesn't, and I think it would be good for her if she did some basic home maintenance. Just basic upkeep.'

Gilpin jolted like an invalid woken from an afternoon nap. 'You're an old-fashioned guy, right? I'm the same way. I tell my wife all the time, "I don't know how to iron, I don't know how to do the dishes. I can't cook. So, sweetheart, I'll catch the bad guys, that I can do, and you throw some clothes in the washer now and then." Rhonda, you were married, did you do the domestic stuff at home?'

Boney looked believably annoyed. 'I catch bad guys too, idiot.'

Gilpin rolled his eyes toward me; I almost expected him to make a joke – *sounds like* someone's *on the rag* – the guy was laying it on so thick.

Gilpin rubbed his vulpine jaw. 'So you just wanted a housewife,' he said to me, making the proposition seem reasonable.

'I wanted – I wanted whatever Amy wanted. I really didn't care.' I appealed to Boney now, Detective Rhonda Boney with the sympathetic air that seemed at least partly authentic. (*It's not*, I reminded myself.) 'Amy couldn't decide what to do here. She couldn't find a job, and she wasn't interested in The Bar. Which is fine, if you want to stay home, that's fine, I said. But when she stayed home, she was unhappy too. And she'd wait for me to fix it. It was like I was in charge of her happiness.'

Boney said nothing, gave me a face expressionless as water.

'And, I mean, it's fun to be hero for a while, be the white knight, but it doesn't really work for long. I couldn't *make* her be happy. She didn't want to be happy. So I thought if she started taking charge of a few practical things—'

'Like the cat box,' said Boney.

'Yeah, clean the cat box, get some groceries, call a plumber to fix the drip that drove her crazy.'

'Wow, that sounds like a real happiness plan there. Lotta yuks.'

'But my point was, *do something*. Whatever it is, do something. Make the most of the situation. Don't sit and wait for me to fix everything for you.' I was speaking loudly, I realized, and I sounded almost angry, certainly righteous, but it was such a relief. I'd started with a lie – the cat box – and turned that into a surprising burst of pure truth, and I realized why criminals talked too much, because it feels so good to tell your story to a stranger, someone who won't call bullshit, someone forced to listen to your side. (Someone *pretending* to listen to your side, I corrected.)

'So the move back to Missouri?' Boney said. 'You moved Amy here against her wishes?'

'Against her wishes? No. We did what we had to do. I had no job, Amy had no job, my mom was sick. I'd do the same for Amy.'

'That's nice of you to *say*,' Boney muttered. And suddenly she reminded me exactly of Amy: the damning below-breath retorts uttered at the perfect level, so I was pretty sure I heard them but couldn't swear to it. And if I asked what I was supposed to ask – *What did you say?* – she'd always say the same: *Nothing.* I glared at Boney, my mouth tight, and then I thought: *Maybe this is part of the plan, to see how you act toward angry, dissatisfied women.* I tried to make myself smile, but it only seemed to repulse her more.

'And you're able to afford this, Amy working, not working, whatever, you could swing it financially?' Gilpin asked.

'We've had some money problems of late,' I said. 'When we first married, Amy was wealthy, like extremely wealthy.'

'Right,' said Boney, 'those *Amazing Amy* books.'

'Yeah, they made a ton of money in the eighties and nineties. But the publisher dropped them. Said *Amy* had run her course. And everything went south. Amy's parents had to borrow money from us to stay afloat.'

'From your wife, you mean?'

'Right, fine. And then we used most of the last of Amy's trust fund to buy the bar, and I've been supporting us since.'

'So when you married Amy, she was very wealthy,' Gilpin said. I nodded. I was thinking of the hero narrative: the husband who sticks by his wife through the horrible decline in her family's circumstances.

'So you had a very nice lifetstyle.'

'Yeah, it was great, it was awesome.'

'And now she's near broke, and you're dealing with a very different lifestyle than what you married into. What you signed on for.'

I realized my narrative was completely wrong.

'Because, okay, we've been going over your finances, Nick, and dang, they don't look good,' Gilpin started, almost turning the accusation into a concern, a worry.

'The Bar is doing decent,' I said. 'It usually takes a new business three or four years to get out of the red.'

'It's those credit cards that got my attention,' Boney said. 'Two hundred and twelve thousand dollars in credit-card debt. I mean, it took my breath away.' She fanned a stack of red-ink statements at me.

My parents were fanatics about credit cards – used only for special purposes, paid off every month. *We don't buy what we can't pay for*; it was the Dunne family motto.

'We don't – I don't, at least – but I don't think Amy would— Can I see those?' I stuttered, just as a low-flying bomber rattled the windowpanes. A plant on the mantel promptly lost five pretty purple leaves. Forced into silence for ten brain-shaking seconds, we all watched the leaves flutter to the ground.

'Yet this great brawl we're supposed to believe happened in here, and not a petal was on the floor then,' Gilpin muttered disgustedly.

I took the papers from Boney and saw my name, only my name, versions of it – Nick Dunne, Lance Dunne, Lance N. Dunne, Lance Nicholas Dunne, on a dozen different credit cards, balances from $62.78 to $45,602.33, all in various states of lateness, terse threats printed in ominous lettering across the top: pay now.

'Holy fuck! This is, like, identity theft or something!' I said. 'They're not mine. I mean, freakin' look at some of this stuff: I don't even golf.' Someone had paid over seven thousand dollars for a set of clubs. 'Anyone can tell you: I *really* don't golf.' I tried to make it sound self-effacing – *yet another thing I'm not good at* – but the detectives weren't biting.

'You know Noelle Hawthorne?' Boney asked. 'The friend of Amy's you told us to check out?'

'Wait, I want to talk about the bills, because they are not mine,' I said. 'I mean, please, seriously, we need to track this down.'

'We'll track it down, no problem,' Boney said, expressionless. 'Noelle Hawthorne?'

'Right. I told you to check her out because she's been all over town, wailing about Amy.'

Boney arched an eyebrow. 'You seem angry about that.'

'No, like I told you, she seems a little too broken up, like in a fake way. Ostentatious. Attention-seeking. A little obsessed.'

'We talked to Noelle,' Boney said. 'Says your wife was extremely troubled by the marriage, was upset about the money stuff, that she worried you'd married her for her money. She says your wife worried about your temper.'

'I don't know why Noelle would say that; I don't think she and Amy ever exchanged more than five words.'

'That's funny, because the Hawthornes' living room is

covered with photos of Noelle and your wife.' Boney frowned. I frowned too: actual real pictures of her and Amy?

Boney continued: 'At the St. Louis zoo last October, on a picnic with the triplets, on a weekend float trip this past June. As in *last month*.'

'Amy has never uttered the name Noelle in the entire time we've lived here. I'm serious.' I scanned my brain over this past June and came upon a weekend I went away with Andie, told Amy I was doing a boys' trip to St. Louis. I'd returned home to find her pink-cheeked and angry, claiming a weekend of bad cable and bored reading on the deck. And she was on a float trip? No. I couldn't think of anything Amy would care for less than the typical midwestern float trip: beers bobbing in coolers tied to canoes, loud music, drunk frat boys, campgrounds dotted with vomit. 'Are you sure it was my wife in those photos?'

They gave each other a *he serious?* look.

'Nick,' Boney said. 'We have no reason to believe that the woman in the photos who looks exactly like your wife and who Noelle Hawthorne, a mother of three, your wife's best friend here in town, says is your wife, is not your wife.'

'Your wife who – I should say – according to Noelle, you married for money,' Gilpin added.

'I'm not joking,' I said. 'Anyone these days can doctor photos on a laptop.'

'Okay, so a minute ago you were sure Desi Collings was involved, and now you've moved on to Noelle Hawthorne,' Gilpin said. 'It seems like you're really casting about for someone to blame.'

'Besides me? Yes, I am. Look, I did not marry Amy for her money. You really should talk more with Amy's parents. They know me, they know my character.' *They don't know everything*, I thought, my stomach seizing. Boney was watching me; she looked sort of sorry for me. Gilpin didn't even seem to be listening.

'You bumped up the life insurance coverage on your wife to one-point-two million,' Gilpin said with mock weariness.

He even pulled a hand over his long, thin-jawed face.

'Amy did that herself!' I said quickly. The cops both just looked at me and waited. 'I mean, I filed the paperwork, but it was Amy's idea. She insisted. I swear, I couldn't care less, but Amy said – she said, given the change in her income, it made her feel more secure or something, or it was a smart business decision. Fuck, I don't know, I don't know why she wanted it. I didn't ask her to.'

'Two months ago, someone did a search on your laptop,' Boney continued. '*Body Float Mississippi River*. Can you explain that?'

I took two deep breaths, nine seconds to pull myself together.

'God, that was just a dumb book idea,' I said. 'I was thinking about writing a book.'

'Huh,' Boney replied.

'Look, here's what I think is happening,' I began. 'I think a lot of people watch these news programs where the husband is always this awful guy who kills his wife, and they are seeing me through that lens, and some really innocent, normal things are being twisted. This is turning into a witch hunt.'

'That's how you explain those credit-card bills?' Gilpin asked.

'I told you, I can't explain the fucking credit-card bills because I have nothing to do with them. It's your fucking job to figure out where they came from!'

They sat silent, side by side, waiting.

'What is currently being done to find my wife?' I asked. 'What leads are you exploring, besides me?'

The house began shaking, the sky ripped, and through the back window, we could see a jet shooting past, right over the river, buzzing us.

'F-10,' Rhonda said.

'Nah, too small,' Gilpin said. 'It's got to be—'

'It's an F-10.'

Boney leaned toward me, hands entwined. 'It's our job to make sure you are in the hundred percent clear, Nick,' she said. 'I know you want that too. Now if you can just help us out with the few little tangles – because that's what they are, they keep tripping us up.'

'Maybe it's time I got a lawyer.'

The cops exchanged another look, as if they'd settled a bet.

AMY ELLIOTT DUNNE
OCTOBER 21, 2011

– Diary entry –

Nick's mom is dead. I haven't been able to write because Nick's mom is dead, and her son has come unmoored. Sweet, tough Maureen. She was up and moving around until days before she died, refusing to discuss any sort of slowdown. 'I just want to live until I can't anymore,' she said. She'd gotten into knitting caps for other chemo patients (she herself was *done done done* after one round, no interest in prolonging life if it meant 'more tubes'), so I'll remember her always surrounded by bright knots of wool: red and yellow and green, and her fingers moving, the needles click-clacking while she talked in her contented-cat voice, all deep, sleepy purr.

And then one morning in September she woke but didn't really wake, didn't become Maureen. She was a bird-sized woman overnight, that fast, all wrinkles and shell, her eyes darting around the room, unable to place anything, including herself. So then came the hospice, a gently lit, cheerful place with paintings of women in bonnets and rolling hills of bounty, and snack machines, and small coffees. The hospice was not expected to fix her or help her but just to make sure she died comfortably, and just three days later, she did. Very matter-of-fact, the way Maureen would have wanted it (although I'm sure she would have rolled her eyes at that phrase: *the way Maureen would have wanted it*).

Her wake was modest but nice – with hundreds of people, her look-alike sister from Omaha bustling by proxy, pouring coffee and Baileys and handing out cookies and telling funny stories about Mo. We buried her on a gusty, warm morning, Go and Nick leaning in to each other as I stood nearby, feeling intrusive. That night in bed, Nick let me put my arms around him, his back to me, but after a few minutes he got up, whispered, 'Got to get some air,' and left the house.

His mother had always *mothered* him – she insisted on coming by once a week and ironing for us, and when she was done ironing, she'd say, 'I'll just help tidy,' and after she'd left, I'd look in the fridge and find she'd peeled and sliced his grapefruit for him, put the pieces in a snap-top container, and then I'd open the bread and discover all the crusts had been cut away, each slice returned half naked. I am married to a thirty-four-year-old man who is still offended by bread crusts.

But I tried to do the same those first weeks after his mom passed. I snipped the bread crusts, I ironed his T-shirts, I baked a blueberry pie from his mom's recipe. 'I don't need to be babied, really, Amy,' he said as he stared at the loaf of skinned breads. 'I let my mom do it because it made her happy, but I know you don't like that nurturing stuff.'

So we're back to black squares. Sweet, doting, loving Nick is gone. Gruff, peeved, angry Nick is back. You are supposed to lean on your spouse in hard times, but Nick seems to have gone even further away. He is a mama's boy whose mama is dead. He doesn't want anything to do with me.

He uses me for sex when he needs to. He presses me against a table or over the back of the bed and fucks me, silent until the last few moments, those few quick grunts, and then he releases me, he puts a palm on the small of my back, his one gesture of intimacy, and he says something that is supposed to make it seem like a game: 'You're so sexy, sometimes I can't control myself.' But he says it in a dead voice.

Quiz: Your husband, with whom you once shared a wonderful sex life, has turned distant and cold – he only wants sex his way, on his time. You:

a) Withhold sex further – he's not going to win this game!

b) Cry and whine and demand answers he's not yet ready to give, further alienating him.
c) Have faith that this is just a bump in a long marriage – he is in a dark place – so try to be understanding and wait it out.

Answer: C. Right?

It bothers me that my marriage is disintegrating and I don't know what to do. You'd think my parents, the double psychologists, would be the obvious people to talk to, but I have too much pride. They would not be good for marital advice: They are soul mates, remember? They are all peaks, no valleys – a single, infinite burst of marital ecstasy. I can't tell them I am screwing up the one thing I have left: my marriage. They'd somehow write another book, a fictional rebuke in which Amazing Amy celebrated the most fantastic, fulfilling, bump-free little marriage ever ... *because she put her mind to it.*

But I worry. All the time. I know I'm already too old for my husband's tastes. Because I used to be his ideal, six years ago, and so I've heard his ruthless comments about women nearing forty: how pathetic he finds them, overdressed, out at bars, oblivious to their lack of appeal. He'd come back from a night out drinking, and I'd ask him how the bar was, whatever bar, and he'd so often say: 'Totally inundated by Lost Causes,' his code for women my age. At the time, a girl barely in her thirties, I'd smirked along with him as if that would never happen to me. Now I am his Lost Cause, and he's trapped with me, and maybe that's why he's so angry.

I've been indulging in toddler therapy. I walk over to Noelle's every day and I let her triplets paw at me. The little plump hands in my hair, the sticky breath on my neck. You can understand why women always threaten to devour children: *She is just to eat! I could eat him with a spoon!* Although watching her three children toddle to her, sleep-stained from their nap, rubbing their eyes while they make their way to Mama, little hands touching her knee or arm as if she were home base, as if they knew they were safe ... it hurts me sometimes to watch.

Yesterday I had a particularly needful afternoon at Noelle's, so maybe that's why I did something stupid.

Nick comes home and finds me in the bedroom, fresh from a shower, and pretty soon he is pushing me against the wall, pushing himself inside me. When he is done and releases me, I can see the wet kiss of my mouth against the blue paint. As he sits on the edge of the bed, panting, he says, 'Sorry about that. I just needed you.'

Not looking at me.

I go to him and put my arms around him, pretending what we'd just done was normal, a pleasant marital ritual, and I say, 'I've been thinking.'

'Yeah, what's that?'

'Well, now might be the right time. To start a family. Try to get pregnant.' I know it's crazy even as I say it, but I can't help myself – I have become the crazy woman who wants to get pregnant because it will save her marriage.

It's humbling, to become the very thing you once mocked.

He jerks away from me. 'Now? Now is about the worst time to start a family, Amy. You have no job—'

'I know, but I'd want to stay home with the baby anyway at first—'

'My mom just died, Amy.'

'And this would be new life, a new start.'

He grips me by both arms and looks me right in the eye for the first time in a week. 'Amy, I think you think that now that my mom is dead, we'll just frolic back to New York and have some babies, and you'll get your old life back. But we don't have enough *money*. We barely have enough money for the two of us to live *here*. You can't imagine how much pressure I feel, every day, to fix this mess we're in. To fucking *provide*. I can't handle you and me *and* a few kids. You'll want to give them everything you had growing up, and *I can't*. No private schools for the little Dunnes, no tennis and violin lessons, no summer homes. You'd hate how poor we'd be. You'd hate it.'

'I'm not that shallow, Nick—'

'You really think we're in a great place right now, to have kids?'

It is the closest we've gotten to discussing our marriage, and I can see he already regrets saying something.

'We're under a lot of pressure, baby,' I say. 'We've had a few bumps, and I know a lot of it is my fault. I just feel so at loose ends here ...'

'So we're going to be one of those couples who has a kid to fix their marriage? Because that always works out so well.'

'We'll have a baby because—'

His eyes go dark, canine, and he grabs me by the arms again.

'Just ... No, Amy. Not right now. I can't take one more bit of stress. I can't handle one more thing to worry about. I am cracking under the pressure. I will snap.'

For once I know he's telling the truth.

The first forty-eight hours are key in any investigation. Amy had been gone, now, almost a week. A candlelight vigil would be held this evening in Tom Sawyer Park, which, according to the press, was 'a favorite place of Amy Elliott Dunne's.' (I'd never known Amy to set foot in the park; despite the name, it is not remotely quaint. Generic, bereft of trees, with a sandbox that's always full of animal feces; it is utterly un-Twainy.) In the last twenty-four hours, the story had gone national – it was everywhere, just like that.

God bless the faithful Elliotts. Marybeth phoned me last night, as I was trying to recover from the bombshell police interrogation. My mother-in-law had seen the *Ellen Abbott* show and pronounced the woman 'an opportunistic ratings whore.' Nevertheless, we'd spent most of today strategizing how to handle the media.

The media (my former clan, my people!) was shaping its story, and the media loved the *Amazing Amy* angle and the long-married Elliotts. No snarky commentary on the dismantling of the series or the authors' near-bankruptcy – right now it was all hearts and flowers for the Elliotts. The media loved them.

Me, not so much. The media was already turning up *items of concern*. Not only the stuff that had been leaked – my lack of alibi, the possibly 'staged' crime scene – but actual personality traits. They reported that back in high school, I'd never dated one girl longer than a few months and thus was clearly a ladies' man. They found out we had my father in Comfort Hill and that I rarely visited, and thus I was an ingrate dad-abandoner. 'It's a problem – they don't like you,'

Go said after every bit of news coverage. 'It's a real, real problem, Lance.' The media had resurrected my first name, which I'd hated since grade school, stifled at the start of every school year when the teacher called roll: 'It's Nick, I go by Nick!' Every September, an opening-day rite: 'Nick-I-go-by-Nick!' Always some smart-ass kid would spend recess parading around like a mincing gallant: 'Hi, I'm Laaaance,' in a flowy-shirted voice. Then it would be forgotten again until the following year.

But not now. Now it was all over the news, the dreaded three-name judgment reserved for serial killers and assassins – Lance Nicholas Dunne – and there was no one I could interrupt.

Rand and Marybeth Elliott, Go and I carpooled to the vigil together. It was unclear how much information the Elliotts were receiving, how many damning updates about their son-in-law. I knew they were aware of the 'staged' scene: 'I'm going to get some of my own people in there, and they'll tell us just the opposite – that it clearly *was* the scene of a struggle,' Rand said confidently. 'The truth is malleable; you just need to pick the right expert.'

Rand didn't know about the other stuff, the credit cards and the life insurance and the blood and Noelle, my wife's bitter best friend with the damning claims: abuse, greed, fear. She was booked on *Ellen Abbott* tonight, post-vigil. Noelle and Ellen could be mutually disgusted by me for the viewing audience.

Not everyone was repulsed by me. In the past week, The Bar's business was booming: Hundreds of customers packed in to sip beers and nibble popcorn at the place owned by Lance Nicholas Dunne, the maybe-killer. Go had to hire four new kids to tend The Bar; she'd dropped by once and said she couldn't go again, couldn't stand seeing how packed it was, fucking gawkers, ghouls, all drinking our booze and swapping stories about me. It was disgusting. Still, Go reasoned, the money would be helpful if . . .

If. Amy gone six days, and we were all thinking in *if*s.

We approached the park in a car gone silent except for Marybeth's constant nail drumming on the window.

'Feels almost like a double date.' Rand laughed, the laughter curving toward the hysterical: high-pitched and squeaky. Rand Elliott, genius psychologist, best-selling author, friend to all, was unraveling. Marybeth had taken to self-medication: shots of clear liquor administered with absolute precision, enough to take the edge off but stay sharp. Rand, on the other hand, was literally losing his head; I half expected to see it shoot off his shoulders on a jack-in-the-box spring – cuckooooooo! Rand's schmoozy nature had turned manic: He got desperately chummy with everyone he met, wrapping his arms around cops, reporters, volunteers. He was particularly tight with our Days Inn 'liaison,' a gawky, shy kid named Donnie who Rand liked to razz and inform he was doing so. 'Ah, I'm just razzing you, Donnie,' he'd say, and Donnie would break into a joyous grin.

'Can't that kid go get validation somewhere else?' I groused to Go the other night. She said I was just jealous that my father figure liked someone better. I was.

Marybeth patted Rand's back as we walked toward the park, and I thought about how much I wanted someone to do that, just a quick touch, and I suddenly let out a gasp-sob, one quick teary moan. I wanted someone, but I wasn't sure if it was Andie or Amy.

'Nick?' Go said. She raised a hand toward my shoulder, but I shrugged her off.

'Sorry. Wow, sorry for that,' I said. 'Weird outburst, very un-Dunne-y.'

'No problem. We're both coming undone-y,' Go said, and looked away. Since discovering my *situation* – which is what we'd taken to calling my infidelity – she'd gotten a bit removed, her eyes distant, her face a constant mull. I was trying very hard not to resent it.

As we entered the park, the camera crews were everywhere,

not just local anymore but network. The Dunnes and the Elliotts walked along the perimeter of the crowd, Rand smiling and nodding like a visiting dignitary. Boney and Gilpin appeared almost immediately, took to our heels like friendly pointer dogs; they were becoming familiar, furniture, which was clearly the idea. Boney was wearing the same clothes she wore to any public event: a sensible black skirt, a gray-striped blouse, barrettes clipping either side of her limp hair. *I got a girl named Bony Moronie* ... The night was steamy; under each of Boney's armpits was a dark smiley face of perspiration. She actually grinned at me as if yesterday, the accusations – they were accusations, weren't they? – hadn't happened.

The Elliotts and I filed up the steps to a rickety makeshift stage. I looked back toward my twin and she nodded at me and pantomimed a big breath, and I remembered to breathe. Hundreds of faces were turned toward us, along with clicking, flashing cameras. *Don't smile*, I told myself. *Do not smile.*

From the front of dozens of *Find Amy* T-shirts, my wife studied me.

Go had said I needed to make a speech ('You need some humanizing, fast') so I did, I walked up to the microphone. It was too low, mid-belly, and I wrestled with it a few seconds, and it raised only an inch, the kind of malfunction that would normally infuriate me, but I could no longer be infuriated in public, so I took a breath and leaned down and read the words that my sister had written for me: 'My wife, Amy Dunne, has been missing for almost a week. I cannot possibly convey the anguish our family feels, the deep hole in our lives left by Amy's disappearance. Amy is the love of my life, she is the heart of her family. For those who have yet to meet her, she is funny, and charming, and kind. She is wise and warm. She is my helpmate and partner in every way.'

I looked up into the crowd and, like magic, spotted Andie, a disgusted look on her face, and I quickly glanced back at my notes.

'Amy is the woman I want to grow old with, and I know this will happen.'

217

PAUSE. BREATHE. NO SMILE. Go had actually written the words on my index card. *Happen happen happen*. My voice echoed out through the speakers, rolling toward the river.

'We ask you to contact us with any information. We light candles tonight in the hope she comes home soon and safely. I love you, Amy.'

I kept my eyes moving anywhere but Andie. The park sparkled with candles. A moment of silence was supposed to be observed, but babies were crying, and one stumbling homeless man kept asking loudly, 'Hey, what is this about? What's it for?' and someone would whisper Amy's name, and the guy would say louder, 'What? It's for *what*?'

From the middle of the crowd, Noelle Hawthorne began moving forward, her triplets affixed, one on a hip, the other two clinging to her skirt, all looking ludicrously tiny to a man who spent no time around children. Noelle forced the crowd to part for her and the children, marching right to the edge of the podium, where she looked up at me. I glared at her – the woman had maligned me – and then I noticed for the first time the swell in her belly and realized she was pregnant again. For one second, my mouth dropped – four kids under four, sweet Jesus! – and later, that look would be analyzed and debated, most people believing it was a one-two punch of anger and fear.

'Hey, *Nick*.' Her voice caught in the half-raised microphone and boomed out to the audience.

I started to fumble with the mike, but couldn't find the off switch.

'I just wanted to see your face,' she said, and burst into tears. A wet sob rolled out over the audience, everyone rapt. 'Where is she? What have you done with Amy? What have you done with your wife!'

Wife, wife, her voice echoed. Two of her alarmed children began to wail.

Noelle couldn't talk for a second, she was crying so hard, she was wild, furious, and she grabbed the microphone stand

and yanked the whole thing down to her level. I debated grabbing it back but *knew* I could do nothing toward this woman in the maternity dress with the three toddlers. I scanned the crowd for Mike Hawthorne – *control your wife* – but he was nowhere. Noelle turned to address the crowd.

'I am Amy's best friend!' *Friend friend friend*. The words boomed out all over the park along with her children's keening. 'Despite my best efforts, the police don't seem to be taking me seriously. So I'm taking our cause to this town, this town that Amy loved, that loved her back! This man, Nick Dunne, needs to answer some questions. He needs to tell us what he did to his wife!'

Boney darted from the side of the stage to reach her, and Noelle turned, and the two locked eyes. Boney made a frantic chopping motion at her throat: *Stop talking!*

'His *pregnant* wife!'

And no one could see the candles anymore, because the flashbulbs were going berserk. Next to me, Rand made a noise like a balloon squeak. Down below me, Boney put her fingers between her eyebrows as if stanching a headache. I was seeing everyone in frantic strobe shots that matched my pulse.

I looked out into the crowd for Andie, saw her staring at me, her face pink and twisted, her cheeks damp, and as we caught each other's eyes, she mouthed, 'Asshole!' and stumbled back away through the crowd.

'We should go.' My sister, suddenly beside me, whispering in my ear, tugging at my arm. The cameras flashing at me as I stood like some Frankenstein's monster, fearful and agitated by the villager torches. *Flash, flash*. We started moving, breaking into two parts: my sister and I fleeing toward Go's car, the Elliotts standing with jaws agape, on the platform, left behind, save yourselves. The reporters pelted the question over and over at me. *Nick, was Amy pregnant? Nick, were you upset Amy was pregnant?* Me, streaking out of the park, ducking like I was caught in hail: *Pregnant, pregnant, pregnant*, the word pulsing in the summer night in time to the cicadas.

AMY ELLIOTT DUNNE
FEBRUARY 15, 2012

– *Diary entry* –

What a strange time this is. I have to think that way, try to examine it from a distance: Ha-*ha*, what an odd period this will be to look back on, won't I be amused when I'm eighty, dressed in faded lavender, a wise, amused figure swilling martinis, and won't this make a *story*? A strange, awful story of something I survived.

Because something is horribly wrong with my husband, of that I am sure now. Yes, he's mourning his mother, but this is something more. It feels directed at me, not a sadness but … I can feel him watching me sometimes, and I look up and see his face twisted in disgust, like he's walked in on me doing something awful, instead of just eating cereal in the morning or combing my hair at night. He's so angry, so unstable, I've been wondering if his moods are linked to something physical – one of those wheat allergies that turn people mad, or a colony of mold spores that has clogged his brain.

I came downstairs the other night and found him at the dining room table, his head in his hands, looking at a pile of credit-card bills. I watched my husband, all alone, under the spotlight of a chandelier. I wanted to go to him, to sit down with him and figure it out like partners. But I didn't, I knew that would piss him off. I sometimes wonder if that is at the root of his distaste for me: He's let me see his shortcomings, and he hates me for knowing them.

He shoved me. Hard. Two days ago, he shoved me, and I fell and banged my head against the kitchen island and

I couldn't see for three seconds. I don't really know what to say about it. It was more shocking than painful. I was telling him I could get a job, something freelance, so we could start a family, have a real life …

'What do you call this?' he said.

Purgatory, I thought. I stayed silent.

'What do you call this, Amy? Huh? What do you call this? This isn't life, according to Miss Amazing?'

'It's not *my* idea of life,' I said, and he took three big steps toward me, and I thought: *He looks like he's going to …* And then he was slamming against me and I was falling.

We both gasped. He held his fist in the other hand and looked like he might cry. He was beyond sorry, he was aghast. But here's the thing I want to be clear on: I knew what I was doing, I was punching every button on him. I was watching him coil tighter and tighter – I wanted him to finally *say* something, *do* something. Even if it's bad, even if it's the worst, *do something, Nick.* Don't leave me here like a ghost.

I just didn't realize he was going to do *that*.

I've never considered what I would do if my husband attacked me, because I haven't exactly run in the wife-beating crowd. (I know, Lifetime movie, I know: Violence crosses all socioeconomic barriers. But still: Nick?) I sound glib. It just seems so incredibly ludicrous: I am a battered wife. *Amazing Amy and the Domestic Abuser.*

He did apologize profusely. (Does anyone do anything *profusely* except apologize? Sweat, I guess.) He's agreed to consider counseling, which was something I never thought could happen. Which is good. He's such a good man, at his core, that I am willing to write it off, to believe it truly was a sick anomaly, brought on by the strain we're both under. I forget sometimes, that as much stress as I feel, Nick feels it too: He bears the burden of having brought me here, he feels the strain of wanting mopey me to be content, and for a man like Nick – who believes strongly in an up-by-the-bootstraps sort of happiness – that can be infuriating.

So the hard shove, so quick, then done, it didn't scare me

in itself. What scared me was the look on his face as I lay on the floor blinking, my head ringing. It was the look on his face as he restrained himself from taking another jab. How much he wanted to shove me again. How hard it was not to. How he's been looking at me since: guilt, and disgust at the guilt. Absolute disgust.

Here's the darkest part. I drove out to the mall yesterday, where about half the town buys drugs, and it's as easy as picking up a prescription; I know because Noelle told me: Her husband goes there to purchase the occasional joint. I didn't want a joint, though, I wanted a gun, just in case. In case things with Nick go really wrong. I didn't realize until I was almost there that it was Valentine's Day. It was Valentine's Day and I was going to buy a gun and then cook my husband dinner. And I thought to myself: *Nick's dad was right about you. You are a dumb bitch. Because if you think your husband is going to hurt you, you* leave. *And yet you can't leave your husband, who's mourning his dead mother. You can't. You'd have to be a bibilically awful woman to do that,* unless *something were truly wrong. You'd have to really believe your husband was going to hurt you.*

But I don't really think Nick would hurt me.

I just would feel safer with a gun.

NICK DUNNE
SIX DAYS GONE

Go pushed me into the car and peeled away from the park. We flew past Noelle, who was walking with Boney and Gilpin toward their cruiser, her carefully dressed triplets bumping along behind her like kite ribbons. We screeched past the mob: hundreds of faces, a fleshy pointillism of anger aimed right at me. We ran away, basically. Technically.

'Wow, ambush,' Go muttered.

'Ambush?' I repeated, brain-stunned.

'You think that was an accident, Nick? Triplet Cunt already made her statement to the police. Nothing about the pregnancy.'

'Or they're doling out bombshells a little at a time.'

Boney and Gilpin had already heard my wife was pregnant and decided to make it a strategy. They clearly really believed I killed her.

'Noelle will be on every cable broadcast for the next week, talking about how you're a murderer and she's Amy's best friend out for justice. Publicity whore. Publicity fucking *whore*.'

I pressed my face against the window, slumped in my seat. Several news vans followed us. We drove silently, Go's breath slowing down. I watched the river, a tree branch bobbing its way south.

'Nick?' she finally said. 'Is it – uh ... Do you—'

'I don't know, Go. Amy didn't say anything to me. If she was pregnant, why would she tell Noelle and not tell me?'

'Why would she try to get a gun and not tell you?' Go said. 'None of this makes sense.'

*

223

We retreated to Go's – the camera crews would be swarming my house – and as soon as I walked in the door my cell phone rang, the real one. It was the Elliotts. I sucked in some air, ducked into my old bedroom, then answered.

'I need to ask you this, Nick.' It was Rand, the TV burbling in the background. 'I need you to tell me. Did you know Amy was pregnant?'

I paused, trying to find the right way to phrase it, the unlikelihood of a pregnancy.

'Answer me, goddammit!'

Rand's volume made me get quieter. I spoke in a soft, soothing voice, a voice wearing a cardigan. 'Amy and I were not trying to get pregnant. She didn't want to be pregnant, Rand, I don't know if she ever was going to be. We weren't even ... we weren't even having relations that often. I'd be ... very surprised if she was pregnant.'

'Noelle said Amy visited the doctor to confirm the pregnancy. The police already submitted a subpoena for the records. We'll know tonight.'

I found Go in the living room, sitting with a cup of cold coffee at my mother's card table. She turned toward me just enough to show she knew I was there, but she didn't let me see me her face.

'Why do you keep lying, Nick?' she asked. 'The Elliotts are not your enemy. Shouldn't you at least tell them that it was you who didn't want kids? Why make Amy look like the bad guy?'

I swallowed the rage again. My stomach was hot with it. 'I'm exhausted, Go. Goddamn. We gotta do this now?'

'We gonna find a time that's better?'

'I did want kids. We tried for a while, no luck. We even started looking into fertility treatments. But then Amy decided she didn't want kids.'

'You told me *you* didn't.'

'I was trying to put a good face on it.'

'Oh, awesome, another lie,' Go said. 'I didn't realize you were such a ... What you're saying, Nick, it makes no sense.

I was there, at the dinner to celebrate The Bar, and Mom misunderstood, she thought you guys were announcing that you were pregnant, and it made Amy cry.'

'Well, I can't explain everything Amy ever did, Go. I don't know why, a fucking year ago, she cried like that. Okay?'

Go sat quietly, the orange of the streetlight creating a rock-star halo around her profile. 'This is going to be a real test for you, Nick,' she murmured, not looking at me. 'You've always had trouble with the truth – you always do the little fib if you think it will avoid a real argument. You've always gone the easy way. Tell Mom you went to baseball practice when you really quit the team; tell Mom you went to church when you were at a movie. It's some weird compulsion.'

'This is very different from baseball, Go.'

'It's a lot different. But you're still fibbing like a little boy. You're still desperate to have everyone think you're perfect. You never want to be the bad guy. So you tell Amy's parents she didn't want kids. You *don't* tell me you're cheating on your wife. You swear the credit cards in your name aren't yours, you swear you were hanging out at a beach when you hate the beach, you swear your marriage was happy. I just don't know what to believe right now.'

'You're kidding, right?'

'Since Amy has disappeared, all you've done is lie. It makes me worry. About what's going on.'

Complete silence for a moment.

'Go, are you saying what I think you're saying? Because if you are, something has fucking died between us.'

'Remember that game you always played with Mom when we were little: *Would you still love me if? Would you still love me if I smacked Go? Would you still love me if I robbed a bank? Would you still love me if I killed someone?*'

I said nothing. My breath was coming too fast.

'I would still love you,' Go said.

'Go, do you really need me to say it?'

She stayed silent.

'I did not kill Amy.'

She stayed silent.

'Do you believe me?' I asked.

'I love you.'

She put her hand on my shoulder and went to her bedroom, shut the door. I waited to see the light go on in the room, but it stayed dark.

Two seconds later, my cell phone rang. This time, it was the disposable cell that I needed to get rid of and couldn't because I always, always, always had to pick up for Andie. *Once a day, Nick. We need to talk once a day.*

I realized I was grinding my teeth.

I took a breath.

Far out on the edge of town were the remains of an Old West fort that was now yet another park that no one ever went to. All that was left was the two-story wooden watchtower, surrounded by rusted swing sets and teeter-totters. Andie and I had met there once, groping each other inside the shade of the watchtower.

I did three long loops around town in my mom's old car to be sure I was not tracked. It was madness to go – it wasn't yet ten o'clock – but I had no say in our rendezvous anymore. *I need to see you, Nick, tonight, right now, or I swear to you, I will lose it.* As I pulled up to the fort, I was hit by the remoteness of it and what it meant: Andie was still willing to meet me in a lonely, unlit place, me the pregnant-wife killer. As I walked toward the tower through the thick, scratchy grass, I could just see her outline in the tiny window of the wooden watchtower.

She is going to undo you, Nick. I quick-stepped the rest of the way.

An hour later I was huddled in the paparazzi-infested house, waiting. Rand said they'd know before midnight whether my wife was pregnant. When the phone rang, I grabbed it immediately only to find it was goddamn Comfort Hill. My father was gone again. The cops had been notified. As always, they made it sound as if I were the jackass. *If this happens again, we are going to have to terminate your father's stay with us.* I had a sickening chill: My dad moving in with me – two pathetic, angry bastards – it would surely make for the worst buddy comedy in the world. The ending would be a murder-suicide. Ba–dum–dum! Cue the laff track.

I was getting off the phone, peering out the back window at the river – *stay calm, Nick* – when I saw a huddled figure down by the boathouse. I thought it must be a stray reporter, but then I recognized something in those balled fists and tight shoulders. Comfort Hill was about a thirty-minute walk straight down River Road. He somehow remembered our house when he couldn't remember me.

I went outside into the darkness to see him dangling a foot over the bank, staring into the river. Less bedraggled than before, although he smelled tangy with sweat.

'Dad? What are you doing here? Everyone's worried.'

He looked at me with dark brown eyes, sharp eyes, not the glazed-milk color some elderly acquire. It would have been less disconcerting if they'd been milky.

'She told me to come,' he snapped. 'She told me to come. This is my house, I can come whenever I want.'

'You walked all the way here?'

'I can come here anytime. You may hate me, but she loves me.'

I almost laughed. Even my father was reinventing a relationship with Amy.

A few photographers on my front lawn began shooting. I had to get my dad back to the home. I could picture the article they'd have to cook up to go along with this exclusive footage: What kind of father was Bill Dunne, what kind of man did he raise? Good God, if my dad started in on one of his harangues against *the bitches* . . . I dialed Comfort Hill, and after some finagling, they sent an orderly to retrieve him. I made a display of walking him gently to the sedan, murmuring reassuringly as the photographers got their shots.

My dad. I smiled as he left. I tried to make it seem very proud-son. The reporters asked me if I killed my wife. I was retreating to the house when a cop car pulled up.

It was Boney who came to my home, braving the paparazzi, to tell me. She did it kindly, in a gentle-fingertip voice.

Amy was pregnant.

My wife was gone with my baby inside her. Boney watched me, waiting for my reaction – make it part of the police report – so I told myself, *Act correctly, don't blow it, act the way a man acts when he hears this news.* I ducked my head into my hands and muttered, *Oh God, oh God*, and while I was doing it, I saw my wife on the floor of our kitchen, her hands around her belly and her head bashed in.

AMY ELLIOTT DUNNE
JUNE 26, 2012

– Diary entry –

I have never felt more alive in my life. It is a bright blue sky day, the birds are lunatic with the warmth, the river outside is gushing past, and I am utterly alive. Scared, thrilled, but *alive*.

This morning when I woke up, Nick was gone. I sat in bed staring at the ceiling, watching the sun golden it a foot at a time, the bluebirds singing right outside our window, and I wanted to vomit. My throat was clenching and unclenching like a heart. I told myself I would not throw up, then I ran to the bathroom and threw up: bile and warm water and one small bobbing pea. As my stomach was seizing and my eyes were tearing and I was gasping for breath, I started doing the only kind of math a woman does, huddled over a toilet. I'm on the pill, but I'd also forgotten a day or two – what does it matter, I'm thirty-eight, I've been on the pill for almost two decades. I'm not going to accidentally get pregnant.

I found the tests behind a locked sheet of glass. I had to track down a harried, mustached woman to unlock the case, and point out one I wanted while she waited impatiently. She handed it to me with a clinical stare and said, 'Good luck.'

I didn't know what would be good luck: plus sign or minus sign. I drove home and read the directions three times, and I held the stick at the right angle for the right number of seconds, and then I set it on the edge of the sink and ran away like it was a bomb. Three minutes, so I turned on the radio and of course it was a Tom Petty song – is there ever a time you turn on the radio and don't hear a Tom Petty song? – so

I sang every word to 'American Girl' and then I crept back into the bathroom like the test was something I had to sneak up on, my heart beating more frantically than it should, and I was pregnant.

I was suddenly running across the summer lawn and down the street, banging on Noelle's door, and when she opened it, I burst into tears and showed her the stick and yelled, 'I'm pregnant!'

And then someone else besides me knew, and so I was scared.

Once I got back home, I had two thoughts.

One: Our anniversary is coming next week. I will use the clues as love letters, a beautiful antique wooden cradle waiting at the end. I will convince him we belong together. As a family.

Two: I wish I'd been able to get that gun.

I get frightened now, sometimes, when my husband gets home. A few weeks ago, Nick asked me to go out on the raft with him, float along in the current under a blue sky. I actually wrapped my hands around our newel post when he asked me this, I clung to it. Because I had an image of him wobbling the raft – teasing at first, laughing at my panic, and then his face going tight, determined, and me falling into the water, that muddy brown water, scratchy with sticks and sand, and him on top of me, holding me under with one strong arm, until I stopped struggling.

I can't help it. Nick married me when I was a young, rich, beautiful woman, and now I am poor, jobless, closer to forty than thirty; I'm not just pretty anymore, I am *pretty for my age*. It is the truth: My value has decreased. I can tell by the way Nick looks at me. But it's not the look of a guy who took a tumble on an honest bet. It's the look of a man who feels swindled. Soon it may be the look of a man who is trapped. He might have been able to divorce me before the baby. But he would never do that now, not Good Guy Nick. He couldn't bear to have everyone in this family-values town believe he's the kind of guy who'd abandon his wife and child. He'd rather stay and suffer with me. Suffer and resent and rage.

I won't have an abortion. The baby is six weeks in my belly today, the size of a lentil, and is growing eyes and lungs and ears. A few hours ago, I went into the kitchen and found a snap-top container of dried beans Maureen had given me for Nick's favorite soup, and I pulled out a lentil and laid it on the counter. It was smaller than my pinkie nail, tiny. I couldn't bear to leave it on the cold countertop, so I picked it up and held it in my palm and petted it with the tip-tip-tip of a finger. Now it's in the pocket of my T-shirt, so I can keep it close.

I won't get an abortion and I won't divorce Nick, not yet, because I can still remember how he'd dive into the ocean on a summer day and stand on his hands, his legs flailing out of the water, and leap back up with the best seashell just for me, and I'd let my eyes get dazzled by the sun, and I'd shut them and see the colors blinking like raindrops on the inside of my eyelids as Nick kissed me with salty lips and I'd think, *I am so lucky, this is my husband, this man will be the father of my children. We'll all be so happy.*

But I may be wrong, I may be very wrong. Because sometimes, the way he looks at me? That sweet boy from the beach, man of my dreams, father of my child? I catch him looking at me with those watchful eyes, the eyes of an insect, pure calculation, and I think: *This man might kill me.*

So if you find this and I'm dead, well . . .

Sorry, that's not funny.

NICK DUNNE
SEVEN DAYS GONE

It was time. At exactly eight a.m. Central, nine a.m. New York time, I picked up my phone. My wife was definitely pregnant. I was definitely the prime – only – suspect. I was going to get a lawyer, *today*, and he was going to be the very lawyer I didn't want and absolutely needed.

Tanner Bolt. A grim necessity. Flip around any of the legal networks, the true-crime shows, and Tanner Bolt's spray-tanned face would pop up, indignant and concerned on behalf of whatever freak-show client he was representing. He became famous at thirty-four for representing Cody Olsen, a Chicago restaurateur accused of strangling his very pregnant wife and dumping her body in a landfill. Corpse dogs detected the scent of a dead body inside the trunk of Cody's Mercedes; a search of his laptop revealed that someone had printed out a map to the nearest landfill the morning Cody's wife went missing. A no-brainer. By the time Tanner Bolt was done, everyone – the police department, two West Side Chicago gang members, a disgruntled club bouncer – was implicated except Cody Olsen, who walked out of the courtroom and bought cocktails all around.

In the decade since, Tanner Bolt had become known as the Hubby Hawk – his specialty was swooping down in high-profile cases to represent men accused of murdering their wives. He was successful over half the time, which wasn't bad, considering the cases were usually damning, the accused extremely unlikable – cheaters, narcissists, sociopaths. Tanner Bolt's other nickname was Dickhead Defender.

I had a two p.m. appointment.

'This is Marybeth Elliott. Please leave a message, and I will return promptly ...' she said in voice just like Amy's. Amy, who would not return promptly.

I was speeding to the airport to fly to New York and meet with Tanner Bolt. When I'd asked Boney's permission to leave town, she seemed amused: *Cops don't really do that. That's just on TV.*

'Hi, Marybeth, it's Nick again. I'm anxious to talk to you. I wanted to tell you ... uh, I truly didn't know about the pregnancy, I'm just as shocked as you must be ... uh, also I'm hiring an attorney, just so you know. I think even Rand had suggested it. So anyway ... you know how bad I am on messages. I hope you call me back.'

Tanner Bolt's office was in midtown, not far from where I used to work. The elevator shot me up twenty-five stories, but it was so smooth that I wasn't sure I was moving until my ears popped. At the twenty-sixth floor, a tight-lipped blonde in a sleek business suit stepped on. She tapped her foot impatiently, waiting for the doors to shut, then snapped at me, 'Why don't you hit close?' I flashed her the smile I give petulant women, the lighten-up smile, the one Amy called the 'beloved Nicky grin,' and then the woman recognized me. 'Oh,' she said. She looked as if she smelled something rancid. She seemed personally vindicated when I scuttled out on Tanner's floor.

This guy was the best, and I needed the best, but I also resented being associated with him in any way – this sleazebag, this showboat, this attorney to the guilty. I pre-hated Tanner Bolt so much that I expected his office to look like a *Miami Vice* set. But Bolt & Bolt was quite the opposite – it was dignified, lawyerly. Behind spotless glass doors, people in very good suits commuted busily between offices.

A young, pretty man with a tie the color of tropical fruit greeted me and settled me down in the shiny glass-and-mirror reception area and grandly offered water (declined), then went back to a gleaming desk and picked up a gleaming phone. I sat on the sofa, watching the skyline, cranes pecking up and down like mechanical birds. Then I unfolded Amy's final clue from my pocket. Five years is wood. Was that going to be the end prize of the treasure hunt? Something for the baby: a carved oak cradle, a wooden rattle? Something for our baby and for us, to start over, the Dunnes redone.

Go phoned while I was still staring at the clue.

'Are we okay?' she asked immediately.

My sister thought I was possibly a wife killer.

'We're as okay as I think we can ever be again, considering.'

'Nick. I'm sorry. I called to say I'm sorry,' Go said. 'I woke up and felt totally insane. And awful. I lost my head. It was a momentary freakout. I really, truly apologize.'

I remained silent.

'You got to give me this, Nick: exhaustion and stress and ... I'm sorry ... truly.'

'Okay,' I lied.

'But I'm glad, actually. It cleared the air—'

'She was definitely pregnant.'

My stomach turned. Again I felt as if I had forgotten something crucial. I had overlooked something and would pay for it.

'I'm sorry,' Go said. She waited a few seconds. 'The fact of the matter is—'

'I can't talk about it. I can't.'

'Okay.'

'I'm actually in New York,' I said. 'I have an appointment with Tanner Bolt.'

She let out a whoosh of breath.

'Thank God. You were able to see him that quick?'

'That's how fucked my case is.' I'd been patched through at once to Tanner – I was on hold all of three seconds after stating my name – and when I told him about my living room interrogation about the pregnancy, he ordered me to hop on the next plane.

'I'm kinda freaking out,' I added.

'You're doing the smart thing. Seriously.'

Another pause.

'His name can't really be Tanner Bolt, can it?' I said, trying to make light.

'I heard it's an anagram for Ratner Tolb.'

'Really?'

'No.'

I laughed, an inappropriate feeling, but good. Then, from the far side of the room, the anagram was walking toward me – black pin-striped suit and lime-green tie, sharky grin. He walked with his hand out, in shake-and-strike mode.

'Nick Dunne, I'm Tanner Bolt. Come with me, let's get to work.'

Tanner Bolt's office seemed designed to resemble the clubroom of an exclusive all-men's golf course – comfortable leather chairs, shelves thick with legal books, a gas fireplace with flames flickering in the air-conditioning. Sit down, have a cigar, complain about the wife, tell some questionable jokes, *just us guys here.*

Bolt deliberately chose not to sit behind his desk. He ushered me toward a two-man table as if we were going to play chess. *This is a conversation for us partners*, Bolt said without having to say it. *We'll sit at our little war-room table and get down to it.*

'My retainer, Mr Dunne, is a hundred thousand dollars. That's a lot of money, obviously. So I want to be clear on what I offer and on what I will expect of you, okay?'

He aimed unblinking eyes at me, a sympathetic smile, and waited for me to nod. Only Tanner Bolt could get away with making me, a *client*, fly to *him*, then tell me what kind of dance I'd need to do in order to give him my money.

'I win, Mr Dunne. I win unwinnable cases, and the case that I think you may soon face is – I don't want to patronize you – it's a tough one. Money troubles, bumpy marriage, pregnant wife. The media has turned on you, the public has turned on you.'

He twisted a signet ring on his right hand and waited for me to show him I was listening. I'd always heard the phrase:

235

At forty, a man wears the face he's earned. Bolt's fortyish face was well tended, almost wrinkle-free, pleasantly plump with ego. Here was a confident man, the best in his field, a man who liked his life.

'There will be no more police interviews without my presence,' Bolt was saying. 'That's something I seriously regret you did. But before we even get to the legal portion, we need to start dealing with public opinion, because the way it's going, we have to assume everything is going to get leaked: your credit cards, the life insurance, the supposedly staged crime scene, the mopped-up blood. It looks very bad, my friend. And so it's a vicious cycle: The cops think you did it, they let the public know. The public is outraged, they demand an arrest. So, one: We've got to find an alternative suspect. Two: We've *got* to keep the support of Amy's parents, I cannot emphasize that piece enough. And three: We've got to fix your image, because should this go to trial, it will influence the juror pool. Change of venue doesn't mean anything anymore – twenty-four-hour cable, Internet, the whole world is your venue. So I cannot tell you how key it is to start turning this whole thing around.'

'I'd like that too, believe me.'

'How are things with Amy's parents? Can we get them to make a statement of support?'

'I haven't spoken with them since it was confirmed that Amy was pregnant.'

'Is pregnant.' Tanner frowned at me. 'Is. She *is* pregnant. Never, ever mention your wife in the past tense.'

'Fuck.' I put my face in my palm for a second. I hadn't even noticed what I'd said.

'Don't worry about it with me,' Bolt said, waving the air magnanimously. 'But everywhere else, worry. Worry hard. From now on, I don't want you to open your mouth if you haven't thought it through. So you haven't spoken to Amy's parents. I don't like that. You've tried to get in touch, I assume?'

'I've left a few messages.'

Bolt scrawled something on a yellow legal pad. 'Okay, we

have to assume this is bad news for us. But you need to track them down. Nowhere public, where some asshole with a cameraphone can film you – we can't have another Shawna Kelly moment. Or send your sister in, a recon mission, see what's going on. Actually, do that, that's better.'

'Okay.'

'I need you to make a list for me, Nick. Of all the nice things you've done for Amy over the years. Romantic things, especially in this past year. You cooked her chicken soup when she was sick, or you sent her love letters while you were on a business trip. Nothing too flashy. I don't care about jewelry unless you guys picked it out on vacation or something. We need real personal stuff here, romantic-movie stuff.'

'What if I'm not a romantic-movie kind of guy?'

Tanner tightened his lips, then blew them back out. 'Come up with something, okay, Nick? You seem like a good guy. I'm sure you did something thoughtful this past year.'

I couldn't think of a decent thing I'd done in the past two years. In New York, those first few years of marriage, I'd been desperate to please my wife, to return to those loose-limbed days when she'd run across a drugstore parking lot and leap into my arms, a spontaneous celebration of her hair-spray purchase. Her face pressed up against mine all the time, her bright blue eyes wide and her yellow lashes catching on mine, the heat of her breath just under my nose, the silliness of it. For two years I tried as my old wife slipped away, and I tried so hard – no anger, no arguments, the constant kowtowing, the capitulation, the sitcom-husband version of me: *Yes, dear. Of course, sweetheart.* The fucking energy leached from my body as my frantic-rabbit thoughts tried to figure out how to make her happy, and each action, each attempt, was met with a rolled eye or a sad little sigh. A *you just don't get it* sigh.

By the time we left for Missouri, I was just pissed. I was ashamed of the memory of me – the scuttling, scraping, hunchbacked toadie of a man I'd turned into. So I wasn't romantic; I wasn't even nice.

'Also, I need a list of people who may have harmed Amy, who may have had something against her.'

'I should tell you, it seems Amy tried to buy a gun earlier this year.'

'The cops know?'

'Yes.'

'Did you know?'

'Not until the guy she tried to buy from told me.'

He took exactly two seconds to think. 'Then I bet their theory is she wanted a gun to protect herself from you,' he said. 'She was isolated, she was scared. She wanted to believe in you, yet she could feel something was very wrong, so she wanted a gun in case her worst fear was correct.'

'Wow, you're good.'

'My dad was a cop,' he said. 'But I do like the gun idea – now we just need someone to match it to besides you. Nothing is too far out. If she argued with a neighbor constantly over a barking dog, if she was forced to rebuff a flirty guy, whatever you got, I need. What do you know about Tommy O'Hara?'

'Right! I know he called the tip line a few times.'

'He was accused of date-raping Amy in 2005.'

I felt my mouth open, but I said nothing.

'She was dating him casually. There was a dinner date at his place, things got out of hand, and he raped her, according to my sources.'

'When in 2005?'

'May.'

It was during the eight months when I'd lost Amy – the time between our New Year's meeting and my finding her again on Seventh Avenue.

Tanner tightened his tie, twisted a diamond-studded wedding band, assessing me. 'She never told you.'

'I haven't heard a single thing about this,' I said. 'From anyone. But especially not from Amy.'

'You'd be surprised, the number of women who still find it a stigma. Ashamed.'

'I can't believe I—'

'I try never to show up to one of these meetings without new information for my client,' he said. 'I want to show you how serious I am about your case. And how much you need me.'

'This guy could be a suspect?'

'Sure, why not,' Tanner said too breezily. 'He has a violent history with your wife.'

'Did he go to prison?'

'She dropped the charges. Didn't want to testify, I assume. If you and I decide to work together, I'll have him checked out. In the meantime, think of *anyone* who took an interest in your wife. Better if it's someone in Carthage, though. More believable. Now—' Tanner crossed a leg, exposed his bottom row of teeth, uncomfortably bunched and stained in comparison with his perfect picket-fence top row. He held his crooked teeth against his upper lip for a moment. 'Now comes the harder part, Nick,' he said. 'I need total honesty from you, it won't work any other way. So tell me everything about your marriage, tell me the worst. Because if I know the worst, then I can plan for it. But if I'm surprised, we're fucked. And if we're fucked, *you're* fucked. Because I get to fly away in my G4.'

I took a breath. Looked him in the eyes. 'I cheated on Amy. I've been cheating on Amy.'

'Okay. With multiple women or just one?'

'No, not multiple. I've never cheated before.'

'So, with *one* woman?' Bolt asked, and looked away, his eyes resting on a watercolor of a sailboat as he twirled his wedding band. I could picture him phoning his wife later, saying, *Just once, just once, I want a guy who's not an asshole.*

'Yes, just one girl, she's very—'

'Don't say *girl*, don't ever say *girl*,' Bolt said. 'Woman. One woman who is very special to you. Is that what you were going to say?'

Of course it was.

'You do know, Nick, special is actually worse than – okay. How long?'

239

'A little over a year.'

'Have you spoken to her since Amy went missing?'

'Yes, on a disposable cell phone. And in person once. Twice. But—'

'In *person.*'

'No one has seen us. I can swear to that. Just my sister.'

He took a breath, looked at the sailboat again. 'And what does this— What's her name?'

'Andie.'

'What is her attitude about all this?'

'She's been great – until the pregnancy ... announcement. Now I think she's a little ... on edge. Very on edge. Very, uh ... *needy* is the wrong word ...'

'Say what you need to say, Nick. If she's needy, then—'

'She's needy. Clingy. Needs lots of reassurance. She's a really sweet girl, but she's young, and it's, it's been hard, obviously.'

Tanner Bolt went to his minibar and pulled out a Clamato. The entire fridge was filled with Clamato. He opened the bottle and drank it in three swallows, then dabbed his lips with a cloth napkin. 'You will need to cut off, completely and forever, all contact with Andie,' he said. I began to speak, and he aimed a palm at me. 'Immediately.'

'I can't cut it off with her just like that. Out of nowhere.'

'This isn't something to debate. *Nick.* I mean, come on, buddy, I really got to say this? You cannot date around while your pregnant wife is missing. You will go to fucking prison. Now, the issue is to do it without turning her against us. Without leaving her with a vendetta, an urge to go public, anything but fond memories. Make her believe that this was the decent thing, make her want to keep you safe. How are you at breakups?'

I opened my mouth, but he didn't wait.

'We'll prep you for the conversation the same way we'd prep you for a cross-exam, okay? Now, if you want me, I'll fly to Missouri, I'll set up camp, and we can really get to work on this. I can be with you as soon as tomorrow if you want me for your lawyer. Do you?'

'I do.'

I was back in Carthage before dinnertime. It was strange, once Tanner swept Andie from the picture – once it became clear that she simply couldn't stay – how quickly I accepted it, how little I mourned her. On that single, two-hour flight, I transitioned from *in love with Andie* to *not in love with Andie*. Like walking through a door. Our relationship immediately attained a sepia tone: the past. How odd, that I ruined my marriage over that little girl with whom I had nothing in common except that we both liked a good laugh and a cold beer after sex.

Of course you're fine with ending it, Go would say. *It got hard.*

But there was a better reason: Amy was blooming large in my mind. She was gone, and yet she was more present than anyone else. I'd fallen in love with Amy because I was the ultimate Nick with her. Loving her made me superhuman, it made me feel alive. At her easiest, she was hard, because her brain was always working, working, working – I had to exert myself just to keep pace with her. I'd spend an hour crafting a casual e-mail to her, I became a student of arcana so I could keep her interested: the Lake Poets, the code duello, the French Revolution. Her mind was both wide and deep, and I got smarter being with her. And more considerate, and more active, and more alive, and almost electric, because for Amy, love was like drugs or booze or porn: There was no plateau. Each exposure needed to be more intense than the last to achieve the same result.

Amy made me believe I was exceptional, that I was up to her level of play. That was both our making and undoing. Because I couldn't handle the demands of greatness. I began craving ease and averageness, and I hated myself for it, and ultimately, I realized, I punished her for it. I turned her into the brittle, prickly thing she became. I had pretended to be one kind of man and revealed myself to be quite another.

241

Worse, I convinced myself our tragedy was entirely her making. I spent years working myself into the very thing I swore she was: a righteous ball of hate.

On the flight home, I'd looked at Clue 4 for so long, I'd memorized it. I wanted to torture myself. No wonder her notes were so different this time: My wife was pregnant, she wanted to start over, return us to our dazzling, happy aliveness. I could picture her running around town to hide those sweet notes, eager as a schoolgirl for me to get to the end – the announcement that she was pregnant with my child. Wood. It had to be an old-fashioned cradle. I knew my wife: It had to be an antique cradle. Although the clue wasn't quite in an expectant-mother tone.

> Picture me: I'm a girl who is very bad
> I need to be punished, and by punished, I mean had
> It's where you store goodies for anniversary five
> Pardon me if this is getting contrived!
> A good time was had right here at sunny midday
> Then out for a cocktail, all so terribly gay.
> So run there right now, full of sweet sighs,
> And open the door for your big surprise.

I was almost home when I figured it out. *Store goodies for anniversary five*: Goodies would be something made of wood. To punish is to take someone to the woodshed. It was the woodshed behind my sister's house – a place to stow lawn-mower parts and rusty tools – a decrepit old outbuilding, like something from a slasher movie where campers are slowly killed off. Go never went back there; she'd often joked of burning it down since she moved into the house. Instead, she'd let it get even more overgrown and cobwebbed. We'd always joked that it would be a good place to bury a body.

It couldn't be.

I drove across town, my face numb, my hands cold. Go's car was in the driveway, but I slipped past the glowing living room window and down the steep downhill slope, and I was soon out of her sight range, out of sight of anyone. Very private.

Back to the far back of the yard, on the edge of the tree line, there was the shed.

I opened the door.

Nonononono.

PART TWO

BOY MEETS GIRL

AMY ELLIOTT DUNNE
THE DAY OF

I'm so much happier now that I'm dead.

Technically, missing. Soon to be presumed dead. But as shorthand, we'll say dead. It's been only a matter of hours, but I feel better already: loose joints, wavy muscles. At one point this morning, I realized my face felt strange, different. I looked in the rearview mirror – dread Carthage forty-three miles behind me, my smug husband lounging around his sticky bar as mayhem dangled on a thin piano wire just above his shitty, oblivious head – and I realized I was smiling. Ha! That's new.

My checklist for today – one of many checklists I've made over the past year – sits beside me in the passenger seat, a spot of blood right next to Item 22: Cut myself. *But Amy is afraid of blood*, the diary readers will say. (The diary, yes! We'll get to my brilliant diary.) No, I'm not, not a bit, but for the past year I've been saying I am. I told Nick probably half a dozen times how afraid I am of blood, and when he said, 'I don't remember you being so afraid of blood,' I replied, 'I've told you, I've told you so many times!' Nick has such a careless memory for other people's problems, he just assumed it was true. Swooning at the plasma center, that was a nice touch. I really did that, I didn't just write that I did. (Don't fret, we'll sort this out: the true and the not true and the might as well be true.)

Item 22: Cut myself has been on the list a long time. Now it's real, and my arm hurts. A lot. It takes a very special discipline to slice oneself past the paper-cut layer, down to the muscle. You want a lot of blood, but not so much that you pass out, get discovered hours later in a kiddie pool of red

247

with a lot of explaining to do. I held a box cutter to my wrist first, but looking at that crisscross of veins, I felt like a bomb technician in an action movie: Snip the wrong line and you die. I ended up cutting into the inside of my upper arm, gnawing on a rag so I wouldn't scream. One long, deep good one. I sat cross-legged on my kitchen floor for ten minutes, letting the blood drizzle steadily until I'd made a nice thick puddle. Then I cleaned it up as poorly as Nick would have done after he bashed my head in. I want the house to tell a story of conflict between true and false. *The living room looks staged, yet the blood has been cleaned up: It can't be Amy!*

So the self-mutilation was worth it. Still, hours later, the slice burns under my sleeves, under the tourniquet. (Item 30: Carefully dress wound, ensuring no blood has dripped where it shouldn't be present. Wrap box cutter and tuck away in pocket for later disposal.)

Item 18: Stage the living room. Tip ottoman. Check.

Item 12: Wrap the First Clue in its box and tuck it just out of the way so the police will find it before dazed husband thinks to look for it. It has to be part of the police record. I want him to be forced to start the treasure hunt (his ego will make him finish it). Check.

Item 32: Change into generic clothes, tuck hair in hat, climb down the banks of the river, and scuttle along the edge, the water lapping inches below, until you reach the edge of the complex. Do this even though you know the Teverers, the only neighbors with a view of the river, will be at church. Do this because you never know. You always take the extra step that others don't, that's who you are.

Item 29: Say goodbye to Bleecker. Smell his little stinky cat breath one last time. Fill his kibble dish in case people forget to feed him once everything starts.

Item 33: Get the fuck out of Dodge.

Check, check, check.

I can tell you more about how I did everything, but I'd like you to know me first. Not Diary Amy, who is a work of fiction (and Nick said I wasn't really a writer, and why did I ever listen to him?), but me, Actual Amy. What kind of woman would do such a thing? Let me tell you a story, a *true* story, so you can begin to understand.

To start: I should never have been born.

My mother had five miscarriages and two stillbirths before me. One a year, in the fall, as if it were a seasonal duty, like crop rotation. They were all girls; they were all named Hope. I'm sure it was my father's suggestion – his optimistic impulse, his tie-dyed earnestness: *We can't give up hope, Marybeth*. But give up Hope is exactly what they did, over and over again.

The doctors ordered my parents to stop trying; they refused. They are not quitters. They tried and tried, and finally came me. My mother didn't count on my being alive, couldn't bear to think of me as an actual baby, a living child, a girl who would get to come home. I would have been Hope 8, if things had gone badly. But I entered the world hollering – an electric, neon pink. My parents were so surprised, they realized they'd never discussed a name, not a real one, for a real child. For my first two days in the hospital, they didn't name me. Each morning my mother would hear the door to her room open and feel the nurse lingering in the doorway (I always pictured her vintage, with swaying white skirts and one of those folded caps like a Chinese take-out box). The nurse would linger, and my mother would ask without even looking up, 'Is she still alive?'

When I remained alive, they named me Amy, because it was a regular girl's name, a popular girl's name, a name a thousand other baby girls were given that year, so maybe the gods wouldn't notice this little baby nestled among the others. Marybeth said if she were to do it again, she'd name me Lydia.

I grew up feeling special, proud. I was the girl who battled oblivion and won. The chances were about 1 percent, but I did it. I ruined my mother's womb in the process – my own prenatal Sherman's March. Marybeth would never have another baby. As a child, I got a vibrant pleasure out of this: just me, just me, only me.

My mother would sip hot tea on the days of the Hopes' birth-deaths, sit in a rocker with a blanket, and say she was just 'taking a little time for myself.' Nothing dramatic, my mother is too sensible to sing dirges, but she would get pensive, she would remove herself, and I would have none of it, needful thing that I was. I would clamber onto my mother's lap, or thrust a crayoned drawing in her face, or remember a permission slip that needed prompt attention. My father would try to distract me, try to take me to a movie or bribe me with sweets. No matter the ruse, it didn't work. I wouldn't give my mother those few minutes.

I've always been better than the Hopes, I was the one who made it. But I've always been jealous too, always – seven dead dancing princesses. They get to be perfect without even trying, without even facing one moment of existence, while I am stuck here on earth, and every day I must try, and every day is a chance to be less than perfect.

It's an exhausting way to live. I lived that way until I was thirty-one.

And then, for about two years, everything was okay. Because of Nick.

Nick *loved* me. A six-o kind of love: He *loooooooved* me. But he didn't love me, me. Nick loved a girl who doesn't exist. I was pretending, the way I often did, pretending to have a personality. I can't help it, it's what I've always done: The way some women change fashion regularly, I change personalities. What persona feels good, what's coveted, what's *au courant*? I think most people do this, they just don't admit it, or else they settle on one persona because they're too lazy or stupid to pull off a switch.

That night at the Brooklyn party, I was playing the girl who was in style, the girl a man like Nick wants: the Cool Girl. Men always say that as *the* defining compliment, don't they? *She's a cool girl.* Being the Cool Girl means I am a hot, brilliant, funny woman who adores football, poker, dirty jokes, and burping, who plays video games, drinks cheap beer, loves threesomes and anal sex, and jams hot dogs and hamburgers into her mouth like she's hosting the world's biggest culinary gang bang while somehow maintaining a size 2, because Cool Girls are above all hot. Hot and understanding. Cool Girls never get angry; they only smile in a chagrined, loving manner and let their men do whatever they want. *Go ahead, shit on me, I don't mind, I'm the Cool Girl.*

Men actually think this girl exists. Maybe they're fooled because so many women are willing to pretend to be this girl. For a long time Cool Girl offended me. I used to see men – friends, coworkers, strangers – giddy over these awful pretender women, and I'd want to sit these men down and calmly say: *You are not dating a woman, you are dating a woman who has watched too many movies written by socially awkward men who'd like to believe that this kind of woman exists and might kiss them.* I'd want to grab the poor guy by his lapels or messenger bag and say: *The bitch doesn't really love chili dogs that much – no one loves chili dogs that much!* And the Cool Girls are even more pathetic: They're not even pretending to be the woman they want to be, they're pretending to be the woman a man wants them to be. Oh, and if you're *not* a Cool Girl, I beg you not to believe that your man doesn't want the Cool Girl. It may be a slightly different version – maybe he's a vegetarian, so Cool Girl loves seitan and is great with dogs; or maybe he's a hipster artist, so Cool Girl is a tattooed, bespectacled nerd who loves comics. There are variations to the window dressing, but believe me, he wants Cool Girl, who is basically the girl who likes every fucking thing he likes and doesn't ever complain. (How do you know you're *not* Cool Girl? Because he says things like: 'I like strong women.' If he says that to you, he will at some point fuck someone else. Because 'I like strong women' is code for 'I hate strong women.')

I waited patiently – *years* – for the pendulum to swing the other way, for men to start reading Jane Austen, learn how to knit, pretend to love cosmos, organize scrapbook parties, and make out with each other while we leer. And then we'd say, *Yeah, he's a Cool Guy.*

But it never happened. Instead, women across the nation

colluded in our degradation! Pretty soon Cool Girl became the standard girl. Men believed she existed – she wasn't just a dreamgirl one in a million. Every girl was supposed to be this girl, and if you weren't, then there was something wrong with *you*.

But it's tempting to be Cool Girl. For someone like me, who likes to win, it's tempting to want to be the girl every guy wants. When I met Nick, I knew immediately that was what he wanted, and for him, I guess I was willing to try. I will accept my portion of blame. The thing is, I was *crazy* about him at first. I found him perversely exotic, a good ole Missouri boy. He was so damn nice to be around. He teased things out in me that I didn't know existed: a lightness, a humor, an ease. It was as if he hollowed me out and filled me with feathers. He helped me be Cool Girl – I couldn't have been Cool Girl with anyone else. I wouldn't have wanted to. I can't say I didn't enjoy some of it: I ate a MoonPie, I walked barefoot, I stopped worrying. I watched dumb movies and ate chemically laced foods. I didn't think past the first step of anything, that was the key. I drank a Coke and didn't worry about how to recycle the can or about the acid puddling in my belly, acid so powerful it could strip clean a penny. We went to a dumb movie and I didn't worry about the offensive sexism or the lack of minorities in meaningful roles. I didn't even worry whether the movie made sense. I didn't worry about anything that came next. Nothing had consequence, I was living in the moment, and I could feel myself getting shallower and dumber. But also happy.

Until Nick, I'd never really felt like a person, because I was always a product. Amazing Amy has to be brilliant, creative, kind, thoughtful, witty, and happy. *We just want you to be happy.* Rand and Marybeth said that all the time, but they never explained how. So many lessons and opportunities and advantages, and they never taught me how to be happy. I remember always being baffled by other children. I would be at a birthday party and watch the other kids giggling and making faces, and I would try to do that, too, but I wouldn't understand *why*. I would sit there with the tight elastic thread of the birthday hat parting the pudge of my underchin, with the grainy frosting of the cake bluing my teeth, and I would try to figure out why it was fun.

With Nick, I understood finally. Because he was so much fun. It was like dating a sea otter. He was the first naturally happy person I met who was my equal. He was brilliant and gorgeous and funny and charming and charmed. People liked him. Women loved him. I thought we would be the most perfect union: the happiest couple around. Not that love is a competition. But I don't understand the point of being together if you're not the happiest.

I was probably happier for those few years – pretending to be someone else – than I ever have been before or after. I can't decide what that means.

But then it had to stop, because it wasn't real, it wasn't me. It wasn't *me*, Nick! I thought you knew. I thought it was a bit of a game. I thought we had a wink-wink, *don't ask, don't tell* thing going. I tried so hard to be easy. But it was unsustainable. It turned out he couldn't sustain his side either: the witty banter, the clever games, the romance, and the wooing. It all started collapsing on itself. I hated Nick for being surprised when I became me. I hated him for not knowing it had to end, for truly believing he had married this creature, this figment of the imagination of a million masturbatory men, semen-fingered and self-satisfied. He truly seemed astonished when I asked him to *listen* to me. He couldn't believe I didn't love wax-stripping my pussy raw and blowing him on request. That I *did* mind when he didn't show up for drinks with my friends. That ludicrous diary entry? *I don't need pathetic dancing-monkey scenarios to repeat to my friends, I am content with letting him be himself.* That was pure, dumb Cool Girl bullshit. What a cunt. Again, I don't get it: If you let a man cancel plans or decline to do things for you, you *lose*. You don't get what you want. It's pretty clear. Sure, he may be happy, he may say you're *the coolest girl ever*, but he's saying it because *he got his way*. He's calling you a Cool Girl to fool you! That's what men do: They try to make it sound like you are the cool girl so you will bow to their wishes. Like a car salesman saying, *How much do you want to pay for this beauty?* when you didn't agree to buy it yet. That awful phrase men use: 'I mean, I know *you* wouldn't mind if I ...' *Yes, I do mind.* Just say it. Don't lose, you dumb little twat.

So it had to stop. Committing to Nick, feeling safe with Nick, being happy with Nick, made me realize that there was a Real Amy in there, and she was so much better, more interesting and complicated and challenging, than Cool Amy. Nick wanted Cool Amy anyway. Can you imagine, finally showing your true self to your spouse, your soul mate, and having him *not like you*? So that's how the hating first began. I've thought about this a lot, and that's where it started, I think.

NICK DUNNE
SEVEN DAYS GONE

I made it a few steps into the woodshed before I had to lean against the wall and catch my breath.

I knew it was going to be bad. I knew it once I figured out the clue: woodshed. Midday fun. Cocktails. Because that description was not me and Amy. It was me and Andie. The woodshed was just one of many strange places where I'd had sex with Andie. We were restricted in our meeting spots. Her busy apartment complex was mostly a no go. Motels show up on credit cards, and my wife was neither trusting nor stupid. (Andie had a MasterCard, but the statement went to her mom. It hurts me to admit that.) So the woodshed, deep behind my sister's house, was very safe when Go was at work. Likewise my father's abandoned home (*Maybe you feel guilty for bringing me here / I must admit it felt a bit queer / But it's not like we had the choice of many a place / We made the decision: We made this our space*), and a few times, my office at school (*I picture myself as your student / With a teacher so handsome and wise / My mind opens up [not to mention my thighs!]*), and once, Andie's car, pulled down a dirt road in Hannibal after I'd taken her for a visit one day, a much more satisfying reenactment of my banal field trip with Amy (*You took me here so I could hear you chat / About your boyhood adventures: crummy jeans and visor hat*).

Each clue was hidden in a spot where I'd cheated on Amy. She'd used the treasure hunt to take me on a tour of all my infidelities. I had a shimmer of nausea as I pictured Amy trailing oblivious me in her car – to my dad's, to Go's, to goddamn Hannibal – watching me fuck this sweet young girl, my wife's lips twisting in disgust and triumph.

Because she knew she'd punish me good. Now at our final stop, Amy was ready for me to know how clever she was. Because the woodshed was packed with about every gizmo and gadget that I swore to Boney and Gilpin I hadn't bought with the credit cards I swore I didn't know anything about. The insanely expensive golf clubs were here, the watches and game consoles, the designer clothes, they were all sitting here, in wait, on my sister's property. Where it looked like I'd stored them until my wife was dead and I could have a little fun.

I knocked on Go's front door, and when she answered, smoking a cigarette, I told her I had to show her something, and I turned around and led her without a word to the woodshed.

'Look,' I said, and ushered her toward the open door.

'Are those— Is that all the stuff ... from the credit cards?' Go's voice went high and wild. She put one hand to her mouth and took a step back from me, and I realized that just for a second, she thought I was making a confession to her.

We'd never be able to undo it, that moment. For that alone, I hated my wife.

'Amy's framing me, Go,' I said. 'Go, Amy bought this stuff. She's *framing* me.'

She snapped to. Her eyelids clicked once, twice, and she gave a tiny shake of her head, as if to rid herself of the image: Nick as wife killer.

'Amy's framing me for her murder. Right? Her last clue, it led me right here, and no, I didn't know about *any* of this stuff. It's her grand statement. *Presenting: Nick Goes to Jail!*' A huge, burpy air bubble formed at the back of my throat – I was going to sob or laugh. I laughed. 'I mean, right? Holy fuck, right?'

So hurry up, get going, please do / And this time I'll teach you a thing or two. The final words of Amy's first clue. How did I not see it?

'If she's framing you, why let you know?' Go was still staring, transfixed by the contents of her shed.

'Because she's done it so perfectly. She always needed that validation, the praise, all the time. She wants me to know I'm

256

being fucked. She can't resist. It wouldn't be fun for her otherwise.'

'No,' Go said, chewing on a nail. 'There's something else. Something more. Have you touched anything in here?'

'No.'

'Good. Then the question becomes ...'

'What does she think I'll do when I find this, this incriminating evidence, on my sister's property,' I said. 'That's the question, because whatever she assumes I'll do, whatever she wants me to do, I have to do the opposite. If she thinks I'll freak out and try to get rid of all this stuff, I guarantee you she has a way I'll get busted with it.'

'Well, you can't leave it here,' Go said. 'You'll definitely get busted that way. Are you sure that was the last clue? Where's your present?'

'Oh. Shit. No. It must be inside somewhere.'

'Don't go in there,' Go said.

'I have to. God knows what else she's got in store.'

I stepped carefully into the dank shed, keeping my hands tight by my sides, walking delicately on tiptoes so as not to leave tread marks. Just past a flat-screen TV, Amy's blue envelope sat on top of a huge gift box, wrapped in her beautiful silvery paper. I took the envelope and the box back outside into the warm air. The object inside the package was heavy, a good thirty pounds, and broken into several pieces that slid with a strange rattle as I set the box on the ground at our feet. Go took an involuntary quick step away from it. I slid open the envelope.

Darling Husband,

Now is when I take the time to tell you that I know you better than you could ever imagine. I know sometimes you think you are moving through this world alone, unseen, unnoticed. But don't believe that for a second. I have made a study of you. I know what you are going to do before you do it. I know where you've been, and I know where you're going. For this anniversary, I've arranged a trip:

257

Follow your beloved river, up up up! And you don't even have to worry about trying to find your anniversary present. This time the present will come to you! So sit back and relax, because you are DONE.

'What's upriver?' Go asked, and then I groaned.

'She's sending me *up the river*.'

'Fuck her. Open the box.'

I knelt down and nudged off the lid with my fingertips, as if expecting an explosion. Silence. I peered inside. At the bottom of the box lay two wooden puppets, side by side. They seemed to be husband and wife. The male was dressed in motley and grinning rabidly, holding a cane or a stick. I pulled the husband figure out, his limbs bouncing around excitedly, a dancer limbering up. The wife was prettier, more delicate, and stiffer. Her face looked shocked, as if she'd seen something alarming. Beneath her was a tiny baby that could be attached to her by a ribbon. The puppets were ancient, heavy, and large, almost as big as ventriloquist dummies. I picked up the male, gripped the thick, clublike handle used to move him, and his arms and legs twitched manically.

'Creepy,' Go said. 'Stop.'

Beneath them lay a piece of buttery blue paper folded over once. Amy's broken-kite handwriting, all triangles and points. It read:

The beginning of a wonderful new story, Nick! 'That's the way to do it!'

Enjoy.

On our mom's kitchen table, we spread all of Amy's treasure-hunt clues and the box containing the puppets. We stared at the objects as if we were assembling a jigsaw puzzle.

'Why bother with a treasure hunt if she was planning ... her plan,' Go said.

Her plan had become immediate shorthand for *faking her disappearance and framing you for murder*. It sounded less insane.

'Keep me distracted, for one thing. Make me believe she still loved me. I'm chasing her little clues all over Christendom, believing my wife was wanting to make amends, wanting to jump-start our marriage ...'

The moony, girlish state her notes had left me in, it sickened me. It embarrassed me. Marrow-deep embarrassment, the kind that becomes part of your DNA, that changes you. After all these years, Amy could still play me. She could write a few notes and get me back completely. I was her little puppet on a string.

I will find you, Amy. Lovesick words, hateful intentions.

'So I don't stop to think: *Hey, it sure looks like I murdered my wife, I wonder why?*'

'And the police would have found it strange – you would have found it strange – if she didn't do the treasure hunt, this tradition,' Go reasoned. 'It would look as if she knew she was going to disappear.'

'This worries me though,' I said, pointing at the puppets. 'They're unusual enough that they have to mean something. I mean, if she just wanted to keep me distracted for a while, the final gift could have been anything wooden.'

Go ran a finger across the male's motley uniform. 'They're clearly very old. Vintage.' She flipped their clothing upside down to reveal the club handle of the male. The female had only a square-shaped gap at her head. 'Is this supposed to be sexual? The male has this giant wooden handle, like a dick. And the female is missing hers. She just has the hole.'

'It's a fairly obvious statement: Men have penises and women have vaginas?'

Go put a finger inside the female puppet's gap, swept around to make sure there was nothing hidden. 'So what is Amy saying?'

'When I first saw them, I thought: *She bought children's toys.* Mom, dad, baby. Because she was pregnant.'

'Is she even pregnant?'

A sense of despair washed over me. Or rather, the opposite. Not a wave coming in, rolling over me, but the ebb of the sea returning: a sense of something pulling away, and me with it.

I could no longer hope my wife was pregnant, but I couldn't bring myself to hope she wasn't either.

Go pulled out the male doll, scrunched her nose, then lightbulb popped. 'You're a puppet on a string.'

I laughed. 'I literally thought those exact words too. But why a male and female? Amy clearly isn't a puppet on a string, she's the puppetmaster.'

'And what's: *That's the way to do it*? To do *what*?'

'Fuck me for life?'

'It's not a phrase Amy used to say? Or some quote from the *Amy* books, or ...' She hurried over to her computer and searched for *That's the way to do it*. Up came lyrics for 'That's the Way to Do It' by Madness. 'Oh, I remember them,' Go said. 'Awesome ska band.'

'Ska,' I said, swerving toward delirious laughter. 'Great.'

The lyrics were about a handyman who could do many types of home-improvement jobs – including electrical and plumbing – and who preferred to be paid in cash.

'God, I fucking hate the eighties,' I said. 'No lyrics ever made sense.'

'"The reflex is an only child,"' Go said, nodding.

'"He's waiting by the park,"' I muttered back automatically.

'So if this is it, what does it mean?' Go said, turning to me, studying my eyes. 'It's a song about a handyman. Someone who might have access to your house, to fix things. Or *rig* things. Who would be paid in cash so there's no record.'

'Someone who installed video cameras?' I asked. 'Amy went out of town a few times during the – the affair. Maybe she thought she'd catch us on tape.'

Go shot a question at me.

'No, never, never at our house.'

'Could it be some secret door?' Go suggested. 'Some secret false panel Amy put in where she's hidden something that will ... I don't know, exonerate you?'

'I think that's it. Yes, Amy is using a Madness song to give me a clue to my own freedom, if only I can decipher their wily, ska-infused codes.'

Go laughed then too. 'Jesus, maybe we're the ones who are bat-shit crazy. I mean, are we? Is this totally insane?'

'It's not insane. She set me up. There is no other way to explain the *warehouse* of stuff in *your* backyard. And it's very Amy to drag you into it, smudge you a little bit with my filth. No, this is Amy. The gift, the fucking giddy, sly note I'm supposed to understand. No, and it has to come back to the puppets. Try the quote with the word *marionettes*.'

I collapsed on the couch, my body a dull throb. Go played secretary. 'Oh my God. Duh! They're Punch and Judy dolls. Nick! We're idiots. That line, that's Punch's trademark. *That's the way to do it!*'

'Okay. The old puppet show – it's really violent, right?' I asked.

'This is so fucked up.'

'Go, it's violent, right?'

'Yeah. Violent. God, she's fucking crazy.'

'He beats her, right?'

'I'm reading ... okay. Punch kills their baby.' She looked up at me. 'And then when Judy confronts him, he beats her. To death.'

My throat got wet with saliva.

'And each time he does something awful and gets away with it, he says, "That's the way to do it!"' She grabbed Punch and placed him in her lap, her fingers grasping the wooden hands as if she were holding an infant. 'He's glib, even as he murders his wife and child.'

I looked at the puppets. 'So she's giving me the narrative of my frame-up.'

'I can't even wrap my brain around this. Fucking *psycho*.'

'Go?'

'Yeah, right: You didn't want her to be pregnant, you got angry and killed her and the unborn baby.'

'Feels anticlimactic somehow,' I said.

'The climax is when you are taught the lesson that Punch never learns, and you are caught and charged with murder.'

'And Missouri has the death penalty,' I said. 'Fun game.'

AMY ELLIOTT DUNNE
THE DAY OF

You know how I found out? I *saw* them. That's how stupid my husband is. One snowy April night, I felt so lonely. I was drinking warm amaretto with Bleecker and reading, lying on the floor as the snow came down, listening to old scratchy albums, like Nick and I used to (that entry was true). I had a burst of romantic cheer: I'd surprise him at The Bar, and we'd have a few drinks and wander through the empty streets together, hand in mitten. We would walk around the hushed downtown and he would press me against a wall and kiss me in the snow that looked like sugar clouds. That's right, I wanted him back so badly that I was willing to re-create that moment. I was willing to pretend to be someone else again. I remember thinking: *We can still find a way to make this work. Faith!* I followed him all the way to Missouri, because I still believed he'd love me again somehow, love me that intense, thick way he did, the way that made everything good. Faith!

I got there just in time to see him leaving with her. I was in the goddamn parking lot, twenty feet behind him, and he didn't even register me, I was a ghost. He didn't have his hands on her, not yet, but I knew. I could tell because he was so *aware* of her. I followed them, and suddenly, he pressed her up against a tree – *in the middle of town* – and kissed her. *Nick is cheating*, I thought dumbly, and before I could make myself say anything, they were going up to her apartment. I waited for an hour, sitting on the doorstep, then got too cold – blue fingernails, chattering teeth – and went home. He never even knew I knew.

I had a new persona, not of my choosing. I was Average

Dumb Woman Married to Average Shitty Man. He had single-handedly de-amazed Amazing Amy.

I know women whose entire personas are woven from a benign mediocrity. Their lives are a list of shortcomings: the unappreciative boyfriend, the extra ten pounds, the dismissive boss, the conniving sister, the straying husband. I've always hovered above their stories, nodding in sympathy and thinking how foolish they are, these women, to let these things happen, how undisciplined. And now to be one of them! One of the women with the endless stories that make people nod sympathetically and think: *Poor dumb bitch.*

I could hear the tale, how everyone would love telling it: how Amazing Amy, the girl who never did wrong, let herself be dragged, penniless, to the middle of the country, where her husband threw her over for a younger woman. How predictable, how perfectly average, how amusing. And her husband? He ended up happier than ever. No. I couldn't allow that. No. Never. Never. He doesn't get to do this to me and still fucking win. No.

I changed *my name* for that piece of shit. Historical records have been *altered* – Amy Elliott to Amy Dunne – like it's nothing. No, he does *not* get to win.

So I began to think of a different story, a better story, that would destroy Nick for doing this to me. A story that would restore my perfection. It would make me the hero, flawless and adored.

Because everyone loves the Dead Girl.

It's rather extreme, framing your husband for your murder. I want you to know I know that. All the tut-tutters out there will say: *She should have just left, bundled up what remained of her dignity. Take the high road! Two wrongs don't make a right!* All those things that spineless women say, confusing their weakness with morality.

I won't divorce him because that's exactly what he'd like. And I won't forgive him because I don't feel like *turning the other cheek.* Can I make it any more clear? I won't find that a satisfactory ending. The bad guy wins? Fuck him.

For over a year now, I've smelled her twat on his fingertips as he slipped into bed next to me. I've watched him ogle himself in the mirror, grooming himself like a horny baboon for their dates. I've listened to his lies, lies, lies – from simplistic child's fibs to elaborate Rube Goldbergian contraptions. I've tasted butterscotch on his dry-kiss lips, a cloying flavor that was never there before. I've felt the stubble on his cheeks that he knows I don't like but apparently she does. I've suffered betrayal with all five senses. For over a year.

So I may have gone a bit mad. I do know that framing your husband for your murder is beyond the pale of what an average woman might do.

But it's so very *necessary*. Nick must be taught a lesson. He's *never* been taught a lesson! He glides through life with that charming-Nicky grin, his beloved-child entitlement, his fibs and shirkings, his shortcomings and selfishness, and no one calls him on *anything*. I think this experience will make him a better person. Or at least a sorrier one. Fucker.

I've always thought I could commit the perfect murder. People who get caught get caught because they don't have patience; they refuse to plan. I smile again as I shift my crappy getaway car into fifth gear (Carthage now seventy-eight miles in the dust) and brace myself for a speeding truck – the car seems ready to take flight every time a semi passes. But I do smile, because this car shows just how smart I am: purchased for twelve hundred dollars cash from a Craigslist posting. Five months ago, so the memory wouldn't be fresh in anyone's mind. A 1992 Ford Festiva, the tiniest, most forgettable car in the world. I met the sellers at night, in the parking lot of a WalMart in Jonesboro, Arkansas. I took the train down with a bundle of cash in my purse – eight hours each way, while Nick was on a boys' trip. (And by boys' trip, I mean *fucking the slut*.) I ate in the train's dining car, a clump of lettuce with two cherry tomatoes that the menu described as a salad. I was seated with a melancholy farmer returning home after visiting his baby granddaughter for the first time.

The couple selling the Ford seemed as interested in discretion as I. The woman remained in the car the whole time, a pacifiered toddler in her arms, watching her husband and me trade cash for keys. (That is the correct grammar, you know: her husband and me.) Then she got out and I got in. That quick. In the rearview mirror, I saw the couple strolling into WalMart with their money. I've been parking it in long-term lots in St. Louis. I go down twice a month and park it somewhere new. Pay cash. Wear a baseball cap. Easy enough.

So that's just an example. Of patience, planning, and ingenuity. I am pleased with myself; I have three hours more until I reach the thick of the Missouri Ozarks and my destination, a small archipelago of cabins in the woods that accepts cash for weekly rentals and has cable TV, a must. I plan to hole up there the first week or two; I don't want to be on the road when the news hits, and it's the last place Nick would think I'd hide once he realizes I'm hiding.

This stretch of highway is particularly ugly. Middle-America blight. After another twenty miles, I see, up on the off-ramp, the remains of a lonesome family gas station, vacant but not boarded up, and when I pull to the side, I see the women's restroom door swung wide. I enter – no electricity, but there's a warped metal mirror and the water is still on. In the afternoon sunlight and the sauna heat, I remove from my purse a pair of metal scissors and bunny-brown hair dye. I shear off large chunks of my hair. All the blond goes into a plastic bag. Air hits the back of my neck, and my head feels light, like a balloon – I roll it around a few times to enjoy. I apply the color, check my watch, and linger in the doorway, looking out over miles of flatland pocked with fast-food restaurants and motel chains. I can feel an Indian crying. (Nick would hate that joke. Derivative! And then he'd add, 'although the word *derivative* as a criticism is itself derivative.' I've got to get him out of my head – he still steps on my lines from a hundred miles away.) I wash my hair in the sink, the warm water making me sweat, and then back in the car with my bag of hair and trash. I put on a pair of outdated wire-rim glasses and look in the rearview mirror and smile again. Nick and I would never have married if I had looked like this when we met. All this could have been avoided if I were less pretty.

Item 34: Change look. Check.

I'm not sure, exactly, how to be Dead Amy. I'm trying to figure out what that means for me, what I become for the next few months. Anyone, I suppose, except people I've already been: Amazing Amy. Preppy '80s Girl. Ultimate-Frisbee Granola and Blushing Ingenue and Witty Hepburnian Sophisticate. Brainy Ironic Girl and Boho Babe (the latest version of Frisbee Granola). Cool Girl and Loved Wife and Unloved Wife and Vengeful Scorned Wife. Diary Amy.

I hope you liked Diary Amy. She was meant to be likable. Meant for someone like you to like her. She's *easy* to like. I've never understood why that's considered a compliment – that just anyone could like you. No matter. I thought the entries turned out nicely, and it wasn't simple. I had to maintain an affable if somewhat naive persona, a woman who loved her husband and could see some of his flaws (otherwise she'd be too much of a sap) but was sincerely devoted to him – all the while leading the reader (in this case, the cops, I am so eager for them to find it) toward the conclusion that Nick was indeed planning to kill me. So many clues to unpack, so many surprises ahead!

Nick always mocked my endless lists. ('It's like you make sure you're never satisfied, that there's always something else to be perfected, instead of just enjoying the moment.') But who wins here? I win, because my list, the master list entitled *Fuck Nick Dunne*, was exacting – it was the most complete, fastidious list that has ever been created. On my list was *Write Diary Entries for 2005 to 2012*. Seven years of diary entries, not every day, but twice monthly, at least. Do you know how much discipline that takes? Would Cool Girl Amy be able to do that? To research each week's current events, to cross-consult with my old daily planners to make sure I forgot nothing important, then to reconstruct how Diary Amy would react to each event? It was fun, mostly. I'd wait for Nick to leave for The Bar, or to go meet his mistress, the ever-texting, gum-chewing, vapid mistress with her acrylic nails and the sweatpants with logos across the butt (she isn't like this, exactly, but she might as well be), and I'd pour some coffee or open a bottle of wine, pick one of my thirty-two different pens, and rewrite my life a little.

It is true that I sometimes hated Nick less while I was doing this. A giddy Cool Girl perspective will do that. Sometimes Nick would come home, stinking of beer or of the hand sanitizer he wiped on his body post-mistress-coitus (never entirely erased the stink, though – she must have one rank pussy), and smile guiltily at me, be all sweet and hangdog with me, and I'd almost think: *I won't go through with this*. And then I'd picture him with her, in her stripper thong, letting him degrade her because she was pretending to be Cool Girl, she was pretending to love blow jobs and football and getting *wasted*. And I'd think, *I am married to an imbecile. I'm married to a man who will always choose that, and when he gets bored with this dumb twat, he'll just find another girl who is pretending to be that girl, and he'll never have to do anything hard in his life.*

Resolve stiffened.

One hundred and fifty-two entries total, and I don't think I ever lose her voice. I wrote her very carefully, Diary Amy. She is designed to appeal to the cops, to appeal to the public should portions be released. They have to read this diary like it's some sort of Gothic tragedy. A wonderful, good-hearted woman – *whole life ahead of her, everything going for her*, whatever else they say about women who die – chooses the wrong mate and *pays the ultimate price*. They have to like me. Her.

My parents are worried, of course, but how can I feel sorry for them, since they made me this way and then deserted me? They never, ever fully appreciated the fact that they were earning money from my existence, that I should have been getting royalties. Then, after they siphoned off *my* money, my 'feminist' parents let Nick bundle me off to Missouri like I was some piece of chattel, some mail-order bride, some property exchange. Gave me a fucking cuckoo clock to remember them by. *Thanks for thirty-six years of service!* They deserve to think I'm dead, because that's practically the state they consigned me to: no money, no home, no friends. They deserve to suffer too. If you can't take care of me while I'm alive, you have made me dead anyway. Just like Nick, who destroyed and rejected the real me a piece at a time – *you're too serious, Amy, you're too uptight, Amy, you overthink things, you analyze too much, you're no fun anymore, you make me feel useless, Amy, you make me feel bad, Amy.* He took away chunks of me with blasé swipes: my independence, my pride, my esteem. I gave, and he took and took. He Giving Treed me out of existence.

That whore, he picked that little whore over me. He killed my soul, which should be a crime. Actually, it is a crime. According to me, at least.

NICK DUNNE
SEVEN DAYS GONE

I had to phone Tanner, my brand-new lawyer, mere hours after I'd hired him, and say the words that would make him regret taking my money: *I think my wife is framing me*. I couldn't see his face, but I could imagine it – the eye roll, the grimace, the weariness of a man who hears nothing but lies for a living.

'Well,' he finally said after a gaping pause, 'I'll be there first thing tomorrow morning, and we will sort this out – everything on the table – and in the meantime, sit tight, okay? Go to sleep and sit tight.'

Go took his advice, she popped two sleeping pills and left me just before eleven, while I literally sat tight, in an angry ball on her couch. Every so often I'd go outside and glare at the woodshed, my hands on my hips, as if it were a predator I could scare off. I'm not sure what I thought I was accomplishing, but I couldn't stop myself. I could stay seated for five minutes, tops, before I'd have to go back outside and stare.

I had just come back inside when a knock rattled the back door. Fucking Christ. Not quite midnight. Cops would come to the front – right? – and reporters had yet to stake out Go's (this would change, a matter of days, hours). I was standing, unnerved, undecided, in the living room when the banging came again, louder, and I cursed under my breath, tried to get myself angry instead of scared. *Deal with it, Dunne*.

I flung open the door. It was Andie. It was goddamn Andie, pretty as a picture, dressed up for the occasion, still not getting it – that she was going to put my neck right in the noose.

'Right in the noose, Andie.' I yanked her inside, and she

stared at my hand on her arm. 'You are going to put my neck right in the fucking noose.'

'I came to the back door,' she said. When I stared her down, she didn't apologize, she steeled herself. I could literally see her features harden. 'I needed to see you, Nick. I told you. I told you I had to see you or talk to you every day, and today you disappeared. Straight to voice mail, straight to voice mail, straight to voice mail.'

'If you don't hear from me, it's because I can't talk, Andie. Jesus, I was in New York, getting a lawyer. He'll be here first thing tomorrow.'

'You got a lawyer. That was what kept you so busy that you couldn't call me for ten seconds?'

I wanted to smack her. I took a breath. I had to cut things off with Andie. It wasn't just Tanner's warning I had in mind. My wife knew me: She knew I'd do almost anything to avoid dealing with confrontation. Amy was depending on me to be stupid, to let the relationship linger – and to ultimately be caught. I had to end it. But I had to do it perfectly. *Make her believe that this was the decent thing.*

'He's actually given me some important advice,' I began. 'Advice I can't ignore.'

I'd been so sweet and doting just last night, at my mandatory meeting in our pretend fort. I'd made so many promises, trying to calm her down. She wouldn't see this coming. She wouldn't take this well.

'Advice? Good. Is it to stop being such an asshole to me?'

I felt the rage rise up; that this was already turning into a high school fight. A thirty-four-year-old man in the middle of the worst night of my life, and I was having a *meet me by the lockers!* squabble with a pissed-off girl. I shook her once, hard, a tiny droplet of spit landing on her lower lip.

'I— You don't get it, Andie. This isn't some joke, this is my life.'

'I just … I need you,' she said, looking down at her hands. 'I know I keep saying that, but I do. I can't do it, Nick. I can't go on like this. I'm falling apart. I'm so scared all the time.'

She was scared. I pictured the police knocking, and here I was with a girl I'd been fucking the morning my wife went missing. I'd sought her out that day – I had never gone to her apartment since that first night, but I went right there that morning, because I'd spent hours with my heart pounding behind my ears, trying to get myself to say the words to Amy: *I want a divorce. I am in love with someone else. We have to end. I can't pretend to love you, I can't do the anniversary thing – it would actually be more wrong than cheating on you in the first place.* (I know: debatable.) But while I was gathering the guts, Amy had preempted me with her speech about still loving me (lying bitch!), and I lost my nerve. I felt like the ultimate cheat and coward, and – the catch-22 – I craved Andie to make me feel better.

But Andie was no longer the antidote to my nerves. Quite the opposite.

The girl was wrapping herself around me even now, oblivious as a weed.

'Look, Andie,' I said, a big exhale, not letting her sit down, keeping her near the door. 'You are such a special person to me. You've handled all this so amazingly well—' *Make her want to keep you safe.*

'I mean ...' Her voice wavered. 'I feel so sorry, for Amy. Which is insane. I know I don't even have a right to feel sad for her, or worried. And on top of feeling sad, I feel so guilty.' She leaned her head against my chest. I retreated, held her at arm's length so she had to look at me.

'Well, that's one thing I think we can fix. I think we need to fix,' I said, pulling up Tanner's exact words.

'We should go to the police,' she said. 'I'm your alibi for that morning, we'll just tell them.'

'You're my alibi for about an hour that morning,' I said. 'No one saw or heard Amy after eleven p.m. the night before. The police can say I killed her before I saw you.'

'That's disgusting.'

I shrugged. I thought, for a second, about telling her about Amy – *my wife is framing me* – and quickly dismissed it. Andie couldn't play the game on Amy's level. She'd want to be my teammate, and she'd drag me down. Andie would be a liability going forward. I put my hands on her arms again, relaunched my speech.

'Look, Andie, we are both under an amazing amount of stress and pressure, and a lot of it is brought on by our feelings of guilt. Andie, the thing is, we are good people. We were attracted to each other, I think, because we both have similar values. Of treating people right, of doing the right thing. And right now we know what we are doing is wrong.'

Her broken, hopeful expression changed – the wet eyes, the gentle touch, they disappeared: a weird flicker, a window shade pulled down, something darker in her face.

'We need to end this, Andie. I think we both know that. It's so hard, but it's the decent thing to do. I think it's the advice we'd give ourselves if we could think straight. As much as I love you, I am still married to Amy. I have to do the right thing.'

'And if she's found?' She didn't say *dead or alive*.

'That's something we can discuss then.'

'Then! And until then, what?'

I shrugged helplessly: *Until then, nothing.*

'What, Nick? I fuck off until then?'

'That's an ugly choice of words.'

'But that's what you mean.' She smirked.

'I'm sorry, Andie. I don't think it's right for me to be with you right now. It's dangerous for you, it's dangerous for me. It doesn't sit well with my conscience. It's just how I feel.'

'Yeah? You know how I feel?' Her eyes burst over, tears streaming down her cheeks. 'I feel like a dumb college girl that you started fucking because you were bored with your wife and I made it extremely convenient for you. You could go home to Amy and eat dinner with her and play around in your little bar that you bought with her money, and then you could meet me at your dying dad's house and jack off on my tits because, poor you, your mean wife would never let you do that.'

'Andie, you know that's not—'

'What a shit you are. What kind of man are you?'

'Andie, please.' *Contain this, Nick.* 'I think because you haven't been able to talk about this stuff, everything has gotten a little bigger in your mind, a little—'

'Fuck you. You think I'm some dumb kid, some pathetic student you can *manage*? I stick by you through all this – this talk about how you might be a *murderer* – and as soon as it's a little tough for you? No, *no*. You don't get to talk about conscience and decency and guilt and feel like you are doing the right thing. Do you understand me? Because you are a cheating, cowardly, selfish *shit*.'

She turned away from me, sobbing, sucking in loud gulps of moist air, and breathing out mewls, and I tried to stop her, I grabbed her by the arm. 'Andie, this isn't how I want to—'

'Hands off me! Hands off me!'

She moved toward the back door, and I could see what would happen, the hatred and embarrassment coming off her like heat, I knew she'd open a bottle of wine, or two, and then she'd tell a friend, or her mother, and it would spread like an infection.

I moved in front of her, barring her way to the door – *Andie, please* – and she reached up to slap me, and I grabbed her arm, just for defense. Our joined arms moved up and down and up and down like crazed dance partners.

'Let me go, Nick, or I swear.'

'Just stay for a minute. Just listen to me.'

'You, let me go!'

She moved her face toward mine like she was going to kiss me. She bit me. I jerked back and she shot out the door.

AMY ELLIOTT DUNNE
FIVE DAYS GONE

You may call me Ozark Amy. I am ensconced in the Hide-A-Way Cabins (has ever there been a more apt name?), and I sit quietly, watching all the levers and latches I put in place do their work.

I have shed myself of Nick, and yet I think about him more than ever. Last night at 10:04 p.m. my disposable cell phone rang. (That's right, Nick, you're not the only one who knows the old 'secret cell phone' trick.) It was the alarm company. I didn't answer, of course, but now I know Nick has made it as far as his dad's house. Clue 3. I changed the code two weeks before I disappeared and listed my secret cell as the first number to call. I can picture Nick, my clue in hand, entering his dad's dusty, stale house, fumbling with the alarm code ... then the time runs out. Beep beep beeeep! His cell is listed as the backup if I can't be reached (and I obviously can't).

So he tripped the alarm, and he talked to someone at the alarm company, and so he's on record as being in his dad's house after my disappearance. Which is good for the plan. It's not foolproof, but it doesn't have to be foolproof. I've already left enough for the police to make a case against Nick: the staged scene, the mopped-up blood, the credit-card bills. All these will be found by even the most incompetent police departments. Noelle will spill my pregnancy news very soon (if she hasn't already). It is enough, especially once the police discover Able Andie (able to suck cock on command). So all these extras, they're just bonus fuck-yous. Amusing booby traps. I love that I am a woman with booby traps.

Ellen Abbott is part of my plan too. The biggest cable crime-news show in the country. I adore Ellen Abbott, I love how protective and maternal she gets about all the missing women on her show, and how rabid-dog vicious she is once she seizes on a suspect, usually the husband. She is America's voice of female righteousness. Which is why I'd really like her to take on my story. The Public must turn against Nick. It's as much a part of his punishment as prison, for darling Nicky – who spends so much time worrying about people liking him – to know he is universally hated. And I need Ellen to keep me apprised of the investigation. Have the police found my diary yet? Do they know about Andie? Have they discovered the bumped-up life insurance? This is the hardest part: waiting for stupid people to figure things out.

I flip on the TV in my little room once an hour, eager to see if Ellen has picked up my story. She has to, I can't see how she could resist. I am pretty, Nick is pretty, and I have the *Amazing Amy* hook. Just before noon, she flares up, promising a special report. I stay tuned, glaring at the TV: Hurry up, Ellen. Or: Hurry up, *Ellen*. We have that in common: We are both people and entities. Amy and *Amy*, Ellen and *Ellen*.

Tampon commercial, detergent commercial, maxipad commercial, Windex commercial. You'd think all women do is clean and bleed.

And finally! There I am! My debut!

I know from the second Ellen shows up, glowering like Elvis, that this is going to be good. A few gorgeous photos of me, a still shot of Nick with his insane *love me!* grin from the first press conference. News: There has been a fruitless multi-site search for 'the beautiful young woman with everything going for her.' News: Nick fucked himself already. Taking candid photos with a townie during a search for me. This is clearly what hooked Ellen, because she is *pissed*. There he is, Nick in his sweetie-pie mode, the *I am the beloved of all women* mode, his face pressed against the strange woman's, as if they're happy-hour buddies.

What an idiot. I love it.

Ellen Abbott is making much of the fact that our backyard leads right to the Mississippi River. I wonder then if it has been leaked – the search history on Nick's computer, which I made sure includes a study on the locks and dams of the Mississippi, as well as a Google search of the words *body float Mississippi River*. Not to put too fine a point on it. It could happen – possibly, unlikely, but there is precedent – that the river might sweep my body all the way to the ocean. I've actually felt sad for myself, picturing my slim, naked, pale body, floating just beneath the current, a colony of snails attached to one bare leg, my hair trailing like seaweed until I reach the ocean and drift down down down to the bottom, my waterlogged flesh peeling off in soft streaks, me slowly disappearing into the current like a watercolor until just the bones are left.

But I'm a romantic. In real life, if Nick had killed me, I think he would have just rolled my body into a trash bag and driven me to one of the landfills in the sixty-mile radius. Just dispose of me. He'd have even taken a few items with him – the broken toaster that's not worth fixing, a pile of old VHS tapes he's been meaning to toss – to make the trip efficient.

I'm learning to live fairly efficiently myself. A girl has to budget when she's dead. I had time to plan, to stockpile some cash: I gave myself a good twelve months between deciding to disappear and disappearing. That's why most people get caught in murders: They don't have the discipline to wait. I have $10,200 in cash. If I'd cleared out $10,200 in a month, that would have been noticed. But I collected cash forwards from credit cards I took out in Nick's name – the cards that would make him look like a greedy little cheat – and I siphoned off another $4,400 from our bank accounts over the months: withdrawals of $200 or $300, nothing to attract attention. I stole from Nick, from his pockets, a $20 here, a $10 there, a slow deliberate stockpile – it's like that budgeting plan where you put the money you'd spend on your morning Starbucks into a jar, and at the end of the year you have $1,500. And I'd always steal from the tip jar when I went to The Bar. I'm sure Nick blamed Go, and Go blamed Nick, and neither of them said anything because they felt too sorry for the other.

But I am careful with money, my point. I have enough to live on until I kill myself. I'm going to hide out long enough to watch Lance Nicholas Dunne become a worldwide pariah, to watch Nick be arrested, tried, marched off to prison, bewildered in an orange jumpsuit and handcuffs. To watch Nick squirm and sweat and swear he is innocent and still be stuck. Then I will travel south along the river, where I will meet up with my body, my pretend floating Other Amy body in the Gulf of Mexico. I will sign up for a booze cruise – something to get me out into the deep end but nothing requiring identification. I will drink a giant ice-wet shaker of gin, and I will swallow sleeping pills, and when no one is looking, I'll drop silently over the side, my pockets full of Virginia Woolf rocks. It requires discipline, to drown oneself, but I have discipline in spades. My body may never be discovered, or it may resurface weeks, months, later – eroded to the point that my death can't be time-stamped – and I will provide a last bit of evidence to make sure Nick is marched to the padded cross, the prison table where he'll be pumped with poison and die.

I'd like to wait around and see him dead, but given the state of our justice system, that may take years, and I have neither the money nor the stamina. I'm ready to join the Hopes.

I did veer from my budget a bit already. I spent about $500 on items to nice-up my cabin – good sheets, a decent lamp, towels that don't stand up by themselves from years of bleaching. But I try to accept what I'm offered. There's a man a few cabins away, a taciturn fellow, a hippie dropout of the Grizzly Adams, homemade-granola variety – full beard and turquoise rings and a guitar he plays on his back deck some nights. His name, he says, is Jeff, just like my name, I say, is Lydia. We smile only in passing, but he brings me fish. A couple of times now, he brings a fish by, freshly stinking but scaled and headless, and presents it to me in a giant icy freezer bag. 'Fresh fish!' he says, knocking, and if I don't open the door immediately, he disappears, leaving the bag on my front doorstep. I cook the fish in a decent skillet I bought at yet another Wal-Mart, and it's not bad, and it's free.

'Where do you get all the fish?' I ask him.

'At the getting place,' he says.

Dorothy, who works the front desk and has already taken a liking to me, brings tomatoes from her garden. I eat the tomatoes that smell like the earth and the fish that smells like the lake. I think that by next year, Nick will be locked away in a place that smells only of the inside. Fabricated odors: deodorant and old shoes and starchy foods, stale mattresses. His worst fear, his own personal panic dream: He finds himself in jail, realizing he did nothing wrong but unable to prove it. Nick's nightmares have always been about being wronged, about being trapped, a victim of forces beyond his control.

He always gets up after these dreams, paces around the house, then puts on clothes and goes outside, wanders along the roads near our house, into a park – a Missouri park, a New York park – going wherever he wants. He is a man of the outdoors, if he is not exactly outdoorsy. He's not a hiker, a camper, he doesn't know how to make fires. He wouldn't know how to catch fish and present them to me. But he likes the option, he likes the choice. He wants to know he can go outside, even if he chooses instead to sit on the couch and watch cage fighting for three hours.

I do wonder about the little slut. Andie. I thought she'd last exactly three days. Then she wouldn't be able to resist *sharing*. I know she likes to share because I'm one of her friends on Facebook – my profile name is invented (Madeleine Elster, ha!), my photo is stolen from a popup ad for mortgages (blond, smiling, benefiting from historically low interest rates). Four months ago, Madeleine randomly asked to be Andie's friend, and Andie, like a hapless puppy, accepted, so I know the little girl fairly well, along with all her minutiae-enthralled friends, who take many naps and love Greek yogurt and pinot grigio and enjoy sharing that with each other. Andie is a good girl, meaning she doesn't post photos of herself 'partying,' and she never posts lascivious messages. Which is unfortunate. When she's exposed as Nick's girlfriend, I'd prefer the media find photos of her doing shots or kissing girls or flashing her thong; this would more easily cement her as the homewrecker she is.

Homewrecker. My home was disheveled but not yet wrecked when she first started kissing my husband, reaching inside his trousers, slipping into bed with him. Taking his cock in her mouth, all the way to the root so he feels extra big as she gags. Taking it in her ass, deep. Taking cum shots to the face and tits, then licking it off, *yum*. Taking, definitely taking. Her type would. They've been together for over a year. Every holiday. I went through his credit-card statements (the real ones) to see what he got her for Christmas, but he's been shockingly careful. I wonder what it feels like to be a woman whose Christmas present must be bought in cash. Liberating. Being an undocumented girl means being the girl who doesn't have to call the plumber or listen to gripes about work or remind and remind him to pick up some goddamn cat food.

I need her to break. I need 1) Noelle to tell someone about my pregnancy; 2) the police to find the diary; 3) Andie to tell someone about the affair. I suppose I had her stereotyped – that a girl who posts updates on her life five times a day for anyone to see would have no real understanding of what a secret is. She's made occasional grazing mentions of my husband online:

Saw Mr Hunky today.

(Oh, do tell!)

(When do we get to meet this stud?)

(Bridget likes this!)

A kiss from a dreamy guy makes everything better.

(Too true!)

(When do we get to meet Dreamy?!)

(Bridget likes this!)

But she's been surprisingly discreet for a girl of her generation. She's a good girl (for a cunt). I can picture her, that heart-shaped face tilted to one side, the gently furrowed brow. *I just want you to know I'm on your side, Nick. I'm here for you.* Probably baked him cookies.

The *Ellen Abbott* cameras are now panning the Volunteer Center, which looks a little shabby. A correspondent is talking about how my disappearance has 'rocked this tiny town,' and behind her, I can see a table lined with homemade casseroles and cakes for poor Nicky. Even now the asshole has women taking care of him. Desperate women spotting an opening. A good-looking, vulnerable man – and fine, he may have killed his wife, but we don't *know* that. Not for sure. For now it's a relief just to have a man to cook for, the fortysomething equivalent of driving your bike past the cute boy's house.

They are showing Nick's grinning cell-phone photo again. I can picture the townie slut in her lonely, glistening kitchen – a trophy kitchen bought with alimony money – mixing and baking while having an imaginary conversation with Nick: *No, I'm forty-three, actually. No, really, I am! No, I don't have men swarming all over me, I really don't, the men in town aren't that interesting, most of them . . .*

I get a burst of jealousy toward that woman with her cheek against my husband's. She is prettier than me as I am now. I eat Hershey bars and float in the pool for hours under a hot sun, the chlorine turning my flesh rubbery as a seal's. I'm tan, which I've never been before – at least not a dark, proud, deep tan. A tanned skin is a damaged skin, and no one likes a wrinkled girl; I spent my life slick with SPF. But I let myself darken a bit before I disappeared, and now, five days in, I'm on my way to brown. 'Brown as a berry!' old Dorothy, the manager says. 'You are brown as a berry, girl!' she says with delight when I come in to pay next week's rent in cash.

I have dark skin, my mouse-colored helmet cut, the smart-girl glasses. I gained twelve pounds in the months before my disappearance – carefully hidden in roomy sundresses, not that my inattentive husband would notice – and already another two pounds since. I was careful to have no photos taken of me in the months before I disappeared, so the public will know only pale, thin Amy. I am definitely not that anymore. I can feel my bottom move sometimes, on its own, when I walk. A wiggle and a jiggle, wasn't that some old saying? I never had either before. My body was a beautiful, perfect economy, every feature calibrated, everything in balance. I don't miss it. I don't miss men looking at me. It's a relief to walk into a convenience store and walk right back out without some hangabout in sleeveless flannel leering as I leave, some muttered bit of misogyny slipping from him like a nacho-cheese burp. Now no one is rude to me, but no one is nice to me either. No one goes out of their way, not overly, not really, not the way they used to.

I am the opposite of Amy.

NICK DUNNE
EIGHT DAYS GONE

As the sun came up, I held an ice cube to my cheek. Hours later, and I could still feel the bite: two little staple-shaped creases. I couldn't go after Andie – a worse risk than her wrath – so I finally phoned her. Voice mail.

Contain, this must be contained.

'Andie, I am so sorry, I don't know what to do, I don't know what's going on. Please forgive me. Please.'

I shouldn't have left a voice mail, but then I thought: *She may have hundreds of my voice mails saved, for all I know.* Good God, if she played a hit list of the raunchiest, nastiest, smittenist ... any woman on any jury would send me away just for that. It's one thing to know I'm a cheat and another to hear my heavy teacher voice telling a young co-ed about my giant, hard—

I blushed in the dawn light. The ice cube melted.

I sat on Go's front steps, began phoning Andie every ten minutes, got nothing. I was sleepless, my nerves barbwired, when Boney pulled in to the driveway at 6:12 a.m. I said nothing as she walked toward me, bearing two Styrofoam cups.

'Hey, Nick, I brought you some coffee. Just came over to check on you.'

'I bet.'

'I know you're probably reeling. From the news about the pregnancy.' She made an elaborate show of pouring two creamers into my coffee, the way I like it, and handed it to me. 'What's that?' she said, pointing to my cheek.

'What do you mean?'

'I mean, Nick, what is wrong with your face? There's a

giant pink . . .' She leaned in closer, grabbed my chin. 'It's like a bite mark.'

'It must be hives. I get hives when I'm stressed.'

'Mm-hmmm.' She stirred her coffee. 'You do know I'm on your side, right, Nick?'

'Right.'

'I am. Truly. I wish you'd trust me. I just – I'm getting to the point where I won't be able to help you if you don't trust me. I know that sounds like a cop line, but it's the truth.'

We sat in a strange semi-companionable silence, sipping coffee.

'Hey, so I wanted you to know before you hear it anywhere,' she said brightly. 'We found Amy's purse.'

'What?'

'Yep, no cash left, but her ID, cell phone. In Hannibal, of all places. On the banks of the river, south of the steamboat landing. Our guess: Someone wanted to make it look like it'd been tossed in the river by the perp on the way out of town, heading over the bridge into Illinois.'

'*Make it look like?*'

'It had never been fully submerged. There are fingerprints still at the top, near the zipper. Now sometimes fingerprints can hold on even in water, but . . . I'll spare you the science, I'll just say, the theory is, this purse was kinda settled on the banks to make sure it was found.'

'Sounds like you're telling me this for a reason,' I said.

'The fingerprints we found were yours, Nick. Which isn't that crazy – men get into their wives' purses all the time. But still—' She laughed as if she got a great idea. 'I gotta ask: You haven't been to Hannibal recently, have you?'

She said it with such casual confidence, I had a flash: a police tracker hidden somewhere in the undercarriage of my car, released to me the morning I went to Hannibal.

'Why, exactly, would I go to Hannibal to get rid of my wife's purse?'

'Say you'd killed your wife and staged the crime scene in your home, trying to get us to think she was attacked by an outsider. But then you realized we were beginning to suspect you, so you wanted to plant something to get us to look outside again. That's the theory. But at this point, some of my guys are so sure you did it, they'd find any theory that fit. So let me help you: You in Hannibal lately?'

I shook my head. 'You need to talk to my lawyer. Tanner Bolt.'

'*Tanner Bolt?* You sure that's the way you want to go, Nick? I feel like we've been pretty fair with you so far, pretty open. Bolt, he's a ... he's a last-ditch guy. He's the guy guilty people call in.'

'Huh. Well, I'm clearly your lead suspect, Rhonda. I have to look out for myself.'

'Let's all get together when he gets in, okay? Talk this through.'

'Definitely – that's our plan.'

'A man with a plan,' Boney said. 'I'll look forward to it.' She stood up, and as she walked away, she called back: 'Witch hazel's good for hives.'

An hour later, the doorbell rang, and Tanner Bolt stood there in a baby-blue suit, and something told me it was the look he wore when he went 'down South.' He was inspecting the neighborhood, eyeing the cars in the driveways, assessing the houses. He reminded me of the Elliotts, in a way – examining and analysing at all times. A brain with no off switch.

'Show me,' Tanner said before I could greet him. 'Point me toward the shed – do not come with me, and do not go near it again. Then you'll tell me everything.'

We settled down at the kitchen table – me, Tanner, and a just-woken Go, huddling over her first cup of coffee. I spread out all of Amy's clues like some awful tarot-card reader.

Tanner leaned toward me, his neck muscles tense. 'Okay, Nick, make your case,' he said. 'Your wife orchestrated this whole thing. Make the case!' He jabbed his index finger on the table. 'Because I'm not moving forward with my dick in one hand and a wild story about a frame-up in the other. Unless you convince me. Unless it works.'

I took a deep breath and gathered my thoughts. I was always better at writing than talking. 'Before we start,' I said, 'you have to understand one very key thing about Amy: She is fucking brilliant. Her brain is so busy, it never works on just one level. She's like this endless archaeological dig: You think you've reached the final layer, and then you bring down your pick one more time, and you break through to a whole new mine shaft beneath. With a maze of tunnels and bottomless pits.'

'Fine,' Tanner said. 'So ...'

'The second thing you need to know about Amy is, she is righteous. She is one of those people who is never wrong, and she loves to teach lessons, dole out punishment.'

'Right, fine, so ...'

'Let me tell you a story, one quick story. About three years ago, we were driving up to Massachusetts. It was awful, road-rage traffic, and this trucker flipped Amy off – she wouldn't let him in – and then he zoomed up and cut her off. Nothing dangerous, but really scary for a second. You know those signs on the back of trucks: *How Am I Driving?* She had me call and give them the license plate. I thought that was the end of it. Two months later – two *months* later – I walked into our bedroom, and Amy was on the phone, repeating that license plate. She had a whole story: She was traveling with her two-year-old, and the driver had nearly run her off the road. She said it was her fourth call. She said she'd even researched the company's routes so she could pick the correct highways for her fake near-accidents. She thought of everything. She was really proud. She was going to get that guy fired.'

'Jesus, Nick,' Go muttered.

'That's a very ... enlightening story, Nick,' Tanner said.

'It's just an example.'

'So, now, help me put this all together,' he said. 'Amy finds out you're cheating. She fakes her death. She makes the supposed crime scene look just fishy enough to raise eyebrows.

285

She's screwed you over with the credit cards and the life insurance and your little man-cave situation out back ...'

'She picks an argument with me the night before she goes missing, and she does it standing near an open window so our neighbor will hear.'

'What was the argument?'

'I am a selfish asshole. Basically, the same one we always have. What our neighbor doesn't hear is Amy apologizing later – because Amy doesn't want her to hear that. I mean, I remember being astonished, because it was the quickest makeup we've ever had. By the morning she was freakin' making me crepes, for crying out loud.'

I saw her again at the stove, licking powdered sugar off her thumb, humming to herself, and I pictured me, walking over to her and shaking her until—

'Okay, and the treasure hunt?' Tanner said. 'What's the theory there?'

Each clue was unfolded on the table. Tanner picked up a few and let them drop.

'Those are all just bonus fuck-yous,' I said. 'I know my wife, believe me. She knew she had to do a treasure hunt or it would look fishy. So she does it, and of course it has eighteen different meanings. Look at the first clue.'

I picture myself as your student,
With a teacher so handsome and wise
My mind opens up (not to mention my thighs!)
If I were your pupil, there'd be no need for flowers
Maybe just a naughty appointment during your office hours
So hurry up, get going, please do
And this time I'll teach you a thing or two.

'It's pure Amy. I read this, I think: *Hey, my wife is flirting with me.* No. She's actually referring to my ... infidelity with Andie. Fuck-you number one. So I go there, to my office, with Gilpin, and what's waiting for me? A pair of women's underwear. Not even close to Amy's size – the cops kept asking

286

everyone what size Amy wore, I couldn't figure out why.'

'But Amy had no way of knowing Gilpin would be with you.' Tanner frowned.

'It's a damn good bet,' Go interrupted. 'Clue One was part of the *actual crime scene* – so the cops would know about it – and she has the words *office hours* right in it. It's logical they'd go there, with or without Nick.'

'So whose panties are they?' Tanner asked. Go squinched her nose at the word *panties*.

'Who knows?' I said. 'I'd assumed they were Andie's, but ... Amy probably just bought them. The main point is they're not Amy's size. They lead anyone to believe something inappropriate happened in my office with someone who is not my wife. Fuck-you number two.'

'And if the cops weren't with you when you went to the office?' Tanner asked. 'Or no one noticed the panties?'

'She doesn't *care*, Tanner! This treasure hunt, it's as much for her amusement as anything. She doesn't need it. She's overdone it all just to make sure there are a million damning little clues in circulation. Again, you've got to know my wife: She's a belt-and-suspenders type.'

'Okay. Clue Two,' Tanner said.

> *Picture me: I'm crazy about you*
> *My future is anything but hazy with you*
> *You took me here so I could hear you chat*
> *About your boyhood adventures: crummy jeans and visor hat*
> *Screw everyone else, for us they're all ditched*
> *And let's sneak a kiss ... pretend we just got hitched.*

'This is Hannibal,' I said. 'Amy and I visited there once, so that's how I read it, but it's also another place where I had ... relations with Andie.'

'And you didn't get a red flag?' Tanner said.

'No, not yet, I was too moony about the notes Amy had written me. God, the girl knows me cold. She knows exactly what I want to hear. You are *brilliant*. You are *witty*. And how fun for her to know that she could fuck with my head like that *still*. Long-distance, even. I mean, I was … Christ, I was practically falling in love with her again.'

My throat hitched for a moment. The goofy story about her friend Insley's half-dressed, disgusting baby. Amy knew that was what I had loved most about us back when I loved us: not the big moments, not the Romantic with capital-R moments, but our secret inside jokes. And now she was using them all against me.

'And guess what?' I said. 'They just found Amy's purse in Hannibal. I'm sure as hell someone can place me there. Hell, I paid for my tour ticket with my credit card. So again, here is this piece of evidence, and Amy making sure I can be linked to it.'

'What if no one found the purse?' Tanner asked.

'Doesn't matter,' Go said. 'She's keeping Nick running in circles, she's amusing herself. I'm sure she was happy just knowing what a guilt trip it must be for Nick to be reading all these sweet notes when he knows he's a cheat and she's gone missing.'

I tried not to wince at her disgusted tone: *cheat*.

'What if Gilpin were still with Nick when he went to Hannibal?' Tanner persisted. 'What if Gilpin were with Nick the whole time, so he knew that Nick didn't plant the purse then?'

'Amy knows me well enough to know I'd ditch Gilpin. She knows I wouldn't want a stranger watching me read this stuff, gauging my reactions.'

'Really? How do you know that?'

'I just do.' I shrugged. I knew, I just knew.

'Clue Three,' I said, and pushed it into Tanner's hand.

Maybe you feel guilty for bringing me here
I must admit it felt a bit queer
But it's not like we had the choice of many a place
We made the decision: We made this our space.
Let's take our love to this little brown house
Gimme some goodwill, you hot lovin' spouse.

288

'See, I misread this, thinking that *bringing me here* meant Carthage, but again, she's referring to my father's house, and—'

'It's yet another place where you fucked this Andie girl,' Tanner said. He turned to my sister. 'Pardon the vulgarity.'

Go gave a no-problem flick of her hand.

Tanner continued: 'So, Nick. There are incriminating women's panties in your office, where you fucked Andie, and there is Amy's incriminating purse in Hannibal, where you fucked Andie, and there is an incriminating treasure trove of secret credit-card purchases in the woodshed, where you fucked Andie.'

'Uh, yeah. Yes, that's right.'

'So what's at your dad's house?'

AMY ELLIOTT DUNNE
SEVEN DAYS GONE

I'm pregnant! Thank you, Noelle Hawthorne, the world knows it now, you little idiot. In the day since she pulled her stunt at my vigil (I do wish she hadn't upstaged my vigil, though – ugly girls can be such thunder stealers), the hatred against Nick has ballooned. I wonder if he can breathe with all that fury building around him.

I knew the key to big-time coverage, round-the-clock, frantic, bloodlust never-ending *Ellen Abbott* coverage, would be the pregnancy. Amazing Amy is tempting as is. Amazing Amy knocked up is irresistible. Americans like what is easy, and it's easy to like pregnant women – they're like ducklings or bunnies or dogs. Still, it baffles me that these self-righteous, self-enthralled waddlers get such special treatment. As if it's so hard to spread your legs and let a man ejaculate between them.

You know what *is* hard? Faking a pregnancy.

Pay attention, because this is impressive. It started with my vacant-brained friend Noelle. The Midwest is full of these types of people: the nice-enoughs. Nice enough but with a soul made of plastic – easy to mold, easy to wipe down. The woman's entire music collection is formed from Pottery Barn compilations. Her bookshelves are stocked with coffee-table crap: *The Irish in America. Mizzou Football: A History in Pictures. We Remember 9/11. Something Dumb with Kittens.* I knew I needed a pliant friend for my plan, someone I could load up with awful stories about Nick, someone who would become overly attached to me, someone who'd be easy to manipulate, who wouldn't think too hard about anything I said because she felt privileged to hear it. Noelle was the obvious choice, and when she told me she was pregnant again – triplets weren't enough, apparently – I realized I could be pregnant too.

A search online: how to drain your toilet for repair.

Noelle invited for lemonade. Lots of lemonade.

Noelle peeing in my drained, unflushable toilet, each of us so terribly embarrassed!

Me, a small glass jar, the pee in my toilet going into the glass jar.

Me, a well-laid history of needle/blood phobia.

Me, the glass jar of pee hidden in my purse, a doctor's appointment (oh, I can't do a blood test, I have a total phobia of needles ... urine test, that'll do fine, thank you).

Me, a pregnancy on my medical record.

Me, running to Noelle with the good news.

Perfect. Nick gets another motive, I get to be sweet missing pregnant lady, my parents suffer even more, *Ellen Abbott* can't resist. Honestly, it was thrilling to be selected finally, officially for *Ellen* among all the hundreds of other cases. It's sort of like a talent competition: You do the best you can, and then it's out of your hands, it's up to the judges.

And, oh, does she hate Nick and *love* me. I wished my parents weren't getting such special treatment, though. I watch them on the news coverage, my mom thin and reedy, the cords in her neck like spindly tree branches, always flexed. I see my dad grown ruddy with fear, the eyes a little too wide, the smile squared. He's a handsome man, usually, but he's beginning to look like a caricature, a possessed clown doll. I know I should feel sorry for them, but I don't. I've never been more to them than a symbol anyway, the walking ideal. Amazing Amy in the flesh. Don't screw up, you are Amazing Amy. Our only one. There is an unfair responsibility that comes with being an only child – you grow up knowing you aren't allowed to disappoint, you're not even allowed to die. There isn't a replacement toddling around; you're it. It makes you desperate to be flawless, and it also makes you drunk with the power. In such ways are despots made.

This morning I stroll over to Dorothy's office to get a soda. It's a tiny wood-paneled room. The desk seems to have no purpose other than holding Dorothy's collection of snow globes from places that seem unworthy of commemoration: Gulf Shores, Alabama, Hilo, Arkansas. When I see the snow globes, I don't see paradise, I see overheated hillbillies with sunburns tugging along wailing, clumsy children, smacking them with one hand, with the other clutching giant nonbiodegradable Styrofoam cups of warm corn-syrupy drinks.

Dorothy has one of those '70s kitten-in-a-tree posters – *Hang in There!* She posts her poster with all sincerity. I like to picture her running into some self-impressed Williamsburg bitch, all Bettie Page bangs and pointy glasses, who owns the same poster ironically. I'd like to listen to them try to negotiate each other. Ironic people always dissolve when confronted with earnestness, it's their kryptonite. Dorothy has another gem taped to the wall by the soda machine, showing a toddler asleep on the toilet – *Too Tired to Tinkle*. I've been thinking about stealing this one, a fingernail under the old yellow tape, while I distract-chat with Dorothy. I bet I could get some decent cash for it on eBay – I'd like to keep some cash coming in – but I can't do it, because that would create an *electronic trail*, and I've read plenty about those from my myriad true-crime books. Electronic trails are bad: Don't use a cell phone that's registered to you, because the cell towers can ping your location. Don't use your ATM or credit card. Use only public computers, well trafficked. Beware of the number of cameras that can be on any given street, especially near a bank or a busy intersection or bodegas. Not that there are any bodegas down here. There are no cameras either, in our cabin complex. I know – I asked Dorothy, pretending it was a safety issue.

'Our clients aren't exactly Big Brother types,' she said. 'Not that they're criminals, but they don't usually like to be on the radar.'

No, they don't seem like they'd appreciate that. There's my friend Jeff, who keeps his odd hours and returns with suspicious amounts of undocumented fish that he stores in massive ice chests. He is literally fishy. At the far cabin is a couple who are probably in their forties, but meth-weathered, so they look at least sixty. They stay inside most of the time, aside from occasional wild-eyed treks to the laundry room – darting across the gravel parking lot with their clothes in trash bags, some sort of tweaky spring cleaning. Hellohello, they say, always twice with two head nods, then continue on their way. The man sometimes has a boa constrictor wrapped around his neck, though the snake is never acknowledged, by me or him. In addition to these regulars, a goodly amount of single women straggle through, usually with bruises. Some seem embarrassed, others horribly sad.

One moved in yesterday, a blond girl, very young, with brown eyes and a split lip. She sat on her front porch – the cabin next to mine – smoking a cigarette, and when we caught each other's eye, she sat up straight, proud, her chin jutted out. No apology in her. I thought: *I need to be like her. I will make a study of her: She is who I can be for a bit – the abused tough girl hiding out until the storm passes over.*

After a few hours of morning TV – scanning for any news on the Amy Elliott Dunne case – I slip into my clammy bikini. I'll go to the pool. Float a bit, take a vacation from my harpy brain. The pregnancy news was gratifying, but there is still so much I don't know. I planned so hard, but there are things beyond my control, spoiling my vision of how this should go. Andie hasn't done her part. The diary may need some help being found. The police haven't made a move to arrest Nick. I don't know what all they've discovered, and I don't like it. I'm tempted to make a call, a tip-line call, to nudge them in the right direction. I'll wait a few more days. I have a calendar on my wall, and I mark three days from now with the words *CALL TODAY*. So I know that's how long I've agreed to wait. Once they find the diary, things will move quickly.

Outside, it's jungle-hot once again, the cicadas closing in. My inflatable raft is pink with mermaids on it and too small for me – my calves dangle in the water – but it keeps me floating aimlessly for a good hour, which is something I've learned 'I' like to do.

I can see a blond head bobbing across the parking lot, and then the girl with the split lip comes through the chain-link gate with one of the bath towels from the cabins, no bigger than a tea towel, and a pack of Merits and a book and SPF 120. Lung cancer but not skin. She settles herself and applies the lotion carefully, which is different from the other beat-up women who come here – they slather themselves in baby oil, leave greasy shadows on the lawn chairs.

The girl nods to me, the nod men give each other when they sit down at a bar. She is reading *The Martian Chronicles* by Ray Bradbury. A sci-fi girl. Abused women like escapism, of course.

'Good book,' I toss over to her, a harmless conversational beach ball.

'Someone left it in my cabin. It was this or *Black Beauty*.' She puts on fat, cheap sunglasses.

'Not bad either. *Black Stallion*'s better, though.'

She looks up at me with sunglasses still on. Two black bee-eyed discs. 'Hunh.'

She turns back to her book, the pointed *I am now reading* gesture usually seen on crowded airplanes. And I am the annoying busybody next to her who hogs the armrest and says things like 'Business or pleasure?'

'I'm Nancy,' I say. A new name – not Lydia – which isn't smart in these cramped quarters, but it comes out. My brain sometimes goes too fast for my own good. I was thinking of the girl's split lip, her sad, pre-owned vibe, and then I was thinking of abuse and prostitution, and then I was thinking of *Oliver!*, my favorite musical as a child, and the doomed hooker Nancy, who loved her violent man right until he killed her, and then I was wondering why my feminist mother and I ever watched *Oliver!*, considering 'As Long as He Needs Me' is basically a lilting paean to domestic violence, and then I was thinking that Diary Amy was also killed by her man, she was actually a lot like—

'I'm Nancy,' I say.

'Greta.'

Sounds made up.

'Nice to meet you, Greta.'

I float away. Behind me I hear the shwick of Greta's lighter, and then smoke wafts overhead like spindrifts.

Forty minutes later, Greta sits down on the edge of the pool, dangles her legs in the water. 'It's hot,' she says. 'The water.' She has a husky, hardy voice, cigarettes and prairie dirt.

'Like bathwater.'

'It's not very refreshing.'

'The lake's not much cooler.'

'I can't swim anyway,' she says.

I've never met anyone who can't swim. 'I can just barely,' I lie. 'Dog paddle.'

She ruffles her legs, the waves gently rocking my raft. 'So what's it like here?' she asks.

'Nice. Quiet.'

'Good, that's what I need.'

I turn to look at her. She has two gold necklaces, a perfectly round bruise the size of a plum near her left breast, and a shamrock tattoo just above her bikini line. Her swimsuit is brand-new, cherry-red, cheap. From the marina convenience store where I bought my raft.

'You on your own?' I ask.

'Very.'

I am unsure what to ask next. Is there some sort of code that abused women use with each other, a language I don't know?

'Guy trouble?'

She twitches an eyebrow at me that seems to be a yes.

'Me too,' I say.

'It's not like we weren't warned,' she says. She cups her

295

hand into the water, lets it dribble down her front. 'My mom, one of the first things she ever told me, going to school the first day: *Stay away from boys. They'll either throw rocks or look up your skirt.*'

'You should make a T-shirt that says that.'

She laughs. 'It's true, though. It's always true. My mom lives in a lesbian village down in Texas. I keep thinking I should join her. Everyone seems happy there.'

'A lesbian village?'

'Like a, a whaddayacallit. A commune. Bunch of lesbians bought land, started their own society, sort of. No men allowed. Sounds just freakin' great to me, world without men.' She cups another handful of water, pulls up her sunglasses, and wets her face. 'Too bad I don't like pussy.'

She laughs, an old woman's angry-bark laugh. 'So, are there any asshole guys here I can start dating?' she says. 'That's my, like, pattern. Run away from one, bump into the next.'

'It's half empty most of the time. There's Jeff, the guy with the beard, he's actually really nice,' I say. 'He's been here longer than me.'

'How long are you staying?' she asks.

I pause. It's odd, I don't know the exact amount of time I will be here. I had planned on staying until Nick was arrested, but I have no idea if he will be arrested soon.

'Till he stops looking for you, huh?' Greta guesses.

'Something like that.'

She examines me closely, frowns. My stomach tightens. I wait for her to say it: You look familiar.

'Never go back to a man with fresh bruises. Don't give him the satisfaction,' Greta intones. She stands up, gathers her things. Dries her legs on the tiny towel.

'Good day killed,' she says.

For some reason, I give a thumbs-up, which I've never done in my life.

'Come to my cabin when you get out, if you want to,' she says. 'We can watch TV.'

*

296

I bring a fresh tomato from Dorothy, held in my palm like a shiny housewarming gift. Greta comes to the door and barely acknowledges me, as if I've been dropping over for years. She plucks the tomato from my hand.

'Perfect, I was just making sandwiches,' she says. 'Grab a seat.' She points toward the bed – we have no sitting rooms here – and moves into her kitchenette, which has the same plastic cutting board, the same dull knife, as mine. She slices the tomato. A plastic disc of lunch meat sits on the counter, the stomachy-sweet smell filling the room. She sets two slippery sandwiches on paper plates, along with handfuls of goldfish crackers, and marches them into the bedroom area, her hand already on the remote, flipping from noise to noise. We sit on the edge of the bed, side by side, watching the TV.

'Stop me if you see something,' Greta says.

I take a bite of my sandwich. My tomato slips out the side and onto my thigh.

The Beverly Hillbillies, Suddenly Susan, Armageddon.

Ellen Abbott Live. A photo of me fills the screen. I am the lead story. Again. I look great.

'You seen this?' Greta asked, not looking at me, talking as if my disappearance were a rerun of a decent TV show. 'This woman vanishes on her five-year wedding anniversary. Husband acts real weird from the start, all smiley and shit. Turns out he bumped up her life insurance, and they just found out the wife was *pregnant*. And the guy didn't want it.'

The screen cuts to another photo of me juxtaposed with *Amazing Amy.*

Greta turns to me. 'You remember those books?'

'Of course!'

'You *like* those books?'

'Everyone likes those books, they're so cute,' I say.

Greta snorts. 'They're so fake.'

Close-up of me.

I wait for her to say how beautiful I am.

'She's not bad, huh, for, like, her age,' she says. 'I hope I look that good when I'm forty.'

Ellen is filling the audience in on my story; my photo lingers on the screen.

'Sounds to me like she was a spoiled rich girl,' Greta says. 'High-maintenance. Bitchy.'

That is simply unfair. I'd left no evidence for anyone to conclude that. Since I'd moved to Missouri – well, since I'd come up with my plan – I'd been careful to be low-maintenance, easygoing, cheerful, all those things people want women to be. I waved to neighbors, I ran errands for Mo's friends, I once brought cola to the ever-soiled Stucks Buckley. I visited Nick's dad so that all the nurses could testify to how nice I was, so I could whisper over and over into Bill Dunne's spiderweb brain: *I love you, come live with us, I love you, come live with us.* Just to see if it would catch. Nick's dad is what the people of Comfort Hill call a roamer – he is always wandering off. I love the idea of Bill Dunne, the living totem of everything Nick fears he could become, the object of Nick's most profound despair, showing up over and over and over on our doorstep.

'How does she seem bitchy?' I ask.

She shrugs. The TV goes to a commercial for air freshener. A woman is spraying air freshener so her family will be happy. Then to a commercial for very thin panty liners so a woman can wear a dress and dance and meet the man she will later spray air freshener for.

Clean and bleed. Bleed and clean.

'You can just tell,' Greta says. 'She just sounds like a rich, bored bitch. Like those rich bitches who use their husbands' money to start, like, *cupcake* companies and *card shops* and shit. *Boutiques.*'

In New York, I had friends with all those kinds of businesses – they liked to be able to say they worked, even though they only did the little stuff that was fun: Name the cupcake, order the stationery, wear the adorable dress that was from *their very own* store.

'She's definitely one of those,' Greta said. 'Rich bitch putting on airs.'

Greta leaves to go to the bathroom, and I tiptoe into her

kitchen, go into her fridge, and spit in her milk, her orange juice, and a container of potato salad, then tiptoe back to the bed.

Flush. Greta returns. 'I mean, all that doesn't mean it's okay that he *killed* her. She's just another woman, made a very bad choice in her man.'

She is looking right at me, and I wait for her to say, 'Hey, wait a minute . . .'

But she turns back to the TV, rearranges herself so she is lying on her stomach like a child, her chin in her hands, her face directed at my image on the screen.

'Oh, shit, here it goes,' Greta says. 'People are hatin' on this guy.'

The show gets underway, and I feel a bit better. It is the apotheosis of Amy.

Campbell MacIntosh, childhood friend: 'Amy is just a nurturing, motherly type of woman. She loved being a wife. And I know she would have been a great mother. But Nick – you just knew Nick was wrong somehow. Cold and aloof and really calculating – you got the feeling that he was definitely aware of how much money Amy had.'

(Campbell is lying: She got all googly around Nick, she absolutely adored him. But I'm sure she liked the idea that he only married me for my money.)

Shawna Kelly North, Carthage resident: 'I found it really, really strange how totally unconcerned he was at the search for his wife. He was just, you know, chatting, passing the time. Flirting around with me, who he didn't know from Adam. I'd try to turn the conversation to Amy, and he would just – just no interest.'

(I'm sure this desperate old slut absolutely did not try to turn the conversation toward me.)

Steven 'Stucks' Buckley, longtime friend of Nick Dunne: 'She was a sweetheart. Sweet. Heart. And Nick? He just didn't seem that worried about Amy being gone. The guy was always like that: self-centered. Stuck up a little. Like he'd made it all big in New York and we should all bow down.'

(I despise Stucks Buckley, and what the fuck kind of name is that?)

Noelle Hawthorne, looking like she just got new highlights: 'I think he killed her. No one will say it, but I will. He abused her, and he bullied her, and he finally killed her.'

(Good dog.)

Greta glances sideways at me, her cheeks smushed up under her hands, her face flickering in the TV glow.

'I hope that's not true,' she says. 'That he killed her. It'd be nice to think that maybe she just got away, just ran away from him, and she's hiding out all safe and sound.'

She kicks her legs back and forth like a lazy swimmer. I can't tell if she's fucking with me.

NICK DUNNE
EIGHT DAYS GONE

We searched every cranny of my father's house, which didn't take long, since it's so pathetically empty. The cabinets, the closets. I yanked at the corners of rugs to see if they came up. I peeked into his washer and dryer, stuck a hand up his chimney. I even looked behind the toilet tanks.

'Very *Godfather* of you,' Go said.

'If it were very *Godfather*, I'd have found what we were looking for and come out shooting.'

Tanner stood in the center of my dad's living room and tugged at the end of his lime tie. Go and I were smeared with dust and grime, but somehow Tanner's white button-down positively glowed, as if it retained some of the strobe-light glamour of New York. He was staring at the corner of a cabinet, chewing on his lip, tugging at the tie, *thinking*. The man had probably spent years perfecting this look: the *Shut up, client, I'm thinking* look.

'I don't like this,' he finally said. 'We have a lot of uncontained issues here, and I won't go to the cops until we're very, very contained. My first instinct is to get ahead of the situation – report that stuff in the shed before we get busted with it. But if we don't know what Amy wants us to find here, and we don't know Andie's mind-set ... Nick, do you have a *guess* about what Andie's mind-set is?'

I shrugged. 'Pissed.'

'I mean, that makes me very, very nervous. We're in a very prickly situation, basically. We need to tell the cops about the woodshed. We have to be on the front end of that discovery. But I want to lay out for you what will happen when we do.

And what will happen is: They will go after Go. It'll be one of two options. One: Go is your accomplice, she was helping you hide this stuff on her property, and in all likelihood, she knows you killed Amy.'

'Come on, you can't be serious,' I said.

'Nick, we'd be lucky with that version,' Tanner said. 'They can interpret this however they want. How about this one: It was Go who stole your identity, who got those credit cards. She bought all that crap in there. Amy found out, there was a confrontation, Go killed Amy.'

'Then we get way, way ahead of all this,' I said. 'We tell them about the woodshed, and we tell them Amy is framing me.'

'I think that is a bad idea in general, and right now it's a really bad idea if we don't have Andie on our side, because we'd have to tell them about Andie.'

'Why?'

'Because if we go to the cops with your story, that Amy framed you—'

'Why do you keep saying *my story*, like it's something I made up?'

'Ha. Good point. If we explain to the cops how Amy is framing you, we have to explain *why* she is framing you. Why: because she found out you have a very pretty, very young girlfriend on the side.'

'Do we really have to tell them that?' I asked.

'Amy framed you for her murder because ... she was ... what, bored?'

I swallowed my lips.

'We have to give them Amy's motive, it doesn't work otherwise. But the problem is, if we set Andie, gift-wrapped, on their doorstep, and they don't buy the frame-up theory, then we've given them your motive for murder. Money problems, check. Pregnant wife, check. Girlfriend, check. It's a murderer's triumvirate. You'll go down. Women will line up to tear you apart with their fingernails.' He began pacing. 'But if we don't do anything, and Andie goes to them on her own ...'

'So what do we do?' I asked.

'I think the cops will laugh us out of the station if we say right now that Amy framed you. It's too flimsy. I believe you, but it's flimsy.'

'But the treasure hunt clues—' I started.

'Nick, even I don't understand those clues,' Go said. 'They're all inside baseball between you and Amy. There's only your word that they're leading you into ... incriminating situations. I mean, seriously: crummy jeans and visor equals Hannibal?'

'Little brown house equals your dad's house, which is *blue*,' Tanner added.

I could feel Tanner's doubt. I needed to really show him Amy's character. Her lies, her vindictiveness, her score-settling. I needed other people to back me up – that my wife wasn't Amazing Amy but *Avenging* Amy.

'Lets see if we can reach out to Andie today,' Tanner finally said.

'Isn't it a risk to wait?' Go asked.

Tanner nodded. 'It's a risk. We have to move fast. If another bit of evidence pops up, if the police get a search warrant for the woodshed, if Andie goes to the cops—'

'She won't,' I said.

'She bit you, Nick.'

'She won't. She's pissed off right now, but she's ... I can't believe she'd do that to me. She knows I'm innocent.'

'Nick, you said you were with Andie for about an hour the morning Amy disappeared, yes?'

'Yes. From about ten-thirty to right before twelve.'

'So where were you between seven-thirty and ten?' Tanner asked. 'You said you left the house at seven-thirty, right? Where did you go?'

I chewed on my cheek.

'Where did you go, Nick – I need to know.'

'It's not relevant.'

'*Nick!*' Go snapped.

'I just did what I do some mornings. I pretended to leave,

then I drove to the most deserted part of our complex, and I ... one of the houses there has an unlocked garage.'

'And?' Tanner said.

'And I read magazines.'

'Excuse me?'

'I read back issues of my old magazine.'

I still missed my magazine – I hid copies like porn and read them in secret, because I didn't want anyone feeling sorry for me.

I looked up, and both Tanner and Go felt very, very sorry for me.

I drove back to my house just after noon, was greeted by a street full of news vans, reporters camped out on my lawn. I couldn't get into my driveway, was forced to park in front of the house. I took a breath, then flung myself out of the car. They set on me like starving birds, pecking and fluttering, breaking formation and gathering again. *Nick, did you know Amy was pregnant? Nick, what is your alibi? Nick, did you kill Amy?*

I made it inside, locked myself in. On each side of the door were windows, so I braved it and quickly pulled down the shades, all the while cameras clicking at me, questions called. *Nick, did you kill Amy?* Once the shades were pulled, it was like covering a canary for the night: The noise out front stopped.

I went upstairs and satisfied my shower craving. I closed my eyes and let the spray dissolve the dirt from my dad's house. When I opened them back up, the first thing I saw was Amy's pink razor on the soap dish. It felt ominous, malevolent. My wife was crazy. I was married to a crazy woman. It's every asshole's mantra: *I married a psycho bitch.* But I got a small, nasty bite of gratification: I really did marry a genuine, bona fide psycho bitch. *Nick, meet your wife: the world's foremost mindfucker.* I was not as big an asshole as I'd thought. An asshole, yes, but not on a grandiose scale. The cheating, that had been preemptive, a subconscious reaction to five years yoked to a madwoman: Of course I'd find myself attracted to an uncomplicated, good-natured hometown girl. It's like when people with iron deficiencies crave red meat.

I was toweling off when the doorbell rang. I leaned out the bathroom door and heard the reporters' voices geared up again: *Do you believe your son-in-law, Marybeth? What does it feel like to know you'll be a grandpa, Rand? Do you think Nick killed your daughter, Marybeth?*

They stood side by side on my front step, grim-faced, their backs rigid. There were about a dozen journalists, paparazzi, but they made the noise of twice that many. *Do you believe your son-in-law, Marybeth? What does it feel like to know you'll be a grandpa, Rand?* The Elliotts entered with mumbled hellos and downcast eyes, and I slammed the door shut on the cameras. Rand put a hand on my arm and immediately removed it under Marybeth's gaze.

'Sorry, I was in the shower.' My hair was still dripping, wetting the shoulders of my T-shirt. Marybeth's hair was greasy, her clothes wilted. She looked at me like I was insane.

'Tanner Bolt? Are you serious?' she asked.

'What do you mean?'

'I mean, Nick: Tanner Bolt, are you serious. He only represents guilty people.' She leaned in closer, grabbed my chin. 'What's on your cheek?'

'Hives. Stress.' I turned away from her. 'That's not true about Tanner, Marybeth. It's not. He's the best in the business. I need him right now. The police – all they're doing is looking at me.'

'That certainly seems to be the case,' she said. 'It looks like a bite mark.'

'It's hives.'

Marybeth released an aggravated sigh, turned the corner into the living room. 'This is where it happened?' she asked. Her face had collapsed into a series of fleshy ridges – eye bags and saggy cheeks, her lips downcast.

'We think. Some sort of . . . altercation, confrontation, also happened in the kitchen.'

'Because of the blood.' Marybeth touched the ottoman, tested it, lifted it a few inches, and let it drop. 'I wish you hadn't fixed everything. You made it look like nothing ever happened.'

'Marybeth, he has to live here,' Rand said.

'I still don't understand how – I mean, what if the police didn't find everything? What if . . . I don't know. It seems like they gave up. If they just let the house go. Open to anyone.'

'I'm sure they got everything,' Rand said, and squeezed her hand. 'Why don't we ask if we can look at Amy's things so you can pick something special, okay?' He glanced at me. 'Would that be all right, Nick? It'd be a comfort to have something of hers.' He turned back to his wife. 'That blue sweater Nana knitted for her.'

'I don't want the goddamn blue sweater, Rand!'

She flung his hand off, began pacing around the room, picking up items. She pushed the ottoman with a toe. 'This is the ottoman, Nick?' she asked. 'The one they said was flipped over but it shouldn't have been?'

'That's the ottoman.'

She stopped pacing, kicked it again, and watched it remain upright.

'Marybeth, I'm sure Nick is exhausted' – Rand glanced at me with a meaningful smile – 'like we all are. I think we should do what we came here for and—'

'This is what I came here for, Rand. Not some stupid sweater of Amy's to snuggle up against like I'm three. I want my daughter. I don't want her stuff. Her stuff means nothing to me. I want Nick to tell us what the hell is going on, because this whole thing is starting to stink. I never, I never – I never felt so foolish in my life.' She began crying, swiping away the tears, clearly furious at herself for crying. 'We trusted you with our daughter. We trusted you, Nick. Just tell us the truth!' She put a quivering index finger under my nose. 'Is it true? Did you not want the baby? Did you not love Amy anymore? Did you hurt her?'

I wanted to smack her. Marybeth and Rand had raised Amy.

306

She was literally their work product. They had created her. I wanted to say the words *Your daughter is the monster here*, but I couldn't – not until we'd told the police – and so I remained dumbfounded, trying to think of what I could say. But I looked like I was stonewalling. 'Marybeth, I would never—'

'*I would never, I could never*, that's all I hear from your goddamn *mouth*. You know, I hate even *looking* at you anymore. I really do. There's something wrong with you. There's something missing inside you, to act the way you've been acting. Even if it turns out you're totally blameless, I will never forgive you for how casually you've taken all of this. You'd think you mislaid a damn umbrella! After all Amy gave up for you, after all she did for you, and this is what she gets in return. It— You – I don't believe you, Nick. That's what I came here to let you know. I don't believe in you. Not anymore.'

She began sobbing, turned away, and flung herself out the front door as the thrilled cameramen filmed her. She got in the car, and two reporters pressed against the window, knocking on it, trying to get her to say something. In the living room, we could hear them repeating and repeating her name. *Marybeth – Marybeth—*

Rand remained, hands in his pockets, trying to figure out what role to play. Tanner's voice – *we have to keep the Elliotts on our side* – was Greek-chorusing in my ear.

Rand opened his mouth, and I headed him off. 'Rand, tell me what I can do.'

'Just say it, Nick.'

'Say *what*?'

'I don't want to ask, and you don't want to answer. I get that. But I need to hear you say it. You didn't kill our daughter.'

He laughed and teared up at the same time. 'Jesus Christ, I can't keep my head straight,' Rand said. He was turning pink, flushed, a nuclear sunburn. 'I can't figure out how this is happening. I can't figure it out!' He was still smiling. A tear dribbled on his chin and fell to his shirt collar. 'Just say it, Nick.'

'Rand, I did not kill Amy or hurt her in any way.' He kept his eyes on me. 'Do you believe me, that I didn't physically *harm* her?'

Rand laughed again. 'You know what I was about to say? I was about to say I don't know what to believe anymore. And then I thought, that's someone else's line. That's a line from a movie, not something I should be saying, and I wonder for a second, am I in a movie? Can I stop being in this movie? Then I know I can't. But for a second, you think, *I'll say something different, and this will all change.* But it won't, will it?'

With one quick Jack Russell headshake, he turned and followed his wife to the car.

Instead of feeling sad, I felt alarmed. Before the Elliotts were even out of my driveway, I was thinking: *We need to go to the cops quickly, soon.* Before the Elliotts started discussing their loss of faith in public. I needed to prove my wife was not who she pretended to be. *Not Amazing Amy: Avenging Amy.* I flashed to Tommy O'Hara – the guy who called the tip line three times, the guy Amy had accused of raping her. Tanner had gotten some background on him: He wasn't the macho Irishman I'd pictured from his name, not a firefighter or cop. He wrote for a humor website based in Brooklyn, a decent one, and his contributor photo revealed him to be a scrawny guy with dark-framed glasses and an uncomfortable amount of thick black hair, wearing a wry grin and a T-shirt for a band called the Bingos.

He picked up on the first ring. 'Yeah?'

'This is Nick Dunne. You called me about my wife. Amy Dunne. Amy Elliott. I have to talk with you.'

I heard a pause, waited for him to hang up on me like Hilary Handy.

'Call me back in ten minutes.'

I did. The background was a bar, I knew the sound well enough: the murmur of drinkers, the clatter of ice cubes, the strange pops of noise as people called for drinks or hailed friends. I had a burst of homesickness for my own place.

'Okay, thanks,' he said. 'Had to get to a bar. Seemed like a

Scotch conversation.' His voice got progressively closer, thicker: I could picture him huddling protectively over a drink, cupping his mouth to the phone.

'So,' I began, 'I got your messages.'

'Right. She's still missing, right? Amy?'

'Yes.'

'Can I ask you what you think has happened?' he said. 'To Amy?'

Fuck it, I wanted a drink. I went into my kitchen – next best thing to my bar – and poured myself one. I'd been trying to be more careful about the booze, but it felt so good: the tang of a Scotch, a dark room with the blinding sun right outside.

'Can I ask you why you called?' I replied.

'I've been watching the coverage,' he said. 'You're fucked.'

'I am. I wanted to talk to you because I thought it was … interesting that you'd try to get in touch. Considering. The rape charge.'

'Ah, you know about that,' he said.

'I know there was a rape charge, but I don't necessarily believe you're a rapist. I wanted to hear what you had to say.'

'Yeah.' I heard him take a gulp of his Scotch, kill it, shake the ice cubes around. 'I caught the story on the news one night. Your story. Amy's. I was in bed, eating Thai. Minding my own business. Totally fucked me in the head. *Her* after all these years.' He called to the bartender for another. 'So my lawyer said no way I should talk to you, but … what can I say? I'm too fucking nice. I can't let you twist. God, I wish you could still smoke in bars. This is a Scotch *and* cigarette conversation.'

'Tell me,' I said. 'About the assault charge. The rape.'

'Like I said, man, I've seen the coverage, the media is shitting all over you. I mean, you're *the guy*. So I should leave well enough alone – I don't need that girl back in my life. Even, like, tangentially. But shit. I wish someone had done me the favor.'

'So do me the favor,' I said.

'First of all, she dropped the charges – you know that, right?'

'I know. Did you do it?'

'Fuck you. Of course I didn't do it. Did *you* do it?'

'No.'

'Well.'

Tommy called again for his Scotch. 'Let me ask: Your marriage was good? Amy was happy?'

I stayed silent.

'You don't have to answer, but I'm going to guess no. Amy was not happy. For whatever reason. I'm not even going to ask. I can guess, but I'm not going to ask. But I know you must know this: Amy likes to play God when she's not happy. Old Testament God.'

'Meaning?'

'She doles out punishment,' Tommy said. 'Hard.' He laughed into the phone. 'I mean, you should see me,' he said. 'I do not look like some alpha-male rapist. I look like a twerp. I am a twerp. My go-to karaoke song is "Sister Christian," for crying out loud. I weep during *Godfather II*. Every time.' He coughed after a swallow. Seemed like a moment to loosen him up.

'Fredo?' I asked.

'Fredo, man, yeah. Poor Fredo.'

'Stepped over.'

Most men have sports as the lingua-franca of dudes. This was the film-geek equivalent to discussing some great play in a famous football game. We both knew the line, and the fact that we both knew it eliminated a good day's worth of *are we copacetic* small talk.

He took another drink. 'It was so fucking absurd.'

'Tell me.'

'You're not taping this or anything, right? No one's listening in? Because I don't want that.'

'Just us. I'm on your side.'

'So I meet Amy at a party – this is, like, seven years ago now – and she's so damn cool. Just hilarious and weird and

... cool. We just clicked, you know, and I don't click with a lot of girls, at least not girls who look like Amy. So I'm thinking ... well, first I'm thinking I'm being punked. Where's the catch, you know? But we start dating, and we date a few months, two, three months, and then I find out the catch: She's not the girl I thought I was dating. She can *quote* funny things, but she doesn't actually like funny things. She'd rather not laugh, anyway. In fact, she'd rather that I not laugh either, or be funny, which is awkward since it's my job, but to her, it's all a waste of time. I mean, I can't even figure out why she started dating me in the first place, because it seems pretty clear that she doesn't even like me. Does that make sense?'

I nodded, swallowed a gulp of Scotch. 'Yeah. It does.'

'So, I start making excuses not to hang out so much. I don't call it off, because I'm an idiot, and she's gorgeous. I'm hoping it might turn around. But you know, I'm making excuses fairly regularly: I'm stuck at work, I'm on deadline, I have a friend in town, my monkey is sick, whatever. And I start seeing this other girl, kinda sorta seeing her, very casual, no big deal. Or so I *think*. But Amy finds out – how, I still don't know, for all I know, she was staking out my apartment. But ... *shit* ...'

'Take a drink.'

We both took a swallow.

'Amy comes over to my place one night – I'd been seeing this other girl like a month – and Amy comes over, and she's all back like she used to be. She's got some bootleg DVD of a comic I like, an underground performance in Durham, and she's got a sack of burgers, and we watch the DVD, and she's got her leg flopped over mine, and then she's nestling into me, and ... sorry. She's your wife. My main point is: The girl knew how to work me. And we end up ...'

'You had sex.'

'*Consensual* sex, yes. And she leaves and everything is fine. Kiss goodbye at the door, the whole shebang.'

'Then what?'

'The next thing I know, two cops are at my door, and they've done a rape kit on Amy, and she has "wounds consistent with forcible rape." And she has ligature marks on her wrists, and when they search my apartment, there on the headboard of my bed are two ties – like, neckties – tucked down near the mattress, and the ties are, quote, "consistent with the ligature marks."'

'Had you tied her up?'

'No, the sex wasn't even that ... *that*, you know? I was totally caught off guard. She must have tied them there when I got up to take a piss or whatever. I mean, I was in some serious shit. It was looking very bad. And then suddenly she dropped the charges. Couple of weeks later, I got a note, anonymous, typed, says: *Maybe next time you'll think twice.*'

'And you never heard from her again?'

'Never heard from her again.'

'And you didn't try to press charges against her or anything?'

'Uh, no. Fuck no. I was just glad she went away. Then last week, I'm eating my Thai food, sitting in my bed, watching the news report. On Amy. On you. Perfect wife, anniversary, no body, a real shitstorm. I swear, I broke out in a sweat. I thought: *That's Amy, she's graduated to murder. Holy shit.* I'm serious, man, I bet whatever she's got cooked up for you, it's drum-fucking-tight. You should be fucking scared.'

AMY ELLIOTT DUNNE
EIGHT DAYS GONE

I am wet from the bumper boats; we got more than five dollars' worth of time because the two sun-stunned teenage girls would rather flip through gossip magazines and smoke cigarettes than try to herd us off the water. So we spent a good thirty minutes on our lawn-mower-motor-propelled ships, ramming each other and turning wild twists, and then we got bored and left of our own accord.

Greta, Jeff, and I, an odd crew in a strange place. Greta and Jeff have become good friends in just a day, which is how people do it here, where there's nothing else to do. I think Greta is deciding whether she'll make Jeff another of her disastrous mating choices. Jeff would like it. He prefers her. She is much prettier than I am, right now, in this place. Cheap pretty. She is wearing a bikini top and jean shorts, with a spare shirt tucked into the back pocket for when she wants to enter a store (T-shirts, wood carvings, decorative rocks) or restaurant (burger, barbecue, taffy). She wants us to get Old West photos taken, but that's not going to happen for reasons aside from the fact that I don't want redneck-lake-person lice.

We end up settling for a few rounds on a decrepit miniature golf course. The fake grass is torn off in patches, the alligators and windmills that once moved mechanically are still. Jeff does the honors instead, twirling the windmill, snapping open and shut the gator jaws. Some holes are simply unplayable – the grass rolled up like carpeting, the farmhouse with its beckoning mousehole collapsed in on itself. So we roam between courses in no particular order. No one is even keeping score.

This would have annoyed Old Amy no end: the haphazardness of it all, the pointlessness. But I'm learning to drift, and I do it quite well. I am overachieving at aimlessness, I am a type-A, alpha-girl lollygagger, the leader of a gang of heartbroken kids, running wild across this lonely strip of amusements, each of us smarting from the betrayals of a loved one. I catch Jeff (cuckolded, divorced, complicated custody arrangement) furrowing his brow as we pass a Love Tester: Squeeze the metal grip and watch the temperature rise from 'just a fling' to 'soulmate.' The odd equation – a crushing clutch means true love – reminds me of poor smacked-around Greta, who often places her thumb over the bruise on her chest like it's a button she can push.

'You're up,' Greta says to me. She's drying her ball off on her shorts – twice she's gone into the cesspool of dirty water.

I get in position, wiggle once or twice, and putt my bright red ball straight into the birdhouse opening. It disappears for a second, then reappears out a chute and into the hole. Disappear, reappear. I feel a wave of anxiety – everything reappears at some point, even me. I am anxious because I think my plans have changed.

I have changed plans only twice so far. The first was the gun. I was going to get a gun and then, on the morning I disappeared, I was going to shoot myself. Nowhere dangerous: through a calf or a wrist. I would leave behind a bullet with my flesh and blood on it. A struggle occurred! Amy was shot! But then I realized this was a little too macho even for me. It would hurt for weeks, and I don't love pain (my sliced arm feels better now, thank you very much). But I still liked the idea of a gun. It made for a nice MacGuffin. Not *Amy was shot* but *Amy was scared*. So I dolled myself up and went to the mall on Valentine's Day, so I'd be remembered. I couldn't get one, but it's not a big deal as far as changed plans go.

The other one is considerably more extreme. I have decided I'm not going to die.

I have the discipline to kill myself, but can't stomach the injustice. It's not fair that I have to die. Not *really* die. I don't want to. I'm not the one who did anything wrong.

The problem now though, is money. It's so ludicrous, that of all things it's money that should be an issue for me. But I have only a finite amount – $9,132 at this point. I will need more. This morning I went to chat with Dorothy; as always, holding a handkerchief so as not to leave fingerprints (I told her it was my grandmother's – I try to give her a vague impression of southern wealth gone to squander, very Blanche DuBois). I leaned against her desk as she told me, in great bureaucratic detail, about a blood thinner she can't afford – the woman is an encyclopedia of denied pharmaceuticals – and then I said, just to test the situation: 'I know what you mean. I'm not sure where I'm going to get rent for my cabin after another week or two.'

She blinked at me, and blinked back toward the TV set, a game show where people screamed and cried a lot. She took a grandmotherly interest in me, she'd certainly let me stay on, indefinitely: The cabins were half empty, no harm.

'You better get a job, then,' Dorothy said, not turning away from the TV. A contestant made a bad choice, the prize was lost, a wuh-waaahhh sound effect voiced her pain.

'A job like what? What kind of job can I get around here?'

'Cleaning, babysitting.'

Basically, I was supposed to be a housewife for pay. Irony enough for a million *Hang in There* posters.

It's true that even in our lowly Missouri state, I didn't ever have to actually budget. I couldn't go out and buy a new car just because I wanted to, but I never had to think about the day-to-day stuff, coupon clipping and buying generic and knowing how much milk costs off the top of my head. My parents never bothered teaching me this, and so they left me unprepared for the real world. For instance, when Greta complained that the convenience store at the marina charged five dollars for a gallon of milk, I winced because the kid there always charged me ten dollars. I'd thought that seemed like a lot, but it hadn't occurred to me that the little pimply teenager just threw out a number to see if I'd pay.

So I'd budgeted, but my budget – guaranteed, according to the Internet, to last me six to nine months – is clearly off. And so I am off.

When we're done with golf – I win, of course I do, I know because I'm keeping score in my head – we go to the hot-dog stand next door for lunch, and I slip around the corner to dig into my zippered money belt under my shirt, and when I glance back, Greta has followed me, she catches me right before I can stuff the thing away.

'Ever heard of a purse, Moneybags?' she cracks. This will be an ongoing problem – a person on the run needs lots of cash, but a person on the run by definition has nowhere to keep the cash. Thankfully, Greta doesn't press the issue – she knows we are both victims here. We sit in the sun on a metal picnic bench and eat hot dogs, white buns wrapped around cylinders of phosphate with relish so green it looks toxic, and it may be the greatest thing I've ever eaten because I am Dead Amy and I don't care.

'Guess what Jeff found in his cabin for me?' Greta says. 'Another book by the *Martian Chronicle* guy.'

'Ray Bradburrow,' Jeff says. *Bradbury*, I think.

'Yeah, right. *Something Wicked This Way Comes*,' Greta says. 'It's good.' She chirps the last bit as if that were all to say about a book: It's good or it's bad. I liked it or I didn't. No discussions of the writing, the themes, the nuances, the structure. Just good or bad. Like a hot dog.

'I read it when I first moved in there,' Jeff says. 'It is good. Creepy.' He catches me watching him and makes a goblin face, all crazy eyes and leering tongue. He isn't my type – the fur on the face is too bristly, he does suspicious things with fish – but he is nice-looking. Attractive. His eyes are very warm, not like Nick's frozen blues. I wonder if 'I' might like sleeping with him – a nice slow screw with his body pressed against mine and his breath in my ear, the bristles on my cheeks, not the lonely way Nick fucks, where our bodies barely connect: right angle from behind, L-shape from the front, and then he's out of bed almost immediately, hitting the shower, leaving me pulsing in his wet spot.

'Cat got your tongue?' Jeff says. He never calls me by name, as if to acknowledge that we both know I've lied. He says *this lady* or *pretty woman* or *you*. I wonder what he would call me in bed. *Baby*, maybe.

'Just thinking.'

'Uh-oh,' he says, and smiles again.

'You were thinking about a boy, I can tell,' Greta says.

'Maybe.'

'I thought we were steering clear of the assholes for a while,' she says. 'Tend to our chickens.' Last night after *Ellen Abbott*, I was too excited to go home, so we shared a six-pack and imagined our recluse life as the token straight girls on Greta's mother's lesbian compound, raising chickens and hanging laundry to dry in the sun. The objects of gentle, platonic courtship from older women with gnarled knuckles and indulgent laughs. Denim and corduroy and clogs and never worrying about makeup or hair or nails, breast size or hip size, or having to pretend to be the understanding wifey, the supportive girlfriend who loves everything her man does.

'Not all guys are assholes,' Jeff says. Greta makes a non-committal noise.

We return to our cabins liquid-limbed. I feel like a water balloon left in the sun. All I want to do is sit under my sputtering window air conditioner and blast my skin with the cool while watching TV. I've found a rerun channel that shows nothing but old '70s and '80s shows, *Quincy* and *The Love Boat* and *Eight Is Enough*, but first comes *Ellen Abbott*, my new favorite show!

Nothing new, nothing new. Ellen doesn't mind speculating, believe me, she's hosted an array of strangers from my past who swear they are my friends, and they all have lovely things to say about me, even the ones who never much liked me. Post-life fondness.

Knock on the door, and I know it will be Greta and Jeff.

I switch off the TV, and there they are on my doorstep, aimless.

'Whatcha doing?' Jeff asks.

'Reading,' I lie.

He sets down a six-pack of beer on my counter, Greta padding in behind. 'Oh, I thought we heard the TV.'

Three is literally a crowd in these small cabins. They are blocking the door for a second, sending a pulse of nervousness through me – why are they blocking the door? – and then they keep moving and they are blocking my bedside table. Inside my bedside table is my money belt packed with eight thousand dollars in cash. Hundreds, fifties, and twenty-dollar bills. The money belt is hideous, flesh-colored and bunchy. I can't possibly wear all my money at once – I leave some scattered around the cabin – but I try to wear most, and when I do, I am as conscious of it as a girl at the beach with a maxipad. A perverse part of me enjoys spending money, because every time I pull off a wad of twenties, that's less money to hide, to worry about being stolen or lost.

Jeff clicks on the TV, and Ellen Abbott – and Amy – buzz into focus. He nods, smiles to himself.

'Want to watch ... Amy?' Greta asks.

I can't tell if she used a comma: *Want to watch, Amy?* or *Want to watch Amy?*

'Nah. Jeff, why don't you grab your guitar and we can sit on the porch?'

Jeff and Greta exchange a look.

'Awww ... but that's what you were watching, right?' Greta says. She points at the screen, and it's me and Nick at a benefit, me in a gown, my hair pulled back in a chignon, and I look more like I look now, with my short hair.

'It's boring,' I say.

'Oh, I don't think it's boring at all,' Greta says, and flops down on my bed.

I think what a fool I am, to have let these two people inside. To have assumed I could control them, when they are feral creatures, people used to finding the angle, exploiting the weakness, always needing, whereas I am new to this. Needing. Those people who keep backyard pumas and living room chimps – this must be how they feel when their adorable pet rips them open.

'You know what, would you guys mind ... I feel kinda crummy. Too much sun, I think.'

They look surprised and a little offended, and I wonder if I've got it wrong – that they are harmless and I'm just paranoid. I'd like to believe that.

'Sure, sure, of course,' Jeff says. They shuffle out of my cabin, Jeff grabbing his beer on the way. A minute later, I hear Ellen Abbott snarling from Greta's cabin. The accusatory questions. *Why did ... Why didn't ... How can you explain ...*

Why did I ever let myself get friendly with anyone here? *Why didn't* I keep to myself? *How can I explain* my actions if I'm found out?

I can't be discovered. If I were ever found, I'd be the most hated woman on the planet. I'd go from being the beautiful, kind, doomed, pregnant victim of a selfish, cheating bastard to being the bitter bitch who exploited the good hearts of all America's citizens. Ellen Abbott would devote show after show to me, angry callers venting their hate: 'This is just another example of a spoiled rich girl doing what she wants, when she wants and not thinking of anyone else's feelings, Ellen. I think she *should* disappear for life – in prison!' Like that, it would go like that. I've read conflicting Internet information on the penalties for faking a death, or framing a spouse for said death, but I know the public opinion would be brutal. No matter what I do after that – feed orphans, cuddle lepers – when I died, I'd be known as That Woman Who Faked Her Death and Framed Her Husband, You Remember.

I can't allow it.

Hours later, I am still awake, thinking in the dark, when my door rattles, a gentle bang, Jeff's bang. I debate, then open it, ready to apologize for my rudeness before. He's tugging on his beard, staring at my doormat, then looks up with amber eyes.

'Dorothy said you were looking for work,' he said.

'Yeah. I guess. I am.'

'I got something tonight, pay you fifty bucks.'

Amy Elliott Dunne wouldn't leave her cabin for fifty bucks, but Lydia and/or Nancy needs work. I have to say yes.

'Coupla hours, fifty dollars.' He shrugs. 'Doesn't make any difference to me, just thought I'd offer.'

'What is it?'

'Fishing.'

I was positive Jeff would drive a pickup, but he guides me to a shiny Ford hatchback, a heartbreaking car, the car of the new college grad with big plans and a modest budget, not the car a grown man should be driving. I am wearing my swimsuit under my sundress, as instructed ('Not the bikini, the full one, the one you can really swim in,' Jeff intoned; I'd never noticed him anywhere near the pool, but he knew my swimwear cold, which was flattering and alarming at the same time).

He leaves the windows down as we drive through the forested hills, the gravel dust coating my stubby hair. It feels like something from a country-music video: the girl in the sundress leaning out to catch the breeze of a red-state summer night. I can see stars. Jeff hums off and on.

He parks down the road from a restaurant that hangs out on stilts over the lake, a barbecue place known for its giant souvenir cups of boozy drinks with bad names: Gator Juice and Bassmouth Blitz. I know this from the discarded cups that float along all the shores of the lake, cracked and neon-colored with the restaurant's logo: Catfish Carl's. Catfish Carl's has a deck that overhangs the water – diners can load up on handfuls of kitty kibble from the crank machines and drop them into the gaping mouths of hundreds of giant catfish that wait below.

'What exactly are we going to do, Jeff?'

'You net 'em, I kill 'em.' He gets out of the car, and I follow him around to the hatchback, which is filled with coolers. 'We put 'em in here, on ice, resell them.'

'Resell them. Who buys stolen fish?'

Jeff smiles that lazy-cat smile. 'I got a clientele of sorts.'

And then I realize: He isn't a Grizzly Adams, guitar-playing, peace-loving granola guy at all. He is a redneck thief who wants to believe that he's more complicated than that.

He pulls out a net, a box of Nine Lives, and a stained plastic bucket.

I have absolutely no intention of being part of this illicit piscine economy, but 'I' am fairly interested. How many women can say they were part of a fish-smuggling ring? 'I' am game. I have become game again since I died. All the things I disliked or feared, all the limits I had, they've slid off me. 'I' can do pretty much anything. A ghost has that freedom.

We walk down the hill, under the deck of Catfish Carl's, and onto the docks, which float slurpily on the wakes of a passing motorboat, Jimmy Buffett blaring.

Jeff hands me a net. 'We need this to be quick – you just jump in the water, scoop the net in, nab the fish, then tilt the net up to me. It'll be heavy, though, and squirmy, so be prepared. And don't scream or nothing.'

'I won't scream. But I don't want to go in the water. I can do it from the deck.'

'You should take off your dress, at least, you'll ruin it.'

'I'm okay.'

He looks annoyed for a moment – he's the boss, I'm the employee, and so far I'm not listening to him – but then he turns around modestly and tugs off his shirt and hands me the box of cat food without fully facing me, as if he's shy. I hold the box with its narrow mouth over the water, and immediately, a hundred shiny arched backs roll toward me, a mob of serpents, the tails cutting across the surface furiously, and then the mouths are below me, the fish roiling over each other to swallow the pellets and then, like trained pets, aiming their faces up toward me for more.

I scoop the net into the middle of the pack and sit down hard on the dock to get leverage to pull the harvest up. When I yank, the net is full of half a dozen whiskery, slick catfish, all frantically trying to get back in the water, their gaping lips opening and shutting between the squares of nylon, their collective tugging making the net wobble up and down.

'Lift it up, lift it up, girl!'

I push a knee below the net's handle and let it dangle there, Jeff reaching in, grabbing a fish with two hands, each encased in terry-cloth manicure gloves for a better grip. He moves his hands down around the tail, then swings the fish like a cudgel, smashing its head on the side of the dock. Blood explodes. A brief sharp pelt of it streaks across my legs, a hard chunk of meat hits my hair. Jeff throws the fish in the bucket and grabs another with assembly-line smoothness.

We work in grunts and wheezes for half an hour, four nets full, until my arms turn rubbery and the ice chests are full. Jeff takes the empty pail and fills it with water from the lake, pours it across the messy entrails and into the fish pens. The catfish gobble up the guts of their fallen brethren. The dock is left clean. He pours one last pail of water across our bloody feet.

'Why do you have to smash them?' I ask.

'Can't stand to watch something suffer,' he says. 'Quick dunk?'

'I'm okay,' I say.

'Not in my car, you're not – come on, quick dunk, you have more crap on you than you realize.'

We run off the dock toward the rocky beach nearby. While I wade ankle-deep in the water, Jeff runs with giant splashy footsteps and throws himself forward, arms wild. As soon as he's far enough out, I unhook my money belt and fold my sundress around it, leave it at the water's edge with my glasses on top. I lower myself until I feel the warm water hit my thighs, my belly, my neck, and then I hold my breath and go under.

I swim far and fast, stay underwater longer than I should to remind myself what it would feel like to drown – I know I could do it if I needed to – and when I come up with a single disciplined gasp, I see Jeff lapping rapidly toward shore, and I have to swim fast as a porpoise back to my money belt and scramble onto the rocks just ahead of him.

NICK DUNNE
EIGHT DAYS GONE

As soon as I hung up with Tommy, I phoned Hilary Handy. If my 'murder' of Amy was a lie, and Tommy O'Hara's 'rape' of Amy was a lie, why not Hilary Handy's 'stalking' of Amy? A sociopath must cut her teeth somewhere, like the austere marble halls of Wickshire Academy.

When she picked up, I blurted: 'This is Nick Dunne, Amy Elliott's husband. I really need to talk to you.'

'Why.'

'I really, really need more information. About your—'

'Don't say *friendship*.' I heard an angry grin in her voice.

'No. I wouldn't. I just want to hear your side. I am not calling because I think you've got anything – *anything* – to do with my wife, her situation, currently. But I would really like to hear what happened. The truth. Because I think you may be able to shed light on a ... pattern of behavior of Amy's.'

'What kind of pattern?'

'When very bad things happen to people who upset her.'

She breathed heavily into the phone. 'Two days ago, I wouldn't have talked to you,' she started. 'But then I was having a drink with some friends, and the TV was on, and you came on, and it was about Amy being pregnant. Everyone I was with, they were so *angry* at you. They *hated* you. And I thought, *I know how that feels*. Because she's not dead, right? I mean, she's still just missing? No body?'

'That's right.'

'So let me tell you. About Amy. And high school. And what happened. Hold on.' On her end, I could hear cartoons playing – rubbery voices and calliope music – then suddenly

323

not. Then whining voices. *Go watch downstairs. Downstairs, please.*

'So, freshman year. I'm the kid from Memphis. *Everyone* else is East Coast, I swear. It felt weird, different, you know? All the girls at Wickshire, it was like they'd been raised communally – the lingo, the clothes, the hair. And it wasn't like I was a pariah, I was just … insecure, for sure. Amy was already The Girl. Like, first day, I remember, everyone knew her, everyone was talking about her. She was Amazing Amy – we'd all read those books growing up – plus, she was just gorgeous. I mean, she was—'

'Yeah, I know.'

'Right. And pretty soon she was showing an interest in me, like, taking me under her wing or whatever. She had this joke that she was Amazing Amy, so I was her sidekick Suzy, and she started calling me Suzy, and pretty soon everyone else did, too. Which was fine by me. I mean, I was a little toadie: Get Amy a drink if she was thirsty, throw in a load of laundry if she needed clean underwear. Hold on.'

Again I could hear the shuffle of her hair against the receiver. Marybeth had brought every Elliott photo album with her in case we needed more pictures. She'd shown me a photo of Amy and Hilary, cheek-to-cheek grins. So I could picture Hilary now, the same butter-blond hair as my wife, framing a plainer face, with muddy hazel eyes.

'Jason, I am on the phone – just give them a few Popsicles, it's not that dang hard.

'Sorry. Our kids are out of school, and my husband never ever takes care of them, so he seems a little confused about what to do for the ten minutes I'm on the phone with you. Sorry. So … so, right, I was little Suzy, and we had this game going, and for a few months – August, September, October – it was great. Like *intense* friendship, we were together all the time. And then a few weird things happened at once that I knew kind of bothered her.'

'What?'

'A guy from our brother school, he meets us both at the fall

324

dance, and the next day he calls *me* instead of Amy. Which I'm sure he did because Amy was too intimidating, but whatever ... and then a few days later, our midterm grades come, and mine are slightly better, like, four-point-one versus four-point. And not long after, one of our friends, she invites me to spend Thanksgiving with her family. Me, not Amy. Again, I'm sure this was because Amy intimidated people. She wasn't easy to be around, you felt all the time like you had to impress. But I can feel things change just a little. I can tell she's really irritated, even though she doesn't admit it.

'Instead, she starts getting me to do things. I don't realize it at the time, but she starts setting me up. She asks if she can color my hair the same blond as hers, because mine's mousy, and it'll look *so nice* a brighter shade. And she starts complaining about her parents. I mean she's always complained about her parents, but now she really gets going on them – how they only love her as an idea and not really for who she is – so she says she wants to mess with her parents. She has me start prank-calling her house, telling her parents I'm the new Amazing Amy. We'd take the train into New York some weekends, and she'd tell me to stand outside their house – one time she had me run up to her mom and tell her I was going to get rid of Amy and be her new Amy or some crap like that.'

'And you did it?'

'It was just dumb stuff girls do. Back before cell phones and cyber-bullying. A way to kill time. We did prank stuff like that all the time, just dumb stuff. Try to one-up each other on how daring and freaky we could be.'

'Then what?'

'Then she starts distancing herself. She gets cold. And I think – I think that she doesn't like me anymore. Girls at school start looking at me funny. I'm shut out of the cool circle. Fine. But then one day I'm called into the principal's office. Amy has had a horrible accident – twisted ankle, fractured arm, cracked ribs. Amy has fallen down this long set of stairs, and she says it was *me* who pushed her. Hold on. *Go*

back downstairs now. Go. Down. Stairs. Goooo downstairs. Sorry,
I'm back. Never have kids.'

'So Amy said you pushed her?'

'Yeah, because I was *craaaazy*. I was obsessed with her, and
I wanted to be Suzy, and then being Suzy wasn't enough –
I had to be Amy. And she had all this evidence that she'd had
me create over the past few *months*. Her parents, obviously,
had seen me *lurking* around the house. I theoretically accosted
her mom. My hair dyed blond and the clothes I'd bought that
matched Amy's – clothes I bought while shopping *with* her,
but I couldn't prove that. All her friends came in, explained
how Amy for the past month had been so frightened of me.
All this shit. I looked *totally insane*. Completely insane. Her
parents got a restraining order on me. And I kept swearing it
wasn't me, but by then I was so miserable that I wanted to
leave school anyway. So we didn't fight the expulsion. I wanted
to get away from her by that time. I mean, the girl *cracked her
own ribs*. I was scared – this little fifteen-year-old, she'd pulled
this off. Fooled friends, parents, teachers.'

'And this was all because of a boy and some grades and a
Thanksgiving invitation?'

'About a month after I moved back to Memphis, I got a
letter. It wasn't signed, it was typed, but it was obviously Amy.
It was a list of all the ways I'd let her down. Crazy stuff:
*Forgot to wait for me after English, twice. Forgot I am allergic to
strawberries, twice.*'

'Jesus.'

'But I feel like the real reason wasn't even on there.'

'What was the real reason?'

'I feel like Amy wanted people to believe she really was
perfect. And as we got to be friends, I got to know her. And
she wasn't perfect. You know? She was brilliant and charming
and all that, but she was also controlling and OCD and a
drama queen and a bit of a liar. Which was fine by me. It just
wasn't fine by her. She got rid of me because I knew she
wasn't perfect. It made me wonder about you.'

'About me? Why?'

'Friends see most of each other's flaws. Spouses see every awful last bit. If she punished a friend of a few months by throwing herself down a flight of stairs, what would she do to a man who was dumb enough to marry her?'

I hung up as one of Hilary's kids picked up the second extension and began singing a nursery rhyme. I immediately phoned Tanner and relayed my conversations with Hilary and Tommy.

'So we have a couple of stories, great,' Tanner said, 'this'll really be great!' in a way that told me it wasn't that great. 'Have you heard from Andie?'

I hadn't.

'I have one of my people waiting for her at her apartment building,' he said. 'Discreet.'

'I didn't know you had people.'

'What we really need is to *find Amy*,' he said, ignoring me. 'Girl like that, I can't imagine she'd be able to stay hidden for too long. You have any thoughts?'

I kept picturing her on a posh hotel balcony near the ocean, wrapped in a white robe thick as a rug, sipping a very good Montrachet, while she tracked my ruin on the Internet, on cable, in the tabloids. While she enjoyed the endless coverage and exultation of Amy Elliott Dunne. Attending her own funeral. I wondered if she was self-aware enough to realize: She'd stolen a page from Mark Twain.

'I picture her near the ocean,' I said. Then I stopped, feeling like a boardwalk psychic. 'No. I have no ideas. She could literally be anywhere. I don't think we'll see her unless she decides to come back.'

'That seems unlikely,' Tanner breathed, annoyed. 'So let's try to find Andie and see where her head is. We're running out of wiggle room here.'

Then it was dinnertime, and then the sun set, and I was alone again in my haunted house. I was thinking about all of Amy's lies and whether the pregnancy was one of them. I'd done the math. Amy and I had sex sporadically enough it was possible. But then she would know I'd do the math.

Truth or lie? If it was a lie, it was designed to gut me.

I'd always assumed that Amy and I would have children. It was one of the reasons I knew I would marry Amy, because I pictured us having kids together. I remember the first time I imagined it, not two months after we began dating: I was walking from my apartment in Kips Bay to a favorite pocket park along the East River, a path that took me past the giant LEGO block of the United Nations headquarters, the flags of myriad countries fluttering in the wind. *A kid would like this*, I thought. All the different colors, the busy memory game of matching each flag to its country. *There's Finland, and there's New Zealand*. The one-eyed smile of Mauritania. And then I realized it wasn't *a* kid, but *our* kid, mine and Amy's, who would like this. Our kid, sprawled on the floor with an old encyclopedia, just like I'd done, but our kid wouldn't be alone, I'd be sprawled next to him. Aiding him in his budding vexillology, which sounds less like a study of flags than a study in annoyance, which would have suited my father's attitude toward me. But not mine toward my son's. I pictured Amy joining us on the floor, flat on her stomach, her feet kicked up in the air, pointing out Palau, the yellow dot just left of center on the crisp blue background, which I was sure would be her favorite.

From then on, the boy was real (and sometimes a girl, but mostly a boy). He was inevitable. I suffered from regular, insistent paternal aches. Months after the wedding, I had a strange moment in front of the medicine cabinet, floss between my teeth, when I thought: *She wants kids, right? I should ask. Of course I should ask.* When I posed the question – roundabout, vague – she said, *Of course, of course, someday*, but every morning she still perched in front of the sink and swallowed her pill. For three years she did this every morning, while I fluttered near the topic but failed to actually say the words: *I want us to have a baby.*

After the layoffs, it seemed like it might happen. Suddenly, there was an uncontestable space in our lives, and one day over breakfast, Amy looked up from her toast and said, *I'm off the pill.* Just like that. She was off the pill three months, and nothing happened, and not long after the move to Missouri, she made an appointment for us to start the medical intervention. Once Amy started a project, she didn't like to dilly-dally: 'We'll tell them we've been trying a year,' she said. Foolishly I agreed – we were barely ever touching each other by then, but we still thought a kid made sense. Sure.

'You'll have to do your part too, you know,' she said on the drive to St. Louis. 'You'll have to give semen.'

'I know. Why do you say it like that?'

'I just figured you'd be too proud. Self-conscious and proud.'

I was a rather nasty cocktail of both those traits, but at the fertility center, I dutifully entered the strange small room dedicated to self-abuse: a place where hundreds of men had entered for no other purpose than to crank the shank, clean the rifle, jerk the gherkin, make the bald man cry, pound the flounder, sail the mayonnaise seas, wiggle the walrus, whitewash with Tom and Huck.

(I sometimes use humor as self-defense.)

The room contained a vinyl-covered armchair, a TV, and a table that held a grab bag of porn and a box of tissues. The porn was early '90s, judging from the women's hair (yes: top and bottom), and the action was midcore. (Another good essay: Who selects the porn for fertility centers? Who judges what will get men off yet not be too degrading to all the women outside the cum-room, the nurses and doctors and hopeful, hormone addled wives?)

I visited the room on three separate occasions – they like to have a lot of backup – while Amy did nothing. She was supposed to begin taking pills, but she didn't, and then she didn't some more. She was the one who'd be pregnant, the one who'd turn over her body to the baby, so I postponed nudging her for a few months, keeping an eye on the pill bottle to see if the level went down. Finally, after a few beers one winter night, I crunched up the steps of our home, shed my snow-crusted clothes, and curled up next to her in bed, my face near her shoulder, breathing her in, warming the tip of my nose on her skin. I whispered the words – *Let's do this, Amy, let's have a baby* – and she said no. I was expecting nervousness, caution, worry – *Nick, will I be a good mom?* – but I got a clipped, cold *no*. A no without loopholes. Nothing dramatic, no big deal, just not something she was interested in anymore. 'Because I realized I'd be stuck doing all the hard stuff,' she reasoned. 'All the diapers and doctors' appointments and discipline, and you'd just breeze in and be Fun Daddy. I'd do all the work to make them good people, and you'd undo it anyway, and they'd love you and hate me.'

I told Amy it wasn't true, but she didn't believe me. I told her I didn't just *want* a child, I *needed* a child. I had to know I could love a person unconditionally, that I could make a little creature feel constantly welcome and wanted no matter what. That I could be a different kind of father than my dad was. That I could raise a boy who wasn't like me.

I begged her. Amy remained unmoved.

A year later, I got a notice in the mail: The clinic would dispose of my semen unless they heard from us. I left the letter on the dining room table, an open rebuke. Three days later, I saw it in the trash. That was our final communication on the subject.

By then I'd already been secretly dating Andie for months, so I had no right to be upset. But that didn't stop my aching, and it didn't stop me from daydreaming about our boy, mine and Amy's. I'd gotten attached to him. The fact was, Amy and I would make a great child.

The marionettes were watching me with alarmed black eyes. I peered out my window, saw that the news trucks had packed it in, so I went out into the warm night. Time to walk. Maybe a lone tabloid writer was trailing me; if so, I didn't care. I headed through our complex, then forty-five minutes out along River Road, then onto the highway that shot right through the middle of Carthage. Thirty loud, fumy minutes –

past car dealerships with trucks displayed appealingly like desserts, past fast-food chains and liquor stores and mini-marts and gas stations – until I reached the turnoff for downtown. I had encountered not a single other person on foot the entire time, only faceless blurs whizzing past me in cars.

It was close to midnight. I passed The Bar, tempted to go in but put off by the crowds. A reporter or two had to be camped out in there. It's what I would do. But I wanted to be in a bar. I wanted to be surrounded by people, having fun, blowing off steam. I walked another fifteen minutes to the other end of downtown, to a cheesier, rowdier, younger bar where the bathrooms were always laced with vomit on Saturday nights. It was a bar that Andie's crowd would go to, and perhaps, who knew, drag along Andie. It would be a nice bit of luck to see her there. At least gauge her mood from across the room. And if she wasn't there then I'd have a fucking drink.

I went as deep into the bar as I could – no Andie, no Andie. My face was partially covered by a baseball cap. Even so, I felt a few pings as I moved past crowds of drinkers: heads abruptly turning toward me, the wide eyes of identification. *That guy! Right?*

Mid-July. I wondered if I'd become so nefarious come October, I'd be some frat boy's tasteless Halloween costume: mop of blond hair, an *Amazing Amy* book tucked under an armpit. Go said she'd received half a dozen phone calls asking if The Bar had an official T-shirt for sale. (We didn't, thank God.)

I sat down and ordered a Scotch from the bartender, a guy about my age who stared at me a beat too long, deciding whether he would serve me. He finally, grudgingly, set down a small tumbler in front of me, his nostrils flared. When I got out my wallet, he aimed an alarmed palm up at me. 'I do not want your money, man. Not at all.'

I left cash anyway. Asshole.

When I tried to flag him for another drink, he glanced my way, shook his head, and leaned in toward the woman he was chatting up. A few seconds later, she discreetly looked toward me, pretending she was stretching. Her mouth turned down as she nodded. *That's him. Nick Dunne.* The bartender never came back.

You can't yell, you can't strong-arm: *Hey, jackass, will you get me a goddamn drink or what?* You can't be the asshole they believe you are. You just have to sit and take it. But I wasn't leaving. I sat with my empty glass in front of me and pretended I was thinking very hard. I checked my cell, just in case Andie had called. No. Then I pulled out my real phone and played a round of solitaire, pretending to be engrossed. My wife had done this to me, turned me into a man who couldn't get a drink in his own hometown. God, I hated her.

'Was it Scotch?'

A girl about Andie's age was standing in front of me. Asian, black shoulder-length hair, cubicle-cute.

'Excuse me?'

'What you were drinking? Scotch?'

'Yeah. Having trouble getting—'

She was gone, to the end of the bar, and she was nosing into the bartender's line of vision with a big *help me* smile, a girl used to making her presence known, and then she was back with a Scotch in an actual big-boy tumbler.

'Take it,' she nudged, and I did. 'Cheers.' She held up her own clear, fizzing drink. We clinked glasses. 'Can I sit?'

'I'm not staying long, actually—' I looked around, making sure no one was aiming a cameraphone at us.

'So, okay,' she said with a shruggy smile. 'I could pretend I don't know you're Nick Dunne, but I'm not going to insult you. I'm rooting for you, by the way. You've been getting a bad rap.'

'Thanks. It's, uh, it's a weird time.'

'I'm serious. You know how, in court, they talk about the *CSI* effect? Like, everyone on the jury has watched so much *CSI* that they believe science can prove anything?'

'Yeah.'

'Well, I think there's an *Evil Husband* effect. Everyone has seen too many true-crime shows where the husband is always, always the killer, so people automatically assume the husband's the bad guy.'

'That's exactly it,' I said. 'Thank you. That is exactly it. And Ellen Abbott—'

'Fuck Ellen Abbott,' my new friend said. 'She's a one-woman walking, talking, man-hating perversion of the justice system.' She raised her glass again.

'What's your name?' I asked.

'Another Scotch?'

'That's a gorgeous name.'

Her name, as it turned out, was Rebecca. She had a ready credit card and a hollow leg. (*Another? Another? Another?*) She was from Muscatine, Iowa (another Mississippi River town), and had moved to New York after undergrad to be a writer (also like me). She'd been an editorial assistant at three different magazines – a bridal magazine, a working-mom magazine, a teen-girl magazine – all of which had shuttered in the past few years, so she was now working for a crime blog called Who-dunnit, and she was (giggle) in town to try to get an interview with me. Hell, I had to love her hungry-kid chutzpah: *Just fly me to Carthage – the major networks haven't gotten him, but I'm sure I can!*

'I've been waiting outside your house with the rest of the world, and then at the police station, and then I decided I needed a drink. And here you walk in. It's just too perfect. Too weird, right?' she said. She had little gold hoop earrings that she kept playing with, her hair tucked behind her ears.

'I should go,' I said. My words were sticky around the edges, the beginnings of a slur.

'But you never told me why you're here,' Rebecca said. 'I have to say, it takes a lot of courage, I think, for you to head out without a friend or some sort of backup. I bet you get a lot of shitty looks.'

I shrugged: *No big deal.*

'People judging everything you do without even knowing you. Like you with the cell phone photo at the park. I mean, you were probably like me: You were raised to be polite. But no one wants the real story. They just want to ... *gotcha*. You know?'

'I'm just tired of people judging me because I fit into a certain mold.'

She raised her eyebrows; her earrings jittered.

I thought of Amy sitting in her mystery control center, wherever the fuck she was, judging me from every angle, finding me wanting even from afar. Was there anything she could see that would make her call off this madness?

I went on, 'I mean, people think we were in a rocky marriage, but actually, right before she disappeared, she put together a treasure hunt for me.'

Amy would want one of two things: for me to learn my lesson and fry like the bad boy I was; or for me to learn my lesson and love her the way she deserved and be a good, obedient, chastised, dickless little boy.

'This wonderful treasure hunt.' I smiled. Rebecca shook her head with a little-V frown. 'My wife, she always did a treasure hunt for our anniversary. One clue leads to a special place where I find the next clue, and so on. Amy ...' I tried to get my eyes to fill, settled for wiping them. The clock above the door read 12:37 a.m. 'Before she went missing, she hid all the clues. For this year.'

'Before she disappeared on your anniversary.'

'And it's been all that's kept me together. It made me feel closer to her.'

Rebecca pulled out a Flip camera. 'Let me interview you. On camera.'

'Bad idea.'

'I'll give it context,' she said. 'That's exactly what you need, Nick, I swear. Context. You need it bad. Come on, just a few words.'

I shook my head. 'Too dangerous.'

'Say what you just said. I'm serious, Nick. I'm the opposite of Ellen Abbott. The anti-Ellen Abbott. You need me in your life.' She held up the camera, its tiny red light eyeing me.

'Seriously, turn it off.'

'Help a girl out. I get the Nick Dunne interview? My career is made. You've done your good deed for the year. Pleeease? No harm, Nick, one minute. Just one minute. I swear I will only make you look good.'

She motioned to a nearby booth where we'd be tucked out of view of any gawkers. I nodded and we resettled, that little red light aimed at me the whole time.

'What do you want to know?' I asked.

'Tell me about the treasure hunt. It sounds romantic. Like, quirky, awesome, romantic.'

Take control of the story, Nick. For both the capital-P public and the capital-C wife. *Right now*, I thought, *I am a man who loves his wife and will find her. I am a man who loves his wife, and I am the good guy. I am the one to root for. I am a man who isn't perfect, but my wife is, and I will be very, very obedient from now on.*

I could do this more easily than feign sadness. Like I said, I can operate in sunlight. Still, I felt my throat tighten as I got ready to say the words.

'My wife, she just happens to be the coolest girl I've ever met. How many guys can say that? *I married the coolest girl I ever met.*'

Youfuckingbitchyoufuckingbitchyoufuckingbitch. Come home so I can kill you.

AMY ELLIOTT DUNNE
NINE DAYS GONE

I wake up feeling immediately nervous. Off. *I cannot be found here*, that's what I wake up thinking, a burst of words, like a flash in my brain. The investigation is not going fast enough, and my money situation is just the opposite, and Jeff and Greta's greedy antennae are up. And I smell like fish.

There was something about Jeff and that race to the shoreline, toward my bundled dress and my money belt. Something about the way Greta keeps alighting on *Ellen Abbott*. It makes me nervous. Or am I being paranoid? I sound like Diary Amy: *Is my husband going to kill me or am I imagining!?!?* For the first time I actually feel sorry for her.

I make two calls to the Amy Dunne tip line, and speak to two different people, and offer two different tips. It's hard to tell how quickly they'll reach the police – the volunteers seem utterly disinterested. I drive to the library in a dark mood. I need to pack up and leave. Clean my cabin with bleach, wipe my fingerprints off everything, vacuum for any hairs. Erase Amy (and Lydia and Nancy) and go. If I go, I'll be safe. Even if Greta and Jeff do suspect who I am, as long as I'm not caught in the flesh, I'm okay. Amy Elliott Dunne is like a yeti – coveted and folkloric – and they are two Ozarks grifters whose blurry story will be immediately debunked. I will leave today. That's what I decide when I walk with my head bowed into the chilly, mostly uninhabited library with its three vacant computers and I go online to catch up on Nick.

Since the vigil, the news about Nick has been on repeat – the same facts on a circuit, over and over, getting louder and louder, but with no new information. But today something is different. I type Nick's name into the search engine, and the blogs are going nuts, because my husband has gotten drunk and done an insane interview, in a bar, with a random girl wielding a Flip camera. God, the idiot never learns.

NICK DUNNE'S VIDEO CONFESSION!!!
NICK DUNNE, DRUNKEN DECLARATIONS!!!

My heart jumps so high, my uvula begins pulsing. My husband has fucked himself again.

The video loads, and there is Nick. He has the sleepy eyes he gets when he's drunk, the heavy lids, and he's got his sideways grin, and he's talking about me, and he looks like a human being. He looks happy. 'My wife, she just happens to be the coolest girl I've ever met,' he says. 'How many guys can say that? *I married the coolest girl I ever met.*'

My stomach flutters delicately. I was not expecting this. I almost smile.

'What's so cool about her?' the girl asks off-screen. Her voice is high, sorority-cheery.

Nick launches into the treasure hunt, how it was our tradition, how I always remembered hilarious inside jokes, and right now this was all he had left of me, so he had to complete the treasure hunt. It was his mission.

'I just reached the end this morning,' he says. His voice is husky. He has been talking over the crowd. He'll go home and gargle with warm salt water, like his mother always made him do. If I were at home with him, he'd ask me to heat the water and make it for him, because he never got the right amount of salt. 'And it made me ... realize a lot. She is the only person in the world who has the power to surprise me, you know? Everyone else, I always know what they're going to say, because everyone says the same thing. We all watch the same shows, we read the same stuff, we recycle everything. But Amy, she is her own perfect person. She just has this *power* over me.'

'Where do you think she is now, Nick?'

My husband looks down at his wedding band and twirls it twice.

'Are you okay, Nick?'

'The truth? No. I failed my wife so entirely. I have been so wrong. I just hope it's not too late. For me. For us.'

'You're at the end of your rope. Emotionally.'

Nick looks right at the camera. 'I want my wife. I want her to be right here.' He takes a breath. 'I'm not the best at showing emotion. I know that. But I love her. I need her to be okay. She has to be okay. I have so much to make up to her.'

'Like what?'

He laughs, the chagrined laugh that even now I find appealing. In better days, I used to call it the talk-show laugh: It was the quick downward glance, the scratching of a corner of the mouth with a casual thumb, the inhaled chuckle that a charming movie star always deploys right before telling a killer story.

'Like, none of your business.' He smiles. 'I just have a lot to make up to her. I wasn't the husband I could have been. We had a few hard years, and I ... I lost my shit. I stopped trying. I mean, I've heard that phrase a thousand times: *We stopped trying*. Everyone knows it means the end of a marriage – it's textbook. But I stopped trying. It was me. I wasn't the man I needed to be.' Nick's lids are heavy, his speech off-kilter enough that his twang is showing. He is past tipsy, one drink before drunk. His cheeks are pink with alcohol. My fingertips glow, remembering the heat of his skin when he had a few cocktails in him.

'So how would you make it up to her?' The camera wobbles for a second; the girl is grabbing her cocktail.

'How *will* I make it up to her. First I'm going to find her and bring her home. You can bet on that. Then? Whatever she needs from me, I'll give her. From now on. Because I reached the end of the treasure hunt, and I was brought to my knees. Humbled. My wife has never been more clear to me than she is now. I've never been so sure of what I needed to do.'

'If you could talk to Amy right now, what would you tell her?'

'I love you. I will find you. I *will* ...'

I can tell he is about to do the Daniel Day-Lewis line from *The Last of the Mohicans*: 'Stay alive ... I *will* find you.' He can't resist deflecting any sincerity with a quick line of movie dialogue. I can feel him teetering right on the edge of it. He stops himself.

'I love you forever, Amy.'

How heartfelt. How unlike my husband.

Three morbidly obese hill people on motorized scooters are between me and my morning coffee. Their asses mushroom over the sides of the contraptions, but they still need another Egg McMuffin. There are literally three people, *parked* in front of me, in line, *inside* the McDonald's.

I actually don't care. I'm curiously cheerful despite this twist in the plan. Online, the video is already spiral-viraling away, and the reaction is surprisingly positive. Cautiously optimistic: *Maybe this guy didn't kill his wife after all*. That is, word for word, the most common refrain. Because once Nick lets his guard down and shows some emotion, it's all there. No one could watch that video and believe he was putting up an act. It was no swallow-the-pain sort of amateur theater. My husband loves me. Or at least last night he loved me. While I was plotting his doom in my crummy little cabin that smells of moldy towel, he loved me.

It's not enough. I know that, of course. I can't change my plan. But it gives me pause. My husband has finished the treasure hunt and he is in love. He is also deeply distressed: on one cheek I swear I could spot a hive.

I pull up to my cabin to find Dorothy knocking on my door. Her hair is wet from the heat, brushed straight back like a Wall Street slickster's. She is in the habit of swiping her upper lip, then licking the sweat off her fingers, so she has her index finger in her mouth like a buttery corncob as she turns to me.

'There she is,' she says. 'The truant.'

I am late on my cabin payment. Two days. It almost makes me laugh: I am late on rent.

'I'm so sorry, Dorothy. I'll come by with it in ten minutes.'

'I'll wait, if you don't mind.'

'I'm not sure if I'm going to stay. I might have to head on.'

'Then you'd still owe me the two days. Eighty dollars, please.'

I duck into my cabin, undo my flimsy money belt. I counted my cash on my bed this morning, taking a good long time doling out each bill, a teasing economic striptease, and the big reveal was that I have, *somehow*, I have only $8,849 left. It costs a lot to live.

When I open the door to hand Dorothy the cash ($8,769 left), I see Greta and Jeff hanging out on Greta's porch, watching the cash exchange hands. Jeff isn't playing his guitar, Greta isn't smoking. They seem to be standing on her porch just to get a better look at me. They both wave at me, *hey, sweetie*, and I wave limply back. I close the door and start packing.

It's strange how little I own in this world when I used to own so much. I don't own an eggbeater or a soup bowl. I own sheets and towels, but I don't own a decent blanket. I own a pair of scissors so I can keep my hair butchered. It makes me smile because Nick didn't own a pair of scissors when we moved in together. No scissors, no iron, no stapler, and I remember asking him how he thought he was possibly civilized without a pair of scissors, and he said of course he wasn't and swooped me up in his arms and threw me on the bed and pounced on top of me, and I laughed because I was still Cool Girl. I laughed instead of thinking about what it meant.

One should never marry a man who doesn't own a decent set of scissors. That would be my advice. It leads to bad things.

I fold and pack my clothes in my tiny backpack – the same three outfits I bought and kept in my getaway car a month ago so I didn't have to take anything from home. Toss in my travel toothbrush, calendar, comb, lotion, the sleeping pills I bought back when I was going to drug and drown myself. My cheap swimsuits. It takes such little time, the whole thing.

I put on my latex gloves and wipe down everything. I pull out the drains to get any trapped hair. I don't really think Greta and Jeff know who I am, but if they do, I don't want to leave any proof, and the whole time I say to myself, *This is what you get for relaxing, this is what you get for not thinking* all the time, all the time. *You deserve to get caught, a girl who acts so stupidly, and what if you left hairs in the front office, then what, and what if there are fingerprints in Jeff's car or Greta's kitchen, what then, why did you ever think you could be someone who didn't worry?* I picture the police scouring the cabins, finding nothing, and then, like a movie, I go in for a close-up of one lone mousy hair of mine, drifting along the concrete floor of the pool, waiting to damn me.

Then my mind swings the other way: *Of course no one is going to show up to look for you here.* All the police have to go on is the claim of a few grifters that they saw the real Amy Elliott Dunne at a cheap broke-down cabin court in the middle of nowhere. Little people wanting to feel bigger, that's what they'd assume.

An assertive knock at the door. The kind a parent gives right before swinging the door wide: *I own this place.* I stand in the middle of my room and debate not answering. Bang bang bang. I understand now why so many horror movies use that device – the mysterious knock on the door – because it has the weight of a nightmare. You don't know what's out there, yet you know you'll open it. You'll think what I think: *No one bad ever knocks.*

Hey, sweetheart, we know you're home, open up!

I strip off my latex gloves, open the door, and Jeff and Greta are standing on my porch, the sun to their backs, their features in shadow.

'Hey, pretty lady, we come in?' Jeff asks.

'I actually – I was going to come see you guys,' I say, trying to sound flippant, harried. 'I'm leaving tonight – tomorrow or tonight. Got a call from back home, got to get going back home.'

'Home Louisiana or home Savannah?' Greta says. She and Jeff have been talking about me.

'Louisi—'

'It doesn't matter,' Jeff says, 'let us in for a second, we come to say goodbye.'

He steps toward me, and I think about screaming or slamming the door, but I don't think either will go well. Better to pretend everything is fine and hope that is true.

Greta closes the door behind them and leans against it as Jeff wanders into the tiny bedroom, then the kitchen, chatting about the weather. Opening doors and cabinets.

'You got to clear everything out; Dorothy will keep your deposit if you don't,' he says. 'She's a stickler.' He opens the refrigerator, peers into the crisper, the freezer. 'Not even a jar of ketchup can you leave. I always thought that was weird. Ketchup doesn't go bad.'

He opens the closet and lifts up the cabin bedding I've folded, shakes out the sheets. 'I always, always shake out the sheets,' he says. 'Just to make sure nothing is inside – a sock or underwear or what have you.'

He opens the drawer of my bedside table, kneels down, and looks all the way to the back. 'Looks like you've done a good job,' he says, standing up and smiling, brushing his hands off on his jeans. 'Got everything.'

He scans me, neck to foot and back up. 'Where is it, sweetheart?'

'What's that?'

'Your money.' He shrugs. 'Don't make it hard. Me 'n her really need it.'

Greta is silent behind me.

'I have about twenty bucks.'

'Lie,' Jeff said. 'You pay for everything, even rent, in cash. Greta saw you with that big wad of money. So hand it over, and you can leave, and we all never have to see each other again.'

'I'll call the police.'

'Go ahead! My guest.' Jeff waits, arms crossed, thumbs in his armpits.

'Your glasses are fake,' Greta says. 'They're just glass.'

I say nothing, stare at her, hoping she'll back down. These two seem just nervous enough they may change their minds, say they're screwing with me, and the three of us will laugh and know otherwise but all agree to pretend.

'And your hair, the roots are coming in, and they're blond, a lot prettier than whatever color you dyed it – *hamster* – and that haircut is awful, by the way,' Greta says. 'You're hiding – from whatever. I don't know if it really is a guy or what, but you're not going to call the police. So just give us the money.'

'Jeff talk you into this?' I ask.

'I talked Jeff into it.'

I start toward the door that Greta's blocking. 'Let me out.'

'Give us the money.'

I make a grab for the door, and Greta swings toward me, shoves me against the wall, one hand smashed over my face, and with the other, she pulls up my dress, yanks off the money belt.

'Don't, Greta, I'm serious! Stop!'

Her hot, salty palm is all over my face, jamming my nose; one of her fingernails scrapes my eye. Then she pushes me back against the wall, my head banging, my teeth coming down on the tip of my tongue. The whole scuffle is very quiet.

I have the buckle end of the belt in my hand, but I can't see to fight her, my eye is watering too much, and she soon rips away my grip, leaving a burning scrape of fingernails on my knuckles. She shoves me again and opens the zipper, fingers through the money.

'Holy shit,' she says. 'This is like' – she counts – 'more'n a thousand, two or three. Holy shit. Damn, girl! You rob a bank?'

'She may *have*,' Jeff says. 'Embezzlement.'

In a movie, one of Nick's movies, I would upthrust my palm into Greta's nose, drop her to the floor bloody and unconscious, then roundhouse Jeff. But the truth is, I don't know how to fight, and there are two of them, and it doesn't seem worth it. I will run at them, and they will grab me by the wrists while I pat and fuss at them like a child, or they will get really angry and beat the crap out of me. I've never been hit. I'm scared of getting hurt by someone else.

'You going to call the police, go ahead and call them,' Jeff says again.

'Fuck you,' I whisper.

'Sorry about this,' Greta says. 'Next place you go, be more careful, okay? You gotta not look like a girl traveling by herself, hiding out.'

'You'll be okay,' Jeff says.

He pats me on the arm as they leave.

A quarter and a dime sit on the bedside table. It's all my money in the world.

NICK DUNNE
NINE DAYS GONE

Good morning!

I sat in bed with my laptop by my side, enjoying the online reviews of my impromptu interview. My left eyeball was throbbing a bit, a light hangover from the cheap Scotch, but the rest of me was feeling pretty satisfied. Last night I cast the first line to lure my wife back in. *I'm sorry, I will make it up to you, I will do whatever you want from now on, I will let the world know how special you are.*

Because I was fucked unless Amy decided to show herself. Tanner's detective (a wiry, clean-cut guy, not the boozy noir gumshoe I'd hoped for) had come up with nothing so far – my wife had disappeared herself perfectly. I had to convince Amy to come back to me, flush her out with compliments and capitulation.

If the reviews were any indication, I made the right call, because the reviews were good. They were very good:

The Iceman Melteth!
I KNEW he was a good guy.
In vino veritas!
Maybe he didn't kill her after all.
Maybe he didn't kill her after all.
Maybe he didn't kill her after all.

And they'd stopped calling me Lance.

Outside my house, the cameramen and journalists were restless, they wanted a statement from the guy who Maybe Didn't Kill Her After All. They were yelling at my drawn blinds: *Hey, Nick, come on out, tell us about Amy. Hey, Nick, tell us about your treasure hunt.* For them it was just a new wrinkle in a ratings bonanza, but it was much better than *Nick, did you kill your wife?*

And then, suddenly, they were yelling Go's name – they loved Go, she had no poker face, you knew if Go was sad, angry, worried; stick a caption underneath, and you had a whole story. *Margo, is your brother innocent? Margo, tell us about … Tanner, is your client innocent? Tanner—*

The doorbell rang, and I opened the door while hiding behind it because I was still disheveled; my spiky hair and wilted boxers would tell their own story. Last night, on camera, I was adorably smitten, a tad tipsy, in vino veritastic. Now I just looked like a drunk. I closed the door and waited for two more glowing reviews of my performance.

'You don't ever – *ever* – do something like that again,' Tanner started. 'What the hell is wrong with you, Nick? I feel like I need to put one of those toddler leashes on you. How stupid can you be?'

'Have you seen all the comments online? People love it. I'm turning around public opinion, like you told me to.'

'You don't do that kind of thing in an uncontrolled environment,' he said. 'What if she worked for Ellen Abbott? What if she started asking you questions that were harder than *What do you want to say to your wife, cutie-pumpkin-pie?*' He said this is a girlish singsong. His face under the orange spray tan was red, giving him a radioactive palette.

'I trusted my instincts. I'm a journalist, Tanner, you have to give me some credit that I can smell bullshit. She was genuinely sweet.'

He sat down on the sofa, put his feet on the ottoman that would never have flipped over on its own. 'Yeah, well, so was your wife once,' he said. 'So was Andie once. How's your cheek?'

It still hurt; the bite seemed to throb as he reminded me of it. I turned to Go for support.

'It wasn't smart, Nick,' she said, sitting down across from Tanner. 'You were *really, really* lucky – it turned out *really* well, but it might not have.'

346

'You guys are *really* overreacting. Can we enjoy a small moment of good news? Just thirty seconds of good news in the past nine days? Please?'

Tanner pointedly looked at his watch. 'Okay, go.'

When I started to talk, he popped his index finger, made the uhp-uhp noise that grown-ups make when children try to interrupt. Slowly, his index finger lowered, then landed on the watch face.

'Okay, thirty seconds. Did you enjoy it?' He paused to see if I'd say anything – the pointed silence a teacher allows after asking the disruptive student: *Are you done talking?* 'Now we need to talk. We are in a place where excellent timing is absolutely key.'

'I agree.'

'Gee, thanks.' He arched an eyebrow at me. 'I want to go to the police very, very soon with the contents of the woodshed. While the hoi polloi is—'

Just hoi polloi, I thought, *not* the *hoi polloi*. It was something Amy had taught me.

'—all loving on you again. Or, excuse me, not *again*. Finally. The reporters have found Go's house, and I don't feel secure leaving that woodshed, its contents, undisclosed much longer. The Elliotts are . . .?'

'We can't count on the Elliotts' support anymore,' I said. 'Not at all.'

Another pause. Tanner decided not to lecture me, or even ask what happened.

'So we need offense,' I said, feeling untouchable, angry, ready.

'Nick, don't let one good turn make you feel indestructible,' Go said. She pressed some extra-strengths from her purse into my hand. 'Get rid of your hangover. You need to be on today.'

'It's going to be okay,' I told her. I popped the pills, turned to Tanner. 'What do we do? Let's make a plan.'

'Great, here's the deal,' Tanner said. 'This is incredibly unorthodox, but that's me. Tomorrow we are doing an interview with Sharon Schieber.'

'Wow, that's … for sure?' Sharon Schieber was as good as I could ask for: the top-rated (ages 30–55) network (broader reach than cable) newswoman (to prove I could have respectful relations with people who have vaginas) working today. She was known for dabbling very occasionally in the impure waters of true-crime journalism, but when she did, she got freakin' righteous. Two years ago, she took under her silken wing a young mother who had been imprisoned for shaking her infant to death. Sharon Schieber presented a whole legal – and very emotional – defense case over a series of nights. The woman is now back home in Nebraska, remarried and expecting a child.

'That's for sure. She got in touch after the video went viral.'

'So the video did help.' I couldn't resist.

'It gave you an interesting wrinkle: Before the video, it was clear you did it. Now there's a slight chance you didn't. I don't know how it is you finally seemed genuine—'

'Because last night it served an actual purpose: Get Amy back,' Go said. 'It was an offensive maneuver. Where before it would just be indulgent, undeserved, disingenuous emotion.'

I gave her a thank-you smile.

'Well, keep remembering that it is serving a purpose,' Tanner said. 'Nick, I'm not fucking around here: This is beyond unorthodox. Most lawyers would be shutting you up. But it's something I've been wanting to try. The media has saturated the legal environment. With the Internet, Facebook, YouTube, there's no such thing as an unbiased jury anymore. No clean slate. Eighty, ninety percent of a case is decided before you get in the courtroom. So why not use it – control the story. But it's a risk. I want every word, every gesture, every bit of information planned out ahead of time. But you have to be natural, likable, or this will all backfire.'

'Oh, that sounds simple,' I said. 'One hundred percent canned yet totally genuine.'

'You have to be extremely careful with your wording, and we will tell Sharon that you won't answer certain questions. She'll ask you anyway, but we'll teach you how to say, *Because*

*of certain prejudicial actions by the police involved in this case,
I really, unfortunately, can't answer that right now, as much as
I'd like to* – and say it convincingly.'

'Like a talking dog.'

'Sure, like a talking dog who doesn't want to go to prison.
We get Sharon Schieber to take you on as a cause, Nick, and
we are golden. This is all incredibly unorthodox, but that's
me,' Tanner said again. He liked the line; it was his theme
music. He paused and furrowed his brow, doing his pretend-
thinking gesture. He was going to add something I wouldn't
like.

'What?' I asked.

'You need to tell Sharon Schieber about Andie – because
it's going to come out, the affair, it just will.'

'Right when people are finally starting to like me. You want
me to undo that?'

'I *swear* to you, Nick – how many cases have I handled? It
always – somehow, some way, always comes out. This way we
have control. You tell her about Andie and you apologize.
Apologize literally as if your life depends on it. You had an
affair, you are a man, a weak, stupid man. *But* you love your
wife, and you will make it up to her. You do the interview,
it'll air the next night. All content is embargoed – so they can't
tease the Andie affair in their ads. They can just use the word
bombshell.'

'So you already told them about Andie?'

'Good God, no,' he said. 'I told them: *We have a nice
bombshell for you.* So you do the interview, and we have about
twenty-four hours. Just before it hits TV, we tell Boney and
Gilpin about Andie and about our discovery in the woodshed.
*Oh my gosh, we've put it all together for you: Amy is alive and
she's framing Nick! She's crazy, jealous, and she is framing Nick!
Oh, the humanity!*'

'Why not tell Sharon Schieber, then? About Amy framing
me?'

'Reason one. You come clean about Andie, you beg forgiveness, the nation is primed to forgive you, they'll feel sorry

for you – Americans love to see sinners apologize. But you can reveal nothing to make your wife look bad; no one wants to see the cheating husband blame the wife for anything. Let someone else do it sometime the next day: *Sources close to the police* reveal that Nick's wife – the one he swore he loved with all his heart – is framing him! It's great TV.'

'What's reason two?'

'It's too complicated to explain exactly how Amy is framing you. You can't do it in a sound bite. It's bad TV.'

'I feel sick,' I said.

'Nick, it's—' Go started.

'I know, I know, it has to be done. But can you imagine, your biggest secret and you have to tell the world about it? I know I have to do it. And it works for us, ultimately, I think. It's the only way Amy might come back,' I said. 'She wants me to be publicly humiliated—'

'Chastened,' Tanner interrupted. 'Humiliated makes it sound like you feel sorry for yourself.'

'—and to publicly apologize,' I continued. 'But it's going to be fucking awful.'

'Before we go forward, I want to be honest here,' Tanner said. 'Telling the police the whole story – Amy's framing Nick – it is a risk. Most cops, they decide on a suspect and they don't want to veer at all. They're not open to any other options. So there's the risk that we tell them and they laugh us out of the station and they arrest you – and then theoretically we've just given them a preview of our defense. So they can plan exactly how to destroy it at trial.'

'Okay, wait, that sounds really, really bad, Tanner,' Go said. 'Like, bad, inadvisable bad.'

'Let me finish,' Tanner said. 'One, I think you're right, Nick. I think Boney isn't convinced you're a killer. I think she would be open to an alternate theory. She has a good reputation as a cop who's actually fair. As a cop who has good instincts. I talked with her. I got a good vibe. I think the evidence is leading her in your direction, but I think her gut is telling her something's off. More important, if we do go to trial, I wouldn't use the Amy frame-up as your defense, anyway.'

'What do you mean?'

'Like I said, it's too complicated, a jury wouldn't be able to follow. If it's not good TV, believe me, it's not for a jury. We'd go with more of an O.J. thing. A simple story line: The cops are incompetent and out to get you, it's all circumstantial, if the glove doesn't fit, blah blah, blah.'

'Blah blah blah, that gives me a lot of confidence,' I said.

Tanner flashed a smile. 'Juries love me, Nick. I'm one of them.'

'You're the opposite of one of them, Tanner.'

'Reverse that: They'd like to think they're one of me.'

Everything we did now, we did in front of small brambles of flashing paparazzi, so Go, Tanner, and I left the house under pops of light and pings of noise ('Don't look down,' Tanner advised, 'don't smile, but don't look ashamed. Don't rush either, just walk, let them take their shots, and shut the door before you call them names. Then you can call them whatever you want.') We were headed down to St. Louis, where the interview would take place, so I could prep with Tanner's wife, Betsy, a former TV news anchor turned lawyer. She was the other Bolt in Bolt & Bolt.

It was a creepy tailgate party: Tanner and I, followed by Go, followed by a half-dozen news vans, but by the time the Arch crept over the skyline, I was no longer thinking of the paparazzi.

By the time we reached Tanner's penthouse hotel suite, I was ready to do the work I needed to nail the interview. Again I longed for my own theme music: the montage of me getting ready for the big fight.

What's the mental equivalent of a speed bag?

A gorgeous six-foot-tall black woman answered the door.

'Hi, Nick, I'm Betsy Bolt.'

In my mind Betsy Bolt was a diminutive blond Southern-belle white girl.

'Don't worry, everyone is surprised when they meet me.'

Betsy laughed, catching my look, shaking my hand. 'Tanner and Betsy, we sound like we should be on the cover of *The Official Preppy Guide*, right?'

'*Preppy Handbook*,' Tanner corrected as he kissed her on the cheek.

'See? He actually knows,' she said.

She ushered us into an impressive penthouse suite – a living room sunlit by wall-to-wall windows, with bedrooms shooting off each side. Tanner had sworn he couldn't stay in Carthage, at the Days Inn, out of respect for Amy's parents, but Go and I both suspected he couldn't stay in Carthage because the closest five-star hotel was in St. Louis.

We engaged in the preliminaries: small talk about Betsy's family, college, career (all stellar, A-list, awesome), and drinks dispersed for everyone (soda pops and Clamato, which Go and I had come to believe was an affectation of Tanner's, a quirk he thought would give him character, like my wearing fake glasses in college). Then Go and I sank down into the leather sofa, Betsy sitting across from us, her legs pressed together to one side, like a slash mark. Pretty/professional. Tanner paced behind us, listening.

'Okay. So, Nick,' Betsy said. 'I'll be frank, yes?'

'Yes.'

'You and TV. Aside from your bar-blog thingie, the Who-dunnit.com thingie last night, you're *awful*.'

'There was a reason I went to print journalism,' I said. 'I see a camera, and my face freezes.'

'Exactly,' Betsy said. 'You look like a mortician, so stiff. I got a trick to fix that, though.'

'Booze?' I asked. 'That worked for me on the blog thingie.'

'That won't work here,' Betsy said. She began setting up a video camera. 'Thought we'd do a dry run first. I'll be Sharon. I'll ask the questions she'll probably ask, and you answer the way you normally would. That way we can know how far off the mark you are.' She laughed again. 'Hold on.' She was wearing a blue sheath dress, and from an oversize leather

352

purse, she pulled a string of pearls. The Sharon Schieber uniform. 'Tanner?'

Her husband fastened the pearls for her, and when they were in place, Betsy grinned. 'I aim for absolute authenticity. Aside from my Georgia accent. And being black.'

'I see only Sharon Schieber before me,' I said.

She turned the camera on, sat down across from me, let out a breath, looked down, and then looked up. 'Nick, there have been many discrepancies in this case,' Betsy said in Sharon's plummy broadcast voice. 'To begin with, can you walk our audience through the day your wife went missing?'

'Here, Nick, you only discuss the anniversary breakfast you two had,' Tanner interrupted. 'Since that is already out there. But you don't give time lines, you don't discuss before and after breakfast. You are emphasizing only this wonderful last breakfast you had. Okay, go.'

'Yes.' I cleared my throat. The camera was blinking red; Betsy had her quizzical-journalist expression on. 'Uh, as you know, it was our five-year anniversary, and Amy got up early and was making crepes—'

Betsy's arm shot out, and my cheek suddenly stung.

'What the hell?' I said, trying to figure out what had happened. A cherry-red jellybean was in my lap. I held it up.

'Every time you tense up, every time you turn that handsome face into an undertaker's mask, I am going to hit you with a jellybean,' Betsy explained, as if the whole thing were quite reasonable.

'And that's supposed to make me *less* tense?'

'It works,' Tanner said. 'It's how she taught me. I think she used rocks with me, though.' They exchanged *oh, you!* married smiles. I could tell already: They were one of those couples who always seemed to be starring in their own morning talk show.

'Now start again, but linger over the crepes,' Betsy said. 'Were they your favorites? Or hers? And what were you doing that morning for your wife while she was making crepes for you?'

'I was sleeping.'

'What had you bought her for a gift?'

'I hadn't yet.'

'Oh, boy.' She rolled her eyes over to her husband. 'Then be really, really, *really* complimentary about those crepes, okay? And about what you were *going* to get her that day for a present. Because I know you were not coming back to that house without a present.'

We started again, and I described our crepe tradition that wasn't really, and I described how careful and wonderful Amy was with picking out gifts (here another jellybean smacked just right of my nose, and I immediately loosened my jaw) and how I, dumb guy ('Definitely play up the doofus-husband stuff,' Betsy advised) was still trying to come up with something dazzling.

'It wasn't like she even liked expensive or fancy presents,' I began, and was hit with a paper ball from Tanner.

'What?'

'Past tense. Stop using fucking past tense about your wife.'

'I understand you and your wife had some bumps,' Betsy continued.

'It had been a rough few years. We'd both lost our jobs.'

'Good, yes!' Tanner called. 'You *both* had.'

'We'd moved back here to help care for my dad, who has Alzheimer's, and my late mother, who had cancer, and on top of that I was working very hard at my new job.'

'Good, Nick, good,' Tanner said.

'Be sure to mention how close you were with your mom,' Betsy said, even though I'd never mentioned my mom to her. 'No one will pop up to deny that, right? No Mommy Dearest or Sonny Dearest stories out there?'

'No, my mom and I were very close.'

'Good,' said Betsy. 'Mention her a lot, then. And that you own the bar with your sister – always mention your sister when you mention the bar. If you own a bar on your own, you're a player; if you own it with your beloved twin sister, you're—'

'Irish.'

'Go on.'

'And so it all built up—' I started.

'No,' Tanner said. 'Implies building up to an explosion.'

'So we had gotten off track a little, but I was considering our five-year anniversary as a time to revive our relationship—'

'*Recommit to our relationship*,' Tanner called. '*Revive* means something was dead.'

'Recommit to our relationship—'

'And so how does fucking a twenty-three-year-old figure in to this rejuvenative picture?' Betsy asked.

Tanner lobbed a jellybean her way. 'A little out of character, Bets.'

'I'm sorry, guys, but I'm a woman, and that smells like bullshit, like mile-away bullshit. Recommit to the relationship, *please*. That girl was still in the picture when Amy went missing. Women are going to hate you, Nick, unless you suck it up. Be up-front, don't stall. You can add it on: *We lost our jobs, we moved, my parents were dying. Then I fucked up. I fucked up huge. I lost track of who I was, and unfortunately, it took losing Amy to realize it.* You have to admit you're a jerk and that everything was all your fault.'

'So, like, what men are supposed to do in general,' I said.

Betsy flung an annoyed look at the ceiling. 'And that's an attitude, Nick, you should be real careful on.'

AMY ELLIOTT DUNNE
NINE DAYS GONE

I am penniless and on the run. How fucking noir. Except that I am sitting in my Festiva at the far end of the parking lot of a vast fast-food complex on the banks of the Mississippi River, the smell of salt and factory-farm meat floating on the warm breezes. It is evening now – I've wasted hours – but I can't move. I don't know where to move to. The car gets smaller by the hour – I am forced to curl up like a fetus or my legs fall asleep. I certainly won't sleep tonight. The door is locked, but I still await the tap on the window, and I know I will peek up and see either a crooked-toothed, sweet-talking serial killer (wouldn't that be ironic, for me to actually be murdered?) or a stern, ID-demanding cop (wouldn't that be worse, for me to be discovered in a parking lot looking like a hobo?). The glowing restaurant signs never go off here; the parking lot is lit like a football field – I think of suicide again, how a prisoner on suicide watch spends twenty-four hours a day under lights, an awful thought. My gas tank is below the quarter mark, an even more awful thought: I can drive only about an hour in any direction, so I must choose the direction carefully. South is Arkansas, north is Iowa, west is back to the Ozarks. Or I could go east, cross the river into Illinois. Everywhere I go is the river. I'm following it or it's following me.

I know, suddenly, what I must do.

NICK DUNNE
TEN DAYS GONE

We spent the day of the interview huddled in the spare bedroom of Tanner's suite, prepping my lines, fixing my look. Betsy fussed over my clothes, then Go trimmed the hair above my ears with nail scissors while Betsy tried to talk me into using makeup – powder – to cut down on shine. We all spoke in low voices because Sharon's crew was setting up outside; the interview would be in the suite's living room, overlooking the St. Louis Arch. Gateway to the West. I'm not sure what the point of the landmark was except to serve as a vague symbol of the middle of the country: *You Are Here*.

'You need at least a little powder, Nick,' Betsy finally said, coming at me with the puff. 'Your nose sweats when you get nervous. Nixon lost an election on nose sweat.' Tanner oversaw it all like a conductor. 'Not too much off that side, Go,' he'd call. 'Bets, be very careful with that powder, better too little than too much.'

'We should have Botoxed him,' she said. Apparently, Botox fights sweat as well as wrinkles – some of their clients got a series of underarm shots before a trial, and they were already suggesting such a thing for me. Gently, subtly suggesting, *should* we go to trial.

'Yeah, I really need the press to get wind that I was having Botox treatments while my wife was missing,' I said. 'Is missing.' I knew Amy wasn't dead, but I also knew she was so far out of my reach that she might as well be. She was a wife in past tense.

'Good catch,' Tanner said. 'Next time do it before it comes out of your mouth.'

At five p.m., Tanner's phone rang, and he looked at the display. 'Boney.' He sent it to voice mail. 'I'll call her after.' He didn't want any new bit of information, interrogation, gossip to force us to reformulate our message. I agreed: I didn't want Boney in my head just then.

'You sure we shouldn't see what she wants?' Go said.

'She wants to fuck with me some more,' I said. 'We'll call her. A few hours. She can wait.'

We all rearranged ourselves, a mass group reassurance that the call was nothing to worry about. The room stayed silent for half a minute.

'I have to say, I'm strangely excited to get to meet Sharon Schieber,' Go finally said. 'Very classy lady. *Not like that Connie Chung.*'

I laughed, which was the intention. Our mother had loved Sharon Schieber and hated Connie Chung – she'd never forgiven her for embarrassing Newt Gingrich's mother on TV, something about Newt calling Hillary Clinton a b-i-t-c-h. I don't remember the actual interview, just our mom's outrage over it.

At six p.m. we entered the room, where two chairs were set up facing each other, the Arch in the background, the timing picked precisely so the Arch would glow but there would be no sunset glare on the windows. One of the most important moments of my life, I thought, dictated by the angle of the sun. A producer whose name I wouldn't remember clicked toward us on dangerously high heels and explained to me what I should expect. Questions could be asked several times, to make the interview seem as smooth as possible, and to allow for Sharon's reaction shots. I could not speak to my lawyer before giving an answer. I could rephrase an answer but not change the substance of the answer. Here's some water, let's get you miked.

We started to move over to the chair, and Betsy nudged my arm. When I looked down, she showed me a pocket of jellybeans. 'Remember ...' she said, and tsked her finger at me.

Suddenly, the suite door swung wide and Sharon Schieber entered, as smooth as if she were being borne by a team of swans. She was a beautiful woman, a woman who had probably never looked girlish. A woman whose nose probably never sweated. She had thick dark hair and giant brown eyes that could look doelike or wicked.

'It's Sharon!' Go said, a thrilled whisper to imitate our mom.

Sharon turned to Go and nodded majestically, came over to greet us. 'I'm Sharon,' she said in a warm, deep voice, taking both of Go's hands.

'Our mother loved you,' Go said.

'I'm so glad,' Sharon said, managing to sound warm. She turned to me and was about to speak when her producer clicked up on high heels and whispered in her ear. Then waited for Sharon's reaction, then whispered again.

'Oh. Oh my God,' Sharon said. When she turned back to me, she wasn't smiling at all.

AMY ELLIOTT DUNNE
TEN DAYS GONE

I have made a call: to make a call. The meeting can't happen until this evening – there are predictable complications – so I kill the day by primping and prepping.

I clean myself in a McDonald's bathroom – green gel on wet paper towels – and change into a cheap, papery sundress. I think about what I'll say. I am surprisingly eager. The shithole life was wearing on me: the communal washing machine with someone's wet underwear always stuck in the rungs at the top, to be peeled out by hesitant pincered fingers; the corner of my cabin rug that was forever mysteriously damp; the dripping faucet in the bathroom.

At 5 o'clock, I begin driving north to the meeting spot, a river casino called Horseshoe Alley. It appears out of nowhere, a blinking neon clump in the middle of a scrawny forest. I roll in on fumes – a cliché I've never put to practice – park the car, and take in the view: a migration of the elderly, scuttling like broken insects on walkers and canes, jerking oxygen tanks toward the bright lights. Sliding in and out of the groups of octogenarians are hustling, overdressed boys who've watched too many Vegas movies and don't know how poignant they are, trying to imitate Rat Pack cool in cheap suits in the Missouri woods.

I enter under a glowing billboard promoting – for two nights only – the reunion of a '50s doo-wop group. Inside, the casino is frigid and close. The penny slots clink and clang, joyful electronic chirps that don't match the dull, drooping faces of the people sitting in front of the machines, smoking cigarettes above dangling oxygen masks. Penny in penny in penny in penny in penny in ding-ding-ding! penny in penny in. The money that they waste goes to the underfunded public schools that their bored, blinking grandchildren attend. Penny in penny in. A group of wasted boys stumble past, a bachelor party, the boys' lips wet from shots; they don't even notice me, husky and Hamill-haired. They are talking about girls, *get us some girls*, but besides me, the only girls I see are golden. The boys will drink away their disappointment and try not to kill fellow motorists on the way home.

I wait in a pocket bar to the far left of the casino entrance, as planned, and watch the aged boy band sing to a large snowy-haired audience, snapping and clapping along, shuffling gnarled fingers through bowls of complimentary peanuts. The skeletal singers, withered beneath bedazzled tuxes, spin slowly, carefully, on replaced hips, the dance of the moribund.

The casino seemed like a good idea at first – right off the highway, filled with drunks and elderly, neither of whom are known for eyesight. But I am feeling crowded and fidgety, aware of the cameras in every corner, the doors that could snap shut.

I am about to leave when he ambles up.

'Amy.'

I've called devoted Desi to my aid (and abet). Desi, with whom I've never entirely lost touch, and who – despite what I've told Nick, my parents – doesn't unnerve me in the slightest. Desi, another man along the Mississippi. I always knew he might come in handy. It's good to have at least one man you can use for anything. Desi is a white-knight type. He loves troubled women. Over the years, after Wickshire, when we'd talk, I'd ask after his latest girlfriend, and no matter the girl, he would always say: 'Oh, she's not doing very well, unfortunately.' But I know it is fortunate for Desi – the eating disorders, the painkiller addictions, the crippling depressions. He is never happier than when he's at a bedside. Not in bed, just perched nearby with broth and juice and a gently starched voice. *Poor darling.*

Now he is here, dashing in a white midsummer suit (Desi changes wardrobes monthly – what was appropriate for June would not work for July – I've always admired the discipline, the precision of the Collings's costuming). He looks good. I don't. I am too aware of my humid glasses, the extra roll of flesh at my waist.

'Amy.' He touches my cheek, then pulls me in for an embrace.

Not a hug, Desi doesn't hug, it's more like being encased by something tailored just to you. 'Sweetheart. You can't imagine. That call. I thought I'd gone insane. I thought I was making you up! I'd daydreamed about it, that somehow you were alive, and then. That call. Are you okay?'

'I am now,' I say. 'I feel safe now. It's been awful.' And then I burst into tears, actual tears, which hadn't been the plan, but they feel so relieving, and they fit the moment so perfectly, that I let myself unravel entirely. The stress drips off me: the nerve of enacting the plan, the fear of being caught, the loss of my money, the betrayal, the manhandling, the pure wildness of being on my own for the first time in my life.

I look quite pretty after a cry of about two minutes – longer than that and the nose goes runny, the puffiness sets in, but up to that, my lips gets fuller, my eyes bigger, my cheeks flushed. I count as I cry into Desi's crisp shoulder, *one Mississippi, two Mississippi* – that river again – and I curb the tears at one minute and forty-eight seconds.

'I'm sorry I couldn't get here earlier, sweetheart,' Desi says.

'I know how full Jacqueline keeps your schedule,' I demur. Desi's mom is a touchy subject in our relationship.

He studies me. 'You look *very* ... different,' he says. 'So full in the face, especially. And your poor hair is—' He catches himself. 'Amy. I just never thought I could be so grateful for anything. Tell me what's happened.'

I tell a Gothic tale of possessiveness and rage, of Midwest steak-and-potato brutality, barefoot pregnancy, animalistic dominance. Of rape and pills and liquor and fists. Pointed cowboy boots in the ribs, fear and betrayal, parental apathy, isolation, and Nick's final telling words: 'You can never leave me. I will kill you. I will find you no matter what. You are mine.'

How I had to disappear for my own safety and the safety of my unborn child, and how I needed Desi's help. My savior. My story would satisfy Desi's craving for ruined women – I was now the most damaged of them all. Long ago, back in boarding school, I'd told him about my father's nightly visits to my bedroom, me in a ruffly pink nightgown, staring at the ceiling until he was done. Desi has loved me ever since the lie, I know he pictures making love to me, how gentle and reassuring he would be as he plunged into me, stroking my hair. I know he pictures me crying softly as I give myself to him.

'I can't ever go back to my old life, Desi. Nick will kill me. I'll never feel safe. But I can't let him go to prison. I just wanted to disappear. I didn't realize the police would think *he* did it.'

I glance prettily toward the band onstage, where a skeletal septuagenarian is singing about love. Not far from our table, a straight-backed guy with a trim mustache tosses his cup toward a trash can near us and bricks (a term I learned from Nick). I wish I'd picked a more picturesque spot. And now the guy is looking at me, tilting his head toward the side, in exaggerated confusion. If he were a cartoon, he'd scratch his head, and it would make a rubbery *wiik-wiik* sound. For some reason, I think: *He looks like a cop.* I turn my back to him.

'Nick is the last thing for you to worry about,' Desi said. 'Give that worry to me and I'll take care of it.' He holds out his hand, an old gesture. He is my worry-keeper; it is a ritual game we played as teens. I pretend to place something in his palm and he closes his fingers over it and I actually feel better.

'No, I won't take care of it. I do hope Nick dies for what he did to you,' he said. 'In a sane society, he would.'

'Well, we're in an insane society, so I need to stay hidden,' I said. 'Do you think that's horrible of me?' I already know the answer.

'Sweetheart, of course not. You are doing what you've been forced to do. It would be madness to do anything else.'

He doesn't ask anything about the pregnancy. I knew he wouldn't.

'You're the only one who knows,' I say.

'I'll take care of you. What can I do?'

I pretend to balk, chew the edge of my lip, look away and then back to Desi. 'I need money to live on for a bit. I thought about getting a job, but—'

'Oh, no, don't do that. You are *everywhere*, Amy – on all the newscasts, all the magazines. Someone would recognize you. Even with this' – he touches my hair – 'new sporty cut of yours. You're a beautiful woman, and it's difficult for beautiful women to disappear.'

'Unfortunately, I think you're right,' I say. 'I just don't want you to think I'm taking advantage. I just didn't know where else to—'

The waitress, a plain brunette disguised as a pretty brunette, drops by, sets our drinks on the table. I turn my face from her and see that the mustached curious guy is standing a little closer, watching me with a half smile. I am off my game. Old Amy never would have come here. My mind is addled by Diet Coke and my own body odor.

'I ordered you a gin and tonic,' I say.

Desi gives a delicate grimace.

'What?' I ask, but I already know.

'That's my spring drink. I'm Jack and gingers now.'

'Then we'll get you one of those, and I'll have your gin.'

'No, it's fine, don't worry.'

The lookiloo appears again in my peripheral. 'Is that guy, that guy with the mustache – don't look now – is he staring at me?'

Desi gives a flick of a glance, shakes his head. 'He's watching the ... *singers*.' He says the word dubiously. 'You don't just want a little bit of cash. You'll get tired of this subterfuge. Not being able to look people in the face. Living among' – he spread his arms out to include the whole casino – 'people with

364

whom I assume you don't have much in common. Living below your means.'

'That's what it is for the next ten years. Until I've aged enough and the story has gone away and I can feel comfortable.'

'Ha! You're willing to do that for *ten* years? Amy?'

'Sh, don't say the name.'

'Cathy or Jenny or Megan or whatever, don't be ludicrous.'

The waitress returns, and Desi hands her a twenty and dismisses her. She walks away grinning. Holding the twenty up like it is novel. I take a sip of my drink. The baby won't mind.

'I don't think Nick would press charges if you return,' Desi says.

'What?'

'He came by to see me. I think he knows that he's to blame—'

'He went to see you? When?'

'Last week. Before I'd talked to you, thank God.'

Nick has shown more interest in me these past ten days than he has in the past few years. I've always wanted a man to get in a fight over me – a brutal, bloody fight. Nick going to interrogate Desi, that's a nice start.

'What did he say?' I ask. 'How did he seem?'

'He seemed like a top-drawer asshole. He wanted to pin it on *me*. Told me some insane story about how I—'

I'd always liked that lie about Desi trying to kill himself over me. He had truly been devastated by our breakup, and he'd been really annoying, creepy, hanging around campus, hoping I'd take him back.

So he might as well have attempted suicide.

'What did Nick say about me?'

'I think he knows that he can never hurt you now that the world knows and cares about who you are. He'd have to let you come back safely, and you could divorce him and marry the right man.' He took a sip. 'At long last.'

'I can't come back, Desi. Even if people believed everything about Nick's abuse. I'd still be the one they hated – I was the one who tricked them. I'd be the biggest pariah in the world.'

'You'd be my pariah, and I'd love you no matter what, and I'd shield you from everything,' Desi said. 'You would never have to deal with any of it.'

'We'd never be able to socialize with anyone again.'

'We could leave the country if you want. Live in Spain, Italy, wherever you like, spend our days eating mangoes in the sun. Sleep late, play Scrabble, flip through books aimlessly, swim in the ocean.'

'And when I died, I'd be some bizarre footnote – a freak show. No. I do have pride, Desi.'

'I'm not letting you go back to the trailer-park life. I'm not. Come with me, we'll set you up in the lake house. It's very secluded. I'll bring groceries and anything you need, anytime. You can hide out, all alone, until we decide what to do.'

Desi's *lake house* was a *mansion*, and *bringing groceries* was *becoming my lover*. I could feel the need coming off him like heat. He was squirming a little under his suit, wanting to make it happen. Desi was a collector: He had four cars, three houses, suites of suits and shoes. He would like knowing I was stowed away under glass. The ultimate white-knight fantasy: He steals the abused princess from her squalid circumstances and places her under his gilded protection in a castle that no one can breach but him.

'I can't do that. What if the police find out somehow and they come to search?'

'Amy, the police think you're dead.'

'No, I should be on my own for now. Can I just have a little cash from you?'

'What if I say no?'

'Then I'll know your offer to help me isn't genuine. That you're like Nick and you just want control over me, however you can get it.'

Desi was silent, swallowing his drink with a tight jaw. 'That's a rather monstrous thing to say.'

'It's a rather monstrous way to act.'

'I'm not acting that way,' he said. 'I'm worried about you.

Try the lake house. If you feel cramped by me, if you feel uncomfortable, you leave. The worst that can happen is you get a few days' rest and relaxation.'

The mustached guy is suddenly at our table, a flickering smile on his face. 'Ma'am, I don't suppose you're any relation to the Enloe family, are you?' he asks.

'No,' I say, and turn away.

'Sorry, you just look like some—'

'We're from Canada, now excuse us,' Desi snaps, and the guy rolls his eyes, mutters a *jeez*, and strolls back to the bar. But he keeps glancing at me.

'We should leave,' Desi says. 'Come to the lake house. I'll take you there now.' He stands.

Desi's lake house would have a grand kitchen, it would have rooms I could traipse around in – I could 'hills are alive' twirl in them, the rooms would be so massive. The house would have Wi-Fi and cable – for all my command-center needs – and a gaping bathtub and plush robes and a bed that didn't threaten to collapse.

It would have Desi too, but Desi could be managed.

At the bar, the guy is still staring at me, less benevolently.

I lean over and kiss Desi gently on the lips. It has to seem like my decision. 'You're such a wonderful man. I'm sorry to put you in this situation.'

'I want to be in this situation, Amy.'

We are on our way out, walking past a particularly depressing bar, TVs buzzing in all corners, when I see the Slut.

The Slut is holding a press conference.

Andie looks tiny and harmless. She looks like a babysitter, and not a sexy porn babysitter but the girl from down the road, the one who actually plays with the kids. I know this is not the real Andie, because I have followed her in real life. In real life she wears snug tops that show off her breasts, and clingy jeans, and her hair long and wavy. In real life she looks fuckable.

Now she is wearing a ruffled shirtdress with her hair tucked behind her ears, and she looks like she's been crying, you can tell by the small pink pads beneath her eyes. She looks exhausted and nervous but very pretty. Prettier than I'd thought before. I never saw her this close up. She has freckles.

'Ohhhh, shit,' says one woman to her friend, a cheap-cabernet redhead.

'Oh noooo, I was actually starting to feel bad for the guy,' says the friend.

'I have crap in my fridge older than that girl. What an asshole.'

Andie stands behind the mike and looks down with dark eyelashes at a statement that leaf-shakes in her hand. Her upper lip is damp; it shines under the camera lights. She swipes an index finger to blot the sweat. 'Um. My statement is this: I did engage in an affair with Nick Dunne from April 2011 until July of this year, when his wife, Amy Dunne, went missing. Nick was my professor at North Carthage Junior College, and we became friendly, and then the relationship became more.'

Andie stops to clear her throat. A dark-haired woman behind her, not much older than I am, hands her a glass of water, which she slurps quickly, the glass shaking.

'I am deeply ashamed of having been involved with a married man. It goes against all my values. I truly believed I was in love' – she begins crying; her voice shivers – 'with Nick Dunne and that he was in love with me. He told me that his relationship with his wife was over and that they would be divorcing soon. I did not know that Amy Dunne was pregnant. I am cooperating with the police in their investigation in the disappearance of Amy Dunne, and I will do everything in my power to help.'

Her voice is tiny, childish. She looks up at the wall of cameras in front of her and seems shocked, looks back down. Two apples turn red on her round cheeks.

'I ... I.' She begins sobbing, and her mother – that woman has to be her mother, they have the same oversize anime eyes – puts an arm on her shoulder. Andie continues reading. 'I am so sorry and ashamed for what I have done. And I want to apologize to Amy's family for any role I played in their pain. I am cooperating with the police in their investi— Oh, I said that already.'

She smiles a weak, embarrassed smile, and the press corps chuckle encouragingly.

'Poor little thing,' says the redhead.

She is a little slut, she is not to be pitied. I cannot believe anyone would feel sorry for Andie. I literally refuse to believe it.

'I am a twenty-three-year-old student,' she continues. 'I ask only for some privacy to heal during this very painful time.'

'Good luck with that,' I mutter as Andie backs away and a police officer declines to take any questions and they walk off camera. I catch myself leaning to the left as if I could follow them.

'Poor little lamb,' says the older woman. 'She seemed terrified.'

'I guess he did do it after all.'

'Over a *year* he was with her.'

'Slimebag.'

Desi gives me a nudge and widens his eyes in a question: Did I know about the affair? Was I okay? My face is a mask of fury – *poor little lamb, my ass* – but I can pretend it is because of this betrayal. I nod, smile weakly. I am okay. We are about to leave when I see my parents, holding hands as always, stepping up to the mike in tandem. My mother looks like she's just gotten her hair cut. I wonder if I should be annoyed that she paused in the middle of my disappearance for personal grooming. When someone dies and the relatives carry on, you always hear them say *so-and-so would have wanted it that way.* I don't want it that way.

My mother speaks. 'Our statement is brief, and we will take no questions afterward. First, thank you for the tremendous outpouring for our family. It seems the world loves Amy as much as we do. Amy: We miss your warm voice and your good humor, and your quick wit and your good heart. You are indeed amazing. We will return you to our family. I know we will. Second, we did not know that our son-in-law, Nick Dunne, was having an affair until this morning. He has been, since the beginning of this nightmare, less involved, less interested, less concerned than he should be. Giving him the benefit of the doubt, we attributed this behavior to shock. With our new knowledge, we no longer feel this way. We have withdrawn our support from Nick accordingly. As we move forward with the investigation, we can only hope that Amy comes back to us. Her story must continue. The world is ready for a new chapter.'

Amen, says someone.

NICK DUNNE
TEN DAYS GONE

The show was over, Andie and the Elliotts gone from view. Sharon's producer kicked the TV off with the point of her heel. Everyone in the room was watching me, waiting for an explanation, the party guest who just shat on the floor. Sharon gave me a too-bright smile, an angry smile that strained her Botox. Her face folded in the wrong spots.

'Well?' she said in her calm, plummy voice. 'What the fuck was that?'

Tanner stepped in. 'That was the bombshell. Nick was and is fully prepared to disclose and discuss his actions. I'm sorry about the timing, but in a way, it's better for you, Sharon. You'll get the first react from Nick.'

'You'd better have some goddamn interesting things to say, Nick.' She breezed away, calling, 'Mike him, we do this now' to no one in particular.

Sharon Schieber, it turned out, fucking adored me. In New York I'd always heard rumors that she'd been a cheat herself and returned to her husband, a very hush-hush inside-journalism story. That was almost ten years ago, but I figured the urge to absolve might still be there. It was. She beamed, she coddled, she cajoled and teased. She pursed those full, glossy lips at me in deep sincerity – a knuckled hand under her chin – and asked me her hard questions, and for once I answered them well. I am not a liar of Amy's dazzling caliber, but I'm not bad when I have to be. I looked like a man who loved his wife, who was shamed by his infidelities and ready to do right. The night before, sleepless and nervy, I'd gone online and watched Hugh Grant on Leno, 1995, apologizing to the nation for getting lewd with a hooker. Stuttering, stammering, squirming as if his skin were two sizes too small. But no excuses: 'I think you know in life what's a good thing to do and what's a bad thing, and I did a bad thing ... and there you have it.' Damn, the guy was good – he looked sheepish, nervous, so shaky you wanted to take his hand and say, *Buddy, it's not that big a deal, don't beat yourself up*. Which was the effect I was going for. I watched that clip so many times, I was in danger of borrowing a British accent.

I was the ultimate hollow man: the husband that Amy always claimed couldn't apologize finally did, using words and emotions borrowed from an actor.

But it worked. *Sharon, I did a bad thing, an unforgivable thing. I can't make any excuses for it. I let myself down – I've never thought of myself as a cheater. It's inexcusable, it's unforgivable, and I just want Amy to come home so I can spend the rest of my life making it up to her, treating her how she deserves.*

Oh, I'd definitely like to treat her how she deserves.

But here's the thing, Sharon: I did not kill Amy. I would never hurt her. I think what's happening here is what I've been calling [a chuckle] *in my mind the* Ellen Abbott *effect. This embarrassing, irresponsible brand of journalism. We are so used to seeing these murders of women packaged as entertainment, which is disgusting, and in these shows, who is guilty? It's always the husband. So I think the public and, to an extent, even the police have been hammered into believing that's always the case. From the beginning, it was practically assumed I had killed my wife – because that's the story we are told time after time – and that's wrong, that's morally wrong. I did not kill my wife. I want her to come home.*

I knew Sharon would like an opportunity to paint Ellen Abbott as a sensationalistic ratings whore. I knew regal Sharon with her twenty years in journalism, her interviews with Arafat and Sarkozy and Obama, would be offended by the very idea of Ellen Abbott. I am (was) a journalist, I know the drill, and so when I said those words – *the Ellen Abbott effect* – I recognized

Sharon's mouth twitch, the delicately raised eyebrows, the lightening of her whole visage. It was the look when you realize: *I got my angle.*

At the end of the interview, Sharon took both my hands in hers – cool, a bit callused, I'd read she was an avid golfer – and wished me well. 'I will be keeping a close eye on you, my friend,' she said, and then she was kissing Go on the cheek and swishing away from us, the back of her dress a battlefield of stickpins to keep the material in front from slouching.

'You fucking did that perfectly,' Go pronounced as she headed to the door. 'You seem totally different than before. In charge but not cocky. Even your jaw is less ... dickish.'

'I unclefted my chin.'

'Almost, yeah. See you back home.' She actually gave me a go-champ punch to the shoulder.

I followed the Sharon Schieber interview with two quickies – one cable and one network. Tomorrow the Schieber interview would air, and then the others would roll out, a domino of apologetics and remorse. I was taking control. I was no longer going to settle for being the possibly guilty husband or the emotionally removed husband or the heartlessly cheating husband. I was the guy everyone knew – the guy many men (and women) have been: *I cheated, I feel like shit, I will do what needs to be done to fix the situation because I am a real man.*

'We are in decent shape,' Tanner pronounced as we wrapped up. 'The thing with Andie, it won't be as awful as it might have been, thanks to the interview with Sharon. We just need to stay ahead of everything else from now on.'

Go phoned, and I picked up. Her voice was thin and high.

'The cops are here with a warrant for the woodshed ... they're at Dad's house too. They're ... I'm scared.'

Go was in the kitchen smoking a cigarette when we arrived, and judging from the overflow in the kitschy '70s ashtray, she was on her second pack. An awkward, shoulderless kid with a crew cut and a police officer's uniform sat next to her on one of the bar stools.

'This is Tyler,' she said. 'He grew up in Tennessee, he has a horse named Custard—'

'Custer,' Tyler said.

'Custer, and he's allergic to peanuts. Not the horse but Tyler. Oh, and he has a torn labrum, which is the same injury baseball pitchers get, but he's not sure how he got it.' She took a drag on the cigarette. Her eyes watered. 'He's been here a long time.'

Tyler tried to give me a tough look, ended up watching his well-shined shoes.

Boney appeared through the sliding glass doors at the back of the house. 'Big day, boys,' she said. 'Wish you'd bothered letting us know, Nick, that you have a girlfriend. Would have saved us all a lot of time.'

'We're happy to discuss that, as well as the contents of the shed, both of which we were on our way to tell you about,' Tanner said. 'Frankly, if you had given us the courtesy of telling us about Andie, a lot of pain could have been forestalled. But you needed the press conference, you had to have the publicity. How disgusting, to put that girl up there like that.'

'Right,' Boney said. 'So, the woodshed. You all want to come with me?' She turned her back on us, leading the way over the patchy end-of-summer grass to the woodshed. A cobweb trailed from her hair like a wedding veil. She motioned impatiently when she saw me not following. 'Come on,' she said. 'Not gonna bite you.'

The woodshed was lit up by several portable lights, making it look even more ominous.

'When's the last time you been in here, Nick?'

'I came in here very recently, when my wife's treasure hunt led me here. But it's not my stuff, and I did not touch anything—'

Tanner cut me off: 'My client and I have an explosive new theory—' Tanner began, then caught himself. The phony TV-speak was so incredibly awful and inappropriate, we all cringed.

374

'Oh, explosive, how exciting,' Boney said.

'We were about to inform you—'

'Really? What convenient timing,' she said. 'Stay there, please.' The door hung loose on its hinges, a broken lock dangling to the side. Gilpin was inside, cataloging the goods.

'These the golf clubs you don't play with?' Gilpin said, jostling the glinting irons.

'None of this is mine – none of this was put there by me.'

'That's funny, because everything in here corresponds with purchases made on the credit cards that aren't yours either,' Boney snapped. 'This is, like, what do they call it, a man cave? A man cave in the making, just waiting for the wife to go away for good. Got yourself some nice pastimes, Nick.' She pulled out three large cardboard boxes and set them at my feet.

'What's this?'

Boney opened them with fingertip disgust despite her gloved hands. Inside were dozens of porn DVDs, flesh of all colors and sizes on display on the covers.

Gilpin chuckled. 'I gotta hand it to you, Nick, I mean, a man has his needs—'

'Men are highly visual, that's what my ex always said when I caught him,' Boney said.

'Men are highly visual, but Nick, this shit made me blush,' Gilpin said. 'It made me a little sick, too, some of it, and I don't get sick too easy.' He spread out a few of the DVDs like an ugly deck of cards. Most of the titles implied violence: *Brutal Anal, Brutal Blowjobs, Humiliated Whores, Sadistic Slut Fucking, Gang-raped Sluts*, and a series called *Hurt the Bitch*, volumes 1–18, each featuring photos of women writhing in pain while leering, laughing men inserted objects into them.

I turned away.

'Oh, now he's embarrassed.' Gilpin grinned.

But I didn't respond because I saw Go being helped into the back of a police car.

We met an hour later at the police station. Tanner advised against it – I insisted. I appealed to his iconoclast, millionaire

375

rodeo-cowboy ego. We were going to tell the cops the truth. It was time.

I could handle them fucking with me – but not my sister.

'I'm agreeing to this because I think your arrest is inevitable, Nick, no matter what we do,' he said. 'If we let them know we're up for talking, we may get some more information on the case they've got against you. Without a body, they'll really want a confession. So they'll try to overwhelm you with the evidence. And they may give us enough to really jumpstart our defense.'

'And we give them everything, right?' I said. 'We give them the clues and the marionettes and Amy.' I was panicked, aching to go – I could picture the cops right now sweating my sister under a bare lightbulb.

'As long as you let me talk,' Tanner said. 'If it's me talking about the frame-up, they can't use it against us at trial … if we go with a different defense.'

It concerned me that my lawyer found the truth to be so completely unbelievable.

Gilpin met us at the steps of the station, a Coke in his hand, late dinner. When he turned around to lead us in, I saw a sweat-soaked back. The sun had long set, but the humidity remained. He flapped his arms once, and the shirt fluttered and stuck right back to his skin.

'Still hot,' he said. 'Supposed to get hotter overnight.'

Boney was waiting for us in the conference room, the one from the first night. The Night Of. She'd French-braided her limp hair and clipped it to the back of her head in a rather poignant updo, and she wore lipstick. I wondered if she had a date. A *meet you after midnight* situation.

'You have kids?' I asked her, pulling out a chair.

She looked startled and held up a finger. 'One.' She didn't say a name or an age or anything else. Boney was in business mode. She tried to wait us out.

'You first,' Tanner said. 'Tell us what you got.'

'Sure,' Boney said. 'Okay.' She turned on the tape recorder, dispensed with the preliminaries. 'It is your contention, Nick, that you never bought or touched the items in the woodshed on your sister's property.'

'That is correct,' Tanner replied for me.

'Nick, your fingerprints are all over almost every item in the shed.'

'That's a lie! I touched *nothing*, not a thing in there! Except for my anniversary present, which *Amy left inside*.'

Tanner touched my arm: *shut the fuck up.*

'Which we have brought here today,' Tanner said.

'Nick, your fingerprints are on the porn, on the golf clubs, on the watch cases, and even on the TV.'

And then I saw it, how much Amy would have enjoyed this: my deep, self-satisfied sleep (which I lorded over her, my belief that if she were only more laid-back, more like me, her insomnia would vanish) turned against me. I could see it: Amy down on her knees, my snores heating her cheeks, as she pressed a fingertip here and there over the course of months. She could have slipped me a mickey for all I knew. I remember her peering at me one morning as I woke up, sleep-wax gumming my lips, and she said, 'You sleep the sleep of the damned, you know. Or the drugged.' I was both and didn't know it.

'Do you want to explain about the fingerprints?' Gilpin said.

'Tell us the rest,' Tanner said.

Boney set a biblically thick leather-covered binder on the table between us, charred all along the edges. 'Recognize this?'

I shrugged, shook my head.

'It's your wife's diary.'

'Um, no. Amy didn't do diaries.'

'Actually, Nick, she did. She did about seven years' worth of diaries,' Boney said.

'Okay.'

Something bad was about to happen. My wife was being clever again.

AMY ELLIOTT DUNNE
TEN DAYS GONE

We drive my car across state lines into Illinois, to a particularly awful neighborhood of some busted river town, and we spend an hour wiping it down, and then we leave it with the keys in the ignition. Call it the circle of strife: The Arkansas couple who drove it before me were sketchy; Ozark Amy was obviously shady; hopefully, some Illinois down-and-outer will enjoy it for a bit too.

Then we drive back into Missouri over wavy hills until I can see, between the trees, Lake Hannafan glistening. Because Desi has family in St. Louis, he likes to believe the area is old, East Coast old, but he is wrong. Lake Hannafan is not named after a nineteenth-century statesman or a Civil War hero. It is a private lake, machine-forged in 2002 by an oily developer named Mike Hannafan who turned out to have a moonlighting job illegally disposing of hazardous waste. The kerfuffled community is scrambling to find a new name for their lake. Lake Collings, I'm sure, has been floated.

So despite the well-planned lake – upon which a few select residents can sail but not motor – and Desi's tastefully grand house – a Swiss château on an American scale – I remain unwooed. That was always the problem with Desi. Be from Missouri or don't, but don't pretend Lake 'Collings' is Lake Como.

He leans against his Jaguar and aims his gaze up at the house so that I have to pause for appreciation also.

'We modeled it after this wonderful little chalet my mother and I stayed at in Brienzersee,' he says. 'All we're missing is the mountain range.'

378

A rather big miss, I think, but I put my hand on his arm and say, 'Show me the inside. It must be fabulous.'

He gives me the nickel tour, laughing at the idea of a nickel. A cathedral kitchen – all granite and chrome – a living room with his-and-hers fireplaces that flows onto an outdoor space (what midwesterners call a deck) overlooking the woods and the lake. A basement entertainment room with a snooker table, darts, surround sound, a wet bar, and its own outdoor space (what midwesterners call another deck). A sauna off the entertainment room and next to it the wine cellar. Upstairs, five bedrooms, the second largest of which he bestows on me.

'I had it repainted,' he says. 'I know you love dusty rose.'

I don't love dusty rose anymore; that was high school. 'You are so lovely, Desi, thank you,' I say, my most heartfelt. My thank-yous always come out rather labored. I often don't give them at all. People do what they're supposed to do and then wait for you to pile on the appreciation – they're like frozen-yogurt employees who put out cups for tips.

But Desi takes to thank-yous like a cat being brushed; his back almost arches with the pleasure. For now it's a worthwhile gesture.

I set my bag down in my room, trying to signal my retirement for the evening – I need to see how people are reacting to Andie's confession and whether Nick has been arrested – but it seems I am far from through with the thank-yous. Desi has ensured I will be forever indebted to him. He smiles a special-surprise smile and takes my hand (*I have something else to show you*) and pulls me back downstairs (*I really hope you like this*) onto a hallway off the kitchen (*it took a lot of work, but it's so worth it*).

'I really hope you like this,' he says again, and flings open the door.

It's a glass room, a greenhouse, I realize. Within are tulips, hundreds, of all colors. Tulips bloom in the middle of July in Desi's lake house. In their own special room for a very special girl.

'I know tulips are your favorite, but the season is so short,' Desi said. 'So I fixed that for you. They'll bloom year-round.'

He puts his arm around my waist and aims me toward the flowers so I can appreciate them fully.

'Tulips any day of the year,' I say, and try to get my eyes to glisten. Tulips were my favorite in high school. They were everyone's favorite, the gerbera daisy of the late '80s. Now I like orchids, which are basically the opposite of tulips.

'Would Nick ever have thought of something like this for you?' Desi breathes into my ear as the tulips sway under a mechanized dusting of water from above.

'Nick never even remembered I liked tulips,' I say, the correct answer.

It is sweet, beyond sweet, the gesture. My own flower room, like a fairy tale. And yet I feel a lilt of nerves: I called Desi only twenty-four hours ago, and these are not newly planted tulips, and the bedroom did not smell of fresh paint. It makes me wonder: the uptick in his letters the past year, their wooful tone ... how long has he been wanting to bring me here? And how long does he think I will stay? Long enough to enjoy blooming tulips every day for a year.

'My goodness, Desi,' I say. 'It's like a fairy tale.'

'Your fairy tale,' he says. 'I want you to see what life can be like.'

In fairy tales, there is always gold. I wait for him to give me a stack of bills, a slim credit card, something of use. The tour loops back around through all the rooms so I can ooh and ahh about details I missed the first time, and then we return to my bedroom, a satin-and-silk, pink-and-plush, marshmallow-and-cotton-candy girl's room. As I peer out a window, I notice the high wall that surrounds the house.

I blurt, nervously, 'Desi, would you be able to leave me with some money?'

He actually pretends to be surprised. 'You don't need money now, do you?' he says. 'You have no rent to pay anymore; the house will be stocked with food. I can bring new clothes for you. Not that I don't like you in bait-shop chic.'

'I guess a little cash would just make me feel more comfortable. Should something happen. Should I need to get out of here quickly.'

He opens his wallet and pulls out two twenty-dollar bills. Presses them gently in my hand. 'There you are,' he says indulgently.

I wonder then if I have made a very big mistake.

I made a mistake, feeling so cocky. Whatever the hell this diary was, it was going to ruin me. I could already see the cover of the true-crime novel: the black-and-white photo of us on our wedding day, the blood-red background, the jacket copy: *including sixteen pages of never-seen photos and Amy Elliott Dunne's actual diary entries – a voice from beyond the grave …* I'd found it strange and kind of cute, Amy's guilty pleasures, those cheesy true-crime books I'd discovered here and there around our house. I thought maybe she was loosening up, allowing herself some beach reading.

Nope. She was just studying.

Gilpin pulled over a chair, sat on it backward, and leaned toward me on crossed arms – his movie-cop look. It was almost midnight; it felt later.

'Tell us about your wife's illness these past few months,' he said.

'Illness? Amy never got sick. Once a year she'd get a cold, maybe.'

Boney picked up the book, turned to a marked page. 'Last month you made Amy and yourself some drinks, sat on your back porch. She writes here that the drinks were impossibly sweet and describes what she thinks is an allergic reaction: *My heart was racing, my tongue was slabbed, stuck to the bottom of my mouth. My legs turned to meat as Nick walked me up the stairs.*' She put a finger down to hold her place in the diary, looked up as if I might not be paying attention. 'When she woke the next morning: *My head ached and my stomach was oily, but weirder, my fingernails were light blue, and when I looked in the mirror, so were my lips. I didn't pee for two days after. I felt so weak.'*

I shook my head in disgust. I'd become attached to Boney; I expected better of her.

'Is this your wife's handwriting?' Boney tilted the book toward me, and I saw deep black ink and Amy's cursive, jagged as a fever chart.

'Yes, I think so.'

'So does our handwriting expert.'

Boney said the words with a certain pride, and I realized: This was the first case these two had ever had that required outside experts, that demanded they get in touch with professionals who did exotic things like analyze handwriting.

'You know what else we learned, Nick, when we showed this entry to our medical expert?'

'Poisoning,' I blurted. Tanner frowned at me: *steady*.

Boney stuttered for a second; this was not information I was supposed to provide.

'Yeah, Nick, thank you: antifreeze poisoning,' she said. 'Textbook. She's lucky she survived.'

'She didn't *survive*, because that never happened,' I said. 'Like you said, it's textbook – it's made up from an Internet search.'

Boney frowned but refused to bite. 'The diary isn't a pretty picture of you, Nick,' she continued, one finger tracing her braid. '*Abuse* – you pushed her around. *Stress* – you were quick to anger. Sexual relations that bordered on *rape*. She was very frightened of you at the end there. It's painful to read. That gun we were wondering about, she says she wanted it because she was afraid of you. Here's her last entry: *This man might kill me. This man might kill me*, in her own words.'

My throat clenched. I felt like I might throw up. Fear, mostly, and then a surge of rage. *Fucking bitch, fucking bitch, cunt, cunt, cunt.*

'What a smart, convenient note for her to end on,' I said. Tanner put a hand on mine to hush me.

'You look like you want to kill her again, right now,' Boney said.

'You've done nothing but lie to us, Nick,' Gilpin said. 'You say you were at the beach that morning. Everyone we talk to says you hate the beach. You say you have no idea what all these purchases are on your maxed-out credit cards. Now we have a shed full of exactly those items, *and they have your fingerprints all over them*. We have a wife suffering from what sounds like antifreeze poisoning weeks before she *disappears*. I mean, come on.' He paused for effect.

'Anything else of note?' Tanner asked.

'We can place you in Hannibal, where your wife's purse shows up a few days later,' Boney said. 'We have a neighbor who overheard you two arguing the night before. A pregnancy you didn't want. A bar borrowed on your wife's money that would revert to her in case of a divorce. And of course, *of course*: a secret girlfriend of more than a year.'

'We can help you right now, Nick,' Gilpin said. 'Once we arrest you, we can't.'

'Where did you find the diary? At Nick's father's house?' Tanner asked.

'Yes,' Boney said.

Tanner nodded to me: *That's what we didn't find.* 'Let me guess: anonymous tip.'

Neither cop said a thing.

'Can I ask where in the house you found it?' I asked.

'In the furnace. I know you thought you burned it. It caught fire, but the pilot light was too weak; it got smothered. So only the outer edges burned,' Gilpin said. 'Extremely good luck for us.'

The furnace – another inside joke from Amy! She'd always proclaimed amazement at how little I understood the things men are supposed to understand. During our search, I'd even glanced at my dad's old furnace, with its pipes and wires and spigots, and backed away, intimidated.

'It wasn't luck. You were meant to find it,' I said.

Boney let the left side of her mouth slide into a smile. She

384

leaned back and waited, relaxed as the star of an iced-tea commercial. I gave Tanner an angry nod: *Go ahead.*

'Amy Elliott Dunne is alive, and she is framing Nick Dunne for her murder,' he said. I clasped my hands and sat up straight, tried to do anything that would lend me an air of reason. Boney stared at me. I needed a pipe, eyeglasses I could swiftly remove for effect, a set of encyclopedias at my elbow. I felt giddy. Do *not* laugh.

Boney frowned. 'What's that again?'

'Amy is alive and very well, and she is framing Nick,' my proxy repeated.

They exchanged a look, hunched over the table: *Can you believe this guy?*

'Why would she do that?' Gilpin asked, rubbing his eyes.

'Because she hates him. Obviously. He was a shitty husband.'

Boney looked down at the floor, let out a breath. 'I'd certainly agree with you there.'

At the same time, Gilpin said: 'Oh, for Christ's sake.'

'Is she *crazy*, Nick?' Boney said, leaning in. 'What you're talking about, it's crazy. You hear me? It would have taken, what, six months, a *year*, to set all this up. She would have had to hate you, to wish you harm – ultimate, serious, horrific harm – for a *year*. Do you know how hard it is to sustain that kind of hatred for that long?'

She could do it. Amy could do it.

'Why not just divorce your ass?' Boney snapped.

'That wouldn't appeal to her . . . sense of justice,' I replied. Tanner gave me another look.

'Jesus Christ, Nick, aren't you tired of all this?' Gilpin said. 'We have it in your wife's own words: *I think he may kill me.*'

Someone had told them at some point: Use the suspect's name a lot, it will make him feel comfortable, known. Same idea as in sales.

'You been in your dad's house lately, Nick?' Boney asked. 'Like on July ninth?'

Fuck. *That's* why Amy changed the alarm code. I battled a new wave of disgust at myself: that my wife played me twice.

Not only did she dupe me into believing she still loved me, she actually *forced me to implicate myself.* Wicked, wicked girl. I almost laughed. Good Lord, I hated her, but you had to admire the bitch.

Tanner began: 'Amy used her clues to force my client to go to these various venues, where she'd left evidence – Hannibal, his father's house – so he'd incriminate himself. My client and I have brought these clues with us. As a courtesy.'

He pulled out the clues and the love notes, fanned them in front of the cops like a card trick. I sweated while they read them, willing them to look up and tell me all was clear now.

'Okay. You say Amy hated you so much that she spent months framing you for her murder?' Boney asked, in the quiet, measured voice of a disappointed parent.

I gave her a blank face.

'This does not sound like an angry woman, Nick,' she said. 'She's falling all over herself to apologize to you, to suggest that you both start again, to let you know how much she loves you: *You are warm – you are my sun. You are brilliant, you are witty.*'

'Oh, for fuck's sake.'

'Once again, Nick, an incredibly strange reaction for an innocent man,' Boney said. 'Here we are, reading sweet words, maybe your wife's last words to you, and you actually look angry. I still remember that very first night: Amy's missing, you come in here, we park you in this very room for forty-five minutes, and you look *bored.* We watched you on surveillance, you practically fell asleep.'

'That has nothing to do with anything—' Tanner started.

'I was trying to stay calm.'

'You looked very, very calm,' Boney said. 'All along, you've acted ... inappropriately. Unemotional, flippant.'

'That's just how I am, don't you see? I'm stoic. To a fault. Amy knows this ... She complained about it all the time. That I wasn't sympathetic enough, that I retreated into myself, that I couldn't handle difficult emotions – sadness, guilt. She *knew* I'd look suspicious as hell. Jesus fucking Christ! Talk to Hilary

Handy, will you? Talk to Tommy O'Hara. I talked to them! They'll tell you what she's like.'

'We have talked to them,' Gilpin said.

'And?'

'Hilary Handy has made two suicide attempts in the years since high school. Tommy O'Hara has been in rehab twice.'

'Probably because of *Amy*.'

'Or because they're deeply unstable, guilt-ridden human beings,' Boney said. 'Let's go back to the treasure hunt.'

Gilpin read aloud Clue 2 in a deliberate monotone.

You took me here so I could hear you chat
About your boyhood adventures: crummy jeans and visor hat
Screw everyone else, for us they're all ditched
And let's sneak a kiss ... pretend we just got hitched.

'You say this was written to force you to go to Hannibal?' Boney said.

I nodded.

'It doesn't say Hannibal anywhere here,' she said. 'It doesn't even imply it.'

'The visor hat, that's an old inside joke between us about—'

'Oh, an inside joke,' Gilpin said.

'What about the next clue, the little brown house?' Boney asked.

'To go to my dad's,' I said.

Boney's face grew stern again. 'Nick, your dad's house is blue.' She turned to Tanner with rolling eyes: *This is what you're giving me?*

'It sounds to me like you're making up "inside jokes" in these clues,' Boney said. 'I mean, you want to talk about convenient: We find out you've been to Hannibal, whaddaya know, this clue secretly means *go to Hannibal*.'

'The final present here,' Tanner said, pulling the box onto the table, 'is a not-so-subtle hint. Punch and Judy dolls. As you know, I'm sure, Punch kills Judy and her baby. This was discovered by my client. We wanted to make sure you have it.'

Boney pulled the box over, put on latex gloves, and lifted the puppets out. 'Heavy,' she said, 'solid.' She examined the lace of the woman's dress, the male's motley. She picked up the male, examined the thick wooden handle with the finger grooves.

She froze, frowning, the male puppet in her hands. Then she turned the female upside down so the skirt flew up.

'No handle for this one.' She turned to me. 'Did there used to be a handle?'

'How should I know?'

'A handle like a two-by-four, very thick and heavy, with built-in grooves to get a really good grip?' she snapped. 'A handle like a goddamn club?'

She stared at me and I could tell what she was thinking: *You are a gameplayer. You are a sociopath. You are a killer.*

AMY ELLIOTT DUNNE
ELEVEN DAYS GONE

Tonight is Nick's much touted interview with Sharon Schieber. I was going to watch with a bottle of good wine after a hot bath, recording at the same time, so I can take notes on his lies. I want to write down every exaggeration, half truth, fib, and bald-facer he utters, so I can gird my fury against him. It slipped after the blog interview – *one* drunken, random interview! – and I can't allow that to happen. I'm not going to soften. I'm not a chump. Still, I am eager to hear his thoughts on Andie now that she has broken. His spin.

I want to watch alone, but Desi hovers around me all day, floating in and out of whatever room I retreat to, like a sudden patch of bad weather, unavoidable. I can't tell him to leave, because it's his house. I've tried this already, and it doesn't work. He'll say he wants to check the basement plumbing or he wants to peer into the fridge to see what food items need purchasing.

This will go on, I think. *This is how my life will be. He will show up when he wants and stay as long as he wants, he'll shamble around making conversation, and then he'll sit, and beckon me to sit, and he'll open a bottle of wine and we'll suddenly be sharing a meal and there's no way to stop it.*

'I really am exhausted,' I say.

'Indulge your benefactor a little bit longer,' he responds, and runs a finger down the crease of his pant legs.

He knows about Nick's interview tonight, so he leaves and returns with all my favorite foods: Manchego cheese and chocolate truffles and a bottle of cold Sancerre and, with a wry eyebrow, he even produces the chili-cheese Fritos I got hooked on back when I was Ozark Amy. He pours the wine. We have an unspoken agreement not to get into details about the baby, we both know how miscarriages run in my family, how awful it would be for me to have to speak of it.

'I'll be interested to hear what the swine has to say for himself,' he says. Desi rarely says *jackfuck* or *shitbag*; he says *swine*, which sounds more poisonous on his lips.

An hour later, we have eaten a light dinner that Desi cooked, and sipped the wine that Desi brought. He has given me one bite of cheese and split a truffle with me. He has given me exactly ten Fritos and then secreted away the bag. He doesn't like the smell; it offends him, he says, but what he really doesn't like is my weight. Now we are side by side on the sofa, a spun-soft blanket over us, because Desi has cranked up the air-conditioning so that it is autumn in July. I think he has done it so he can crackle a fire and force us together under the blankets; he seems to have an October vision of the two of us. He even brought me a gift – a heathery violet turtleneck sweater to wear – and I notice it complements both the blanket and Desi's deep green sweater.

'You know, all through the centuries, pathetic men have abused strong women who threaten their masculinity,' Desi is saying. 'They have such fragile psyches, they need that control ...'

I am thinking of a different kind of control. I am thinking about control in the guise of caring: *Here is a sweater for the cold, my sweet, now wear it and match my vision.*

Nick, at least, didn't do this. Nick let me do what I wanted.

I just want Desi to sit still and be quiet. He's fidgety and nervous, as if his rival is in the room with us.

'Shhh,' I say as my pretty face comes on the screen, then another photo and another, like falling leaves, an Amy collage.

'She was the girl that *every* girl wanted to be,' said Sharon's voiceover. 'Beautiful, brilliant, inspiring, and very wealthy.'

'He was the guy that all men admired ...'

'Not this man,' Desi muttered.

'... handsome, funny, bright, and charming.'

'But on July fifth, their seemingly perfect world came crashing in when Amy Elliott Dunne disappeared on their fifth wedding anniversary.'

Recap recap recap. Photos of me, Andie, Nick. Stock photos of a pregnancy test and unpaid bills. I really did do a nice job. It's like painting a mural and stepping back and thinking: *Perfect*.

'Now, exclusively, Nick Dunne breaks his silence, not only on his wife's disappearance but on his infidelity and *all those rumors*.'

I feel a gust of warmth toward Nick because he's wearing my favorite tie that I bought for him, that he thinks, or thought, was too girly-bright. It's a peacocky purple that turns his eyes almost violet. He's lost his satisfied-asshole paunch over the last month: His belly is gone, the fleshiness of his face has vanished, his chin is less clefty. His hair has been trimmed but not cut – I have an image of Go hacking away at him just before he went on camera, slipping into Mama Mo's role, fussing over him, doing the saliva-thumb rubdown on some spot near his chin. He is wearing my tie and when he lifts his hand to make a gesture, I see he is wearing my watch, the vintage Bulova Spaceview that I got him for his thirty-third birthday, that he never wore because it *wasn't him*, even though it was completely him.

'He's wonderfully well groomed for a man who thinks his wife is missing,' Desi snipes. 'Glad he didn't skip a manicure.'

'Nick would never get a manicure,' I say, glancing at Desi's buffed nails.

'Let's get right to it, Nick,' Sharon says. 'Did you have anything to do with your wife's disappearance?'

'No. No. Absolutely, one hundred percent not,' Nick says, keeping well-coached eye contact. 'But let me say, Sharon, I am far, far from being innocent, or blameless, or a good husband. If I weren't so afraid for Amy, I would say this was a good thing, in a way, her disappearing—'

'Excuse me, Nick, but I think a lot of people will find it hard to believe you just said that when your wife is missing.'

'It's the most awful, horrible feeling in the world, and I want her back more than anything. All I am saying is that it has been the most brutal eye-opener for me. You hate to believe that you are such an awful man that it takes something like this to pull you out of your selfishness spiral and wake you up to the fact that you are the luckiest bastard in the world. I mean, I had this woman who was my equal, my *better*, in every way, and I let my insecurities – about losing my job, about not being able to care for my family, about getting older – cloud all that.'

'Oh, please—' Desi starts, and I shush him. For Nick to admit to the world that he is not a good guy – it's a small death, and not of the *petite mort* variety.

'And Sharon, let me say it. Let me say it right now: I cheated. I disrespected my wife. I didn't want to be the man that I had become, but instead of working on myself, I took the easy way out. I cheated with a young woman who barely knew me. So I could *pretend* to be the big man. I could *pretend* to be the man I wanted to be – smart and confident and successful – because this young woman didn't know any different. This young girl, she hadn't seen me crying into a towel in the bathroom in the middle of the night because I lost my job. She didn't know all my foibles and shortcomings. I was a fool who believed if I wasn't perfect, my wife wouldn't love me. I wanted to be Amy's hero, and when I lost my job, I lost my self-respect. I couldn't be that hero anymore. Sharon, I know right from wrong. And I just – I just did wrong.'

'What would you say to your wife, if she is possibly out there, able to see and hear you tonight?'

'I'd say: Amy, I love you. You are the best woman I have ever known. You are more than I deserve, and if you come back, I will spend the rest of my life making it up to you. We will find a way to put all this horror behind us, and I will be the best man in the world to you. Please come home to me, Amy.'

Just for a second, he places the pad of his index finger in the cleft of his chin, our old secret code, the one we did back in the day to swear we weren't bullshitting each other – the dress really did look nice, that article really was solid. *I am absolutely, one hundred percent sincere right now – I have your back, and I wouldn't fuck with you.*

Desi leans in front of me to break my contact with the screen and reaches for the Sancerre. 'More wine, sweetheart?' he says.

'Shhhh.'

He pauses the show. 'Amy, you are a good-hearted woman. I know you are susceptible to ... pleas. But everything he is saying is lies.'

Nick is saying exactly what I want to hear. *Finally.*

Desi moves around so he is staring at me full-face, completely obstructing my vision. 'Nick is putting on a pageant. He wants to come off as a good, repentant guy. I'll admit he's doing a bang-up job. But it's not real – he hasn't even mentioned beating you, violating you. I don't know what kind of hold this guy has on you. It must be a Stockholm-syndrome thing.'

'I know,' I say. I know exactly what I am supposed to say to Desi. 'You're right. You're absolutely right. I haven't felt so safe in so long, Desi, but I am still ... I see him and ... I'm fighting this, but he hurt me ... for years.'

'Maybe we shouldn't watch any more,' he says, twirling my hair, leaning too close.

'No, leave it on,' I say. 'I have to face this. With you. I can do it with you.' I put my hand in his. *Now shut the fuck up.*

I just want Amy to come home so I can spend the rest of my life making it up to her, treating her how she deserves.

Nick forgives me – *I screwed you over, you screwed me over, let's make up.* What if his code is true? Nick wants me back. Nick wants me back so he can treat me right. So he can spend the rest of his life treating me the way he should. It sounds rather lovely. We could go back to New York. Sales for the *Amazing Amy* books have skyrocketed since my disappearance – three generations of readers have remembered how much they love me. My greedy, stupid, irresponsible parents can finally pay back my trust fund. With interest.

Because I want to go back to my old life. Or my old life with my old money and my New Nick. Love-Honor-and-Obey Nick. Maybe he's learned his lesson. Maybe he'll be like he was before. Because I've been daydreaming – trapped in my Ozarks cabin, trapped in Desi's mansion compound, I have a lot of time to daydream and what I've been daydreaming of is Nick, in those early days. I thought I would daydream more about Nick getting ass-raped in prison, but I haven't so much, not so much, lately. I think about those early, early days, when we would lie in bed next to each other, naked flesh on cool cotton, and he would just stare at me, one finger tracing my jaw from my chin to my ear, making me wriggle, that light tickling on my lobe, and then through all the seashell curves of my ear and into my hairline, and then he'd take hold of one lock of hair, like he did that very first time we kissed, and pull it all the way to the end and tug twice, gently, like he was ringing a bell. And he'd say, 'You are better than any storybook, you are better than anything anyone could make up.'

Nick fastened me to the earth. Nick wasn't like Desi, who brought me things I wanted (tulips, wine) to make me do the things *he* wanted (love him). Nick just wanted me to be happy, that's all, very pure. Maybe I mistook that for laziness. *I just want you to be happy, Amy.* How many times did he say that and I took it to mean: *I just want you to be happy, Amy, because that's less work for me.* But maybe I was unfair. Well, not unfair but confused. No one I've loved has ever not had an agenda. So how could I know?

It really is true. It took this awful situation for us to realize it. Nick and I fit together. I am a little too much, and he is a little too little. I am a thornbush, bristling from the overattention of my parents, and he is a man of a million little fatherly stab wounds, and my thorns fit perfectly into them.

I need to get home to him.

NICK DUNNE
FOURTEEN DAYS GONE

I woke up on my sister's couch with a raging hangover and an urge to kill my wife. This was fairly common in the days after the Diary Interview with the police. I'd imagine finding Amy tucked away in some spa on the West Coast, sipping pineapple juice on a divan, her cares floating way, far away, above a perfect blue sky, and me, dirty, smelly from an urgent cross-country drive, standing in front of her, blocking the sun until she looks up, and then my hands around her perfect throat, with its cords and hollows and the pulse thumping first urgently and then slowly as we look into each other's eyes and at last have some understanding.

I was going to be arrested. If not today, tomorrow; if not tomorrow, the next day. I had taken the fact that they let me walk out of the station as a good sign, but Tanner had shut me down: 'Without a body, a conviction is incredibly tough. They're just dotting the I's, crossing the T's. Spend these days doing whatever you need to do, because once the arrest happens, we'll be busy.'

Just outside the window, I could hear the rumbling of camera crews – men greeting each other good morning, as if they were clocking in at the factory. Cameras click-click-clicked like restless locusts, shooting the front of Go's house. Someone had leaked the discovery of my 'man cave' of goods on my sister's property, my imminent arrest. Neither of us had dared to so much as flick at a curtain.

Go walked into the room in flannel boxers and her high

395

school Butthole Surfers T-shirt, her laptop in the crook of an arm. 'Everyone hates you again,' she said.

'Fickle fucks.'

'Last night someone leaked the information about the shed, about Amy's purse and the diary. Now it's all: *Nick Is a Liar, Nick Is a Killer, Nick Is a Lying Killer.* Sharon Schieber just released a statement saying she was *very shocked and disappointed* with the direction the case was taking. Oh, and everyone knows all about the porn – *Kill the Bitches.*'

'*Hurt the Bitch.*'

'Oh, excuse me,' she said. 'Hurt *the Bitch.* So *Nick Is a Lying Killer-slash-Sexual Sadist.* Ellen Abbott is going to go fucking rabid. She's crazy anti-porn lady.'

'Of course she is,' I said. 'I'm sure Amy is very aware of that.'

'Nick?' she said in her *wake up* voice. 'This is bad.'

'Go, it doesn't matter what anyone else thinks, we need to remember that,' I said. 'What matters right now is what Amy is thinking. If *she's* softening toward me.'

'Nick. You really think she can go that fast from hating you so much to falling in love with you again?'

It was the fifth anniversary of our conversation on this topic.

'Go, yeah, I do. Amy was never a person with any sort of bullshit detector. If you said she looked beautiful, she knew that was a fact. If you said she was brilliant, it wasn't flattery, it was her due. So yeah, I think a good chunk of her truly believes that if I can only see the error of my ways, of *course* I'll be in love with her again. Because why in God's name wouldn't I be?'

'And if it turns out she's developed a bullshit detector?'

'You know Amy; she needs to win. She's less pissed off that I cheated than that I picked someone else over her. She'll want me back just to prove that she's the winner. Don't you agree? Just seeing me begging her to come back so I can worship her properly, it will be hard for her to resist. Don't you think?'

'I think it's a decent idea,' she said in the way you might wish someone good luck on the lottery.

396

'Hey, if you've got something better, by all fucking means.'

We snapped like that at each other now. We'd never done that before. After the police found the woodshed, they grilled Go, hard, just as Tanner had predicted: *Did she know? Did she help?*

I'd expected her to come home that night, brimming with curse words and fury, but all I got was an embarrassed smile as she slipped past me to her room in the house she had double-mortgaged to cover Tanner's retainer.

I had put my sister in financial and legal jeopardy because of my shitty decisions. The whole situation made Go feel resentful and me ashamed, a lethal combination for two people trapped in small confines.

I tried a different subject: 'I've been thinking about phoning Andie now that—'

'Yeah, that would be genius-smart, Nick. Then she can go back on *Ellen Abbott*—'

'She didn't go on *Ellen Abbott*. She had a press conference that *Ellen Abbott* carried. She's not evil, Go.'

'She gave the press conference because she was pissed at you. I sorta wish you'd just kept fucking her.'

'Nice.'

'What would you even say to her?'

'I'm sorry.'

'You are definitely fucking sorry,' she muttered.

'I just – I hate how it ended.'

'The last time you saw Andie, she *bit* you,' Go said in an overly patient voice. 'I don't think the two of you have anything else to say. You are the prime suspect in a murder investigation. You have forfeited the right to a smooth breakup. For fuck's sake, Nick.'

We were growing sick of each other, something I never thought could happen. It was more than basic stress, more than the danger I'd deposited on Go's doorstep. Those ten seconds just a week ago, when I'd opened the door of the woodshed, expecting Go to read my mind as always, and what Go had read was that I'd killed my wife: I couldn't get over that, and neither could she. I caught her looking at me now and then with the same steeled chill with which she looked at our father: just another shitty male taking up space. I'm sure I looked at her through our father's miserable eyes sometimes: just another petty woman resenting me.

I let out a gust of air, stood up, and squeezed her hand, and she squeezed back.

'I think I should head home,' I said. I felt a wave of nausea. 'I can't stand this anymore. Waiting to be arrested, I can't stand it.'

Before she could stop me, I grabbed my keys, swung open the door, and the cameras began blasting, the shouts exploded from a crowd that was even larger than I'd feared: *Hey, Nick, did you kill your wife? Hey, Margo, did you help your brother hide evidence?*

'Fucking shitbags,' Go spat. She stood next to me in solidarity, in her Butthole Surfers T-shirt and boxers. A few protesters carried signs. A woman with stringy blond hair and sunglasses shook a poster board: *Nick, where is AMY?*

The shouts got louder, frantic, baiting my sister: *Margo, is your brother a wife killer? Did Nick kill his wife and baby? Margo, are you a suspect? Did Nick kill his wife? Did Nick kill his baby?*

I stood, trying to hold my ground, refusing to let myself step back into the house. Suddenly, Go was crouching behind me, cranking the spigot near the steps. She turned on the hose full-bore – a hard, steady jet – and blasted all those cameramen and protesters and pretty journalists in their TV-ready suits, sprayed them like animals.

She was giving me covering fire. I shot into my car and tore off, leaving them dripping on the front lawn, Go laughing shrilly.

It took ten minutes for me to nudge my car from my driveway into my garage, inching my way slowly, slowly forward, parting the angry ocean of human beings – there were at least twenty protesters in front of my home, in addition to the camera crews. My neighbor Jan Teverer was one of them. She and I made eye contact, and she aimed her poster at me: *WHERE IS AMY, NICK?*

Finally, I was inside, and the garage door came buzzing down. I sat in the heat of the concrete space, breathing.

Everywhere felt like a jail now – doors opening and closing and opening and closing, and me never feeling safe.

I spent the rest of my day picturing how I'd kill Amy. It was all I could think of: finding a way to end her. Me smashing in Amy's busy, busy brain. I had to give Amy her due: I may have been dozing the past few years, but I was fucking wide awake now. I was electric again, like I had been in the early days of our marriage.

I wanted to do something, make something happen, but there was nothing to be done. By late evening, the camera crews were all gone, though I couldn't risk leaving the house. I wanted to walk. I settled for pacing. I was wired dangerously tight.

Andie had screwed me over, Marybeth had turned against me, Go had lost a crucial measure of faith. Boney had trapped me. Amy had destroyed me. I poured a drink. I took a slug, tightened my fingers around the curves of the tumbler, then hurled it at the wall, watched the glass burst into fireworks, heard the tremendous shatter, smelled the cloud of bourbon. Rage in all five senses. *Those fucking bitches.*

I'd tried all my life to be a decent guy, a man who loved and respected women, a guy without hang-ups. And here I was, thinking nasty thoughts about my twin, about my mother-in-law, about my mistress. I was imagining bashing in my wife's skull.

A knock came at the door, a loud, furious bang-bang-bang that rattled me out of my nightmare brain.

I opened the door, flung it wide, greeting fury with fury.

It was my father, standing on my doorstep like some awful specter summoned by my hatefulness. He was breathing heavily and sweating. His shirtsleeve was torn and his hair was wild, but his eyes had their usual dark alertness that made him seem viciously sane.

'Is she here?' he snapped.

'Who, Dad, who are you looking for?'

'You know who.' He pushed past me, started marching through the living room, trailing mud, his hands balled, his gravity far forward, forcing him to keep walking or fall down, muttering *bitchbitchbitch*. He smelled of mint. Real mint, not manufactured, and I saw a smear of green on his trousers, as if he'd been stomping through someone's garden.

Little bitch that little bitch, he kept muttering. Through the dining room, into the kitchen, flipping on lights. A waterbug scuttled up the wall.

I followed him, trying to get him to calm down, *Dad, Dad, why don't you sit down, Dad, do you want a glass of water, Dad* ... He stomped downstairs, clumps of mud falling off his shoes. My hands turtled into fists. Of course this bastard would show up and actually make things worse.

'Dad! Goddammit, Dad! No one is here but me. Just me.' He flung open the guest room door, then went back up to the living room, ignoring me – 'Dad!'

I didn't want to touch him. I was afraid I'd hit him. I was afraid I'd cry.

I blocked him as he tried to go upstairs to the bedroom. I placed one hand on the wall, one on the banister – human barricade. 'Dad! Look at me.'

His words came out in a furious spittle.

'You tell her, you tell that little ugly bitch it's not over. She's not better than me, you tell her. She's not too good for me. She doesn't get to have a *say*. That ugly bitch will have to learn—'

I swear I saw a blank whiteness for just a second, a moment of complete, jarring clarity. I stopped trying to block my father's voice for once and let it throb in my ears. I was not that man: I didn't hate and fear all women. I was a one-woman misogynist. If I despised only Amy, focused all my fury and rage and venom on the one woman who deserved it, that didn't make me my father. That made me sane.

Little bitch little bitch little bitch.

I had never hated my father more for making me truly love those words.

Fucking bitch fucking bitch.

I grabbed him by the arm, hard, and herded him into the car, slammed the door. He repeated the incantation all the way to Comfort Hill. I pulled up to the home in the entry reserved for ambulances, and I went to his side, swung open the door, yanked him out by the arm, and walked him just inside the doors.

Then I turned my back and went home.

Fucking bitch fucking bitch.

But there was nothing I could do except beg. My bitch wife had left me with *nothing* but my sorry dick in my hand, begging her to come home. Print, online, TV, wherever, all I could do was hope my wife saw me playing good husband, saying the words she wanted me to say: *capitulation, complete. You are right and I am wrong, always. Come home to me (you fucking cunt). Come home so I can kill you.*

AMY ELLIOTT DUNNE
TWENTY-SIX DAYS GONE

Desi is here again. He is here almost every day now, simpering around the house, standing in the kitchen as the setting sun lights up his profile so I can admire it, pulling me by the hand into the tulip room so I can thank him again, reminding me how safe and loved I am.

He says I'm safe and loved even though he won't let me leave, which doesn't make me feel safe and loved. He's left me no car keys. Nor house keys nor the gate security code. I am literally a prisoner – the gate is fifteen feet high, and there are no ladders in the house (I've looked). I could, I suppose, drag several pieces of furniture over to the wall, pile them up, and climb over, drop to the other side, limp or crawl away, but that's not the point. The point is, I am his valued, beloved guest, and a guest should be able to leave when she wants. I brought this up a few days ago. 'What if I need to leave. Immediately?'

'Maybe I should move in here,' he counters. 'Then I could be here all the time and keep you safe, and if anything happens, we could leave together.'

'What if your mom gets suspicious and comes up here and you're found hiding me? It would be awful.'

His mother. I would die if his mother came up here, because she would report me immediately. The woman despises me, all because of that incident back in high school – so long ago, and she still holds a grudge. I scratched up my face and told Desi she attacked me (the woman was so possessive, and so cold to me, she might as well have). They didn't talk for a month. Clearly, they've made up.

'Jacqueline doesn't know the code,' he says. 'This is *my* lake house.' He pauses and pretends to think. 'I really should move up here. It's not healthy for you to spend so many hours by yourself.'

But I'm not by myself, not that much. We have a bit of a routine established in just two weeks. It's a routine mandated by Desi, my posh jailer, my spoiled courtier. Desi arrives just after noon, always smelling of some expensive lunch he's devoured with Jacqueline at some white-linened restaurant, the kind of restaurant he could take me to if we moved to Greece. (This is the other option he repeatedly presents: We could move to Greece. For some reason, he believes I will never be identified in a tiny little fishing village in Greece where he has summered many times, and where I know he pictures us sipping the wine, making lazy sunset love, our bellies full of octopus.) He smells of lunch as he enters, he wafts it. He must dab goose liver behind his ears (the way his mother always smelled vaguely vaginal – food and sex, the Collings reek of, not a bad strategy).

He enters, and he makes my mouth water. The smell. He brings me something nice to eat, but not as nice as what he's had: He's thinning me up, he always preferred his women waify. So he brings me lovely green star fruit and spiky artichokes and spiny crab, anything that takes elaborate preparation and yields little in return. I am almost my normal weight again, and my hair is growing out. I wear it back in a headband he brought me, and I have colored it back to my blond, thanks to hair dye he also brought me: 'I think you will feel better about yourself when you start looking more like yourself, sweetheart,' he says. Yes, it's all about my well-being, not the fact that he wants me to look exactly like I did before. Amy circa 1987.

I eat lunch as he hovers near me, waiting for the compliments. (To never have to say those words – *thank you* – again. I don't remember Nick ever pausing to allow me – force me – to thank him.) I finish lunch, and he tidies up as best as he knows how. We are two people unaccustomed to cleaning up after ourselves; the place is beginning to look lived in – strange stains on countertops, dust on windowsills.

Lunch concluded, Desi fiddles with me for a while: my hair, my skin, my clothes, my mind.

'Look at you,' he'll say, tucking my hair behind my ears the way he likes it, unbuttoning my shirt one notch and loosening it at the neck so he can look at the hollow of my clavicle. He puts a finger in the little indentation, filling the gap. It is obscene. 'How can Nick have hurt you, have not loved you, have cheated on you?' He continually hits these points, verbally poking a bruise. 'Wouldn't it be so lovely to just forget about Nick, those awful five years, and move on? You have that chance, you know, to completely start over with the right man. How many people can say that?'

I do want to start over with the right man, the New Nick. Things are looking bad for him, dire. Only I can save Nick from me. But I am trapped.

'If you ever left here and I didn't know where you were, I'd have to go to the police,' he says. 'I'd have no choice. I'd need to make sure you were safe, that Nick wasn't ... holding you somewhere against your will. Violating you.'

A threat disguised as concern.

I look at Desi with outright disgust now. Sometimes I feel my skin must be hot with repulsion and with the effort to keep that repulsion hidden. I'd forgotten about him. The manipulation, the purring persuasion, the delicate bullying. A man who finds guilt erotic. And if he doesn't get his way, he'll pull his little levers and set his punishment in motion. At least Nick was man enough to go stick his dick in something. Desi will push and push with his waxy, tapered fingers until I give him what he wants.

I thought I could control Desi, but I can't. I feel like something very bad is going to happen.

NICK DUNNE
THIRTY-THREE DAYS GONE

The days were loose and long, and then they smashed into a wall. I went out to get groceries one August morning, and I came home to find Tanner in my living room with Boney and Gilpin. On the table, inside a plastic evidence bag, was a long thick club with delicate grooves for fingers.

'We found this just down the river from your home on that first search,' Boney said. 'Didn't look like anything at the time, really. Just some of the weird flotsam on a river bank, but we keep everything in a search like that. After you showed us your Punch and Judy dolls, it clicked. So we got the lab to check it out.'

'And?' I said. Toneless.

Boney stood up, looked me right in the eye. She sounded sad. 'We were able to detect Amy's blood on it. This case is now classified as a homicide. And we believe this to be the murder weapon.'

'Rhonda, come on!'

'It's time, Nick,' she said. 'It's time.'

The next part was starting.

AMY ELLIOTT DUNNE
FORTY DAYS GONE

I have found a piece of old twine and an empty wine bottle, and I've been using them for my project. Also some vermouth, of course. I am ready.

Discipline. This will take discipline and focus. I am up to the task.

I array myself in Desi's favorite look: delicate flower. My hair in loose waves, perfumed. My skin has paled after a month inside. I am almost without makeup: a flip of mascara, pink-pink cheeks, and clear lip gloss. I wear a clingy pink dress he bought me. No bra. No panties. No shoes, despite the air-conditioned chill. I have a fire crackling and perfume in the air, and when he arrives after lunch without invitation, I greet him with pleasure. I wrap my arms around him and bury my face in his neck. I rub my cheek against his. I have been increasingly sweeter to him the past few weeks, but this is new, this clinging.

'What's this, sweetheart?' he says, surprised and so pleased that I almost feel ashamed.

'I had the worst nightmare last night,' I whisper. 'About Nick. I woke up, and all I wanted was to have you here. And in the morning ... I've spent all day wishing you were here.'

'I can always be here, if you like.'

'I would,' I say, and I turn my face up to him and let him kiss me. His kiss disgusts me; it's nibbly and hesitant, like a fish. It's Desi being respectful of his raped, abused woman. He nibbles again, wet cold lips, his hands barely on me, and I just want this all over, I want it done, so I pull him to me and push his lips open with my tongue. I want to bite him.

He pulls back. 'Amy,' he says. 'You've been through a lot. This is fast. I don't want you to do this fast if you don't want to. If you're not sure.'

I know he's going to have to touch my breasts, I know he's going to have to push himself inside me, and I want it over, I can barely restrain myself from scratching him: the idea of doing this slowly.

'I'm sure,' I say. 'I guess I've been sure since we were sixteen. I was just afraid.'

This means nothing, but I know it will get him hard.

I kiss him again, and then I ask him if he will take me into *our* bedroom.

In the bedroom, he begins undressing me slowly, kissing parts of my body that have nothing to do with sex – my shoulder, my ear – while I delicately guide him away from my wrists and ankles. Just fuck me, for Christ's sake. Ten minutes in and I grab his hand and thrust it between my legs.

'Are you sure?' he says, pulling back from me, flushed, a loop of his hair falling over his forehead, just like in high school. We could be back in my dorm room, for all the progress Desi has made.

'Yes, darling,' I say, and I reach modestly for his cock.

Another ten minutes and he's finally between my legs, pumping gently, slowly, slowly, *making love*. Pausing for kisses and caresses until I grab him by the buttocks and begin pushing him. 'Fuck me,' I whisper, 'fuck me hard.'

He stops. 'It doesn't have to be like that, Amy. I'm not Nick.'

Very true. 'I know, darling, I just want you to … to fill me. I feel so empty.'

That gets him. I grimace over his shoulder as he thrusts a few more times and comes, me realizing it almost too late – *Oh, this is his pathetic cum-sound* – and faking quick oohs and ahhs, gentle kittenish noises. I try to work up some tears because I know he imagines me crying with him the first time.

'Darling, you're crying,' he says as he slips out of me. He kisses a tear.

407

'I'm just happy,' I say. Because that's what those kinds of women say.

I have mixed up some martinis, I announce – Desi loves a decadent afternoon drink – and when he makes a move to put on his shirt and fetch them, I insist he stay in bed.

'I want to do something for you for a change,' I say.

So I scamper into the kitchen and get two big martini glasses, and into mine I put gin and a single olive. Into his I put three olives, gin, olive juice, vermouth, and the last of my sleeping pills, three of them, crushed.

I bring the martinis, and there is snuggling and nuzzling, and I slurp my gin while this happens. I have an edge that must be dulled.

'Don't you like my martini?' I ask when he has only a sip. 'I always pictured being your wife and making you martinis. I know that's silly.'

I begin a pout.

'Oh, darling, not silly at all. I was just taking my time, enjoying. But—' He guzzles the whole thing down. 'If it makes you feel better!'

He is giddy, triumphant. His cock is slick with conquest. He is, basically, like all men. Soon he is sleepy, and after that he is snoring.

And I can begin.

PART THREE

BOY GETS GIRL BACK
(OR VICE VERSA)

NICK DUNNE
FORTY DAYS GONE

Out on bond, awaiting trial. I'd been processed and released –
the depersonalized in-and-outing of jail, the bond hearing, the
fingerprints and photos, the rotating and the shuffling and the
handling, it didn't make me feel like an animal, it made me
feel like a product, something created on an assembly line.
What they were creating was Nick Dunne, Killer. It would be
months until we'd begin my trial (my trial: the word still
threatened to undo me completely, turn me into a high-pitched
giggler, a madman). I was supposed to feel privileged to be
out on bond: I had stayed put even when it was clear I was
going to be arrested, so I was deemed no flight risk. Boney
might have put a good word in for me, too. So I got to be in
my own home for a few more months before I was carted off
to prison and killed by the state.

Yes, I was a lucky, lucky man.

It was mid-August, which I found continually strange: *It's
still summer*, I'd think. *How can so much have happened and it's
not even autumn?* It was brutally warm. Shirtsleeve weather,
was how my mom would have described it, forever more
concerned with her children's comfort than the actual Fahr-
enheit. Shirtsleeve weather, jacket weather, overcoat weather,
parka weather – the Year in Outerwear. For me this year, it
would be handcuff weather, then possibly prison-jumpsuit
weather. Or funeral-suit weather, because I didn't plan on
going to prison. I'd kill myself first.

Tanner had a team of five detectives trying to track Amy
down. So far, nothing. Like trying to catch water. Every day
for weeks, I'd done my little shitty part: videotape a message

to Amy and post it on young Rebecca's Whodunnit blog. (Rebecca, at least, had remained loyal.) In the videos, I wore clothes Amy had bought me, and I brushed my hair the way she liked, and I tried to read her mind. My anger toward her was like heated wire.

The camera crews parked themselves on my lawn most mornings. We were like rival soldiers, rooted in shooting distance for months, eyeing each other across no-man's-land, achieving some sort of perverted fraternity. There was one guy with a voice like a cartoon strongman whom I'd become attached to, sight unseen. He was dating a girl he really, really liked. Every morning his voice boomed in through my windows as he analyzed their dates; things seemed to be going very well. I wanted to hear how the story ended.

I finished my evening taping to Amy. I was wearing a green shirt she liked on me, and I'd been telling her the story of how we first met, the party in Brooklyn, my awful opening line, *just one olive*, that embarrassed me every time Amy mentioned it. I talked about our exit from the oversteamed apartment out into the crackling cold, with her hand in mine, the kiss in the cloud of sugar. It was one of the few stories we told the same way. I said it all in the cadence of a bedtime tale: soothing and familiar and repetitive. Always ending with *Come home to me, Amy*.

I turned off the camera and sat back on the couch (I always filmed while sitting on the couch under her pernicious, unpredictable cuckoo clock, because I knew if I didn't show her cuckoo clock, she'd wonder whether I had finally gotten rid of her cuckoo clock, and then she'd stop wondering whether I had finally gotten rid of her cuckoo clock and simply come to believe it was true, and then no matter what sweet words came out of my mouth, she'd silently counter with: '*and yet he tossed out my cuckoo clock*'). The cuckoo was, in fact, soon to pop out, its grinding windup beginning over my head – a sound that inevitably made my jaw tense – when the camera crews outside emitted a loud, collective, oceanic wushing. Somebody was here. I heard the seagull cries of a few female news anchors.

Something is wrong, I thought.

The doorbell rang three times in a row: Nick-nick! Nick-nick! Nick-nick!

I didn't hesitate. I had stopped hesitating over the past month: Bring on the trouble posthaste.

I opened the door.

It was my wife.

Back.

Amy Elliott Dunne stood barefoot on my doorstep in a thin pink dress that clung to her as if it were wet. Her ankles were ringed in dark violet. From one limp wrist dangled a piece of twine. Her hair was short and frayed at the ends, as if it had been carelessly chopped by dull scissors. Her face was bruised, her lips swollen. She was sobbing.

When she flung her arms out toward me, I could see her entire midsection was stained with dried blood. She tried to speak; her mouth opened, once, twice, silent, a mermaid washed ashore.

'Nick!' she finally keened – a wail that echoed against all the empty houses – and fell into my arms.

I wanted to kill her.

Had we been alone, my hands might have found their place around her neck, my fingers locating perfect grooves in her flesh. To feel that strong pulse under my fingers ... but we weren't alone, we were in front of cameras, and they were realizing who this strange woman was, they were coming to life as sure as the cuckoo clock inside, a few clicks, a few questions, then an avalanche of noise and light. The cameras were blasting us, the reporters closing in with microphones, everyone yelling Amy's name, screaming, literally screaming. So I did the right thing, I held her to me and howled her name right back: 'Amy! My God! My God! My darling!' and buried my face in her neck, my arms wrapped tight around her, and let the cameras get their fifteen seconds, and I whispered deep inside her ear,

'You fucking bitch.' Then I stroked her hair, I cupped her face in my two loving hands, and I yanked her inside.

Outside our door, a rock concert was demanding its encore: *Amy! Amy! Amy!* Someone threw a scattering of pebbles at our window. *Amy! Amy! Amy!*

My wife took it all as her due, fluttering a dismissive hand toward the rabble outside. She turned to me with a worn but triumphant smile – the smile on the rape victim, the abuse survivor, the bed burner in the old TV movies, the smile where the bastard has finally received due justice and we know our heroine will be able to move on with *life*! Freeze frame.

I gestured to the twine, the hacked hair, the dried blood. 'So, what's your story, wife?'

'I'm back,' she whimpered. 'I made it back to you.' She moved to put her arms around me. I moved away.

'What is your *story*, Amy?'

'Desi,' she whispered, her lower lip trembling. 'Desi Collings took me. It was the morning. Of. Of our anniversary. And the doorbell rang, and I thought . . . I don't know, I thought maybe it was flowers from you.'

I flinched. Of course she'd find a way to work in a gripe: that I hardly ever sent her flowers, when her dad had sent her mom flowers each week since they'd been married. That's 2,444 bouquets of flowers vs. 4.

'Flowers or . . . something,' she continued. 'So I didn't think, I just flung open the door. And there he stood, Desi, with this look on his face. Determined. As if he'd been girding himself up for this all along. And I was holding the handle . . . to the Judy puppet. Did you find the puppets?' She smiled up at me tearily. She looked so sweet.

'Oh, I found everything you left for me, Amy.'

'I had just found the handle to the Judy puppet – it had fallen off – I was holding it when I opened the door, and I tried to hit him, and we struggled, and he clubbed me with it. Hard. And the next thing I knew . . .'

'You had framed me for murder and disappeared.'

'I can explain everything, Nick.'

I stared at her a long hard moment. I saw *days under the hot sun* stretched across the sand of the beach, her hand on my chest, and I saw *family dinners* at her parents' house, with Rand always refilling my glass and patting me on the shoulder, and I saw us *sprawled on the rug* in my crummy New York apartment, talking while staring at the lazy ceiling fan, and I saw *mother of my child* and the stunning life I'd planned for us once. I had a moment that lasted two beats, *one, two*, when I wished violently that she were telling the truth.

'I actually don't think you can explain everything,' I said. 'But I am going to love watching you try.'

'Try me now.'

She tried to take my hand, and I flung her off. I walked away from her, took a breath, and then turned to face her. My wife must always be faced.

'Go ahead, Nick. Try me now.'

'Okay, sure. Why was every clue of the treasure hunt hidden in a place where I had ... relations with Andie?'

She sighed, looked at the floor. Her ankles were raw. 'I didn't even know about Andie until I saw it on TV ... while I was tied to Desi's bed, hidden away in his lake house.'

'So that was all ... coincidence?'

'Those were all places that were meaningful to us,' she said. A tear slid down her face. 'Your office, where you reignited your passion for journalism.'

I snuffed.

'Hannibal, where I finally understood how much this area means to you. Your father's house – confronting the man who hurt you so much. Your mother's house, which is now Go's house, the two people who made you such a good man. But ... I guess it doesn't surprise me that you'd like to share those places with someone you' – she bowed her head – 'had fallen in love with. You always liked repeats.'

'Why did each of those places end up including clues that implicated me in your murder? Women's undies, your purse, your *diary*. Explain your *diary*, Amy, with all the lies.'

She just smiled and shook her head like she was sorry for me. 'Everything, I can explain everything,' she said.

I looked in that sweet tear-stained face. Then I looked down at all the blood. 'Amy. Where's Desi?'

She shook her head again, a sad little smile.

I moved to call the police, but a knock on our door told me they were already here.

AMY ELLIOTT DUNNE
THE NIGHT OF THE RETURN

I still have Desi's semen inside me from the last time he raped me, so the medical examination goes fine. My rope-wreathed wrists, my damaged vagina, my bruises – the body I present them is textbook. An older male doctor with humid breath and thick fingers performs the pelvic exam – scraping and wheezing in time – while Detective Rhonda Boney holds my hand. It is like being clutched by a cold bird claw. Not comforting at all. Once she breaks into a grin when she thinks I'm not looking. She is absolutely thrilled that Nick isn't a bad guy after all. Yes, the women of America are collectively sighing.

Police have been dispatched to Desi's home, where they'll find him naked and drained, a stunned look on his face, a few strands of my hair in his clutches, the bed soaked in blood. The knife I used on him, and on my bonds, will be nearby on the floor where I dropped it, dazed, and walked barefoot, carrying nothing out of the house but his keys – to the car, to the gate – and climbed, still slick with his blood, into his vintage Jaguar and returned like some long-lost faithful pet, straight back home to my husband. I'd been reduced to an animal state; I didn't think of anything but getting back to Nick.

The old doctor tells me the good news; no permanent damage and no need for a D&C – I miscarried too early. Boney keeps clutching my hand and murmuring, *My God, what you've been through, do you think you feel up to answering a few questions?* That fast, from condolences to brass tacks. I find ugly women are usually overly deferential or incredibly rude.

You are Amazing Amy, and you've survived a brutal

417

kidnapping involving repeated assaults. You've killed your captor, and you've made it back to a husband you've discovered was cheating. You:

a) Put yourself first and demand some time alone to collect yourself.
b) Hold it together just a little longer so you can help the police.
c) Decide which interview to give first – you might as well get something out of the ordeal, like a book deal.

Answer: B. Amazing Amy always puts others first.

I'm allowed to clean myself up in a private room in the hospital, and I change into a set of clothes Nick put together for me from the house – jeans with creases from being folded too long, a pretty blouse that smells of dust. Boney and I drive from the hospital to the police station in near silence. I ask weakly after my parents.

'They're waiting for you at the station,' Boney says. 'They wept when I told them. With joy. Absolute joy and relief. We'll let them get some good hugs in with you before we do our questions, don't worry.'

The cameras are already at the station. The parking lot has that hopeful, overlit look of a sports stadium. There is no underground parking, so we have to pull right up front as the madding crowd closes in: I see wet lips and spittle as everyone screams questions, the pops of flashbulbs and camera lights. The crowd pushes and pulls en masse, jerking a few inches to the right, then the left as everyone tries to reach me.

'I can't do this,' I say to Boney. A man's meaty palm smacks against the car window as a photographer tries to keep his balance. I grab her cold hand. 'It's too much.'

She pats me and says, *wait*. The station doors open, and every officer in the building files down the stairs and forms a line on either side of me, holding the press back, creating an honor guard for me, and Rhonda and I run in holding hands like reverse newlyweds, rushing straight up to my parents who are waiting just inside the doorway, and everyone gets the photos of us clutching each other with my mom whispering *sweetgirlsweetgirlsweetgirl* and my dad sobbing so loudly he almost chokes.

There is more whisking away of me, as if I haven't been whisked away quite enough already. I am deposited in a closet of a room with comfortable but cheap office chairs, the kind that always seem to have bits of old food woven into the fabric. A camera blinking up in the corner and no windows. It is not what I pictured. It is not designed to make me feel safe.

I am surrounded by Boney, her partner, Gilpin, and two FBI agents up from St. Louis who remain nearly silent. They give me water, and then Boney starts.

B: Okay, Amy, first we have to thank you sincerely for talking with us after what you've been through. In a case like this, it's very important to get everything down while the memory is fresh. You can't imagine how important that is. So it's good to talk now. If we can get all these details down, we can close the case, and you and Nick can go back to your lives.

A: I'd definitely like that.

B: You deserve that. So if you're ready to begin, can we start with the time line: What time did Desi arrive at your door? Do you remember?

A: About ten a.m. A little after, because I remember hearing the Teverers talking as they walked to their car for church.

B: What happened when you opened the door?

A: Something felt wrong immediately. First of all, Desi has written me letters all my life. But his obsession seemed to have become less intense over the years. He seemed to think of himself as just an old friend, and since the police couldn't do anything about it, I made my peace with that. I never felt like he meant me active harm, although I really didn't like being this close to him. Geographically. I think that's what put him over the edge. Knowing I was so close. He walked into my house with ... He was sweaty and sort of nervous but also determined-looking. I'd been upstairs, I'd been about to iron my dress when I noticed the big wooden handle of the Judy puppet on the floor – I guess it had fallen off. Bummer because I'd already hidden the puppets in the woodshed. So I grabbed the handle, and I had that in my hand when I opened the door.

B: Very good memory.

A: Thank you.

B: What happened next?

A: Desi barged in, and he was pacing around the living room, all flustered and kind of frantic, and he said, *What are you doing for your anniversary?* It frightened me, that he knew today was our anniversary, and he seemed angry about it, and then his arm flashed out and he had me by the wrist and was twisting it behind my back, and we struggled. I put up a real fight.

B: What next?

A: I kicked him and got away for a second and ran to the kitchen, and we struggled more and he clubbed me once with the big wooden Judy handle, and I went flying and then he hit me two or three more times. I remember not being able to see for a second, just dizzy, my head was throbbing and I tried to grab for the handle and he stabbed my arm with this pocketknife he was carrying. I still have the scar. See?

B: Yes, that was noted in your medical examination. You were lucky it was only a flesh wound.

420

A: It doesn't feel like a flesh wound, believe me.

B: So he stabbed you? The angle is—

A: I'm not sure if he did it on purpose, or if I thrust myself onto the blade accidentally – I was so off balance. I remember the club falling to the floor, though, and I looked down and saw my blood from the stab wound pooling over the club. I think I passed out then.

B: Where were you when you woke up?

A: I woke up hog-tied in my living room.

B: Did you scream, try to get the neighbors' attention?

A: Of course I screamed. I mean, did you hear me? I was beaten, stabbed, and hog-tied by a man who had been obsessed with me for decades, who once tried to kill himself in my dorm bedroom.

B: Okay, okay, Amy, I'm sorry, that question was not intended in the least to sound like we are blaming you, we just need to get a full picture here so we can close the investigation and you can get on with your life. Do you want another water, or coffee or something?

A: Something warm would be nice. I'm so cold.

B: No problem. Can you get her a coffee? So what happened then?

A: I think his original plan was to subdue me and kidnap me and let it look like a runaway-wife thing, because when I wake up, he's just finished mopping the blood in the kitchen, and he's straightened the table of little antique ornaments that fell over when I ran to the kitchen. He's gotten rid of the club. But he's running out of time, and I think what must have happened is: He sees this disheveled living room – and so he thinks, *Leave it. Let it look like something bad happened here.* So he throws the front door open, and then he knocks a few more things over in the living room. Overturns the ottoman. So that's why the scene looked so weird: It was half true and half false.

B: Did Desi plant incriminating items at each of the treasure hunt sites: Nick's office, Hannibal, his dad's house, Go's woodshed?

A: I don't know what you mean?

B: There was a pair of women's underwear, not your size, in Nick's office.

A: I guess it must have been the girl he was ... dating.

B: Not hers either.

A: Well, I can't help on that one. Maybe he was seeing more than one girl.

B: Your diary was found in his father's house. Partly burned in the furnace.

A: Did you *read* the diary? It's awful. I'm sure Nick did want to get rid of it – I don't blame him, considering you guys zeroed in on him so quickly.

B: I wonder why he would go to his father's to burn it.

A: You should ask him. (Pause.) Nick went there a lot, to be alone. He likes his privacy. So I'm sure it didn't feel that odd to him. I mean he couldn't do it at our house, because it's a crime scene – who knows if you guys will come back, find

422

something in the ashes. At his dad's, he has some discretion. I thought it was a smart move, considering you guys were basically railroading him.

B: The diary is very, very concerning. The diary alleges abuse and your fears that Nick didn't want the baby, that he might want to kill you.

A: I really do wish that diary had burned. (Pause.) Let me be honest: The diary includes some of Nick's and my struggles these past few years. It doesn't paint the greatest picture of our marriage or of Nick, but I have to admit: I never wrote in the diary unless I was super-happy, *or* I was really, really unhappy and wanted to vent and then … I can get a little dramatic when it's just me stewing on things. I mean, a lot of that is the ugly truth – he did shove me once, and he didn't want a baby, and he did have money problems. But me being afraid of him? I have to admit, it *pains* me to admit, but that's my dramatic streak. I think the problem is, I've been stalked several times – it's been a lifelong issue – people getting obsessed with me – and so I get a little paranoid.

B: You tried to buy a gun.

A: I get a lot paranoid, okay? I'm sorry. If you had my history, you'd understand.

B: There's an entry about a night of drinks when you suffered from what sounds like textbook antifreeze poisoning.

A: (Long silence.) That's bizarre. Yes, I did get ill.

B: Okay, back to the treasure hunt. You did hide the Punch and Judy dolls in the woodshed?

A: I did.

B: A lot of our case has focused on Nick's debt, some extensive credit-card purchases, and our discovery of all those items hidden in the woodshed. What did you think when you opened the woodshed and saw all this stuff?

A: I was on Go's property, and Go and I aren't especially close, so mostly, I felt like I was nosing around in something that wasn't my business. I remember thinking at the time that it must have been her stuff from New York. And then I saw on the news – Desi made me watch everything – that it corresponded with Nick's purchases, and ... I knew Nick had some money troubles, he was a spender. I think he was probably embarrassed. Impulse purchases he couldn't undo, so he hid them from me until he could sell them online.

B: The Punch and Judy puppets, they seem a little ominous for an anniversary present.

A: I know! Now I know. I didn't remember the whole backstory of Punch and Judy. I was just seeing a husband and wife and a baby, and they were made of wood, and I was pregnant. I scanned the Internet and saw Punch's line: *That's the way to do it!* And I thought it was cute – I didn't know what it meant.

B: So you were hog-tied. How did Desi get you to the car?

A: He pulled the car into the garage and lowered the garage door, dragged me in, threw me in the trunk, and drove away.

B: And did you yell then?

A: Yes, I fucking yelled. I am a complete coward. And if I'd known that, every night for the next month, Desi was going to rape me, then snuggle in next to me with a martini and a sleeping pill so he wouldn't be awakened by my *sobbing*, and that the police were going to actually interview him and *still* not have a clue, still sit around with their thumbs up their asses, I might have yelled harder. Yes, I might have.

B: Again, my apologies. Can we get Ms Dunne some tissues, please? And where's her coff— Thank you. Okay, where did you go from there, Amy?

A: We drove toward St. Louis, and I remember on the way there he stopped at Hannibal – I heard the steamboat whistle. He threw my purse out. It was the one other thing he did so it would look like foul play.

B: This is so interesting. There seem to be so many strange coincidences in this case. Like, that Desi would happen to toss out the purse right at Hannibal, where your clue would make Nick go – and we in turn would believe that Nick tossed the purse there. Or how you decided to hide a present in the very place where Nick was hiding goods he'd bought on secret credit cards.

A: Really? I have to tell you, none of this sounds like coincidence to me. It sounds like a bunch of cops who got hung up on my husband being guilty, and now that I am alive and he's clearly not guilty, they look like giant idiots, and they're scrambling to cover their asses. Instead of accepting responsibility for the fact that, if this case had been left in your extremely fucking incompetent hands, Nick would be on death row and I'd be chained to a bed, being raped every day from now until I died.

B: I'm sorry, it's—

A: I saved myself, which saved Nick, which saved your sorry fucking asses.

B: That is an incredibly good point, Amy. I'm sorry, we're so ... We've spent so long on this case, we want to figure out every detail that we missed so we don't repeat our mistakes. But you're absolutely right, we're missing the big picture, which is: You are a hero. You are an absolute hero.

A: Thank you. I appreciate you saying that.

NICK DUNNE
THE NIGHT OF THE RETURN

I went to the station to fetch my wife and was greeted by the press like a rock star – landslide president – first moonwalker all in one. I had to resist raising clasped hands above my head in the universal victory shake. *I see*, I thought, *we're all pretending to be friends now.*

I entered a scene that felt like a holiday party gone awry – a few bottles of champagne rested on one desk, surrounded by tiny paper cups. Backslapping and cheers for all the cops, and then more cheers for me, as if these people hadn't been my persecutors a day before. But I had to play along. Present the back for slapping. *Oh yes, we're all buddies now.*

All that matters is that Amy is safe. I'd been practicing that line over and over. I had to look like the relieved, doting husband until I knew which way things were going to go. Until I was sure the police had sawed through all her sticky cobwebby lies. *Until she is arrested* – I'd get that far, *until she is arrested*, and then I could feel my brain expand and deflate simultaneously – my own cerebral Hitchcock zoom – and I'd think: *My wife* murdered *a man.*

'Stabbed him,' said the young police officer assigned as the family liaison. (I hoped never to be liaisoned again, with anyone, for any reason.) He was the same kid who'd yammered on to Go about his horse and torn labrum and peanut allergy. 'Cut him right through the jugular. Cut like that, he bleeds out in, like, sixty seconds.'

Sixty seconds is a long time to know you are dying. I could picture Desi wrapping his hands around his neck, the feel of his own blood spurting between his fingers with each pulse,

427

and Desi getting more frightened and the pulsing only quickening . . . and then slowing, and Desi knowing the slowing was worse. And all the time Amy standing just out of reach, studying him with the blameful, disgusted look of a high school biology student confronted with a dripping pig fetus. Her little scalpel still in hand.

'Cut him with a big ole butcher knife,' the kid was saying. 'Guy used to sit right next to her on the bed, cut up her meat for her, and *feed* her.' He sounded more disgusted by this than by the stabbing. 'One day the knife slips off the plate, he never notices—'

'How'd she use the knife if she was always tied up?' I asked.

The kid looked at me as if I'd just told a joke about his mother. 'I don't know, Mr Dunne, I'm sure they're getting the details right now. The point is, your wife is safe.'

Hurray. Kid stole my line.

I spotted Rand and Marybeth through the doorway of the room where we'd given our first press conference six weeks ago. They were leaning in to each other, as always, Rand kissing the top of Marybeth's head, Marybeth nuzzling him back, and I felt such a keen sense of outrage that I almost threw a stapler at them. *You two worshipful, adoring assholes created that* thing *down the hall and set her loose on the world.* Lo, how jolly, what a perfect monster! And do they get punished? No, not a single person had come forth to question their characters; they'd experienced nothing but an outpouring of love and support, and Amy would be restored to them and everyone would love her more.

My wife was an insatiable sociopath before. What would she become now?

Step carefully, Nick, step very carefully.

Rand caught my eye and motioned me to join them. He shook my hand for a few exclusive reporters who'd been granted an audience. Marybeth held her ground: I was still the man who'd cheated on her daughter. She gave a curt nod and turned away.

Rand leaned in close to me so I could smell his spearmint

gum. 'I tell you, Nick, we are so relieved to have Amy back. We owe you an apology too. Big one. We'll let Amy decide how she feels about your marriage, but I want to at least apologize for where things went. You've got to understand—'

'I do,' I said. 'I understand everything.'

Before Rand could apologize or engage further, Tanner and Betsy arrived together, looking like a *Vogue* spread – crisp slacks and jewel-toned shirts and gleaming gold watches and rings – and Tanner leaned toward my ear and whispered, *Let me see where we are*, and then Go was rushing in, all alarmed eyes and questions: *What does this mean? What happened to Desi? She just showed up on your doorstep? What does this mean? Are you okay? What happens next?*

It was a bizarre gathering – the feel of it: not quite reunion, not quite hospital waiting room, celebratory yet anxious, like some parlor game where no one had all the rules. Meanwhile, the two reporters the Elliotts had allowed into the inner sanctum kept snapping questions at me: *How great does it feel to have Amy back? How wonderful do you feel right now? How relieved are you, Nick, that Amy has returned?*

I'm extremely relieved and very happy, I was saying, crafting my own bland PR statement, when the doors parted and Jacqueline Collings entered, her lips a tight red scar, her face powder lined with tears.

'Where is she?' she said to me. 'The lying little bitch, where is she? She killed my son. My *son*.' She began crying as the reporter snapped a few photos.

How do you feel that your son was accused of kidnap and rape? one reporter asked in a stiff voice.

'How do I *feel*?' she snapped. 'Are you actually serious? Do people really answer questions like that? That nasty, *soulless* girl manipulated my son his entire life – *write this down* – she manipulated and lied and finally murdered him, and now, even after he's dead, she's still using him—'

'Ms Collings, we're Amy's parents,' Marybeth was beginning. She tried to touch Jacqueline on the shoulder, and Jacqueline shook her off. 'I am sorry for your pain.'

'But not my loss.' Jacqueline stood a good head taller than Marybeth; she glared down on her. 'But *not* my *loss*,' she reasserted.

'I'm sorry about ... everything,' Marybeth said, and then Rand was next to her, a head taller than Jacqueline.

'What are you going to do about your daughter?' Jacqueline asked. She turned toward our young liaison officer, who tried to hold his ground. 'What is being done about Amy? Because she is lying when she says my son kidnapped her. She is lying. She killed him, she *murdered* him in his sleep, and no one seems to be taking this seriously.'

'It's all being taken very, very seriously, ma'am,' the young kid said.

'Can I get a quote, Ms Collings?' asked the reporter.

'I just gave you my quote. *Amy Elliott Dunne murdered my son.* It was not self-defense. She *murdered* him.'

'Do you have proof of that?'

Of course she didn't.

The reporter's story would chronicle my husbandly exhaustion (*his drawn face telling of too many nights forfeited to fear*) and the Elliotts' relief (*the two parents cling to each other as they wait for their only child to be officially returned to them*). It would discuss the incompetence of the cops (*it was a biased case, full of dead ends and wrong turns, with the police department focused doggedly on the wrong man*). The article would dismiss Jacqueline Collings in a single line: *After an awkward run-in with the Elliott parents, an embittered Jacqueline Collings was ushered out of the room, claiming her son was innocent.*

Jacqueline was indeed ushered out of the room into another, where her statement would be recorded and she would be kept out of the way of the much better story: the Triumphant Return of Amazing Amy.

When Amy was released to us, it all began again. The photos and the tears, the hugging and the laughter, all for strangers who wanted to see and to know: *What was it like? Amy, what does it feel like to escape your captor and return to your husband? Nick, what does it feel like to get your wife back, to get your freedom back, all at once?*

I remained mostly silent. I was thinking my own questions, the same questions I'd thought for years, the ominous refrain of our marriage: *What are you thinking, Amy? How are you feeling? Who are you? What have we done to each other? What will we do?*

It was a gracious, queenly act for Amy to want to come home to our marriage bed with her cheating husband. Everyone agreed. The media followed us as if we were a royal wedding procession, the two of us whizzing through the neon, fast-food-cluttered streets of Carthage to our McMansion on the river. What grace Amy has, what moxie. A storybook princess. And I, of course, was the lickspittle hunchback of a husband who would bow and scrape the rest of my days. Until she was arrested. If she ever got arrested.

That she was released at all was a concern. More than a concern, an utter shock. I saw them all filing out of the conference room where they questioned her for *four* hours and then let her go: two FBI guys with alarmingly short hair and blank faces; Gilpin, looking like he'd swallowed the greatest steak dinner of his life; and Boney, the only one with thin, tight lips and a little V of a frown. She glanced at me as she walked past, arched an eyebrow, and was gone.

Then, too quickly, Amy and I were back in our home, alone in the living room, Bleecker watching us with shiny eyes. Outside our curtains, the lights of the TV cameras remained, bathing our living room in a bizarrely lush orange glow. We looked candlelit, romantic. Amy was absolutely beautiful. I hated her. I was afraid of her.

'We can't really sleep in the same house—' I began.

'I want to stay here with you.' She took my hand. 'I want to be with my husband. I want to give you the chance to be the kind of husband you want to be. I forgive you.'

'You *forgive* me? Amy, why did you come back? Because of what I said in the interviews? The videos?'

'Wasn't that what you wanted?' she said. 'Wasn't that the point of the videos? They were perfect – they reminded me of what we used to have, how special it was.'

'What I said, that was just me saying what you wanted to hear.'

'I know – that's how well you know me!' Amy said. She beamed. Bleecker began figure-eighting between her legs. She picked him up and stroked him. His purr was deafening. 'Think about it, Nick, we *know* each other. Better than anyone in the world now.'

It was true that I'd had this feeling too, in the past month, when I wasn't wishing Amy harm. It would come to me at strange moments – in the middle of the night, up to take a piss, or in the morning pouring a bowl of cereal – I'd detect a nib of admiration, and more than that, fondness for my wife, right in the middle of me, right in the gut. To know exactly what I wanted to hear in those notes, to woo me back to her, even to predict all my wrong moves … the woman knew me cold. Better than anyone in the world, she knew me. All this time I'd thought we were strangers, and it turned out we knew each other intuitively, in our bones, in our blood.

It was kind of romantic. Catastrophically romantic.

'We can't just pick up where we were, Amy.'

'No, not where we were,' she said. 'Where we are now. Where you love me and you'll never do wrong again.'

'You're crazy, you're literally crazy if you think I'm going to stay. You *killed* a man,' I said. I turned my back to her, and then I pictured her with a knife in her hand and her mouth growing tight as I disobeyed her. I turned back around. Yes, my wife must always be faced.

'To escape him.'

'You killed Desi so you had a new story, so you could come back and be beloved Amy and not ever have to take the blame for what you did. Don't you get it, Amy, the irony? It's what you always hated about me – that I never dealt with the consequences of my actions, right? Well, my ass has been well and duly consequenced. So what about you? You *murdered* a

432

man, a man I assume loved you and was helping you, and now you want me to step in his place and love you and help you, and ... I can't. I cannot do it. I won't do it.'

'Nick, I think you've gotten some bad information,' she said. 'It doesn't surprise me, all the rumors that are going about. But we need to forget all that. If we are to go forward. And we will go forward. All of America wants us to go forward. It's the story the world needs right now. Us. Desi's the bad guy. No one wants two bad guys. They *want* to *like* you, Nick. The only way you can be loved again is to stay with me. It's the only way.'

'Tell me what happened, Amy. Was Desi helping you all along?'

She flared at that: She didn't need a man's help, even though she clearly had needed a man's help. 'Of course not!' she snapped.

'Tell me. What can it hurt, tell me everything, because you and I can't go forward with this pretend story. I'll fight you every step of the way. I know you've thought of everything. I'm not trying to get you to slip up – I'm tired of trying to outthink you, I don't have it in me. I just want to know what happened. I was a step away from death row, Amy. You came back and saved me, and I thank you for that – do you hear me? I *thank* you, so don't say I didn't later on. I *thank* you. But I need to know. You know I need to know.'

'Take off your clothes,' she said.

She wanted to make sure I wasn't wearing a wire. I undressed in front of her, removed every stitch, and then she surveyed me, ran a hand across my chin and my chest, down my back. She palmed my ass and slipped her hand between my legs, cupped my testicles and gripped my limp cock, held it in her hand for a moment to see if anything happened. Nothing happened.

'You're clean,' she said. It was meant as a joke, a wisecrack, a movie reference we'd both laugh at. When I said nothing, she stepped back and said, 'I always did like looking at you naked. That made me happy.'

433

'Nothing made you happy. Can I put my clothes back on?'

'No. I don't want to worry about hidden wires in the cuffs or the hems. Also, we need to go in the bathroom and run the water. In case you bugged the house.'

'You've seen too many movies,' I said.

'Ha! Never thought I'd hear you say that.'

We stood in the bathtub and turned on the shower. The water sprayed my naked back and misted the front of Amy's shirt until she peeled it off. She pulled off all her clothes, a gleeful striptease, and tossed them over the shower stall in the same grinning, game manner she had when we first met – *I'm up for anything!* – and she turned to me, and I waited for her to swing her hair around her shoulders like she did when she flirted with me, but her hair was too short.

'Now we're even,' she said. 'Seemed rude to be the only one clothed.'

'I think we're past etiquette, Amy.'

Look only at her eyes, do not touch her, do not let her touch you.

She moved toward me, put a hand on my chest, let the water trickle between her breasts. She licked a shower teardrop off her upper lip and smiled. Amy hated shower spray. She didn't like getting her face wet, didn't like the feel of water pelleting her flesh. I knew this because I was married to her, and I'd pawed her and harassed her many times in the shower, always to be turned down. (*I know it seems sexy, Nick, but it's actually not, it's something people only do in movies.*) Now she was pretending just the opposite, as if she forgot that I knew her. I backed away.

'Tell me everything, Amy. But first: Was there ever a baby?'

The baby was a lie. It was the most desolate part for me. My wife as a murderer was frightening, repulsive, but the baby as a lie was almost impossible to bear. The baby was a lie, the fear of blood was a lie – during the past year, my wife had been mostly a lie.

'How did you set Desi up?' I asked.

'I found some twine in one corner of his basement. I used a steak knife to saw it into four pieces—'

'He let you keep a knife?'

'We were friends. You forget.'

She was right. I was thinking of the story she'd told the police: that Desi had held her captive. I did forget. She was that good a storyteller.

'Whenever Desi wasn't around, I'd tie the pieces as tight as I could around my wrists and ankles so they'd leave these grooves.'

She showed me the lurid lines on her wrists, like bracelets.

'I took a wine bottle, and I abused myself with it every day, so the inside of my vagina looked ... right. Right for a rape victim. Then today I let him have sex with me so I had his semen, and then I slipped some sleeping pills into his martini.'

'He let you keep sleeping pills?'

She sighed: I wasn't keeping up.

'Right, you were friends.'

'Then I—' She pantomimed slicing his jugular.

'That easy, huh?'

'You just have to decide to do it and then do it,' she said. 'Discipline. Follow through. Like anything. You never understood that.'

I could feel her mood turning stony. I wasn't appreciating her enough.

'Tell me more,' I said. 'Tell me how you did it.'

An hour in, the water went cold, and Amy called an end to our discussion.

'You have to admit, it's pretty brilliant,' she said.

I stared at her.

'I mean, you have to admire it just a little,' she prompted.

'How long did it take for Desi to bleed to death?'

'It's time for bed,' she said. 'But we can talk more tomorrow if you want. Right now we should sleep. Together. I think it's important. For closure. Actually, the opposite of closure.'

'Amy, I'm going to stay tonight because I don't want to deal

435

with all the questions if I don't stay. But I'll sleep downstairs.'

She cocked her head to one side, studied me.

'Nick, I can still do very bad things to you, remember that.'

'Ha! Worse than what you've already done?'

She looked surprised. 'Oh, definitely.'

'I doubt that, Amy.'

I began walking out the door.

'Attempted murder,' she said.

I paused.

'That was my original plan early on: I'd be a poor, sick wife with repeated episodes, sudden intense bouts of illness, and then it turns out that all those cocktails her husband prepared her . . .'

'Like in the diary.'

'But I decided *attempted* murder wasn't good enough for you. It had to be bigger than that. Still, I couldn't get the poisoning idea out of my head. I liked the idea of you working up to the murder. Trying the cowardly way first. So I went through with it.'

'You expect me to believe that?'

'All that vomit, so shocking. An innocent, frightened wife might have saved some of that vomit, just in case. You can't blame her, being a little paranoid.' She gave a satisfied smile. 'Always have a backup plan to the backup plan.'

'You actually poisoned yourself.'

'Nick, please, you're shocked? I *killed* myself.'

'I need a drink,' I said. I left before she could speak.

I poured myself a Scotch and sat on the living room couch. Beyond the curtains, the strobes of the cameras were lighting up the yard. Soon it would no longer be night. I'd come to find the morning depressing, to know it would come again and again.

Tanner picked up on the first ring.

'She killed him,' I said. 'She killed Desi because he was basically . . . he was annoying her, he was power-playing her, and she realized she could kill him, and it was her way back to her old life, and she could blame everything on him. She

436

murdered him, Tanner, she just told me this. She *confessed*.'

'I don't suppose you were able to … record any of it somehow? Cell phone or something?'

'We were naked with the shower running, and she whispered everything.'

'I don't even want to ask,' he said. 'You two are the most fucked-up people I have ever met, and I specialize in fucked-up people.'

'What's going on with the police?'

He sighed. 'She foolproofed everything. It's ludicrous, her story, but no more ludicrous than our story. Amy's basically exploiting the sociopath's most reliable maxim.'

'What's that?'

'The bigger the lie, the more they believe it.'

'Come on, Tanner, there's got to be something.'

I paced over to the staircase to make sure Amy was nowhere nearby. We were whispering, but still. I had to be careful now.

'For now we need to toe the line, Nick. She left you looking fairly bad: Everything in the diary was true, she says. All the stuff in the woodshed was you. You bought the stuff with those credit cards, and you're too embarrassed to admit it. She's just a sheltered little rich girl, what would she know about acquiring secret credit cards in her husband's name? And my goodness, that pornography!'

'She told me there was never a baby, she faked it with Noelle Hawthorne's pee.'

'Why didn't you say— That's huge! We'll lean on Noelle Hawthorne.'

'Noelle didn't know.'

I heard a deep sigh on the other end. He didn't even bother asking how. 'We'll keep thinking, we'll keep looking,' he said. 'Something will break.'

'I can't stay in this house with that *thing*. She's threatening me with—'

'Attempted murder … the antifreeze. Yeah, I heard that was in the mix.'

'They can't arrest me on that, can they? She says she still

437

has some vomit. Evidence. But can they really—'

'Let's not push it for now, okay, Nick?' he said. 'For now, play nice. I hate to say it, I hate to, but that's my best legal advice for you right now: Play nice.'

'Play nice? That's your advice? My one-man legal dream team: *Play nice*? Fuck you.'

I hung up in full fury.

I'll kill her, I thought. *I will fucking kill the bitch.*

I plunged into the dark daydream I'd indulged over the past few years when Amy had made me feel my smallest: I daydreamed of hitting her with a hammer, smashing her head in until she stopped talking, *finally*, stopped with the words she suctioned to me: average, boring, mediocre, unsurprising, unsatisfying, unimpressive. *Un*, basically. In my mind, I whaled on her with the hammer until she was like a broken toy, muttering *un, un, un* until she sputtered to a stop. And then it wasn't enough, so I restored her to perfection and began killing her again: I wrapped my fingers around her neck – she always did crave intimacy – and then I squeezed and squeezed, her pulse—

'Nick?'

I turned around, and Amy was on the bottom stair in her nightgown, her head tilted to one side.

'Play nice, Nick.'

AMY ELLIOTT DUNNE
THE NIGHT OF THE RETURN

He turns around, and when he sees me standing there, he looks scared. That's something useful. Because I'm not going to let him go. He may think he was lying when he said all those nice things to lure me home. But I know different. I know Nick can't lie like that. I know that as he recited those words, he realized the truth. *Ping!* Because you can't be as in love as we were and not have it invade your bone marrow. Our kind of love can go into remission, but it's always waiting to return. Like the world's sweetest cancer.

You don't buy it? Then how about this? He did lie. He didn't mean a fucking thing he said. Well, then, screw him, he did too good a job, because I want him, exactly like that. The man he was pretending to be – women love that guy. I love that guy. That's the man I want for my husband. That's the man I signed up for. That's the man I deserve.

So he can choose to truly love me the way he once did, or I will bring him to heel and make him be the man I married. I'm sick of dealing with his bullshit.

'Play nice,' I say.

He looks like a child, a furious child. He bunches his fists.

'No, Amy.'

'I can ruin you, Nick.'

'You already did, Amy.' I see the rage flash over him, a shiver. 'Why in God's name do you even want to be with me? I'm boring, average, uninteresting, uninspiring. I'm not up to par. You spent the last few years telling me this.'

'Only because you stopped *trying*,' I say. 'You were so perfect, with me. We were so perfect when we started, and then you stopped trying. Why would you do that?'

'I stopped loving you.'

'*Why?*'

'You stopped loving me. We're a sick, fucking toxic Möbius strip, Amy. We weren't ourselves when we fell in love, and when we became ourselves – surprise! – we were poison. We complete each other in the nastiest, ugliest possible way. You don't really love *me*, Amy. You don't even like me. Divorce me. Divorce me, and let's try to be happy.'

'I won't divorce you, Nick. I won't. And I swear to you, if you try to leave, I will devote *my* life to making *your* life as awful as I can. And you know I can make it awful.'

He begins pacing like a caged bear. 'Think about it, Amy, how bad we are for each other: the two most needful human beings in the world stuck with each other. I'll divorce you if you don't divorce me.'

'Really?'

'I will divorce you. But you should divorce me. Because I know what you're thinking already, Amy. You're thinking it won't make a good story: Amazing Amy finally kills her crazed-rapist captor and returns home to ... a boring old divorce. You're thinking it's not triumphant.'

It's *not* triumphant.

'But think of it this way: Your story is not some drippy, earnest survivor story. TV movie circa 1992. It's not. You are a tough, vibrant, independent woman, Amy. You killed your kidnapper, and then you kept on cleaning house: You got rid of your idiot cheat of a husband. Women would *cheer* you. You're not a scared little girl. You're a badass, take-no-prisoners *woman*. Think about it. You know I'm right: The era of forgiveness is over. It's passé. Think of all the women – the politicians' wives, the actresses – every woman in the public who's been cheated on, they don't stay with the cheat these days. It's not *stand by your man* anymore, it's *divorce the fucker.*'

I feel a rush of hate toward him, that he's still trying to wriggle out of our marriage even though I've told him – three times now – that he can't. He still thinks he has power.

'And if I don't divorce you, you'll divorce me?' I ask.

'I don't want to be married to a woman like you. I want to be married to a normal person.'

Piece of shit.

'I see. You want to revert to your lame, limp *loser* self? You want to just *walk away*? No! You don't get to go be some boring-ass middle American with some boring-ass girl next door. You tried it already – remember, baby? Even if you wanted to, you couldn't do that now. You'll be known as the philandering asshole who left his kidnapped, raped wife. You think any *nice* woman will touch you? You'll only get—'

'Psychos? Crazy psycho bitches?' He's pointing at me, jabbing the air.

'Don't call me that.'

'Psycho bitch?'

It'd be so easy, for him to write me off that way. He'd love that, to be able to dismiss me so simply.

'Everything I do, I do for a reason, Nick,' I say. 'Everything I do takes planning and precision and discipline.'

'You are a petty, selfish, manipulative, disciplined psycho bitch—'

'You are a man,' I say. 'You are an average, lazy, boring, cowardly, *woman-fearing* man. Without me, that's what you would have kept on being, ad nauseam. But I made you into something. You were the best man you've *ever* been with me. And you know it. The only time in your life you've ever *liked* yourself was *pretending to be* someone *I* might like. Without me? You're just your dad.'

'Don't say that, Amy.' He balls up his fists.

'You think he wasn't hurt by a woman, too, just like you?' I say it in my most patronizing voice, as if I'm talking to a puppy. 'You think he didn't believe he deserved better than he got, just like you? You really think your mom was his first choice? Why do you think he hated you all so much?'

He moves toward me. 'Shut up, Amy.'

'Think, Nick, you know I'm right: Even if you found a

nice, regular girl, you'd be thinking of *me* every day. Tell me you wouldn't.'

'I wouldn't.'

'How quickly did you forget little Able Andie once you thought I loved you again?' I say it in my poor-baby voice. I even stick out my lower lip. 'One love note, sweetie? Did one love note do it? Two? Two notes with me swearing I *loved* you and I wanted you *back*, and I thought you were just *great* after all – was that it for you? You are *WITTY*, you are *WARM*, you are *BRILLIANT*. You're so pathetic. You think you can ever be a normal man again? You'll find a nice girl, and you'll still think of me, and you'll be so completely dissatisfied, trapped in your boring, normal life with your regular wife and your two average kids. You'll think of me and then you'll look at your wife, and you'll think: *Dumb bitch*.'

'Shut up, Amy. I mean it.'

'Just like your dad. We're all bitches in the end, aren't we, Nick? Dumb bitch, psycho bitch.'

He grabs me by the arm and shakes me hard.

'I'm the bitch who makes you better, Nick.'

He stops talking then. He is using all his energy to keep his hands at his side. His eyes are wet with tears. He is shaking.

'I'm the *bitch* who makes you a man.'

Then his hands are on my neck.

NICK DUNNE
THE NIGHT OF THE RETURN

Her pulse was finally throbbing beneath my fingers, the way I'd imagined. I pressed tighter and brought her to the ground. She made wet clucking noises and scratched at my wrists. We were both kneeling, in face-to-face prayer for ten seconds.

You fucking crazy bitch.

A tear fell from my chin and hit the floor.

You murdering, mind-fucking, evil, crazy bitch.

Amy's bright blue eyes were staring into mine, unblinking.

And then the strangest thought of all clattered drunkenly from the back of my brain to the front and blinded me: *If I kill Amy, who will I be?*

I saw a bright white flash. I dropped my wife as if she were burning iron.

She sat hard on the ground, gasped, coughed. When her breath came back, it was in jagged rasps, with a strange, almost erotic squeak at the end.

Who will I be then? The question wasn't recriminatory. It wasn't like the answer was the pious: *Then you'll be a killer, Nick. You'll be as bad as Amy. You'll be what everyone thought you were.* No. The question was frighteningly soulful and literal: Who would I be without Amy to react to? Because she was right: As a man, I had been my most impressive when I loved her – and I was my next best self when I hated her. I had known Amy only seven years, but I couldn't go back to life without her. Because she was right: I couldn't return to an average life. I'd known it before she'd said a word. I'd already pictured myself with a regular woman – a sweet, normal girl next door – and I'd already pictured telling this regular woman the story of Amy, the lengths she had gone to – to punish me and to return to me. I already pictured this sweet and mediocre girl saying something uninteresting like *Oh, nooooo, oh my God*, and I already knew part of me would be looking at her and thinking: *You've never murdered for me. You've never framed me. You wouldn't even know how to begin to do what Amy did. You could never possibly care that much.* The indulged mama's boy in me wouldn't be able to find peace with this normal woman, and pretty soon she wouldn't just be normal, she'd be substandard, and then my father's voice – *dumb bitch* – would rise up and take it from there.

Amy was exactly right.

So maybe there was no good end for me.

Amy was toxic, yet I couldn't imagine a world without her entirely. Who would I be with Amy just gone? There were no options that interested me anymore. But she had to be brought to heel. Amy in prison, that was a good ending for her. Tucked away in a box where she couldn't inflict herself on me but where I could visit her from time to time. Or at least imagine her. A pulse, my pulse, left out there somewhere.

It had to be me who put her there. It was my responsibility. Just as Amy took the credit for making me my best self, I had to take the blame for bringing the madness to bloom in Amy. There were a million men who would have loved, honored, and obeyed Amy and considered themselves lucky to do so. Confident, self-assured, real men who wouldn't have forced her to pretend to be anything but her own perfect, rigid, demanding, brilliant, creative, fascinating, rapacious, megalomaniac self.

Men capable of being uxorious.

Men capable of keeping her sane.

Amy's story could have gone a million other ways, but she met me, and bad things happened. So it was up to me to stop her.

Not kill her but stop her.

Put her in one of her boxes.

AMY ELLIOTT DUNNE
FIVE DAYS AFTER THE RETURN

I know, I know for sure now, that I need to be more careful about Nick. He's not as tame as he used to be. Something in him is electric; a switch has turned on. I like it. But I need to take precautions.

I need one more spectacular precaution.

It will take some time to put in place, this precaution. But I've done it before, the planning. In the meantime, we can work on our rebuilding. Start with the facade. We will have a happy marriage if it kills him.

'You're going to have to try again to love me,' I told him. The morning after he almost killed me. It happened to be Nick's thirty-fifth birthday, but he didn't mention it. My husband has had enough of my gifts.

'I forgive you for last night,' I said. 'We were both under a lot of stress. But now you're going to have to try again.'

'I know.'

'Things will have to be different,' I said.

'I know,' he said.

He doesn't really know. But he will.

My parents have visited daily. Rand and Marybeth and Nick lavish me with attention. Pillows. Everyone wants to offer me pillows: We are all laboring under a mass psychosis that my rape and miscarriage have left me forever achy and delicate. I have a permanent case of sparrow's bones – I must be held gently in the palm, lest I break. So I prop my feet on the infamous ottoman, and I tread delicately over the kitchen floor where I bled. We must take good care of me.

Yet I find it strangely tense to watch Nick with anyone but

me. He seems on the edge of blurting all the time – as if his lungs are bursting with words about me, damning words.

I need Nick, I realize. I actually need him to back my story. To stop his accusations and denials and admit that it was him: the credit cards, the goodies in the woodshed, the bump in insurance. Otherwise I will carry that waft of uncertainty forever. I have only a few loose ends, and those loose ends are people. The police, the FBI, they are sifting through my story. Boney, I know, would love to arrest me. But they botched everything so badly before – they look like such fools – that they can't touch me unless they have proof. And they don't have proof. They have Nick, who swears he didn't do the things I swear he did, and that's not much, but it's more than I'd like.

I've even prepared in case my Ozarks friends Jeff and Greta show up, nosing around for acclaim or cash. I've already told the police: Desi didn't drive us straight to his home. He kept me blindfolded and gagged and drugged for several days – I *think* it was several days – in some room, maybe a motel room? Maybe an apartment? I can't be sure, it's all such a blur. I was so frightened, you know, and the sleeping pills. If Jeff and Greta show their pointy, lowdown faces and somehow convince the cops to send a tech team down to the Hide-A-Way, and one of my fingerprints or a hair is found, that simply solves part of the puzzle. The rest is them telling lies.

So Nick is really the only issue, and soon I'll return him to my side. I was smart, I left no other evidence. The police may not entirely believe me, but they won't do anything. I know from the petulant tone in Boney's voice – she will live in permanent exasperation from now on, and the more annoyed she gets, the more people will dismiss her. She already has the righteous, eye-rolling cadence of a conspiracy crackpot. She might as well wrap her head in foil.

Yes, the investigation is winding down. But for Amazing Amy, it's quite the opposite. My parents' publisher placed an abashed plea for another *Amazing Amy* book, and they acquiesced for a lovely fat sum. Once again they are squatting on my psyche, earning money for themselves. They left Carthage this morning. They say it's important for Nick and me (the correct grammar) to have some time alone and heal. But I know the truth. They want to get to work. They tell me they are trying to 'find the right tone.' A tone that says: *Our daughter was kidnapped and repeatedly raped by a monster she had to stab in the neck ... but this is in no way a cash grab.*

I don't care about the rebuilding of their pathetic empire, because every day I get calls to tell *my* story. My story: mine, mine, mine. I just need to pick the very best deal and start writing. I just need to get Nick on the same page so that we both agree how this story will end. Happily.

I know Nick isn't in love with me yet, but he will be. I do have faith in that. Fake it until you make it, isn't that an expression? For now he acts like the old Nick, and I act like the old Amy. Back when we were happy. When we didn't know each other as well as we do now. Yesterday I stood on the back porch and watched the sun come up over the river, a strangely cool August morning, and when I turned around, Nick was studying me from the kitchen window, and he held up a mug of coffee with a question: *You want a cup?* I nodded, and soon he was standing beside me, the air smelling of grass, and we were drinking our coffee together and watching the water, and it felt normal and good.

He won't sleep with me yet. He sleeps in the downstairs guest room with the door locked. But one day I will wear him down, I will catch him off guard, and he will lose the energy for the nightly battle, and he will get in bed with me. In the middle of the night, I'll turn to face him and press myself against him. I'll hold myself to him like a climbing, coiling vine until I have invaded every part of him and made him mine.

NICK DUNNE
THIRTY DAYS AFTER THE RETURN

Amy thinks she's in control, but she's very wrong. Or: She will be very wrong.

Boney and Go and I are working together. The cops, the FBI, no one else is showing much interest anymore. But yesterday Boney called out of the blue. She didn't identify herself when I picked up, just started in like an old friend: *Take you for a cup of coffee?* I grabbed Go, and we met Boney back at the Pancake House. She was already at the booth when we arrived, and she stood and smiled somewhat weakly. She'd been getting pummeled in the press. We did an awkward, group-wide hug-or-handshake shuffle. Boney settled for a nod.

First thing she said to me once we got our food: 'I have one daughter. Thirteen years old. Mia. For Mia Hamm. She was born the day we won the World Cup. So, that's my daughter.'

I raised my eyebrows: *How interesting. Tell me more.*

'You asked that one day, and I didn't … I was rude. I'd been sure you were innocent, and then … everything said you weren't, so I was pissed. That I could be that fooled. So I didn't even want to say my daughter's name around you.' She poured us out coffee from the thermos.

'So, it's Mia,' she said.

'Well, thank you,' I said.

'No, I mean … Crap.' She exhaled upward, a hard gust that fluttered her bangs. 'I mean: I know Amy framed you. I know she murdered Desi Collings. I *know* it. I just can't prove it.'

'What is everyone else doing while you're actually working the case?' Go asked.

'There is no case. They're moving on. Gilpin is totally checked out. I basically got the word from on high: Shut this shit *down*. Shut it down. We look like giant, rube, redneck jackasses in the national media. I can't do anything unless I get something from you, Nick. You got *anything*?'

I shrugged. 'I got everything you got. She confessed to me, but—'

'She *confessed*?' she said. 'Well, hell, Nick, we'll wire you.'

'It won't work. It won't work. She thinks of everything. I mean, she knows police procedure cold. She studies, Rhonda.'

She poured electric-blue syrup over her waffles. I stuck the tines of my fork in my bulbous egg yolk and swirled it, smearing the sun.

'It drives me crazy when you call me Rhonda.'

'She studies, Ms Detective Boney.'

She blew her breath upward, fluttered her bangs again. Took a bite of pancake. 'I couldn't get a wire anyway at this point.'

'Come on, there has to be something, you guys,' Go snapped. 'Nick, why the hell are you staying in that house if you aren't getting something?'

'It takes time, Go. I have to get her to trust me again. If she starts telling me things casually, when we're not both stark naked—'

Boney rubbed her eyes and addressed Go: 'Do I even want to ask?'

'They always have their talks naked in the shower with the water running,' Go said. 'Can't you bug the shower somewhere?'

'She whispers in my ear, on top of the shower running,' I said.

'She does study,' Boney said. 'She really does. I went over that car she drove back, Desi's Jag. I had 'em check the trunk, where she swore Desi had stowed her when he kidnapped her. I figured there'd be nothing there – we'd catch her in a lie. She rolled around in the trunk, Nick. Her scent was detected

449

by our dogs. And we found three long blond hairs. *Long* blond hairs. Hers before she cut it. How she did that—'

'Foresight. I'm sure she had a bag of them so if she needed to leave them somewhere to damn me, she could.'

'Good God, can you imagine having her for a mother? You could never fib. She'd be three steps ahead of you, always.'

'Boney, can you imagine having her for a wife?'

'She'll crack,' she said. 'At some point, she'll crack.'

'She won't,' I said. 'Can't I just testify against her?'

'You have no credibility,' Boney said. 'Your only credibility comes from Amy. She's single-handedly rehabilitated you. And she can single-handedly undo it. If she comes out with the antifreeze story . . .'

'I need to find the vomit,' I said. 'If I got rid of the vomit and we exposed more of her lies . . .'

'We should go through the diary,' Go said. 'Seven years of entries? There have to be discrepancies.'

'We asked Rand and Marybeth to go through it, see if anything seemed off to them,' Boney said. 'You can guess how that went. I thought Marybeth was going to scratch my eyes out.'

'What about Jacqueline Collings, or Tommy O'Hara, or Hilary Handy?' Go said. 'They all know the real Amy. There has to be something there.'

Boney shook her head. 'Believe me, it's not enough. They're all less credible than Amy. It's pure public opinion, but right now that's what the department is looking at: public opinion.'

She was right. Jacqueline Collings had popped up on a few cable shows, insisting on her son's innocence. She always started off steady, but her mother's love worked against her: She soon came across as a grieving woman desperate to believe the best of her son, and the more the hosts pitied her, the more she snapped and snarled, and the more unsympathetic she became. She got written off quickly. Both Tommy O'Hara and Hilary Handy called me, furious that Amy remained unpunished, determined to tell their story, but no one wanted to hear from two unhinged *former* anythings. *Hold tight*, I told

450

them, we're working on it. Hilary and Tommy and Jacqueline and Boney and Go and I, we'd have our moment. I told myself I believed it.

'What if we at least got Andie?' I asked. 'Got her to testify that everywhere Amy hid a clue was a place where we'd, you know, had sex? Andie's credible; people love her.'

Andie had reverted to her old cheery self after Amy returned. I know that only from the occasional tabloid snapshot. From these, I know she has been dating a guy her age, a cute, shaggy kid with earbuds forever dangling from his neck. They look nice together, young and healthy. The press adored them. The best headline: *Love Finds Andie Hardy!*, a 1938 Mickey Rooney movie pun only about twenty people would get. I sent her a text: *I'm sorry. For everything.* I didn't hear back. Good for her. I mean that sincerely.

'Coincidence.' Boney shrugged. 'I mean, weird coincidence, but … it's not impressive enough to move forward. Not in this climate. You need to get your wife to tell you something useful, Nick. You're our only chance here.'

Go slammed down her coffee. 'I can't believe we're having this conversation,' she said. 'Nick, I don't want you in that house anymore. You're not an undercover cop, you know. It's not your job. You are living with a murderer. Fucking leave. I'm sorry, but who gives a shit that she killed Desi? I don't want her to kill *you*. I mean, someday you burn her grilled cheese, and the next thing you know, my phone's ringing and you've taken an awful fall from the roof or some shit. *Leave.*'

'I can't. Not yet. She'll never really let me go. She likes the game too much.'

'Then stop playing it.'

I can't. I'm getting so much better at it. I will stay close to her until I can bring her down. I'm the only one left who can do it. Someday she'll slip and tell me something I can use. A week ago I moved into our bedroom. We don't have sex, we barely touch, but we are husband and wife in a marital bed, which appeases Amy for now. I stroke her hair. I take a strand between my finger and thumb, and I pull it to the end and tug, like I'm ringing a bell, and we both like that. Which is a problem.

We pretend to be in love, and we do the things we like to do when we're in love, and it feels almost like love sometimes, because we are so perfectly putting ourselves through the paces. Reviving the muscle memory of early romance. When I forget – I can sometimes briefly forget who my wife is – I actually like hanging out with her. Or the *her* she is pretending to be. The fact is, my wife is a murderess who is sometimes really fun. May I give one example? One night I flew in lobster like the old days, and she pretended to chase me with it, and I pretended to hide, and then we both *at the same time* made an *Annie Hall* joke, and it was so perfect, so the way it was supposed to be, that I had to leave the room for a second. My heart was beating in my ears. I had to repeat my mantra: *Amy killed a man, and she will kill you if you are not very, very careful.* My wife, the very fun, beautiful murderess, will do me harm if I displease her. I find myself jittery in my own house: I will be making a sandwich, standing in the kitchen midday, licking the peanut butter off the knife, and I will turn and find Amy in the same room with me – those quiet little cat feet – and I will quiver. Me, Nick Dunne, the man who used to forget so many details, is now the guy who replays conversations to make sure I didn't offend, to make sure I never hurt her feelings. I write down everything about her day, her likes and dislikes, in case she quizzes me. I am a great husband because I am very afraid she may kill me.

We've never had a conversation about my paranoia, because we're pretending to be in love and I'm pretending not to be frightened of her. But she's made glancing mentions of it: *You know, Nick, you can sleep in bed with me, like, actually sleep. It will be okay. I promise. What happened with Desi was an isolated incident. Close your eyes and sleep.*

But I know I'll never sleep again. I can't close my eyes when I'm next to her. It's like sleeping with a spider.

AMY ELLIOTT DUNNE
EIGHT WEEKS AFTER THE RETURN

No one has arrested me. The police have stopped questioning. I feel safe. I will be even safer very soon.

This is how good I feel: Yesterday I came downstairs for breakfast, and the jar that held my vomit was sitting on the kitchen counter, empty. Nick – the scrounger – had gotten rid of that little bit of leverage. I blinked an eye, and then I tossed out the jar.

It hardly matters now.

Good things are happening.

I have a book deal: I am officially in control of our story. It feels wonderfully symbolic. Isn't that what every marriage is, anyway? Just a lengthy game of he-said, she-said? Well, *she* is saying, and the world will listen, and Nick will have to smile and agree. I will write him the way I want him to be: romantic and thoughtful and very very repentant – about the credit cards and the purchases and the woodshed. If I can't get him to say it out loud, he'll say it in my book. Then he'll come on tour with me and smile and smile.

I'm calling the book simply: *Amazing*. Causing great wonder or surprise; astounding. That sums up my story, I think.

NICK DUNNE
NINE WEEKS AFTER THE RETURN

I found the vomit. She'd hidden it in the back of the freezer in a jar, inside a box of Brussels sprouts. The box was covered in icicles; it must have been sitting there for months. I know it was her own joke with herself: *Nick won't eat his vegetables, Nick never cleans out the fridge, Nick won't think to look here.*

But Nick did.

Nick knows how to clean out the refrigerator, it turns out, and Nick even knows how to defrost: I poured all that sick down the drain, and I left the jar on the counter so she'd know.

She tossed it in the garbage. She never said a word about it.

Something's wrong. I don't know what it is, but something's very wrong.

My life has begun to feel like an epilogue. Tanner picked up a new case: A Nashville singer discovered his wife was cheating, and her body was found the next day in a Hardee's trash bin near their house, a hammer covered with his fingerprints beside her. Tanner is using me as a defense. *I know it looks bad, but it also looked bad for Nick Dunne, and you know how that turned out.* I could almost feel him winking at me through the camera lens. He sent the occasional text: *U OK?* Or: *Anything?*

No, nothing.

Boney and Go and I hung out in secret at the Pancake House, where we sifted the dirty sand of Amy's story, trying to find something we could use. We scoured the diary, an elaborate anachronism hunt. It came down to desperate nit-pickings like: 'She makes a comment here about Darfur, was that on the radar in 2010?' (Yes, we found a 2006 newsclip with George Clooney discussing it.) Or my own best worst: 'Amy makes a joke in the July 2008 entry about killing a hobo, but I feel like dead-hobo jokes weren't big until 2009.' To which Boney replied: 'Pass the syrup, freakshow.'

People peeled away, went on with their lives. Boney stayed. Go stayed.

Then something happened. My father finally died. At night, in his sleep. A woman spooned his last meal into his mouth, a woman settled him into bed for his last rest, a woman cleaned him up after he died, and a woman phoned to give me the news.

'He was a good man,' she said, dullness with an obligatory injection of empathy.

'No, he wasn't,' I said, and she laughed like she clearly hadn't in a month.

I thought it would make me feel better to have the man vanished from the earth, but I actually felt a massive, frightening hollowness open up in my chest. I had spent my life comparing myself to my father, and now he was gone, and there was only Amy left to bat against. After the small, dusty, lonely service, I didn't leave with Go, I went home with Amy, and I clutched her to me. That's right, I went home with my wife.

I have to get out of this house, I thought. *I have to be done with Amy once and for all.* Burn us down, so I couldn't ever go back.

Who would I be without you?

I had to find out. I had to tell my own story. It was all so clear.

The next morning, as Amy was in her study clicking away at the keys, telling the world her *Amazing* story, I took my laptop downstairs and stared at the glowing white screen.

I started on the opening page of my own book.

I am a cheating, weak-spined, woman-fearing coward, and I am the hero of your story. Because the woman I cheated on — my wife, Amy Elliott Dunne — is a sociopath and a murderer.

Yes. I'd read that.

AMY ELLIOTT DUNNE
TEN WEEKS AFTER THE RETURN

Nick still pretends with me. We pretend together that we are happy and carefree and in love. But I hear him clicking away late at night on the computer. Writing. Writing his side, I know it. I *know* it, I can tell by the feverish outpouring of words, the keys clicking and clacking like a million insects. I try to hack in when he's asleep (although he sleeps like me now, fussy and anxious, and I sleep like him). But he's learned his lesson, that he's no longer beloved Nicky, safe from wrong – he no longer uses his birthday or his mom's birthday or Bleecker's birthday as a password. I can't get in.

Still, I hear him typing, rapidly and without pause, and I can picture him hunched over the keyboard, his shoulders up, his tongue clamped between his teeth, and I know that I was right to protect myself. To take my precaution.

Because he isn't writing a love story.

NICK DUNNE
TWENTY WEEKS AFTER THE RETURN

I didn't move out. I wanted this all to be a surprise to my wife, who is never surprised. I wanted to give her the manuscript as I walked out the door to land a book deal. Let her feel that trickling horror of knowing the world is about to tilt and dump its shit all over you, and you can't do anything about it. No, she may never go to prison, and it will always be my word against hers, but my case was convincing. It had an emotional resonance, if not a legal one.

So let everyone take sides. Team Nick, Team Amy. Turn it into even more of a game: Sell some fucking T-shirts.

My legs were weak when I went to tell Amy: I was no longer part of her story.

I showed her the manuscript, displayed the glaring title: *Psycho Bitch*. A little inside joke. We both like our inside jokes. I waited for her to scratch my cheeks, rip my clothes, bite me.

'Oh! What perfect timing,' she said cheerfully, and gave me a big grin. 'Can I show you something?'

I made her do it again in front of me. Piss on the stick, me squatting next to her on the bathroom floor, watching the urine come out of her and hitting the stick and turning it pregnant-blue.

Then I hustled her into the car and drove to the doctor's office, and I watched the blood come out of her – because she isn't really afraid of blood – and we waited the two hours for the test to come back.

Amy was pregnant.

'It's obviously not mine,' I said.

'Oh, it is.' She smiled back. She tried to snuggle into my arms. 'Congratulations, Dad.'

'Amy—' I began, because of course it wasn't true, I hadn't touched my wife since her return. Then I saw it: the box of tissues, the vinyl recliner, the TV and porn, and my semen in a hospital freezer somewhere. I'd left that will-destroy notice on the table, a limp guilt trip, and then the notice disappeared, because my wife had taken action, as always, and that action wasn't to get rid of the stuff but to save it. Just in case.

I felt a giant bubble of joy – I couldn't help it – and then the joy was encased in a metallic terror.

'I'll need to do a few things for my security, Nick,' she said. 'Just because, I have to say, it's almost impossible to trust you. To start, you'll have to delete your book, obviously. And just to put that other matter to rest, we'll need an affidavit, and you'll need to swear that it was you who bought the stuff in the woodshed and *hid* the stuff in the woodshed, and that you did once think I was framing you, but *now* you love me and I love you and everything is good.'

'What if I refuse?'

She put her hand on her small, swollen belly and frowned. 'I think that would be awful.'

We had spent years battling for control of our marriage, of our love story, our life story. I had been thoroughly, finally outplayed. I created a manuscript, and she created a life.

I could fight for custody, but I already knew I'd lose. Amy would relish the battle – God knew what she already had lined up. By the time she was done, I wouldn't even be an every-other-weekend dad; I would interact with my child in strange rooms with a guardian nearby sipping coffee, watching me. Or maybe not even that. I could suddenly see the accusations – of molestation or abuse – and I would never see my baby, and I would know that my child was tucked away far from me, Mother whispering, whispering lies into that tiny pink ear.

'It's a boy, by the way,' she said.

I was a prisoner after all. Amy had me forever, or as long

459

as she wanted, because I needed to save my son, to try to unhook, unlatch, debarb, undo everything that Amy did. I would literally lay down my life for my child, and do it happily. I would raise my son to be a good man.

I deleted my story.

Boney picked up on the first ring.

'Pancake House? Twenty minutes?' she said.

'No.'

I informed Rhonda Boney that I was going to be a father and so could no longer assist in any investigation – that I was, in fact, planning to retract any statement I'd made concerning my misplaced belief that my wife had framed me, and I was, also ready to admit my role in the credit cards.

A long pause on the line. 'Hunh,' she said. 'Hunh.'

I could picture Boney running her hand through her slack hair, chewing on the inside of her cheek.

'You take care of yourself, okay, Nick?' she said finally. 'Take good care of the little one too.' Then she laughed. 'Amy I don't really give a fuck about.'

I went to Go's house to tell her in person. I tried to frame it as happy news. A baby, you can't be that upset about a baby. You can hate a situation, but you can't hate a child.

I thought Go was going to hit me. She stood so close I could feel her breath. She jabbed me with an index finger.

'You just want an excuse to stay,' she whispered. 'You two, you're fucking addicted to each other. You are literally going to be a nuclear family, you do know that? You will explode. You will fucking detonate. You really think you can possibly do this for, what, the next eighteen years? You don't think she'll kill you?'

'Not as long as I am the man she married. I wasn't for a while, but I can be.'

'You don't think you'll kill *her*? You want to turn into Dad?'

'Don't you see, Go? This is my guarantee *not* to turn into Dad. I'll have to be the best husband and father in the world.'

Go burst into tears then – the first time I'd seen her cry

since she was a child. She sat down on the floor, straight down, as if her legs gave out. I sat down beside her and leaned my head against hers. She finally swallowed her last sob and looked at me. 'Remember when I said, Nick, I said I'd still love you *if*? I'd love you no matter what came after the *if*?'

'Yes.'

'Well, I still love you. But this breaks my heart.' She let out an awful sob, a child's sob. 'Things weren't supposed to turn out this way.'

'It's a strange twist,' I said, trying to turn it light.

'She won't try to keep us apart, will she?'

'No,' I said. 'Remember, she's pretending to be someone better too.'

Yes, I am finally a match for Amy. The other morning I woke up next to her, and I studied the back of her skull. I tried to read her thoughts. For once I didn't feel like I was staring into the sun. I'm rising to my wife's level of madness. Because I can feel her changing me again: I was a callow boy, and then a man, good and bad. Now at last I'm the hero. I am the one to root for in the never-ending war story of our marriage. It's a story I can live with. Hell, at this point, I can't imagine my story without Amy. She is my forever antagonist.

We are one long frightening climax.

AMY ELLIOTT DUNNE
TEN MONTHS, TWO WEEKS, SIX DAYS
AFTER THE RETURN

I was told love should be unconditional. That's the rule, everyone says so. But if love has no boundaries, no limits, no conditions, why should anyone try to do the right thing ever? If I know I am loved no matter what, where is the challenge? I am supposed to love Nick despite all his shortcomings. And Nick is supposed to love me despite my quirks. But clearly, neither of us does. It makes me think that everyone is very wrong, that love should have many conditions. Love should require both partners to be their very best at all times. Unconditional love is an undisciplined love, and as we all have seen, undisciplined love is disastrous.

You can read more about my thoughts on love in *Amazing*. Out soon!

But first: motherhood. The due date is tomorrow. Tomorrow happens to be our anniversary. Year six. Iron. I thought about giving Nick a nice pair of handcuffs, but he may not find that funny yet. It's so strange to think: A year ago today, I was undoing my husband. Now I am almost done reassembling him.

Nick has spent all his free time these past months slathering my belly with cocoa butter and running out for pickles and rubbing my feet, and all the things good fathers-to-be are supposed to do. Doting on me. He is learning to love me unconditionally, under all my conditions. I think we are finally on our way to happiness. I have finally figured it out.

We are on the eve of becoming the world's best, brightest nuclear family.

We just need to sustain it. Nick doesn't have it down perfect.

This morning he was stroking my hair and asking what else he could do for me, and I said: 'My gosh, Nick, why are you so wonderful to me?'

He was supposed to say: *You deserve it. I love you.*

But he said, 'Because I feel sorry for you.'

'Why?'

'Because every morning you have to wake up and be you.'

I really, truly wish he hadn't said that. I keep thinking about it. I can't stop.

I don't have anything else to add. I just wanted to make sure I had the last word. I think I've earned that.

ACKNOWLEDGMENTS

I've got to start with Stephanie Kip Rostan, whose smart advice, sound opinions, and good humor have seen me through three books now. She's also just really fun to hang out with. Thanks for all the excellent guidance over the years. Many thanks also to Jim Levine and Daniel Greenberg and everyone at Levine Greenberg Literary Agency.

My editor, Lindsay Sagnette, is a dream: Thank you for lending me your expert ear, for letting me be just the right amount of stubborn, for challenging me to do better, and for cheering me on during that last stretch – if it weren't for you, I'd have remained '82.6 per cent done' forever.

Much thanks to Crown publisher Molly Stern for the feedback, the support, the sage comments, and the endless energy.

Gratitude also to Annsley Rosner, Christine Kopprasch, Linda Kaplan, Rachel Meier, Jay Sones, Karin Schulze, Cindy Berman, Jill Flaxman, and E. Beth Thomas. Thanks as always to Kirsty Dunseath and the gang at Orion.

For my many questions about police and legal procedures, I turned to some very gracious experts. Thanks to my uncle, the Hon. Robert M. Schieber, and to Lt. Emmet B. Helrich for always letting me run ideas by them. Huge thanks this round to defense attorney Molly Hastings in Kansas City, who explained her job with great grace and conviction. And endless gratitude to Det. Craig Enloe of the Overland Park Police Department for answering my 42,000 emails (modest estimate) over the past two years with patience, good humor, and exactly the right amount of information. Any mistakes are mine.

Thanks, for many and varied reasons, to: Trish and Chris Bauer, Katy Caldwell, Jessica and Ryan Cox, Sarah and Alex Eckert, Wade Elliott, Ryan Enright, Mike and Paula Hawthorne, Mike Hillgamyer, Sean Kelly, Sally Kim, Sarah Knight, Yocunda Lopez, Kameren and Sean Miller, Adam Nevens, Josh Noel, Jess and Jack O'Donnell, Lauren "Fake Party We're Awesome" Oliver, Brian "Map App" Raftery, Javier Ramirez, Kevin Robinett, Julie Sabo, gg Sakey, Joe Samson, Katie Sigelman, Matt Stearns, Susan and Errol Stone, Deborah Stone, Tessa and Gary Todd, Jenny Williams, Josh Wolk, Bill and Kelly Ye, Chicago's Inner Town Pub (home of the Christmas Morning), and the unsinkable Courtney Maguire.

For my wonderful Missouri family – all the Schiebers, the Welshes, the Flynns, and branches thereof. Thanks for all the love, support, laughs, pickle rolls, and bourbon slush ... basically for making Missouri, as Nick would say, 'a magical place'.

I received some incredibly helpful feedback from a few readers who are also good friends. Marcus Sakey gave me sharp advice about Nick early on over beer and Thai food. David MacLean and Emily Stone (deareth!) were kind enough to read *Gone Girl* in the months leading up to their wedding. It doesn't seem to have harmed you guys in the least, and it made the book a lot better, so thanks. Nothing will stop you from getting to the Caymans!

Scott Brown: Thanks for all the writing retreats during the Gone Girl Years, especially the Ozarks. I'm glad we didn't sink the paddleboat after all. Thanks for your incredibly insightful reads, and for always swooping in and helping me articulate what the hell it is I'm trying to say. You are a good Monster and a wonderful friend.

Thanks to my brother, Travis Flynn, for always being around to answer questions about how things actually work. Much love to Ruth Flynn, Brandon Flynn, and Holly Bailey.

To my in-laws, Cathy and Jim Nolan, Jennifer Nolan, Megan, Pablo, and Xavy Marroquin – and all the Nolans and Samsons: I am very aware of how lucky I am to have married

465

into your family. Thanks for everything. Cathy, we always knew you had one hell of a heart, but this past year proved it in so many ways.

To my parents, Matt and Judith Flynn. Encouraging, thoughtful, funny, kind, creative, supportive, and still madly in love after more than forty years. I am, as always, in awe of you both. Thanks for being so good to me and for always taking the time to harass strangers into buying my books. And thank you for being so lovely with Flynn – I become a better parent just watching you.

Finally, my guys.

Roy: Good kitty.

Flynn: Beloved boy, I adore you! Also, if you are reading this before the year 2024, you are too little. Put it down and pick up Frumble!

Brett: Husband! Father of my child! Dance partner, emergency grilled-cheese maker. The kind of fellow who knows how to pick the wine. The kind of fellow who looks great in a tux. Also a zombie-tux. The guy with the generous laugh and the glorious whistle. The guy who has the answer. The man who makes my child laugh till he falls down. The man who makes me laugh till I fall down. The guy who lets me ask all sorts of invasive, inappropriate, and intrusive questions about being a guy. The man who read and reread and reread and then reread, and not only gave advice, but gave me a bourbon app. You're it, baby. Thanks for marrying me.

Two words, always.